CRITICAL PRAISE
LYNDA CURNYN

ENGAGING MEN

"Curnyn delivers another fun and frothy crowd-pleaser."
> —*Booklist*

"The author of *Confessions of an Ex-Girlfriend* has done it again with *Engaging Men*...a truly funny and thoroughly enjoyable read."
> —*Romance Reviews Today*

"This dose of chick lit features entertaining supporting characters and may inspire readers to think about what they really want out of relationships and life."
> —*Romantic Times*

"Angie's emotional adventures will strike a chord with women of all ages. *Engaging Men* is a great read..."
> —Barbara Fielding, *The Word on Romance*

CONFESSIONS OF AN EX-GIRLFRIEND

"...Curnyn pens an easy, breezy first novel that's part *Sex and the City* with more heart and part Bridget Jones with less booze."
> —*Publishers Weekly*

"A diverse cast of engaging, occasionally offbeat characters, the hilarious sayings attributed to them, and a fast-paced style facilitated by Emma's pithy sound-bite 'confessions' add to the fun in a lively Manhattan-set story..."
> —*Library Journal*

"Readers will eagerly turn the pages."
> —*Booklist*

"...absolutely hilarious secondary characters. They alone are worth the cover price."
> —*Romantic Times*

In memory of my father,
James Curnyn

Bombshell

Lynda Curnyn

RED
DRESS
INK
™

First edition May 2004

BOMBSHELL

A Red Dress Ink novel

ISBN 0-373-25057-6

© 2004 by Lynda Curnyn.

Photograph of the author © by Julie Ann Coney.

This book is a work of fiction. The names, characters, incidents and places
are the products of the author's imagination, and are not to be construed
as real. While the author was inspired in part by actual events, none of the
characters in the book is based on an actual person. Any resemblance to
persons living or dead is entirely coincidental and unintentional.

www.RedDressInk.com

Printed in U.S.A.

ACKNOWLEDGMENTS

This book truly wouldn't have been possible without the amazing people in my life who inspire me endlessly.

Richard Hoelderlin, whose own search for his birth parents first drew me to the idea for this book. You are gone, dear friend, but your good heart is not forgotten.

The story was brought back to me by another friend, Julie Ann Coney, who shared with me the sad, beautiful story of her search for her birth mother, and gave Grace's story its shape.

Thanks to my dearest friend, Linda Guidi, a true beauty with a big heart, for her generous support and inspiration.

Dora Hoelderlin for providing background on adoptive search. Gerry Zdenek for the scoop on the beauty biz. Javier Castillo, for the scoop on the world of advertising (mistakes are mine). Robert Clegg for showing me some chess moves and for providing the most logical (and amusing) explanation of why people fall in love.

My family, especially my brother Jim, who kept it all together for us during a year when everything seemed to fall apart; my brother Brian, who is my biggest fan; Kim Castellano-Curnyn, Upper West Side Bombshell; Trina K. Curnyn (the K is for Killer Wit); and Dave Webber, who always seems to have answers to my obscure questions.

Sarah Mlynowski, fabulous writer and savvy editor, for reading my drafts.

My wonderful editor, Joan Marlow Golan, who loved Grace from the very first chapter. All the talented people behind Red Dress Ink, especially Margaret, Laura, Stephanie, Margie, Tara and Tania.

And of course, my mother, the original bombshell, and the best friend this girl could have.

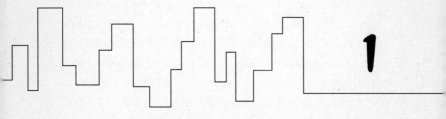

1

"When you lie down with dogs, you get up
with fleas."
—Jean Harlow

It amazed me to discover my relationship with Ethan was
only as strong as the latex between us.

"Oh, God," he said as he looked down at me, just moments
after what I had assumed was his orgasm. But what I had taken
for a look of euphoria on his face turned out to be utter panic.

"What's wrong?" I asked, gazing down at where he knelt
between my legs. He was studying me in a way that made me
feel vaguely embarrassed, despite the fact that we had been dating six months and were, by most standards, in a relationship.

"It's…gone," he said with disbelief.

"Gone?"

"The condom. It's disappeared. Inside you."

Alarmed, I immediately sat up.

"No, no, no—don't move," he said, squinting down at me as if about to perform surgery.

With a sigh, I swung away from him, slid off the bed.

"Where are you going?" he demanded.

"To get it out," I replied, heading for the bathroom.

A sudden calm descended over me, probably because Ethan was panicking so much, I didn't feel the need. But once I was in the bathroom alone, I was scared. I sat down on the side of the tub and, a bit frantically I'll admit, investigated. I was relieved, momentarily, when I fished out the errant bit of latex. And horrified when, upon closer examination, I discovered the damning tear.

I leaned back against the tiled wall, the "what ifs" whirling through my mind. And I discovered, with something resembling surprise, that my chief reason for alarm—the possibility that Ethan and I—that is, the idea of a *baby*—was not so…alarming. I was thirty-four years old. I was a Senior Product Manager for Roxanne Dubrow cosmetics and made damn good money. I had a somewhat posh one bedroom on the Upper West Side. If I wasn't ready now…

Okay, so it wasn't perfect timing. I was about to start work on Roxanne Dubrow's next big campaign, which I was hoping would lead to bigger things for my career. And then there was Ethan. Things were going just fine between us, but a baby? I tried to imagine Ethan, with his pinstripe suits and wire-rimmed glasses, cuddling a child. At first, the image was a bit peculiar. All I could come up with was the look of disgust on Ethan's face as the imaginary child upended its breakfast on his Italian silk tie. But then I mentally put Ethan in a T-shirt and jeans, set him in a lush suburban backyard tossing a ball to a tow-headed little boy and, suddenly, a warmth swept through me, taking me by surprise. I could do this. If I had to.

In this quasi-calm state I returned to the bedroom. Ethan sat up on the bed, looking at me with anticipation. Though he was still naked, he had put his glasses on, and I felt a sudden urge to laugh. What was it about a naked man in glasses that looked so surreal? I wondered as I flopped down on the bed beside him, a kind of gleefulness swimming inside me. Then I looked up at Ethan's handsome, well-chiseled face, studied his usually cool gray eyes and saw the panic still frozen there.

"Well?" he said, staring down at me.

Oh, right. The condom. I remembered the issue at hand. The issue that up until ten minutes ago might have caused me the same kind of terror I saw in Ethan's eyes.

"I found it," I said, gazing up at his usually adorable face and suddenly realizing how very much like a hamster he looked when he was nervous, all pursed mouth and squinty eyes. I rolled over, burying my face in the pillow to hide the smile that threatened to tug at my lips. After all, I didn't want him to think I wasn't worried. I was—in a fashion.

I gathered myself together. Then confessed. "It was… torn."

"Torn?"

I turned to look at him over my shoulder. "Down the middle." Then I shrugged, as if to say, *These things happen.*

I felt him lift off the bed, heard him pad out of the bedroom, then across the living room. Knew when he had reached the bathroom with all the damning evidence in the faux marble wastebasket I kept there. "Oh, *God,*" he said again.

I was surprised at how quickly the hurt stabbed at me. I knew we hadn't planned this. It wasn't something we discussed while sharing moonlit walks and cozy little dinners at all the best restaurants New York had to offer. Yet, I never expected Ethan to react as if I'd just passed him a venereal disease. Just what, exactly, was so horrifying about the idea of us having a child?

By the time he came back to the bedroom and stood before me in all his bespectacled naked glory, I was angry.

"What do we *do?*" he said.

"*Do?*"

"Maybe you should…rinse or something."

"Or something," I replied, my voice thick with sarcasm.

"Hey, isn't there that pill? What's it called again? It's just for emergencies like this," he began, his face filled with a frantic hope. "Yes—the morning-after pill. How do we get our hands on something like that?"

The hamster suddenly morphed into a rat. I wondered what I had ever found so incredibly handsome about Ethan Lederman the Third, as he called himself whenever he got pompous after a few martinis.

Then his face changed, as if he remembered something. That something quickly became apparent when he kneeled next to me on the bed. "I'm sorry, Gracie, I didn't mean…it's not that I didn't *want*…that is… We can't have a baby together. *I* can't. It's just not part of the plan…."

But it was too late. The wall had risen up, thick and unyielding. And I did the only thing a self-respecting woman could do.

I threw him out.

"You *broke up* with him?" Lori said, gawking at me from her desk just outside my office.

"Not exactly *broke up,*" I replied. I instantly regretted sharing this bit of news with my admin, who had inquired about my Saturday night date with Ethan the moment I walked into the office. With a shrug that I hoped made my indifference obvious, I had blithely replied, "He's history."

Now I realized that I had opened myself up to a conversation I didn't want to have. Trying to deflect Lori away from the subject that had caused her perky little features to go slack with shock, I placed the bag I carried on her desk. "Guess what I brought us?" I said, pulling out one of the two giant muffins I'd bought. "Your favorite—chocolate banana chip," I continued, setting it before her.

"Thanks," she mumbled, barely acknowledging the muffin, which I had spontaneously decided to pick up this morning. Things at work were so hectic lately, I'd decided we could use a treat. The powers-that-be at Roxanne Dubrow, the family-owned cosmetic line we all slaved for, had been calling meetings two and three times a month, all in the name of a new product line and—hopefully—higher profit margins. Though my boss, Claudia Stewart, was under the most pressure, as she was supposed to come up with the next Big Idea, Lori often took the brunt of the workload, as Claudia and I had been sharing her ever since Jeannie, Claudia's own assistant, had gone on maternity leave. I sometimes felt guilty. After all, Lori was twenty-three years old and made a third of what I made—and probably a quarter of what Claudia made.

"So what *happened?*" Lori asked, jumping up and going to the coffee machine to make a pot.

I sighed, dropping my pocketbook onto an empty chair and sliding off the light jacket I wore as a concession to the surprisingly cool September morning before I headed for the hall closet to hang it up. What could I tell her?

That I realized Ethan was a selfish bastard who cared nothing about anyone but himself? That there was a possibly—albeit a remote one—that I was carrying this cretin's *child?* That the very idea of sharing anything grander than body fluids had nearly caused dear Ethan to lose the filet mignon he'd dropped a wad of cash on at dinner all over the Italian loafers he'd parked under my bed?

She was too young for the truth. It would only disillusion her. And since I firmly believed a woman needed *some* illusions in order to have any sort of romance in this fine city, I lied.

"He got a job offer," I improvised, "in Fiji." A smile almost curved my lips as I tried to imagine Ethan, with his pasty white skin and perspiring brow, weathering a tropical climate. What had I ever found attractive about him anyway?

"Do they even have accounting firms there?" Lori asked, bewildered.

"He's, uh, he's going private."

"Oh," she said, still studying me. She turned away to the coffee machine, but I could sense that the wheels were still churning in her head. Pulling the now-full coffeepot off the warmer, she filled two mugs and handed me one. Hoping to make my escape with my muffin and my sanity, I thanked her for the coffee and stepped toward my office door. But her next words stopped me.

"He didn't ask you to go *with* him?"

I paused in my doorway, realizing I was getting in too deep with this story meant to keep me from getting in too deep. "He, uh, he wanted to make a clean break," I said, realizing how much more accurately those words applied to me. "You are the queen of the pre-emptive breakup," Claudia was fond

of telling me, commenting on my knack for ending it all succinctly with my man of the moment before said man could
do the deed himself.

This answer seemed to satisfy Lori, for she sat down at her
desk and began thoughtfully picking a chocolate chip off the
top of her muffin. Still, the sight of her concerned frown filled
me with unease. I crouched down by her desk and looked
up at her. "You okay?" I asked.

She nodded. "I'm fine. I just thought you and Ethan were,
like, meant to be." Then she blushed, causing a strange ache
to fill my chest. "I guess I'm just a dopey romantic, huh?"
She forced a smile that did not reach her eyes. Eyes in which
I found myself searching for all those emotions I couldn't
somehow muster up myself about Ethan.

Thankfully, Claudia stormed in at that moment, prevent-
ing me from pursuing any dangerous thoughts. I could tell
by the way Claudia blew past us with barely a glance that she
was not in a good mood. Which didn't bode well for
Lori…or me.

I decided to take the bull by the horns, and after giving
Lori's hand a quick, comforting squeeze, I abandoned my
breakfast on her desk and headed for Claudia's office, which
stood opposite mine.

"Hey," I said, as I stood in the doorway. Claudia had already tossed her coat onto the low black sofa that lined one
wall and was scrutinizing herself in the mirror that lined the
other. The way she was studying her tall, pencil-thin, black-
clad figure said she wasn't satisfied with what she saw, although she looked like her usual well-kept self. "How did
spa-ing with the bigwigs go?" I asked. Claudia had just come
back from an exclusive spa in Switzerland, where, while sip-
ping flavored waters and sitting half-naked, she attended

meetings to decide the fate of Roxanne Dubrow cosmetics. Though the company prided itself on being able to attract an older, wealthier client, sales had recently begun to wane. So Dianne Dubrow, CEO and daughter of the company's founder, had decided that a week at a Swiss spa brainstorming with all her top execs would result in a brilliant new direction for the company—or at least a well-pampered upper management.

But Claudia apparently didn't feel very well-pampered. Smoothing a newly manicured hand over her long, dark hair with dissatisfaction, she stepped behind her desk, glared hard for a moment at the sleek black surface before looking up.

Her eyes roamed over me, taking in my blouse, my flared pants, my pointy-toed pumps, as if assessing their worthiness. It was the kind of once-over I could never get used to, despite the fact that she did it fairly regularly. It was as if Claudia were measuring me to make sure I met the high fashion standards of the illustrious firm of Roxanne Dubrow. Or at least to see if I were someone worthy of taking on as a confidante, even a friend, as Claudia was wont to do, especially when things weren't going her way.

"There should be a four-letter word for beauty," she said finally.

"Tell me," I said, sitting down in the chair across from her desk and preparing to hear about whatever brave new innovations the executives at Roxanne Dubrow had decided upon.

She sighed, gazing out her window and studying the generous glimpse of skyline it afforded. "They've chosen the new face for Roxanne Dubrow," she said, turning to face me once more, "and she's sixteen."

"*What?*" I asked, completely confused. Roxanne Dubrow cosmetics were devoted to the *mature* woman. As in: edging toward forty. In fact, Priscilla, the model who was last year's face, was a bit too young at age twenty-five. "I don't get it. How are they going to pull off 'Beauty beyond thirty' with a sixteen-year-old?"

"That's just it," Claudia replied. "Roxanne Dubrow is creating a new image. A new, *younger* image." She sniffed. "I suppose it's only a matter of time before they replace *us* with sixteen-year-olds. After all, who better to tell a woman how she should look than someone with a Ph.D. in benzyl peroxide?"

"Hmmm…" Studying Claudia's frown, I wondered if perhaps the younger image worried her on a more personal level. With her dark eyes and the shiny brunette hair she dared, at age forty-two, to wear longer than shoulder length, Claudia was a beautiful woman. But she was incredibly age-conscious.

"So tell me what that child was sniveling about out there," Claudia continued, confirming my suspicions. Ever since I had hired Lori fresh out of college a year and a half ago, Claudia had taken an immediate dislike to her. A dislike that seemed to have nothing to do with her work and everything to do with the fact that Lori was younger than Claudia had probably ever been.

"Oh, boy trouble," I said vaguely.

"Poor girl," she replied sarcastically. "Did Dennis the Menace discover someone else while playing in the sandbox?"

Knowing Claudia was about to take her anger at the top brass at Roxanne Dubrow out on Lori, I decided to sacrifice someone a bit more thick-skinned. Myself. "I broke up with Ethan."

This got an eyebrow raise. "*Pourquoi,* darling? Do tell."

"I discovered what a self-absorbed jerk he was."

This got a laugh. "Oh, Grace, don't tell me it took you—how long have you been with him, six months?—to figure *that* out?"

"Yeah, well. I must be getting soft in my old age," I replied.

She studied me for a moment, then a savage smile creased her well-lined lips. "Alas for Ethan. Another hapless victim of Grace's axe."

"Stop that," I replied, worried that she might be right. I quickly did a mental checklist of my most recent dating history. Before Ethan there was Drew, who was as utterly eligible as Ethan had appeared to be, but just as emotionally unavailable, I had discovered. Like Ethan, Drew had only lasted six months. In fact, six months might be my record since Kevin, my college boyfriend, whom I'd kept around for a solid two years before giving him the boot. I had been pretty brutal back then, too, I thought, cringing at the memory of how I had dropped every T-shirt, cassette tape and pair of boxer shorts Kevin had ever left at my place in the hall outside his dorm room, just moments before graduation. The truth was, I had an intuition for when I thought a guy would break up with me, and I never, ever let a man get the better of me. The only time that had happened was with my high school boyfriend, who had thrown me over for a cheerleader in a vain effort to win more votes for homecoming king. Still, he hadn't gotten away without enduring a few cutting barbs from me in front of the entire football team. Because even at the tender age of sixteen, I had a knack for laying a man low.

"It's not like he didn't deserve it," I muttered now, then realized there was no way in hell I could reveal to Claudia the cause of my breakup with Ethan. Because even though, statistically speaking, there was only a minute chance that last night's incident could have resulted in pregnancy, I didn't want to give my boss any food for thought. Losing her assistant to baby fever was hard enough. Having her Senior Product Manager go on maternity leave during Roxanne Dubrow's next major marketing campaign would be nothing less than betrayal in Claudia's eyes.

Fortunately, she had her own beef against Ethan. "He used too many hair products. What was with that Brylcreem look he sported to dinner that night?" she said, referring to one of the few times I had put my sharp-tongued boss and my well-groomed boyfriend in the same room together.

"I think he was going for Antonio Banderas in *The Mask of Zorro.*"

"He looked more like Pee Wee Herman on his latest adventure."

I laughed. I couldn't help myself. "He had more facial moisturizers in his medicine cabinet than we carry in our winter product line."

"There is nothing worse than a man with more beauty products than a woman."

"Nothing," I agreed, laughing harder, until Claudia's office was echoing with the sound of our mutual glee.

Until I remembered that there *was* one thing worse than a man addicted to skin care. And that was no man.

"I'm never going to have sex again," I said with a sigh.

"Please. As if a blond bombshell like you has ever had to worry about *that,*" she said.

She was right, I realized as I stood to leave her office a short while later. With a glance in the mirror on my way out the door, I felt my courage return. There I was, Grace Noonan, blond, busty and single for about the sixth time in as many

years. Was it because a five-foot-nine-inch blonde with a
38-C chest and legs up to her eyebrows could afford to be
choosy? Or was it because I couldn't afford *not* to be?

I got my answer when I found myself in the foyer outside Claudia's office once more, watching in horror as Lori
struggled to swipe away the tears that were gushing from
her eyes.

Alarmed, I rushed forward, crouching beside the chair
where she sat, her thin arms folded against her narrow frame.
"Lori, honey, what's wrong?" I asked.

"I'm s-so s-sorry, Grace," she sputtered. "I just thought, you
know, that some people were meant to be together." She burst
into a fresh avalanche of tears that I found, frankly, bewildering. But not one to turn away a fellow female in distress,
I took her hand in mine.

"Lori, honey, it's okay. Things with Ethan and me…were
kind of going nowhere anyway," I began tentatively, "We're
both…very different. There was no way it would have
worked."

Lori snuffled, then raised her gaze to me. "I thought…I
thought he was the…one," she said, and then, as if the very
thought that Ethan Lederman the Third wasn't Prince
Charming destroyed her, she released a fresh torrent of tears.

Though I was surprised at this sudden display of emotion
over a man who couldn't even remember my admin's name,
although she had fielded enough of his daily phone calls to
me, I wrapped my arms around her.

And as I rubbed a comforting hand over her back, I wondered if maybe I had jumped the gun with Ethan. After all,
I never did let a man get the best of me in the whole breakup
scenario, which often left me alone on more Saturday nights
than I cared to count. But as I listened to Lori babble into

my now-tear-stained silk blouse about true love and soul mates, I began to suspect her lamentations might not be about me and Ethan. She lifted her head, gazed at me with reddened eyes and said, "I know it's only been a year and a half, but I really thought he was the *one*...."

Now I was positive this watery display had nothing to do with me and Ethan. After all, we had only been dating six months.

"What's going on with you and Dennis?" I asked, honing in on her.

"Oh, Gracie, he's applied to graduate school. In...in London! I know it's something he's wanted, like, forever, but I thought—well, I just don't know what's going to happen to us!"

As I pulled Lori back into my embrace for a soothing hug, I felt a depth of yearning I had not known for a long time. For the kind of love that could break hearts. For the courage to even seek it.

2

"There aren't any hard women, just soft men."
—*Raquel Welch*

Though I have mastered the art of the breakup, the aftermath always kills me. I'm not talking about regret. I'm not the kind of woman to cry over a man. I do just fine with these things. It's everyone else I can't deal with.

Like my friend Angela.

"Gracie, what the hell happened this time?" she said when she caught me on the phone, which I had been avoiding. I never call friends in the post-breakup period. Too much explaining when there really isn't much to explain. Besides, I hate it when women overanalyze relationships. And though I love Angie dearly—have ever since I dated her older brother during our shared term at Marine Park Junior High in Brooklyn—she suffers from this particularly female malady.

I gave her the snapshot version.

"Asshole," she said, succinctly summing up Ethan. At least I could count on Angela to agree with me, once given the facts. She wouldn't have me accept anything less than worship from a man, now that she had settled in with her own worshipful partner, her roommate and best friend-turned-lover, Justin. Of course, she wasn't about to let a little thing like one of my umpteen breakups slide, either. "I'm coming over."

"No!" I replied, then realizing my abrupt rejection of her brand of girlfriend comfort had probably hurt her feelings, I hedged. "I mean, I'm tired. I have a big day at work tomorrow…." The last thing I wanted was to be soothed and coddled. I was fine, really. In fact, I felt almost…relieved. I was back to my natural state. Alone.

Knowing I wouldn't be able to hang up the phone without agreeing to a least an hour of the sympathetic cooing and all-out Ethan-blasting on my behalf, I finally made plans to meet her for drinks that Thursday.

Then, because there was one other person to whom I felt some obligation to at least give the larger details of my life to, I called my mother.

As usual, I was not afforded the luxury of speaking with her alone, because as soon as she heard my voice, she beckoned my father to the phone. "Thomas, sweetheart, pick up the extension. Gracie's on the phone!"

My parents had retired and moved to their dream house just outside Albuquerque, New Mexico, four years ago, and though I was happy for them, I hadn't had a private conversation with my mother since. Maybe it was because her naturally frugal nature demanded that a long-distance call involve more than two speakers, but she seemed to treat my every phone call as some wondrous event she couldn't resist sharing with my father. Or maybe it was just that she shared *everything* with my father. He was, as she would often tell me over a glass of wine that would inevitably turn her dreamy-eyed and nostalgic, the love of her life.

"Grace?" my father's deep baritone boomed over the line, a voice that up until his retirement had filled the awestruck college students who had frequented his seminars with reverence.

"Hi, Dad," I replied, a reluctant smile edging the corners of my mouth. It wasn't that I didn't love talking to my father. It was just that breakups resulting from sexual mishaps weren't the kind of thing I felt I could confide in him.

So I described our demise as a couple as a desire for a "clean break." "We didn't really have the same goals," I said, realizing that this was probably true. I mean, I did want to have a baby. Always imagined I would—someday. But I hadn't realized the extent of my desire until the other night. Funny how something like a little broken latex can bring so much…clarity.

"Better you realize that now, Grace, rather than later," my mother said, turning my recent relationship disaster into a triumph, as was her nature. Though she had been happily married to one man since the age of twenty-five, my mother seemed to have a different prescription for happiness for me. "Besides, you have your career to focus on now," she said, as she'd been saying ever since I had landed the Senior Product Manager position at Roxanne Dubrow three years ago. In her mind, I was the single career woman she never was. My mother had studied the cello since she was nine and dreamed of joining the symphony. But she had given up that dream shortly after her marriage to my father, settling instead for a life as a music teacher in the public schools. She hadn't, however, given up her belief that a woman's first duty was to herself and her goals. She never failed to tell me how proud she was of me for staying true to mine. "If the girls at Hewlett High could see you now," she always said, referring to my rebellious youth and somewhat colorful reputation. If my yearbook had allowed for those colorful attributions of yesteryear, mine would have read, "Girl most likely to single-handedly destroy her life."

Yet now I was a shining beacon of success. Sophisticated. Cosmopolitan. Successful.

Even my father gave one of his familiar murmurs of assent—it was the only thing that reminded me he was still on the line—whenever my mother went off on how exalted my position at Roxanne Dubrow was, how magnificent my life.

I suppose it was pretty magnificent, I thought, once I hung up the phone and glanced around my apartment. At least from a real-estate point of view.

I live in a doorman building on the Upper West Side. That's code for mega rent, though mine wasn't up to current astronomical rates since I had snagged this apartment almost six years ago.

Six years. I had been twenty-eight at the time, and had just landed my first job managing my own product. Granted it was for a pharmaceutical company—not as glamorous a position as my current one—but I was jubilant. I finally had a salary fat enough to leave behind my third floor walk-up in the nowhereland of Kip's Bay. I even had an assistant, though I barely knew what to do with her back then. I was moving toward my thirties still buoyant with the belief that I was entering the best part of a woman's life, sexually, emotionally, financially. By thirty-five, I'd been told once by a college professor whom I admired, a woman usually has everything she wants.

I looked around my living room, decorated in soft whites.

It was the kind of space I had always dreamed of having: lush, romantic, inviting. I thought about the fact that just this past summer, at our annual company summer outing at the Southampton Yacht Club, Dianne had told me that she thought I had "vision"—the kind of vision, she implied, that upper management at Roxanne Dubrow appreciated.

Yes, I did have a lot going for me, I thought. Then my eye fell upon two ticket stubs that had been left on the coffee table from the opera Ethan and I had attended the other night....

My stomach clenched, and I ran my hand soothingly over what Ethan had once referred to as my Botticelli belly—like the goddesses depicted by the old masters, I was a bit more rounded about the hips and breasts than today's waif standard. Yes, Ethan had always liked my body. Just as I had liked his. And it had been enough, I supposed.

Until last Saturday night.

What had I expected of him, really? I wondered, finally rousing myself from the sofa and grabbing the ticket stubs to toss before I hit the bathroom for my nightly cleansing and moisturizing ritual.

I had expected nothing.

And that was exactly what I got.

"Morning Mist," Claudia said when I stepped into her office the next day and found her gazing at a tiny glass jar with branding I recognized to be that of Olga Parks, our main competitor in the older woman's market.

"Morning to you, too," I said, wondering at the gleam in her eye.

Claudia shook her head, picking up the glass vial in one hand and holding it before me. "Have you seen this yet?" she demanded.

I glanced at the bottle, hearing the reprimand in her voice. One of my jobs was to keep an eye on the competition, and clearly Claudia thought I had been remiss in this area.

I decided to set her straight. "Olga Parks. Spring line. Two years ago." I remembered the product well, as I myself had been seeking something to restore the dewy look that seemed to disappear just after my thirtieth birthday. At $65 for two ounces, Morning Mist hadn't promised to restore moisture—that was the job of the $85 moisturizer it had been paired with. Morning Mist had more of a cosmetic purpose; sprayed on my face, it added a sheen that suggested I had run a mini-marathon during a ninety-degree NYC day. That was a little too much dewiness for me, and I had mentioned that in my report to Claudia, also two years ago.

But my manager had already moved beyond ire to fascination. "Why didn't we latch on to this concept? It's pure genius!" she said, spraying the back of her hand and studying the resultant sheen. "Look!" she said, holding out her hand to me, as if the evidence were clear. "When was the last time you saw that kind of glow on your skin?"

"At the gym. It looks like sweat, Claudia. Besides, aren't we supposed to be focusing now on products for women who are still suffering from excess oils?"

I saw a shudder roll through her, as if the very idea of catering to our younger counterparts disturbed her. "Speaking of which, where is our slick little admin this morning? It's ten o'clock and she has yet to make an appearance. I need her to run off some sales figures for me."

I knew from the soft-spoken voice mail waiting for me on the phone this morning that Lori had been feeling a bit under the weather and was going to try to be in by noon. Though I detected in her somewhat despondent message that whatever ailed her was probably more emotional than physical, I covered for her. "She has a touch of a stomach virus. She said she'll be in by noon."

"Girls today," Claudia said with disgust. "Bunch of wimps." She shook her head. "They'll never be what we once were, will they, Grace?"

And we'll never be what they are now, I thought. Ever again.

Not wanting to dwell on that, I decided to steer Claudia back to the purpose of our meeting, which was to debrief me on the corporate agenda that had been hashed out in the Swiss Alps. "I'm ready for the debrief if you are," I said, eyeing Claudia as she gazed with a mixture of fondness and disgust at the pretty little jar.

"Right," she said, a look of resignation descending over her aristocratic features. "Well, first I should tell you it wasn't so much a brainstorming as a corporate screwover. They didn't invite us up there to come up with the new vision for Roxanne Dubrow, but to cram their new mandate down our throats. I guess Dianne figured her distasteful little plan would go down easier with a little sparkling water and pâté."

"Don't tell me Burkeston finally got the go-ahead from Dianne on that product line she's been testing forever?" Winona Burkeston, Director of Research, was a bit of a maverick. Though she was close to fifty herself, she had been pushing to get a youth line at the company's forefront for years.

"What, are you living in a cave, Grace? Burkeston's gone. Has been for what—two months now? They called it a resignation, but I think she was forced out. Dianne sent down the memo herself. Surely you must have—" Claudia frowned. "Maybe I didn't pass it on to you." She shrugged, as if the fact that she repeatedly forgot to pass on vital corporate info really wasn't an issue. "Anyway, she's been replaced. By a pretty little Brit named Courtney Manchester, who looks like she's all of sixteen herself and fresh from London with some fancy degree and a pair of tits I'd swear were silicone if I hadn't caught sight of them in the steam room." Her eyes narrowed. "You know, I wouldn't be surprised if those perky tits helped push her agenda through. You know how Michael is when it comes to a fresh piece of ass."

That sent an unexpected stab of heat through me. And why shouldn't it? Because Michael Dubrow, the baby of the Dubrow clan and only son, had once claimed *me* as his piece of ass, for a brief, passionate period in my early history at Roxanne Dubrow. But just as quickly as we got caught up in the perilously romantic idea of our being together despite the company-wide stir an affair between the Dubrow heir and the new—well, I was new at the time—Senior Product Manager would create, we were weighted down by those same facts. Well, Michael was, anyway.

"C'mon, Grace, you can't be serious," he had said when, during a romantic weekend rendezvous in the Hamptons, I had speculated on the future. "You and I are friends," he declared, his only acknowledgment of the deeper intimacy I thought we shared indicated by the way he squeezed my hands in his. "Besides we *work* together. Think of what people might say…."

In truth, the only thing I had been thinking of until that point was that I had found my soul mate. Yes, even *I* had fallen under the spell of that foolish notion once. In fact, I was so enthralled by the idea of Michael and myself as the future golden couple of the Dubrow clan that I was blind to the reality of us. Instead I was focused on the moment when I could tell the world that I was in love—yes, in *love*—with

Michael Dubrow. But that moment never came. Because as soon as I realized that Michael wasn't dreaming of an "us," the very notion effectively ended in my mind.

Ironically, there was no drama at the end, despite the strength of feeling I had developed for him during our short affair. No damning speech. Not even a real breakup. I ended things just as easily as they had started over cocktails at a sales conference four months earlier. Not two weeks after our debacle in the Hamptons, Michael and Dianne came to New York for a few days of meetings. When, at the end of the first day of strategizing in the corporate boardroom, he discreetly suggested we sneak away for an after-work drink, which was usually code for "Let's go fuck," I politely declined, saying I needed to get to bed early that night if I hoped to be fresh for our next round of meetings in the morning. It was a clever blow-off on my part. Michael Dubrow considered himself a model employer, and I knew he would never argue with good employee behavior. As predicted, he didn't argue. And after a while, he stopped asking. Soon enough our relationship went from intensely personal to coolly professional. As if everything that had come before didn't matter. As if he didn't matter to me.

Now I knew that, on some level at least, he had.

"What in God's name is wrong with you?" Claudia asked, startling me out of my reverie.

I quickly composed myself, masking whatever dismay might have shown on my face with a lame excuse about not getting enough sleep the night before. I had to. No one knew about me and Michael. Not Claudia. Not even Angela. And whether out of some warped loyalty to Michael, or a desire not to reveal that bit of romantic foolishness on my part, I wanted to keep it that way.

Fortunately, Claudia was too wound up by the evil she saw in our new corporate direction to be bothered inquiring into my feelings.

"You know that little product line we bought from that floundering U.K. company? Sparkle?" Claudia said, referring to the makeup line we acquired a year ago when the idea of getting into a younger market was just a sparkle in Dianne's eye. "Dianne—and Michael, I suspect—have decided that this line is going to save Roxanne Dubrow." She rolled her eyes. "The vision is to rename it in a way that subtly links it to the mother brand—hence, the 'child' brand revitalizes the 'mother.'"

"Makes sense," I said. "Kind of like how *Teen People* revitalized *People* magazine."

Her eyes narrowed on me, as if I had betrayed her by simply pointing out the rationale of the plan.

I backpedaled a bit, not wanting to get on the wrong side of Claudia so early in the workweek. "So does this 'child' have a name?" I said with what I hoped was the right amount of disdain in my voice.

"Oh, it does," Claudia said, turning her gaze full on me. "Roxy D."

It was good. And I said as much.

"Well, I'm glad you agree," Claudia said, her tone thick with irony. "Because a full two-thirds of our marketing budget for this year is now being redirected toward making Roxy D a household name—or should I say a dorm-room name."

"Hmmm," I muttered noncommittally, while the impact of that sank in. For the past three years, my role, under Claudia's leadership, had been to develop marketing and advertising that positioned Roxanne Dubrow as the premiere mature woman's cosmetic company.

"Now they've brought in this little chippy from the U.K., and apparently she's cast a spell over the whole Dubrow clan—or at least Michael. But you know how Dianne listens to everything her brother says as if he were some sort of marketing genius." This earned another roll of Claudia's eyes, as she hated the fact that Michael, simply by virtue of his role as heir to the Dubrow crown, frequently imposed his point of view on everything from marketing to packaging to color palettes. He was very hands-on, and though I was loath to admit it, it was one of the things I had admired about him. His passion for the business. His ambition.

"Suddenly Dianne is positively *dazzled* by the idea that the Roxy D brand is going to lure all those twentysomethings back to the Roxanne Dubrow counters. And she's wagering big on that assumption," Claudia finished, naming a figure that had me sucking in my breath.

The last time our department had seen that kind of money was during the heyday of Roxanne Dubrow's Youth Elixir— not that I had been around to witness that. Created in the early eighties, Youth Elixir was the moisturizer that Roxanne Dubrow had made its reputation on. Youth Elixir promised to refresh, refine and, most of all, restore all the vital moisture that started to seep out of the skin the moment a woman reached the big 3-0. It was a pretty good product. In fact, I might have been tempted to drop $65 for two ounces of the stuff if I didn't get it by the case for free.

"So what about the Youth Elixir campaign?" I asked, bewildered about where the money for the advertising for this would come. Youth Elixir had been such a perennial bestseller for Roxanne Dubrow that just six months ago, Dianne had advocated making the moisturizer the center of the Spring campaign. During a corporate strategy meeting held right here in the New York office, she had stated that putting the company's flagship product on the front lines once more would remind consumers of the powerhouse product that had made Roxanne Dubrow what it is today, and hopefully convince new consumers to try it. But apparently that had all changed.

"It's on the backburner," Claudia replied, giving me a look weighted with meaning. As if she saw this as the beginning of some end I could not yet fathom. "The idea is that if we successfully lure the younger market to the counter with Roxy D, they'll eventually graduate to Roxanne Dubrow."

"Hmmm," I said again, wondering at the implications of this for me. After all, the Youth Elixir campaign was to be my campaign to run, under Claudia's leadership, of course.

As if in answer to my unasked question, Claudia continued, "You and I are going to have our hands full over the next few months working on this dreadful new campaign."

I looked at her, feeling a bit of relief that I was to have a role in the campaign that was to be the company's lifeblood, judging from the amount of money we were sinking into it. I had seen the careers of product managers of yesteryear shrink to nothing during budget changes. Though Roxanne Dubrow had acquired other brands over the years, I always felt fortunate to be working on the signature brands, especially when budget time came.

"We need to do some testing, develop a new package," Claudia was saying now. "Line up the talent for the print campaign…."

My mind immediately began to roam over the current crop of models out there. "Well, there's no shortage of younger models," I said finally, realizing that the youth fever had already taken over in most marketplaces. That Roxanne

Dubrow might, in fact, be a little late in jumping on this particular bandwagon.

"Oh, Dianne has already made her decision," Claudia said now, and I could tell how much it irked her to receive all her marching orders from on high. "She wants Irina Barbalovich," she declared.

I quickly wrapped my mind around that. Irina had been embraced by the fashion world ever since she had been plucked from her parents' farm in rural Russia to walk the runways of Paris at the tender age of seventeen. In fact, in the past six months, she had gotten more magazine covers than Cindy Crawford at the height of her career. Which meant we were going to pay through the nose for her. Now I understood where most of that budget was going. Irina was the next generation of supermodel, and the fact that Dianne hoped to head up our spring campaign with her was big. Roxanne Dubrow usually chose a no-name stunner they inevitably turned into a star. Now it looked like Dianne was hoping to harness the power of the industry's latest supermodel. "Didn't you say they wanted a sixteen-year-old?" I asked, somewhat inanely, still trying to figure out the implications of this for us in marketing. "I think Irina's closer to nineteen by now…" I continued, remembering a profile I had read of her when she did a recent cover for *Cosmo.*

"Sixteen, nineteen. Whatever," Claudia said, waving a hand dismissively, as if anyone under the age of twenty was not worthy of her regard. "She's the next big thing, and if we don't bring her on board soon, my dear Grace, we may find ourselves without a campaign at all."

I didn't miss the threat beneath her words, but I took it with a grain of salt. Claudia was forever hinting at the annihilation of our jobs. I sometimes wondered if it was the only thing that motivated her to get out of bed and come to work these days.

"We'll get her," I said, ready to take on the challenge. After all, there is nothing like a full work life to keep a woman from remembering how empty her love life has suddenly become.

3

"Give a man a free hand and he'll run it all over you."
—Mae West

If Roxanne Dubrow's new marketing plan sent a shudder through Claudia, it was like a balm to my soul. As I put together an agenda for the coming month, filled with meetings with New Product Development, entertaining bids from ad firms, talking with the sales reps about in-store positioning, I knew I was going to be okay. Even Lori seemed to shrug off her own personal crisis when I filled her in on what needed to be done for the new campaign. Maybe it was the excitement of seeing the new product that would one day be Roxy D, as boxes of Sparkle had already been shipped in from the Dubrow compound on Long Island for us to review. Or maybe it was the dozen long-stems Dennis had sent, which seemed to ameliorate any wounds his newly announced future plans had caused. For a brief moment, I even hoped for my own long-stems—not that I wanted Ethan back, but a girl did like a man to grovel a bit. Although I hardly expected that from Ethan. One of the few things he and I had in common was a stubborn streak a mile wide.

Besides, I had already begun to build up a wall of indifference to him.

So I was dually armed when I found myself sitting before the one person whose whole purpose, at least for the forty-five minutes a week we spent together, was to probe at whatever feelings she believed I was having.

Shelley Longford, my therapist.

"You *broke up* with him?" Shelley said after I had blithely related the story of my mishap with Ethan, after spending more than half the session seated in the chair across from her in a tiny, nondescript office on the fourth floor of an equally nondescript office building on W. 72nd Street, relating the more mundane details of my life. The new campaign at Roxanne Dubrow. The fact that I was having trouble getting my super to come up and fix a crack that had begun in the ceiling of my pretty, albeit ancient, bathroom. I think I was starting to bore myself, which probably made me blurt out the news of my breakup.

In truth, I took a certain satisfaction in the shock that wreathed Shelley's normally composed features. I had been seeing her just four months, and this was the first time I seemed to get some sort of rise out of her. The most I had seen before was a nervous tuck of that shiny dark hair behind her ear, or a narrowing of her dark eyes. Now, after her somewhat harried exclamation, I felt a sort of…triumph.

"Well, what would you have done?" I asked now, knowing she would somehow find a way to turn the question back on me. This therapy business was so tricky, and if it hadn't been for the endless prodding of the social worker on my case, I wouldn't even be here. It was so pointless somehow. I had been coming once a week for four months now, sitting across from a woman I didn't know—and didn't want to know, judging by the tastefully drab decor of her office, her bad haircut, her aloof manner and the fact that I was paying her $140 for forty-five minutes of relative silence while she asked questions that seemed to have nothing to do with me. Questions that always seemed to lead to one answer—an answer I refused to give her.

"Well, there are a lot of things one could do in a situation like the one you experienced with Ethan," Shelley began, carefully leaving herself out of the answer as I'm sure she was trained to do. See what I mean? How can you *warm up* to someone like this?

I raised my eyebrows, stubbornly resisting the impulse to make life easier for her as I waited for her to fill me on all these options I allegedly had now that Ethan Lederman the Third had accidentally let a few of his precious sperm loose in a woman he had been sleeping with for months, yet somehow couldn't see himself actually propagating with.

"You could have talked," she said, after a lengthy pause. A pause that cost me quite a few bucks at these rates. I could have invested in the new Stila lip shade with more result.

"About?" I said, not wanting to give her anything.

"Your options," she said.

"*Options?*" I began, feeling my temper suddenly—and surprisingly—spike. "Let's see, what exactly were the options that Ethan Lederman the Third presented me with? Ah, yes. There was the douche—very clever on his part. Made me wonder if he'd ever been down this road before. Oh, and then there was the morning-after pill. That's right. Get rid of it before it even gets started. Nice clean solution. Better than say, throwing it in the Hudson after it was born…."

When I saw I had not managed to make a dent in that composure of hers, I continued, "Look, the bottom line is he wanted nothing to do with anything *real* between us. It was all too glaringly apparent that he didn't want a child with me. That he didn't want…me."

This last word came out on a squeak, making me realize how dangerously close to tears I was. I grabbed the arms of the chair to take the tremble out of my fingers. *Don't cry, don't cry, don't cry,* a voice inside me chanted. Within moments, I managed to swallow back whatever emotions threatened. But it was too late.

Shelley Longford had seen it all. And I knew exactly where she was going to go with it.

As it turned out, I only had to endure another ten minutes of therapy. Ten minutes of avoiding the truth Shelley tried to gently guide me to, but which I strictly avoided at all costs. I even hated the words: *fear of rejection.* Her next maneuver was to try and—gently but persistently—tie it all back to my mother. Not my mother, really. My mother was a perfectly nice, perfectly respectable music teacher, now retired and living with my perfectly respectable father in New Mexico. What Shelley wanted to talk about was the woman who gave birth to me. Kristina Morova, who, as I learned three years ago after months of digging through public records, resided a train ride away from me in Sheepshead Bay, Brooklyn. And refused to acknowledge my existence. The only response I had gotten to the certified letter I had finally gotten up the courage to send to her seven months ago was the return receipt with her signature on it. A hastily scrawled "K. Morova" that I had run my fingers over at least a dozen times since I had found it in my mailbox. No note inviting me to meet her at some mutually acceptable location, so that I might get answers to all those questions that had plagued me for most of my life and, for some reason, even more so after I turned thirty. No tearful phone call to express her joy at the possibility of meeting the child she'd given up, for reasons as yet unknown to me, at the age of seventeen.

Nothing.

I had been told ahead of time by the search agency that this was one possible outcome. In fact, this was the reasoning behind sending a certified letter in the first place, so that I could be assured that the letter had been received and that I would, at least, be saved from any emotional trauma caused by a random postal error. Yes, now I knew that whatever emotional trauma I was allegedly dealing with, according to Shelley, had to do with the simple fact that my mother knew I was alive but didn't want to know me.

I had accepted this realization with the same type of angry calm with which I had tossed Ethan out of my apartment a week earlier. Fuck him, I had thought as I watched him angrily pull on his clothes and make tracks out my front door.

Fuck her, I had thought after enduring the two weeks of complete silence that followed the sending of my letter. Yes, I had been disappointed, but even more, I had been mad. Mad at her for not caring. So mad, in fact, that I had taken a car service out to her modest two-family house in Sheepshead Bay, only to stand outside filled with a desire to take the pretty little planter at the center of her neatly edged lawn and toss it through her front window.

I didn't, of course.

Instead, I had gotten back into the car, sinking into comfortable anonymity behind the tinted windows, and had gone to see Barbara, the social worker who assisted me with my search. And after listening to me rail for half an hour over everything from Kristina Morova's impossibly well-kept flower bed to her frailty as a human being, Barbara had finally managed to convince me to do what she had been trying to get me to do since I had taken up my search. Seek counseling.

Not that the sixteen weeks I had been seeing Ms. Shelley Longford, C.S.W., with a specialization in psychotherapy, had made a bit of difference.

Even now as I carefully let myself out of her office after assuring her that yes, I would be there the following Wednesday at six-thirty, I wondered why I bothered.

I was fine really. I had all the information I really needed to know about Kristina Morova. That she was one of two daughters. That there was no real history of disease in her family, other than a few diabetics and some spotty cancer.

I mean, strictly speaking, I really didn't need to know anything else, right?

"How are you *really,* Grace?" Angie said as we sat over drinks the following evening at Bar Six, a little bistro in the West Village.

"I'm *fine,*" I assured her for the third time since we'd sat down, martinis before us. I didn't want to get into an analysis of the demise of my recent relationship, knowing full well that Ethan had likely not even given it a second thought himself. That was the annoying little difference between men and women. When a man exited a relationship, no matter who ended it, it was as if the woman was erased from his mind. Women, on the other hand, could be borderline obsessive, measuring every perceived slight, every phone call or lack thereof, and coming up with a complex analysis of his emotional makeup.

I decided to take the male tack, effectively erasing Ethan from my own mind and turning the conversation to what I hoped would be a more fruitful subject. Angie. "So what's going on with the show?"

Angie was an actor and had, a year earlier, gotten her first big break when she'd landed a primetime drama on *Lifetime,* playing Lisa Petrelli, single mom and NYPD cop. Though the show hadn't garnered huge ratings, Angie had gotten a nice bit of critical notice for what *Entertainment Weekly* had called her "endearingly anxious" portrayal of a woman struggling to raise two kids and save the world, or at least the New York City precinct that was her beat, from crime. The funny thing was that all of that endearing anxiety came from the fact that Angie herself had never encountered child-rearing first hand and was mostly struggling to keep from being railroaded by the two child actors who played her kids.

"The network is reviewing its programming as we speak. But it's looking like a second season might be too much to hope for," she said, fresh anxiety washing over her features. With her large, dark eyes, heart-shaped face and deep brown shoulder-length locks, my friend Angie is almost a dead ringer for Marisa Tomei. Not that I ever would say that to her—she's heard it often enough over the years. But she made her peace with it once she earned some critical acclaim of her own as Angie DiFranco, obsessive-compulsive-yet-utterly-charming actor. That boost to her career has resulted in a subsequent boost to her self-esteem. I have known Angie since we shared secrets and sorrows at Marine Park, where I lived until my parents decided that Brooklyn was turning me into too much of a bad-ass teen and dragged me off to Long Island at age sixteen. Angie and I stayed friends, spending our summers together on the beach, then once I got my driver's license, weekends filled with shopping, club-hopping and, when we both managed to have boyfriends at the same time, double-dating. In all the years I have known her, I have never seen Angie look so radiant. It was as if her life were finally coming together, though the nervous frown now marring her pretty features suggested otherwise. Sometimes my friend Angie, who had an acting career on the rise, an amazing boyfriend and a rent-stabilized two bedroom in the East Village, needed to be reminded of just how magnificent her life was.

"Maybe that's for the best," I said. "Aren't you supposed to start working on Justin's film in the spring?" Her boyfriend was a screenwriter who had received much critical acclaim himself for the feature-length film he'd made as a film student years ago. Now he had a brand-new screenplay and a leading lady, as he'd written a part especially for Angie.

"Yeah, we're starting in April…." she said, beginning to gnaw at her lower lip at the very thought.

It wasn't that Angie didn't believe in her talented boyfriend. It was just that, despite the steadying assurance his love gave her, she was given to panic over anything that she didn't know the outcome of beforehand. Which was just about everything, I supposed.

"Well, then, there you go," I said. "Your future's so bright, you're gonna have to go out and purchase a pair of Ray•Bans."

"I guess," she said, unconvinced. I had known Angie so long, I could practically read her mind. See the little hamsters of anxiety on the wheel of her thoughts, running frantically on those "what ifs" that plagued her. What if I can't carry the role? What if I get some life-threatening disease? Her father had died of cancer and like her equally neurotic mother, Angie seemed to think her own death by malignant cell growth was a foregone conclusion. And, most importantly and probably the real source of her anxiety, what if I'm a complete and utter failure?

"You're going to do great," I said, picking the anxious thought out of her brain before she could voice it. I had heard the spiel one too many times: It happened whenever Angie embarked on a new gig.

She gave me a sheepish smile. "But what about you, Grace?"

"What about me?" I said. "I have a new campaign at work," I said, reminding her of Roxanne Dubrow's new mission, which I had filled her in on earlier. "And since Claudia's in denial about the whole younger, brighter, better schtick the powers that be are on, I may have to shoulder a lot of the burden of developing it myself."

"I mean what are you going to do about Ethan?"

"What's to be done?" I replied with a shrug. "It's over."

She pursed her lips, as if aware she was treading on territory I didn't want to traverse. "I mean, don't you think you guys should talk? For closure?"

"I got all the closure I need," I said. Like Ethan, I was capable of walking away without a backward glance. Which was why I was sure Ethan was doing just fine without me. Just like Michael Dubrow was apparently, I thought, the reminder of Claudia's suggestion that he had moved on to his next "piece of ass" sending a surprising flood of anger through me. I shrugged it off. I guess that was just the kind of man I was attracted to: independent or, as all the self-help books Angie had tried to foist on me of late put it, "emotionally unavailable."

"Well, what does Shelley think?" she asked. Now I *knew* Angie was desperate to probe my inner state. Because in the months I'd been seeing Shelley, Angie had acted a bit like my therapist was the enemy, siding with me whenever I found fault, which was often, with the woman I was paying 140 bucks a session to cure me from whatever she believed ailed me. I secretly thought Angie was a bit jealous of Shelley. I guess she figured I should be able to confess all to her and get the advice I needed. She was, after all, my best friend.

"Oh, you know her," I said. "She's always trying to tie everything back to Kristina. Some perceived slight she thinks I've suffered from a woman I've never met." I waved a hand in the air, hoping to communicate the blandness I felt inside. "I thought I was safe from all that crap when I went to a psychoanalyst. Maybe I'm not remembering my Freud right, but isn't it my father who's supposed to fuck up my emotional life?" I sputtered out a mirthless laugh. What father? The original birth certificate I had managed to track down hadn't listed one. And the father who raised me was probably a candidate for Man of the Year, judging by the way everyone—my mother, his students, even the neighbors—worshiped him.

Now Angie was studying me as if, for a change, she thought my therapist might be on to something. "Another martini?" I said, downing the last of mine.

She frowned.

"C'mon, Ange," I said, trying to rouse her. "This is New York City. There are plenty of men—" I waved a hand at our waiter, who I noticed was a particularly fine example of the breed "—and Stolichnaya to go around."

And plenty of work to do, I realized. But I was feeling more than up to it. It was a good thing, too, because

Claudia had picked up the smoking habit she had given up months earlier after she had discovered a new line in her upper lip. Apparently she had bigger things to worry about now that Roxanne Dubrow had ruined her life, as she alleged whenever she returned reeking of smoke from the handicapped bathroom. I didn't mind her frequent absences, seeing as I felt like I could run this campaign single-handedly, with the assistance of Lori, of course.

But Claudia roused herself from her nicotine stupor just in time for the focus group testing. Because if we hoped to understand the desires, and insecurities, of the 18-to-24-year-old set just as keenly as we understood the desires, and insecurities, of the over-30 set, we needed to do some research. Even Dianne left the Dubrow family enclave in Old Brookville, Long Island, where she ran the Dubrow empire practically from the comfort of her home, to personally conduct the research. Although the building complex that housed Research and Development and one of our manufacturing complexes was only a short drive away in Bethpage, the market tests would be conducted in Cincinnati and Minneapolis. As VP of Marketing, Claudia had gone, too.

Though I was surprised I hadn't been invited this time, I didn't mind. In truth, I always found focus group research, although necessary in many ways, borderline ridiculous. As if the New Yorker in me, the woman who had been born and bred in the shopping mecca of the world, couldn't completely wrap my mind around the idea that a bunch of women from Middle America were going to tell me something about what women truly craved in cosmetic products.

So I was happy enough to maintain the Roxanne Dubrow fort on Park Avenue while Claudia and Dianne headed off to the Midwest to observe a hand-selected segment of 18-to-24-year-olds who had been deemed our new target market.

I was equally glad when Claudia came back, as Lori had started to angst again over Dennis's pending applications. "What if he gets in? He doesn't even talk about what that will mean for us...." she whined during those moments when I clearly hadn't dumped enough work on her. I found myself nodding sympathetically at the appropriate intervals, all the while wondering if what Dennis did or ultimately didn't do mattered at all. Lori would either go with him or move on. Life went on no matter how much we angsted over it. This was one of the wisdoms that age had brought me. I took some measure of comfort in the idea that I was free from all the pining that came from being twenty-three. It was all so useless in the long run, wasn't it?

But as much as I hoped to disregard the pinings of youth, once Claudia dumped the focus group findings on me to review, I found myself deluged in information about what the 18-to-24-year-old female wanted most. At least when it came to her appearance.

She wanted color. Lots of it. Shine, sparkle, glitter.

She wanted to stand out. Be unique.

She wanted to be strong, yet feminine. A lithe athlete in strawberry-scented lip gloss.

She owned an average of two Juicy Couture outfits, spent more time surfing the Internet than she did watching TV and preferred cosmetics called "Don't Quit Your Day Job" to the more descriptive "Passionfruit Pink."

I also learned that the person she most aspired to be was Irina Barbalovich.

Which is exactly why Roxanne Dubrow, or more specifically, Dianne, wanted her to be their new face.

And so the wooing began. It was simple enough at first. Not many people in the fashion industry turned down a personal phone call from Dianne Dubrow, least of all Mimi Blaustein, CEO of Turner Modeling Agency and agent to its current star property, Irina.

As with most relationships, the courtship began with food. Lunch was promptly arranged. And because a lot was riding on this relationship, restaurant selection was of the utmost importance. Lori was promptly sent on a mission to uncover Irina's preferences.

This was not such a difficult mission. The Internet was rife with interviews and sites devoted to Irina. Apparently the entire universe wanted to know what Irina wanted, and I had to assume, since no one knew Irina from any other nineteen-year-old up until recently, this desire was that her hips were slight enough and her abs tight enough to make her irresistible in a pair of low-slung jeans; that her bust-to-hip ratio made her absolutely stunning in most any fabric a designer draped on her.

What Lori uncovered was that Irina was a vegan of the worst kind. Nondairy. Wheat-free. And wholly organic.

Thank God we were in New York City, probably the only place in the world where you could find a restaurant that was up-to-the-moment chic yet capable of creating well-presented plates featuring food that had not been tortured during its lifespan, sprayed with pesticides, kept alive by antibiotics or mishandled in any way, shape or form.

That restaurant was Mandela, a short walk away on Madison Avenue, and usually a month-long wait for a reservation. Unless you happened to be dining with Irina, of course.

Miraculously, or not so miraculously depending on how you looked at it, Mandela just so happened to have an opening during the very two-hour spread that Mimi's assistant had allotted for Irina to make herself available to Dianne Dubrow and Co.

The reservation was made for six people, according to the hastily scrawled note Claudia had left lying on Lori's desk, which I had come across while dropping off some files.

Six? It seemed like a curious number. Irina and her agent. Claudia, Dianne and me. Who was the sixth? I wondered.

It certainly wasn't Lori, because although she had, through her administrative support, probably worked as hard as I had to prepare us for this meeting, she never got to enjoy the perks like Claudia and I did. It could have been Lana Jacobs, though we generally didn't bring in PR at this point—not until we had the prospective model on board. Mark Sulzberg from Legal? Way too soon for that. It wasn't like Irina was ready to sign a contract with us yet, especially since we weren't the only players in the fashion industry vying for Irina's hand.

It could have been Phillip Landau, the up-and-coming photographer who had first captured Irina for *Vogue*. The two had become almost inseparable since that career-boosting fashion spread, and their constant camaraderie might have sparked rumors of romance, if not for the fact that Phillip was gay.

Still curious, I popped my head into Claudia's office. "So who's going to lunch next week?" I inquired.

Claudia looked up from the issue of *W* she'd been poring over, whether because she was trend-spotting or simply gathering ammunition for her next shopping spree I wasn't sure.

"Lunch?" Claudia said, gazing up at me in what looked like a drug-induced fog. She was shopping, I decided. Nothing else could put a glaze like the one I saw in Claudia's eyes right now like the pursuit of the latest handbag or cut of trouser.

"With Irina?"

Her gaze sharpened up immediately, as if the very utterance of Irina's name put all her senses on full alert. "Well, Irina and Mimi, of course. Me and Dianne," she said, ticking off each name on the tips of her manicured fingers. "Michael—"

"Michael Dubrow?" I asked, startled. "Why is he coming?"

Claudia eyed me speculatively. I must have been showing a little more emotion than the situation warranted.

Hoping to dispel any suspicion I may have caused, I said, "It just seems peculiar that the vice president of our Overseas Division is attending a lunch to woo our latest model, don't you think?" Even as I said the words with the veneer of cool indifference that had become my trademark, new anxiety washed over me. I hadn't seen Michael at close range for quite some time. Shortly after our affair, he had taken over management of the Overseas Division, which kept him out of the country a lot. When he was in the States, he usually worked out of the Long Island office, and even if he did come to New York, he was easy enough to avoid, seeing as the doors to the family town house in Sutton Place weren't exactly open to all. The few times I did find myself in meetings with him in our Park Avenue offices, there were enough other people in the room for me to maintain a cool, corporate indifference to him from across the room. But the intimacy of sitting across a table in a restaurant from Michael suddenly seemed like too much to bear. It surprised me to what extent he could unravel me after all this time. Maybe I *was* getting soft in my old age.

"I believe he's coming to escort Courtney," she said, feasting her gaze once more on the magazine before her.

"Courtney?"

"Courtney Manchester. The new director of R & D?" she said, looking at me again. "I guess he feels responsible for her. Or something," she continued. "After all, he did, in a sense, *acquire* her, right along with the Sparkle line. Knowing him, he probably wants to claim the company's new baby as his own so he can reap all the glory once Roxy D takes off." She snorted. "But I suppose with the amount of money this company is dropping on this product, *something* glorious is bound to happen."

As Claudia moved on to her typical rant about how Michael—or even Dianne, for that matter—didn't know a thing about successfully marketing a product beyond throwing a bunch of money at it, I nodded absently, my mind whirling with the implications of what she had just told me. For a brief moment, I wasn't even sure what bothered me more: the fact that I suspected Michael was openly wooing his next conquest or the fact that, clearly, I was not a main player in Roxanne Dubrow's next big campaign. I hadn't even been invited to this fucking lunch.

Before the steam visibly shot out of my ears, I interrupted Claudia's tirade with a hurried excuse about a call I needed to make to a sales rep, then headed straight for my office, closing the door behind me.

And while I sat there contemplating the fact that my future at Roxanne Dubrow was not as rosy as I had once thought, I found myself clicking on the e-mail archive where I had filed the semiannual corporate newsletters we received.

Glancing through the file, I quickly located the newsletter announcing Roxanne Dubrow's acquisition of Sparkle and opened it up, my eyes seeking out the article—and more specifically, the photo of Courtney Manchester I had barely glanced at when it first arrived. But I took it all in now.

Like Courtney Manchester's winning smile. Her russet hair and sparkling green eyes.

Michael always was a sucker for a pretty face. And this one was downright irresistible to him, I was sure.

If he wasn't sleeping with her yet, it was only a matter of time.

To think I had once let this man inside me without a condom.

But not even my anger could squash the sinking feeling in the pit of my stomach. Why did this bother me so much? I had dumped better men than Michael since, at least in terms of how available Drew or Ethan had made themselves to me.

Because you loved him, a little voice whispered, as I remembered how many nights I had lain awake during our affair, wishing he weren't so powerful, so ambitious, so hard to nail down for more than just some fleeting yet utterly intimate encounters.

Is that what love was? Longing followed by pain and loss?

If that was true, I didn't want any part of it.

4

"A man in love is incomplete until he is married. Then he is finished."

—Zsa Zsa Gabor

If I could have flung myself wholeheartedly into the new campaign, I would have. Anything to avoid thinking about what a disappointment the men in my life were.

But since Claudia had carefully excluded me from any meaningful role in the Roxy D campaign, I no longer felt compelled to work late reviewing advertising firms and drafting proposals. If Claudia wanted this baby all to herself, then she could deal with it all by herself.

I had better things to do. It wasn't like Roxanne Dubrow was going to survive next year on the strength of Roxy D alone. There was still, according to our market research, a whole segment of women in the 35-to-50-year-old range who had yet to discover the wonders of Youth Elixir, our flagship moisturizer. I decided to concern myself once more with the demographic that needed me most, at least from a skincare perspective. Besides, the Youth Elixir campaign needed all my creative energy if I hoped to keep it afloat now that the budget for it had been cut nearly in half.

I had carefully explained to Shelley the challenge of promoting the Youth Elixir on a drastically reduced budget that week during our session. I could see she was looking for an opening to talk about something with a bit more emotional depth than whether or not I could single-handedly raise Youth Elixir to new sales heights, but I didn't give her the chance. What was the point of wallowing in whatever problems she imagined remained beneath the surface?

Still, I was aware of some lingering malaise over Michael, one I could not erase as effectively as I had Ethan.

No less than three times that week, I caught myself fantasizing about some big scene in which, with one or two killing statements, I revealed to Courtney as well as to Michael's doting sister, Dianne, that Michael Dubrow was a womanizing jerk. Which was why I decided to disappear for the few hours that I lived in danger of running into Michael and his entourage.

So, at eleven-thirty on the appointed day—a full forty-five minutes before the Dubrow clan was due to arrive via car service from Long Island—I went to Bloomingdale's.

In case you think I was shirking my duties out of emotional distress, trust me, I did have some competitive shopping to do. Some of the major manufacturers had come out with new gift packages, and I needed to see what Roxanne Dubrow's competitors were up to, didn't I?

The fact that I dawdled in the designer section on Two once I was done in cosmetics had nothing to do with anything. After all, September was now fully upon us, and I could already feel the cooler weather creeping in. I needed to stock up on this season's trousers and sweaters if I hoped to make it through the coming winter.

By the time I left Bloomingdale's a full two hours later, I was armed with enough shopping bags to make my time away from the office look suspiciously like a personal shopping spree. So I opted for a quick cab ride across town to my apartment, where I relieved myself of all non-work-related expenditures, and took a few moments to dust powder over my face and freshen up my lipstick. Because if I was unfortunate enough to run into Michael, I needed to look gorgeous enough to fill him with a pang of regret that he would never, ever, have me in the horizontal—or otherwise—again.

Take that, I said, standing before the full-length mirror in my bedroom and studying the way my light sweater hugged my curves, the way my narrow skirt accentuated my legs. My well-cut jacket that balanced the vamp element the skirt lent the whole outfit, setting me firmly in the tastefully-corporate-yet-supremely-feminine camp. A dab of lipstick (just a refresher, mind you—I didn't want to look like I was trying too hard) and I left the apartment, more than ready to face whatever Michael Dubrow had to dish out.

Of course, one glance at my watch as the cab rolled toward Park Avenue indicated that I had been gone almost three hours and was likely in no danger of running into any of the Dubrows. The way I calculated it, lunch had ended by two o'clock and Dianne et al. were on the L.I.E. no later than two-fifteen.

Which was why my eyes practically popped out of my head when my cab pulled up and I spotted the Dubrows' shiny dark luxury sedan parked in front of the building. The

driver sat inside reading a newspaper, as if he didn't antici-
pate leaving anytime soon.

I paid my cab fare and stepped out onto the sidewalk,
knowing full well there was no way I could avoid the
Dubrow clan any longer.

The first thing I noticed when I entered the office was that
it was eerily empty—and surprisingly quiet. Lori's desk was
vacant, and if not for the furious tapping of keys that I heard
coming from Claudia's office, I would have thought the
building had been evacuated.

I stopped in her doorway. "What's going on?"

She glanced up. "Where have you *been?*"

"Bloomingdale's," I replied, holding up the single bag I had
brought back to the office with me, which contained an as-
sortment of offerings from our main competitors. "The winter gift packages are in stores," I replied by way of explanation.

"Dianne has got everyone gathered in the conference
room," Claudia said. "We're about to have a champagne
toast."

"Don't tell me you got Mimi Blaustein to sign over her
star property during lunch?"

"No, no," Claudia said, shaking her head. "Please. You
should have seen the way everyone was fawning over that
Irina at lunch. Disgusting. As if anyone was really interested
in what a girl barely out of her training bra had to say, which
wasn't much." She rolled her eyes. "No, Irina and Mimi are
long gone. Something about a plane Irina had to catch to
Paris." I saw a hint of bleariness in her well-made-up eyes
and realized that Claudia was likely exhausted from having
to curb her irritation with the girl-barely-out-of-training-
bra for the sake of the company's agenda. "I just wanted to

get this e-mail out before the end of day and I was hoping to buy *you* some extra time…."

"Time for what?" I blinked.

"Oh, God knows. Dianne has some sort of announcement she wants to make."

Everyone was already assembled, from PR and Sales to the marketing teams for all three of the brands. I spotted Michael right away, chatting merrily with Doug Rutherford, the Director of Sales, who kept an office at the other end of our U-shaped space for when he was in town. In that one fleeting glance I allowed myself, I saw that Michael was just as handsome as ever, with his dark brown hair and thickly lashed blue eyes. Although he had just passed the forty-two mark, he somehow seemed younger-looking than ever. Michael epitomized the phrase "boyishly handsome," with his (seemingly) guileless features and somewhat petulant mouth and jutting chin. It suited his position as the late-in-life baby, born a full twelve years after Dianne—much to the delight of Roxanne Dubrow and her late husband, Ambrose. And Michael was every bit as spoiled and selfish as that position in life allowed, I had realized just after he had carelessly made love to me as if it didn't matter. As if I didn't matter.

Not allowing myself to dwell on that face—or the surprising tremor of feeling that radiated through me, even after all this time—I made my eyes flit about the room until they fell on Dianne, who stood at the helm, her shiny brown hair framing her perfectly made-up face and flawless skin—well, as flawless as a woman of fifty-four could look. She was, as always, dressed to perfection in a fitted ivory suit (the season's new black, as of last week's issue of *W*), and looking like the petite but exquisite queen of the Dubrow clan that she had become when her mother had gone into retirement over a decade ago. The sight of her filled me with a strange sort of relief, as it occurred to me that I had not seen Dianne in probably months. Though she had always ruled the roost from the Long Island office, previously she had made her presence in the New York office felt through frequent visits. I wondered now what had kept her away.

"Makes you want to puke, doesn't she?" Claudia said, startling me as she came to stand at my side.

"Puke?" I asked, confused.

"Courtney Manchester. The redhead talking to Dianne...."

I shifted my gaze, taking in the woman who stood by Dianne's side, smiling up at her with perfectly made-up porcelain features. I hadn't even recognized her. Probably because she looked even more beautiful than she did in that little photo I had dug up.

I decided to play neutral. What choice did I have? "Well, she's a beautiful woman," I replied, as if this explained everything, right down to the tremble my body could barely contain.

Claudia snorted. "*Please*. Wait until you see her teeth. She's a Brit, remember?"

I tried to focus on this one seeming flaw as I made my way across the room to greet Dianne. I couldn't very well avoid the CEO of Roxanne Dubrow just because my heart felt like someone had just placed a large boulder on it. Besides, Dianne had already spotted me across the room and had gently waved me over, her face wreathed in the kind of gracious warmth that was a perk of her deluxe lifestyle.

"Grace Noonan!" Dianne said, holding out one well-manicured hand to me and pulling me into a cheek-grazing embrace. Dianne treated her employees as if they were family, only somehow I never truly felt like a member, no matter how many corporate hugs and Christmas gifts I'd collected over time. "We missed you at lunch today. Claudia said you had another appointment…?"

Before I could turn to send my boss a querying glance, Dianne introduced me to the lovely Courtney, who smiled pleasantly up at me. She was a tiny little thing—probably no more than five-four.

Suddenly there I was, smiling just as cordially back and extending a hand. Was this the woman who would convince Michael Dubrow that a relationship with one of his employees wouldn't destroy the Dubrow empire? I wondered, gazing on her pretty features, yes, there was the matter of a turned front tooth, but it really was quite charming, and listening to the pleasantries she uttered in that beautiful British accent. I took some small measure of comfort in the idea that maybe Michael's interest had more to do with the profit he saw in the merger between Sparkle and Roxanne Dubrow. Perhaps it was this small ray of hope that gave me strength when Michael himself finally made his way over to us.

Balls, I thought, as he gazed frankly at me, a confident smile on that well-shaped mouth. If nothing else, Michael Dubrow had a set of balls on him, I thought. I felt anew the desire to cut him down to size in front of Dianne, who gazed at him fondly as he stepped into our circle, and Courtney, who looked like she was about to fawn all over him, judging from the way her features softened when he stopped next to her.

"Grace, good to see you," he said, nodding at me before turning to Courtney. "I assume you've met Courtney," he continued, not taking his gaze from her, as if she were some precious jewel that had caught his eye.

And apparently, she was. Because no sooner had Michael

locked gazes with the lovely Courtney than Dianne suddenly remembered that she had gathered us all here for a reason. "It's time," she said, with a clap of her hands that commanded the attention of everyone in the room and sent Lori, who, I noticed, had been circulating with a champagne-laden tray, to our circle. Once we had grabbed the remaining five glasses and Lori had tucked the tray beneath the conference table, Dianne stood center stage.

"I'm sure you are all wondering why I have gathered you here today," she said, flashing us that gracious smile. "As it turns out, I have a wonderful announcement to make. Two, in fact," she continued, her proud glance flitting over to Michael and Courtney.

"As you all know, last year we acquired the wonderful Sparkle line headed up by Courtney Manchester out of the U.K. And it is our fervent hope that by placing this line under the Roxanne Dubrow umbrella, the future of our great line will be secure. That's why I am proud to announce that Courtney Manchester, who will oversee the transformation of this new product under Roxanne Dubrow, has been promoted to the position of Vice President of Product Development."

The room erupted in a smattering of applause, small enough for me to hear Claudia mutter, "As if we didn't see *that* coming."

Then, as if the other thing that was coming was just as obvious, Dianne continued, "And I am also happy to announce another merger, this one a bit more personal." Raising her glass she said, "To Michael and Courtney, who have just, this past weekend, announced their engagement."

5

"We are all tied to our destiny and there is no way to liberate ourselves."

—Rita Hayworth

I stopped at Zabar's on the way home, feeling a burning need to chop, sauté and simmer. It wasn't often that I cooked, and on some level, I knew its value for me was more therapeutic than culinary. I had decided on stir fry, mostly because I understood that after the emotionally harrowing events of the afternoon, I would have to chop a gardenful of vegetables to soothe what ailed me. And chop I would, having picked up three peppers, a monstrous eggplant, a head of broccoli, a slew of mushrooms and more garlic than one should consume on Friday night if one hopes to find oneself in the company of others. But I had already decided I didn't want to socialize. Claudia had pressed me for a post-work cocktail on my way out of the office, but I didn't feel like standing at some bar, listening to my more-bitter-by-the-hour boss rail against the injustice of Courtney's sudden rise to the right hand of the Dubrow family, especially when the place she had taken in Michael's heart still stung. And how it stung. Even more so when I saw the way Dianne embraced the happy couple, welcoming Courtney to the family in a way that filled me with a strange longing. I knew now why I never felt a part of the Dubrow "family." Because I wasn't. And never would be.

That thought sent me straight to the liquor store after Zabar, to pick up a bottle of wine. I had felt a determination to make this evening alone just as pleasurable and relaxing as it might have been had I spent it with someone else. I even splurged on a French Bordeaux.

So it was with a bag of produce and a bottle of wine that I sailed through my front lobby. I even winked at Malakai, my ever-friendly and ever-accommodating doorman, who graciously held open the door, eyeing my purchases as I glided through. "Is my tall friend coming by?" he asked cheerfully, referring to Ethan. Malakai always referred to the men in my life by some physical characteristic. My last boyfriend, Drew, had been his "blond friend." Even Michael, despite the fact that his visits were few and far between, had earned the moniker of Malakai's "blue-eyed friend."

This was the problem with doormen. You couldn't hide your love life—or lack thereof—from them. Though we only had one and he only worked five to midnight, Malakai's shift covered that crucial period of the evening when everything did—or didn't—happen in a woman's life.

"No, no one's coming by," I said, with a bracing smile as I transferred my bags to one arm and headed for the line of mailboxes at the other end of the lobby, trying to escape

Malakai's inevitable teasing comment about how he would never let me spend an evening alone if he were twenty years younger.

I knew he meant well, in the way that aging uncle of yours meant well when he sang you the Miss America song when you were six. But I just wasn't in the mood.

Once at the mailboxes, I slid my key in, then grabbed out the handful of catalogs, bills and credit card offers that were my daily due, when a letter caught my eye, the return address as familiar to me by now as my own.

K. Morova. Brooklyn, NY.

I knew that handwriting, though I did not know the writer herself. Had traced my finger often enough over the signature that had come back on the return receipt for the letter I had sent Kristina Morova, all those months ago.

My mother, at least in biological fact.

The woman whom I had believed, up until this moment, had no interest in meeting me.

I ignored the pulse of pure fear that constricted my throat and quickly slid the letter between the pages of a Pottery Barn catalog, as if to protect myself from its contents, then headed for the bank of elevators that flanked the lobby.

"Finally getting that nice cool weather," came a voice, startling me out of whatever scattered thoughts I was having. I looked up to see Mrs. Brandemeyer, who lived a floor below me and had been a tenant of 122 W. 86th Street since the sixties. Her long-term residency, combined with her elderly status, seemed to give her certain inalienable rights. Like laundry room usage (you always forfeited the remaining dryer to Mrs. Brandemeyer, who was "too old to be riding up and down, up and down") or the proprietary air she took when it came to Malakai.

She had treated me rather suspiciously when I had first moved in six years earlier. "I don't like loud music," she proclaimed just moments after she had learned I was not only single but living in the apartment above hers. Once she discovered that I wasn't going to be having raucous parties every weekend, she immediately bestowed upon me neighborly chatter about such subjects as the weather, the number of menus she received underneath her door on any given day or the condition of the carpeting in the hallways.

I was never one for small talk, and this evening it seemed especially burdensome, when I had something large looming between the pages of the shopping catalog I held. So I just nodded and smiled while she speculated about the sudden drop in temperatures.

"It's going to be a cold, cold winter," she said with satisfaction as she stepped off, leaving me to ride that last story alone.

I felt a momentary surprise when I stepped into my apartment and discovered it was exactly the same as I had left it that morning, except for the fading evening light that was now slanting through the gauzy ivory curtains. Outside the city glittered, and I took solace in the fact that regardless of whatever Kristina Morova had decided to write in her letter to me, New York City would still be just outside my window, waiting for me like an old friend.

Maybe it was that letter and its unknown contents that sent me into the next flurry of activity: putting the produce in the kitchen, hanging up my coat, straightening the stack of magazines that I had yet to review, wiping down the kitchen counters. Then curiosity must have won over the fear throbbing through me, and I found myself slipping out of my shoes, curling up on the couch and taking that letter in hand with the sense of fatalism that had been subtly stalking me ever since I had sent my own letter seven months ago.

I carefully broke the seal on the envelope, pulled out a single sheet of ivory stationery decorated with flowers at the top. My first thought was that it reminded me of the stationery my grandmother used. The second was that there was only one page of loopy scrawl. I briefly wondered at that, then settled in to read.

Dear Grace Noonan,

I thank you much for your letter some months back and I write to tell you how sorry I am that I did not make my reply sooner but so much has happened. I have news of my sister, Kristina Morova, to share, but I am so sorry to tell you it is not good. My sister died this past December, of breast cancer. I am sorry to bring you such sad news but I know my sister would want you to know.

I also write to tell you that you have a sister, Sasha, just sixteen years old. She is with me now, in Brooklyn.

I am not sure if you still want to meet with us, but I want to honor my sister's wish and I want to invite you to come to our home. I give you my number in Brooklyn and hope to hear from you about this matter.

Sincerely,
Katerina Morova

I read the letter three times before the contents sank in. Before the cruel truth beneath that shaky cursive and stilted grammar broke through.

She was gone. Kristina Morova was gone.

I felt a momentary relief that at least there was a reason for all the silence of the past months. Followed by a disappointment so keen, tears rushed to my eyes.

Gone. *Gone.*

Still, no tears fell. Maybe because for me, she had never really been there. Could I really mourn someone I did not technically know?

I stood up from the couch with some idea that I should do something. But uncertain what that thing was, I walked woodenly to the kitchen, stared at the bags of produce I'd left there and, as if on autopilot, pulled out the cutting board. Grabbing a head of garlic from the bag, I peeled away the crisp outer shell on one of the cloves and began to chop, with some idea that this meal must be prepared, come hell or high water. Not that I was hungry, but I needed some sense of purpose, even if it was simply to keep this newly purchased bag of produce from rotting, neglected, in the bottom drawer of my fridge.

It wasn't until I got to my eighth clove of garlic—about four cloves more than I actually needed—that I came out of my dense fog. And this only because I had somehow managed, in all my stoical chopping, to take a sliver off my index finger.

"Fuck!"

And then, because I felt a rush of tears that was most definitely more than this little cut could possibly provoke, I stopped, took a deep breath, and after dousing the wound with cold water, wrapped my finger in a napkin and grabbed the phone.

"Angie, it's Grace," I said into my best friend's machine. When she picked up the extension, I felt a noticeable relief wash over me.

"What's up?" she said urgently, as if she sensed some underlying emotion in the three words I'd uttered on her machine. More likely she was just surprised to hear from me. It wasn't like me to call her on a Friday night to chat.

Then, as casually as I might convey a car accident I had witnessed from the safety of the curb, I told her everything.

"Good God, Grace, are you okay?" she sputtered. Then, "Never mind. Don't answer that. I'm coming over."

I didn't have the energy to argue. Or, maybe for once I didn't want to. Because whatever feelings I thought I should or shouldn't be having about Kristina Morova's death, I did at least sense that something momentous had occurred. Something that couldn't be glossed over in my usual fashion.

And so I let Angie march into my apartment that night, even felt emotion clog my throat when she hugged me fiercely. It was this, more than anything else, that convinced me I should allow her to console me, to sit on the couch and regale me with advice because I somehow couldn't bring myself to talk about it. And when she was done with that, to feed me.

"How can you tell if the chicken is done?" she called from the kitchen. She had insisted on finishing the meal— I think the way I sat mutely on the couch during her consolatory speech convinced her that she needed to do *something* for me. So I had curled up on the couch with the glass of wine she poured me, only to remember that when it came to matters of the kitchen, Angie was one who should have stayed in the living room with the glass of wine.

I felt a smile trace its way across my mouth as I uncurled

myself from the couch and meandered into the kitchen. A smile I quickly lost the moment I saw the havoc Angie's latest culinary attempt had wreaked: mutilated vegetable carcasses littered the counter while strips of what looked like chicken fat swam in an olive oil spill near the stove. The meal itself looked like a disaster in the making. The vegetables were cooking just fine—in fact, they were probably overcooking. But the chicken was still in huge, cutlet-size hunks.

Apparently, Angie had never made stir fry before.

"Mmmm…I'm not sure it's going to cook that way," I said, stepping in and taking over. Once I began pulling the chicken out of the pan and cutting it into smaller strips, I felt better. All of Angie's coddling had only made me feel helpless, and that wasn't a feeling I liked to cultivate.

Now Angie stood by helplessly but also visibly relieved that I had taken over, though she kept apologizing.

"Maybe we should order in," she muttered, eyeballing the still-pink flesh of the chicken as I began to toss the strips into the pan. Angie had a fear of death by microbacteria.

"Don't worry, I'll make it edible," I said, slicing up the last cutlet and stirring it into the mix.

By the time we sat down to eat, I was feeling like myself again. In control. Satisfied. And no longer in the mood to dwell on things that might have been. I hadn't really lost anything. I was still the same Grace Noonan I was the day before. There was no funeral to attend, no condolences to accept. I wasn't, technically, the grieving family. So technically, there was nothing to grieve, right?

I had also come to a decision, despite Angie's prodding that I meet this newfound aunt and sister. Although I was more curious about them than I let on, I decided I didn't want to know them. Didn't want to care for the family who had only contacted me out of a sense of obligation.

"That was delicious, Grace," Angie said, leaning back in her chair, having eaten so heartily of the stir fry once she had been assured the chicken wouldn't kill her, she looked ready for a cab ride downtown and a pillow. That was fine with me. I was more than ready to be alone.

Unfortunately, Angie had other ideas. "So, I brought over a toothbrush and a change of underwear…." she began.

"Oh, Angie, you don't need to stay," I immediately protested. But feeling bad at the hurt look in her eyes, I relented.

She beamed. "Great. I'll run out and get us some Double Chocolate Häagen-Dazs. This is gonna be fun, Gracie. Just like old times when we used to do sleepovers back in Brooklyn…."

It was more like old times than even I expected, especially when Angie forewent the sofa bed, insisting instead on sharing my bed.

So there we were, lying side by side in the dark, just like when we were in junior high. We had indulged ourselves on ice cream while Angie talked excitedly about the location Justin had found to shoot the opening scene in his film. We eventually moved on to other topics we shared in common, like men.

Angie listened quietly while I expressed my relief over having Ethan out of my life. "I don't think he would have handled this whole business with Kristina Morova very well…." I said, unexpectedly bringing up the subject I had studiously avoided all evening.

I felt Angie's eyes on me in the dark. As if she sensed the

unease I was feeling. Without saying a word, she took my
hand in hers. And despite this independent front I was trying to put on, I was painfully glad I wasn't alone right then.
Even so, it wasn't until I heard Angie's breath fall in the deep,
rhythmic pattern of sleep that I allowed myself to weep.

I'm not sure how long I let the tears roll quietly down my
face, my body shaking with the effort of holding back any
sobs that might wake Angie, but the tide eventually stopped,
allowing me to turn and look at my sleeping friend with a
sad smile. I really hadn't lost a thing, had I? I still had my best
friend. My family, whom, I realized with a sudden shiver of
unexpected anxiety, I needed to call.

There was no hurry, I thought as I felt myself slip into
sleep. And I was nearly submerged in a blissfully unconscious
state when the sound of a cell phone ringing jarred me
awake once more.

"Shit," I heard Angie mutter. She glanced at me as I eye-
balled her groggily. "Sorry, Grace," she said, scrambling from
the bed.

I watched her shadowy form move across the bedroom
and out the door, which in her hurry to get out of the room,
she had left ajar. Open just enough for me to hear her rum-
mage through her pocketbook, locate the still-ringing phone
and silence it.

"Hey, sweetheart…" I heard her say.

Justin, I realized drowsily.

"I know, I know. I miss you, too, baby…."

I felt my insides soften along with Angie's voice as I imagined Justin in their apartment alone, longing for Angie just
as surely as she was longing for him.

To be so loved—

My heart sank with sudden swiftness.

I realized I *had* lost something tonight. Something even greater than a fifty-one-year-old woman I had never known, yet was bound to in the most intimate of ways.

Hope.

6

*"You may admire a girl's curves on the first intro-
duction, but the second meeting shows up new
angles."*

—Mae West

The last person I expected to revive my spirit was Irina Barbalovich, but when I stepped into the office on Monday
morning and found a seven-foot-tall cardboard effigy of her
staring me in the face, I felt oddly bolstered. Maybe it was
the way her pretty blond hair blew in the nonexistent wind,
or the way she stood, hip jutting, chin tilted as if she had every
reason in the world to be happy.

I suppose she did, judging by the amount of money the
Dubrow clan was dangling before her pretty blue eyes, hoping to lure her in.

"What's with the Irina doll in the lobby?" I asked Lori,
who was already at her desk.

"Dianne ordered it," Lori replied. "I think she's planning on inviting Irina up to the offices for a tour."

I nodded at this bit of information, studying the face of the woman everybody wanted to call their own.

"She's pretty amazing, huh?" Lori said, coming to stand beside me. Her gaze roamed from Irina's cardboard face to mine. "You know, you could be her mother."

Her *mother?* Alarm shot through me and my hand went to my cheek, as if my advancing age was suddenly apparent for the entire world to see.

Lori blushed, probably because she realized her comment had landed right on my thirty-four-year-old ego. "What I meant was, you two kinda look alike. You know, similar coloring, the shape of the face…"

I smiled. As a face-saving comment, it was a good one. I suppose it's not every day a woman gets compared to the reigning supermodel.

I studied the image more closely, then realized that whatever faint resemblance Lori saw likely had to do with the fact that we both had roots in Eastern Europe. I guess there was a similarity in our facial structure and in the slight tilt to our eyes, but she looked more Slavic than I did. "My mother was Ukrainian," I said, unthinkingly. Then I realized that was probably the first time in my life I had ever referred to Kristina Morova as my mother. And in light of the new revelations I had had over the weekend, the word stabbed at me.

Lori blinked, then frowned. "Really? Didn't you tell me your parents were Irish?"

Now I was frowning. I suddenly remembered that no one in the office knew I was adopted. Mostly because I didn't feel a need to share my personal history with anyone, outside of Angie, Justin, the DiFranco family and the few boyfriends I

had allowed myself to open up to. According to ninety per-
cent of the world, my parents were Thomas and Serena
Noonan, a retired history professor and his lovely musician
wife, living in New Mexico.

"My father is Irish," I said, backpedaling. That was true.
Black Irish. My adoptive mother was, technically, a mix of
Irish and German and a bit of English thrown in. I bit back
a sigh as I thought of my parents, realizing that I still needed
to call them—had assured Angie I would do so.

But suddenly I wondered what telling them would ac-
complish. Nothing had changed in my life. Not really. In fact,
once I let go of the harrowing disappointment the letter sent
through me, I found myself feeling lighter. More free. I suppose there was something to the notion of living without ex-
pectation. If you had nothing to look forward to, you had
nothing to lose.

"Her hair's longer than yours. And not as blond," Lori was
saying now.

"Yeah, well, that's a good hairdresser for you," I said, a hand
moving to my chin-length locks as I tried to engage myself.
"Her eyes are bluer," I added absently, my thoughts still on
all that I did not want to talk about.

"Still, there's something there," Lori persisted, as if sensing
some unease in me and hoping to cover it over by raising me
to the heights of Irina's beauty.

I stared hard at the effigy, suddenly wanted to resist any
link to the supermodel. Any link that might somehow tie
me to Kristina. But as I studied Irina's cool confidence, I realized there was something I could learn from her. What was
Irina Barbalovich but a farm girl from Russia with a pretty
face? She had started her life afresh the moment she had
landed in this country. I could start anew, too.

It was all marketing, after all.

So I quickly put aside any lingering emotions and refashioned myself as Grace Noonan, daughter of Thomas and Serena Noonan. Brooklyn born. Long Island bred. Columbia University educated, compliments of my father's tenure in the history department. Talented, successful, smart.

It was a good thing I did, too. Because despite the fact that Claudia had tried to claim the Roxy D campaign for herself, she needed me.

And, I discovered, I needed this campaign, too. If only to forget…

Forget I did. I even canceled my therapy sessions in favor of the soothing rhythms of work. In fact, I worked so hard, it got to the point where I didn't even know what day it was.

"Lori, did that agency ever get back to us with a bid?" I said, stepping out of the whirl of paper that had become my office over the past two weeks. I glanced down at the proposal I still held in my hand. "Says here they have to get back to us by October second. Maybe you ought to give them a reminder call—"

Lori giggled, causing me to finally look up at her.

"Grace, it's the ninth already," she said, her exasperation apparent. Lori thought it was hysterical how I could sweep through blocks of time without ever realizing what month we were in, or what day we were on. I don't know why it happened—I didn't question it. Maybe I figured it might keep me younger longer if I completely ignored the passing of time.

I glanced down at my watch, as if to verify the truth of her words. I frowned. "Ummm, would you give them a follow-up call?" I said. Then, turning on my heel, I headed back to my office, filled with a vague sense that some other event, momentous or otherwise, should have taken place in this time frame.

I was about to consult my day planner when realization hit. My period. My fucking period.

It was…late.

A flurry of other realizations followed. Like that persistent ache in my breasts of late, with no follow-up act. And my cramps—was it my imagination, or did they feel different?

My gaze dropped to the half-eaten corn muffin slathered in butter that sat on my desk. I never ate corn muffins. This morning I'd had a raging lust for one. With butter, no less. I never ate butter except when I was in restaurants and couldn't resist the bread basket. This morning it was all I could think about. It was all I craved…

Suddenly the half-muffin I had already ingested felt in danger of making a reappearance.

I sat down, rolling the rest of that muffin right back up into its wrapping and depositing it promptly in the wastebasket next to my desk.

It didn't mean anything, I told myself, consulting my day planner and trying frantically to remember when I'd had my last period. I never really kept track, but I could usually figure out approximate dates by events in my life, as what I wore was sometimes impacted by the period factor. Ah…here, we go, I thought, spying the words "Met Fund-Raiser" written into the last week of August. I remembered I didn't want to wear my silver-blue dress because of the old bloat factor— that Botticelli belly of mine sometimes bordered on blubber right before my period. Then came the weekend with Ethan, when he opted out of sex because I was menstruating (he was a bit squeamish—another reason to be glad *he* was out of the picture). My finger skittered forward to the next event

I'd marked. That dreadful Wagner opera that even Ethan hadn't wanted to endure any longer, so we snuck out, went back to my place and—

"Fuck!"

"Grace, are you all right?" Lori called.

I leaped from my seat, startled. Then, as if by instinct, I strode toward the door. "I'm fine...fine," I said, nodding distractedly at her. "I, ummm, need to... Uh, hold all my calls."

I shut the door, went back to my desk, stared down at my day planner once more and began to calculate, counting the days between my period and that ill-fated night. Oh, dear God. I could have been ovulating, for chrissakes.

Of all the nights for the latex to give out...

I put my hand on my stomach, gazing down as if I could divine what was going on inside my body just by looking at it. I tried to imagine a child growing inside me, and suddenly I saw it, alive and nestled in my lap. I could almost feel the warm weight of her—I felt certain that it was a her—against my body.

And I got that feeling again. That warm wash through my veins that I had felt that night with Ethan. Except this time it felt more like...longing.

"That's insanity," I insisted to myself, and then, as if to punctuate my words, my intercom buzzed, indicating I had a call from someone in the office. Claudia, I thought, recognizing the extension that lit up my caller ID screen.

I picked up. "What's up?"

"What do you mean, what's up? We have an eleven o'clock. It's 11:05. Not that I want to *disturb* you."

I bit back the retort I wanted to make, letting Claudia's sarcasm slide. I sometimes think she takes delight in seeing me fuck up, which isn't often. But could anyone blame me for forgetting we were meeting with a prospective ad agency this morning?

Needless to say, I was a bit preoccupied.

My preoccupation did not end with my eleven o'clock. Because it was leaning toward eleven-forty-five when I finally began to emerge from the dense fog that had descended over my brain ever since I'd done my little calculation. I was utterly useless during the meeting. Well, not totally useless. I mutely handed over the focus group research while Claudia pontificated on what we hoped to bring to the younger market to the two reps who had come from the Sterling Agency. Not even the chiseled good looks of the elder of the two—Laurence Bennett, approximately thirty-eight, approximately one position away from agency president and, depending on how you viewed his presentation style, practically flaunting that ringless left hand at us—could revive me.

I might not even have noticed his good looks, had it not been for the gleam I saw come into Claudia's eye when, after she had gone over the slides laying out the desires, the hopes, the dreams and, more importantly, the buying habits of the 18-to-24-year-old set, Laurence winked and jokingly suggested that he was glad *he* wasn't so young anymore.

From then on, I saw a new tension in Claudia's movements as she went through the rest of the slides. In fact, if she'd had a tail, it would have been riding straight up into the air the way my mother's cat's had whenever some randy tom meandered through our yard.

Not that Larry noticed, I was sure. If nothing else, Claudia was subtle about her desires, or that desire was even part of her makeup. Nine times out of ten, the guy never even noticed she was female, much less attracted to him. Which probably accounted for the fact that Claudia hadn't gotten laid since her husband left her for a younger woman five years ago.

Somehow the sight of her preening today filled me with a sadness I could not fathom. What was the point? I wondered as I watched their heads lean together to examine a chart Lori had created which summed up the research. It all would result in nothing anyway, I thought.

My hand went to my stomach reflexively.

Whereas this…this was…*something*.

What it was, exactly, had yet to be determined. And probably could have been determined sooner rather than later by a simple stop at Duane Reade for a pregnancy test. Yet somehow I was reluctant to verify what my body seemed to be saying.

Instead I fed it. Quite literally.

I went home that night and ate an entire pint of butter pecan ice cream. And that wasn't the only indulgence I caved into. There was the bag of jalapeño cheddar potato chips I devoured, quite guiltlessly, along with lunch the next day. The Fettuccine Alfredo I grazed on at a café on my way home from work.

By the time I came home at week's end, a tub of chocolate-covered pretzels in tow, I realized something else.

I liked the solitude of my life. The sight of my message-less answering machine did not bother me. Not even the memory of Michael's confident grin as he gazed lovingly at Courtney had the power to hurt me. Nothing did. Not even Kristina Morova, I thought, carefully tucking her sister's letter in my desk drawer, certain now there was no real reason to reply.

Six chocolate-covered pretzels later, I slid out of my work

clothes in the small dressing area in my bathroom, seeking out the soft cotton yoga pants that had become my evening uniform as of late. As I began to slide them on, I caught a glance at my naked body in the mirror on the back of the door and stood, hesitantly turning sideways to check for any visible changes.

And began to imagine that the roundness I saw in my abdomen had nothing to do with my recent indulgences and everything to do with the longing that had taken over my mind.

A baby, I thought, running a hand over the small swell.

Suddenly everything seemed…possible.

A cold breeze accompanied me up the steps of the building where Shelley Longford, C.S.W., kept her neat little office, and as I climbed them I felt, for the first time in weeks, a sense of anticipation. Maybe it was because, for the first time since I had been coming to see her, I was actually looking forward to it.

I had news to share, after all.

"So what makes you think you're pregnant?" Shelley said, finally breaking the silence she had fallen into ever since I cheerfully made my announcement, effectively sidetracking her interrogation as to why I had canceled my recent appointments. And as I embellished my story with the dates of my last ovulation, the bloatedness I felt, the tenderness in my breasts, I saw her usually placid expression purse with suspicion.

Clearly she wasn't buying it. "The symptoms you describe could easily be premenstrual."

I bristled. "I think after nearly thirty-five years, I know my body," I argued, suddenly aware that I *was* arguing. In a somewhat calmer tone, I added, "I mean, have you ever been pregnant?"

Suddenly my question seemed inappropriate. For I had never broached the subject of her personal life in a session before. It had never been an issue before and I suppose it wasn't now, I thought, glancing at her ringless left hand. A flutter of questions rose in me about the stranger who sat before me and I stared at her, hoping she'd give me some information for a change.

Of course, she didn't. "Have you ever missed a period before?"

"Never," I said—a bit smugly, considering the fact that I couldn't entirely remember if this was true. "And I've never had a condom break inside me," I continued, finding the validation I was looking for in the facts of this particular case. "Besides, I feel…different. My body feels different." It was true. Ever since my period had failed to show up in its usual clockwork fashion, my body seemed to have shifted onto a new timetable. I was aware of myself in a way I hadn't been before. I woke up in the morning with a heaviness in my limbs that I couldn't attribute to sadness, for my mind felt suddenly clear.

Now here I was, sitting before a licensed professional and finally giving voice to that which my body already believed, and growing ever more suspicious of her by the second.

Just who the fuck did she think she was, telling me I had cramps? You see, that was the whole problem with this therapy business. As if anyone else could truly tell you what the hell was going on inside of you.

"I'm just saying it's a possibility you are simply suffering from PMS," was all she replied to my protest.

I retreated then, deciding I didn't give a shit what she

thought, and moved on to the subject of Claudia, who, pre-
dictably, had already started to pine for Laurence Bennett, Eligible Bachelor Number 6,785.

"I just don't get her," I said. "If she wants the fucking guy,
she should just go after him. But instead, just like she always
does when she meets a guy, she's going to go on and on about
how hot he is. Then, when he doesn't notice the way she's
gawking at him across a meeting room, whine, whine, whine
to me about how no one appreciates her for the goddess she
is, how she's better off alone, when what she really needs is
to get fucking laid."

I should mention that Shelley did not utter so much as a
word during my discourse on Claudia. This was another
thing I found irritating about her. How do you have a conversation with someone who seems to have no response to
anything you have to say? It's so fucking ridiculous. And because she was really getting on my nerves today, I decided to
tell her so.

"What makes you think I don't care about what you're saying?" she replied.

"You should see yourself," I said, angrily trying to pull together a prim yet blank expression for her benefit. "It's clear
to me you don't give a shit about what I just told you about
Claudia."

"Maybe *you* don't give a shit about what you just told me
about Claudia."

That silenced me. Probably because I had never heard
Miss Priss utter a swear word—or any other word my mother
might deem distasteful. Or maybe it was that she was right.
I didn't give a shit—not *really*—about Claudia's love life. Or
lack thereof. Then what the hell was I blabbering on about
it for, especially at these prices?

So I moved on. Or thought I moved on, anyway, to the new campaign, the work I suddenly found myself deluged in. Until I came back around to someone else again, this time Lori. And just as I was summing up my assistant's weepy little love fest, I realized I was doing it again. Going on and on about nonsense. What the hell was wrong with me? I had more important things to think about. Like the fact that I could be a mother in less than a year.

But knowing that wouldn't yield the response I wanted from Shelley, and because she indicated in her usual miserly way that our time was up, I decided not to go *there* again. I mean, couldn't the woman throw in an extra five minutes of therapy once in a while, for chrissakes?

When I stood up, I suddenly realized I was exhausted. Probably from the effort of talking. I couldn't remember the last time I had spoken so much in a session.

Then, as if I couldn't resist getting in one last little bit, I turned to Shelley once I reached the door. "Oh, I guess I should tell you. I got a letter back from K. Morova." Then I laughed mirthlessly, as if finding humor in the fact that I had been all but obsessing over a signature I had believed belonged to my biological mother, but had in fact belonged to my aunt, who was equally a stranger to me. "As it turned out, K. Morova is also my biological aunt—Katerina, I think she signed it." Then, as quietly and simply as I might have commented on the weather, I said, "Kristina would have written herself, I suppose, except she died last year. Cancer." Then I shrugged, tugging my pocketbook more firmly onto my shoulder and reaching for the doorknob. "So I guess I'll see you next—"

"Grace, do you realize what you've just done?" Shelley said, stopping me as I made my exit.

I looked at her, a bit startled that she'd ask me a question and allow me even an extra minute of her precious time. "What?" I replied, feeling like a recalcitrant child.

She paused, as if carefully planning her next words, which inevitably put me on guard. I didn't trust people who thought that much before they spoke.

"You told me about Kristina's passing as you were walking out the door. Why do you think you did that?"

I shrugged, though I was starting to squirm a bit inside. I guess, to be fair, I should have given the death of the woman who gave me life more than a passing mention. But then, Kristina Morova obviously hadn't thought all that much about me while she was alive, had she?

"I'll tell you why," Shelley offered, startling me out my thoughts. Now this was getting interesting. I'd been fattening up this woman's bank account for months, and up until this moment, she had yet to offer me one bit of advice.

This better be good, I thought, standing firm as I looked down at her.

"I think you waited to talk about the most important thing that's happened in your life recently until you knew there was no more time left in the session to talk about it. In fact, I'd guess that you canceled the last two appointments for the same reason."

I should have known she was going to turn it into one of those crazy little paradoxes. I let out the breath I hadn't realized I'd been holding. Then, because for a change I didn't have a proper retort, I merely shrugged again. "Maybe," I said, giving in a hair. "But I don't think so."

"No?" she said, her dark eyes meeting mine as if she were…challenging me.

"Nope," I said, more firmly now.

"Let me ask you something, Grace. Have you talked to anyone since you've received that letter?"

"Of course," I replied. "I told my friend Angie."

"No one else? Your parents, for example?"

"Look, I'm a grown woman. I don't have to tell my parents everything."

This got an eyebrow raise from her. Then, whether because she was too cheap to carry this conversation on for another minute, or because this was some stupid tactic of hers to get me good and mad, she simply said, "Why don't we pick up with this topic next week?"

"Sure," I said, with a final shrug, then waltzed out the door as if I didn't have a care in the world.

I called my mother that night. I told myself I was just doing my usual dutiful check-in, but an undercurrent of anticipation swirled through me that I couldn't deny. In my heart, I had decided to tell my parents about Kristina Morova. I mean, they *knew* about her, had stood by me as I tracked her down. They deserved to know that she was…gone.

Besides, I was still irritated by Shelley's implication that there was some deep psychological reason why I hadn't talked about this with my parents. It wasn't as if I weren't *close* to my parents….

"Gracie, what a surprise!" my mother declared once she picked up.

I found myself taking offense at her words. It wasn't as if I never called.

"Tom!" I heard her bellow, "It's Grace."

"Is everything all right?" my mother asked, concern evident in her voice.

Suddenly everything didn't feel all right. The weight of

all I needed to say suddenly slammed down on me, and I felt an urge to cry. "Everything's fine," I protested, if only to convince myself.

"'Lo, Grace," my father intoned into the phone a moment later. Something about his chipper tone had me biting my tongue.

I quickly made a decision. There was no way I could saddle them with this information on a Wednesday night. I knew my mother would cluck and murmur sympathetically, all the while working out a way she could be by my side as quickly and inexpensively as possible—because although my mother's maternal instincts always outweighed her miserly ones, she couldn't help fretting over fares. She'd be surfing the Internet all night, and she and my father would be on the first flight she could find that didn't wipe out his retirement fund.

It just seemed like too much to ask on a weeknight. "Everything's fine," I said again. "I just called… I just called to say hello."

My father grunted at this, and I tried not to allow this to rankle beneath my painfully—and surprisingly—thin skin.

"We're so glad you did," my mother chirped, the obvious merriment in her voice making me feel the distance between us all the more keenly. "We have news. Tom, tell Gracie about the panel you've been invited to speak on."

I felt an ease flowing back into my body as my father started regaling me with the details of the paper he was to give. Though he'd retired four years ago, he was still revered as one of the top scholars in his field for his research on the Age of Revolutions and occasionally lectured at some of the local colleges near Albuquerque. I smiled as I listened to him go on for a few moments, taking comfort in the fact that I could rely on my father always to take satisfaction in his discipline.

My mother, on the other hand, was getting impatient. "Tom, never mind that, tell Grace where you're giving the paper!"

"Oh, right," my father said, as if remembering himself. "Paris."

"All expenses paid, Grace," my mother chimed in. "And just in time for our fortieth wedding anniversary!"

The full import of her words struck me then. My parents had met in Paris. My mother had been a promising young cellist fresh out of Julliard and traveling with a small symphony orchestra. My father had been on sabbatical, writing the book that would seal his career as a history professor and, ultimately, land him the tenured position he was to hold most of his life at Columbia University. It had always seemed the grandest of ironies that though they were both New Yorkers living within miles of one another for most of their lives, they had met in Paris. And what a meeting it had been. The way my mother told it, my father had approached her at an art opening featuring Paris's newest crop of artists, and within an hour of taking her hand in his and kissing it so fervently my mother claimed she blushed with embarrassment, he had declared to her that he would one day make her his wife. She had laughed mercilessly at him. Less than a year later they stood before a priest in St. Patrick's Cathedral on Fifth Avenue, promising to love and cherish each other forever.

"That's wonderful news," I said. And it was. So wonderful, in fact, that I felt my own news fading away. I was glad I hadn't told them tonight. Now was clearly not the time for such ugly declarations about wasted lives. So I swallowed it down firmly, listening as my mother waxed poetic about the museums she couldn't wait to revisit, the sights she hoped to take in, the streets she longed to walk on again, arm in arm with my father, just as if it had been four days since they'd met, rather than forty years.

I smiled, feeling the familiar ache roll through me. Though my parents' lifelong love affair filled me with a certain happy wistfulness, it often made me feel like an interloper. Except now I didn't feel like the third wheel. I felt invisible. I don't think they even remembered I was on the line.

Well, my mother did. Eventually. "Gracie, there's only one problem," she said. "We need to leave on December twelfth in order to be there in time for the symposium on the fifteenth. And then we'd hoped to stay on for our anniversary, which means we'd be there through Christmas…."

My parents had married two days after Christmas, filled with the notion that their love was the greatest gift they could give one another. "Oh, don't worry about me," I said immediately. "I can always go to Angie's for Christmas."

"Are you sure, Grace?" my mother said.

"Of course I'm sure," I said. "I'll be fine."

And in that moment, I was sure I would be. In fact, I was almost relieved not to have to hike to New Mexico for the holidays this year. I love Christmas in Manhattan. And Christmas with Angie's family was almost as good as Christmas with my own.

Yes, I would be just fine. I always was, wasn't I? And besides, I thought, my hand coming to rest on the swell of my stomach. I might not be so alone after all….

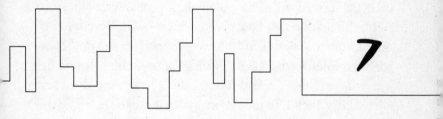

7

"I've got plenty of time to daydream and I'd rather daydream than do anything in the world."
—Jane Russell

Some might say I had sunk into a world of fantasy. Perhaps I had, seeing as I felt no need to seek out the truth of my physical condition, which some voice sounding annoyingly like Shelley's told me I should do. Instead, I chose solitude, wearing it like a protective shell. I spent Friday night alone and was quite content to do so. I didn't even need vegetables to chop or bills to pay. Not even Malakai's inquiries after my absent boy *du jour* could distill the comfort I had found in being alone.

Because I no longer felt alone.

And whether this child I was convinced grew inside me was a fantasy or not, it was something I wanted—needed—to cling to for the moment.

So I clung, curling up on the couch in my fluffiest robe

with a salty box of Chinese takeout and settling in to watch an even saltier woman. Mae West in *I'm No Angel,* which I stumbled across while channel surfing.

I didn't bother to answer the phone, letting the machine pick up instead. Claudia called first, probably looking for some affirmation that Laurence Bennett—who had followed up our meeting with a full-blown proposal for the new campaign coupled with a vague promise of cocktails—found her just as desirable as she had found him. There were also a few hang-ups, which I would normally attribute to the ex, in this case, Ethan, but I had no need to imagine desire where there wasn't desire. One message was from Angie—and I almost picked up, as she sounded kind of desperate. But since she went on to assure me that nothing was wrong, I decided it was just Angie's usual drama. Whatever she had to tell me could wait.

So I waited, going to bed early and rolling into a lazy Saturday morning. I ignored the paperwork I'd dragged home, barely even glanced at the newspaper after plucking it up from my doormat. Instead, I indulged in a hearty bowl of fruit and yogurt, then took a long, hot shower, feeling for the first time in ages, a certain comfort in my skin.

I no longer felt compelled to do anything—strive, socialize, mate. It was as if some great pressure had been lifted.

I discovered, that very afternoon, where that sudden release of pressure had come from.

My period.

Never had I felt such a rush of pure disappointment. But as I let out a long sigh, I realized deep down I had been expecting it along. Did I really think I was going to get what I wanted simply because I desired it?

★ ★ ★

"Why didn't you call me back?" Angie complained when I finally did pick up the phone on Sunday night.

I started to make up some plausible excuse when she cut me off.

"Listen, I was gonna invite you over for drinks to tell you, but now it's Sunday night and I know you have work tomorrow, and Justin and I are getting up early to scout out a location. I'm not even sure we're going to be able to get to use it for the movie. God only knows why we have to get there at six—"

"Angie, what's up?" I asked. I knew whenever she started to babble like she was right now, *something* was up.

She paused, then, as if finding no other way to frame it, she said, "Gracie, Friday night, Justin—that is, we're engaged!"

My stomach dipped and tears rushed to my eyes. "Oh, God, Angie…that's—that's wonderful. Congratulations!" I exclaimed, and despite my joy for her, I felt myself overcompensating. "Wow, I almost can't believe it. I mean, not that I can't believe it—" I stopped short, not understanding what I was feeling but suddenly flooded with a throat-clogging emotion. My God. Angie was getting married. The girl I had shared everything with since the age of twelve was going to share her life with someone else….

"I can't believe it either, Grace. I mean, I knew Justin and I would always be together, but *now* he decides to get engaged? We're going to start shooting in April!"

But she put whatever anxiety this clearly had produced in her aside as she proceeded to explain how he had proposed. "We're at the movies on Friday night—we went to see the new Nicole Kidman movie. Which was excellent, by the way…."

I had to bite back a smile as the expected movie review came. As she was just about to comment on the art direction, I said, "Angie, the engagement? What happened next?"

"Right. Okay, so we're walking out of the theater—you know, the AMC theater on 42nd Street? Anyway, I'm heading for the escalator down when Justin starts tugging me toward the escalator up and I don't know what he's doing but you know how he loves exploring buildings, so we go up to one of the top floors—you know how big that theater is, right? And then he's dragging me through these doors outside that I've never seen before and I'm a little nervous, you know, because no one up is up there, but he's looking around like we're about to get in trouble and I realize this is because we probably aren't *supposed* to be using these doors, and suddenly we're standing on some kind of balcony. It overlooked 42nd Street and we could see the lights of Times Square in the distance and it was so beautiful. Except I don't think we're supposed to be out there, and I turn around to tell Justin this and suddenly I don't see him. I mean, I do see him, but he's no longer eye level. He's on one knee and suddenly he's taking my hand in his—" She broke off on a sob.

"Why are you crying?" I said, concerned.

"Oh, I don't know, Gracie. It's just that…it was like everything I ever dreamed of was suddenly happening. Like, out of nowhere. I mean I had no *idea*."

I smiled. It wasn't exactly out of nowhere. She and Justin had known each other for five years and lived together for most of them. It was true that they hadn't technically become a couple until a little over a year ago, but by the time of their first kiss, I imagined, they were already in love and hadn't even realized it.

"You should have seen my mother when we told her the

news," Angie continued once she got control over her emotions once more. "We went out to Brooklyn this afternoon as usual," she said, referring to the weekly four-course meal her mother served up for the family on Sunday and which Angie now went to on a fairly regular basis, probably because she wouldn't deny Justin a taste of her mother's fabulous red sauce. "Justin was gonna wait until he had a chance to crack open the bottle of champagne we brought with us to tell them, but it was like my mother had some kind of crazy radar on. She spotted the ring from the second I stepped into the kitchen. Next thing you know, she's crying and laughing and she and my grandmother—hell, everyone—was suddenly hugging us and screaming. It was a nuthouse."

I smiled, remembering that nuthouse well.

"One glass of champagne later and my mother is really crying," Angie continued. "She starts talking about my dad, how she wished he had lived to see his only daughter get married.…"

A tremor moved through me at her words, and I felt a sense of loss I couldn't define.

"But she got over it the minute Sonny and Vanessa showed up with my adorable goddaughter.…"

Sonny was Angie's older brother—and one of my first boyfriends. He was married now to Vanessa, and they had just had their first baby girl a year ago. Sonny always had been a wiseass. Which was probably why our preteen romance had ended amicably. It was hard to get broken up over a boy who kept you chronically breaking up with laughter. Or maybe it was because I hadn't truly lost anything when I lost Sonny as a boyfriend. After all, I had gained a best friend—and her family.

"Anyway, now my mother is already starting to talk about

the wedding. Justin and I haven't even set the date yet, and all of a sudden she's putting together this list, and it's getting bigger by the minute. I mean, I always knew my family was big, but she's pulling relatives I never heard of out of the woodwork. Did you know I have a cousin Mildred in Staten Island? Anyway, it's insanity! My mother was up to 150 people by the time we left, and that's not even including Justin's family...."

I had nothing to say to all this. Because I suddenly realized the true source of the sadness that had pierced me the moment she told me her happy news.

While Angie's family was growing larger, the little family I had suddenly seemed to be fading away....

I came to work the next morning a bit later than usual, feeling a sluggishness in my bones that made dragging myself out of bed difficult, and found a bottle of Dom Perignon on my desk.

Not feeling particularly jubilant—and somewhat wary of whatever joyful news would be heaped on me today—I paused in the doorway. Turning to Lori, who was already busy at her desk, I asked, "What's with the champagne?"

"Dianne sent it over for everyone in Marketing," Lori replied cheerfully. "Well, you and Claudia, at least," she continued. "Apparently, Mimi Blaustein called Dianne on Friday, and Irina's going to sign on with us for the new campaign."

Well, at least someone was getting what they wanted, I thought, heading into to my office. I studied the fancy label, remembered the last time I had had Dom (with Michael, on the beach). Then, as if I could will that memory away, I grabbed the bottle by the neck and was about to tuck it into my bottom drawer when Claudia showed up in my doorway.

"I guess you heard the news," she said, smiling crisply at me.

"Yes, I did. That's fabulous, Claudia. Congratulations," I replied, my tone belying my enthusiasm.

Not that Claudia noticed. "Don't open it," she said, as if that had been my intention. "She hasn't signed the contract yet. In fact, Dianne is personally giving Mimi and her insufferable client a tour of the Long Island compound this week. Something about Irina being some kind of animal activist and wanting assurances that our facilities are on the up and up." She rolled her eyes. "But by the look of things, we should have a contract as early as next week. In fact, we're planning a reception for Irina here as soon as a deal is signed, to welcome her into the Dubrow family." Another roll of the eyes, followed by a somewhat gleeful smile. "Oh, fuck it. Let's open it."

I glanced at the clock on my desk. "Claudia, it's barely 10:00 a.m."

"Oh, come on, Grace. Don't be such a party poop."

Yes, Claudia Stewart, my supremely sophisticated boss, actually said "poop."

My antennae went up. Even more so when she disappeared, only to return moments later with two champagne flutes in her hands and a smile on her face that looked positively…*merry.* Well, for Claudia, that is. She closed the door behind her, shutting out the sight of Lori, who had been looking just as curious as I was about Claudia's sudden uplift in spirits.

I mean, yeah, I was sure she was relieved to have the talent practically secured for the new campaign, but it had been clear from the start that Claudia despised everything the nineteen-year-old supermodel stood for. Surely it couldn't be Irina who brought the glow to her eyes….

As it turned out, I was right.

"So I reviewed Larry's proposal."

"Oh, Larry, is it?" I asked, remembering how a week earlier, Claudia had been railing against the very same Laurence Bennett, who had yet to follow up on his promise of drinks with her, though his assistant had already called two times to see if we'd had a chance to look at his bid to win the Roxy D campaign.

She ignored my implication, focusing instead on the wire at the neck of the bottle as she carefully twisted it off. "His ideas are very good. In fact, we're having drinks on Wednesday to discuss them further."

"Is that right?" I said, studying her features, which were now slightly flushed. I had a feeling that flush had little to do with the exertion she was now putting into opening that bottle. "So he finally called?"

"Actually, I called him," she said, freeing the bottle of the wire. "You know, to talk to him about the proposal, of course," she added quickly, as if she feared she might look like she was chasing after the man.

"Oh, of course," I said, studying her.

"Anyway, we got to talking, and I told him I was passing his proposal on to Dianne for a look, and one thing led to another and he suggested we meet for drinks."

I stared back at her, understanding suddenly just how Laurence Bennett was about to win probably the biggest ad campaign—at least in terms of budget dollars allotted—from the usually formidable VP of Marketing at Roxanne Dubrow.

He had hit Claudia right where she was most vulnerable. Her feminine ego.

"Claudia, you do realize that we can't make a decision on this until we consider other agencies."

She glared at me, her hands poised around the neck of the bottle. "I know *that*." Then she smiled again, a bit dreamily. "But I have to say, this proposal from Larry's agency looks very...*promising*."

The cork came flying out, nearly decapitating the cardboard cutout of Priscilla, last year's only-25-and-now-discarded model, which I had allowed Lori to prop up against one of my walls, as I found myself unable to toss it out.

I bit my tongue, not wanting to dispel the happiness on Claudia's face as she filled our two glasses. Who was I to tell her how to run her campaign—or her love life, for that matter? It wasn't as if I were any shining role model in either department.

She held up her glass, narrowing her eyes as she carefully considered her toast. Then, clinking her flute gracefully into mine, she said, "To getting what we want."

Then, apparently satisfied that she was going to get all *she* wanted, she downed that glass of Dom in one fell swoop.

"So what do you think of Pete?" Angie asked, as we lounged together on the couch that bordered the back wall of Three of Cups, the East Village bar that she and Justin had chosen for their friends to gather together in for an informal celebration of their engagement on Tuesday night.

I guess I was grateful for the change in subject, as Angie had just been badgering me about contacting Katerina and my half sister. After resolutely defending my decision not to get involved, I was happy enough to turn my attention to Justin's friend, who stood over at the bar with Justin.

Pete Jordan was, admittedly, a good-looking guy. Lean, well-muscled, with sandy-brown hair that had that tousled, just-got-out-of-bed look. The goatee, combined with the somewhat obscure tattoo that graced his forearm, gave him the edgy look of an East Village slacker. Except Pete wasn't a slacker. In fact, he directed most of the commercials and corporate videos he and Justin worked on at Justin's "day job" as a grip at a production studio in Long Island City. I knew from Angie that, like Justin, Pete had ambitions to direct a feature-length film. Although Pete had yet to make a move toward that goal, he seemed to feel no resentment that Justin was just about to realize that dream this spring, judging by the way he and Justin were yucking it up together at the bar.

"Not my type," I said finally. Not anymore. There was a time, just after college, when I adored artistic men. Even imagined I would fuck one such man into superstardom once, when I found myself in a tangle with a particularly ambitious—and deliciously well-endowed—example of the breed just after graduation from college. But now the thought of even getting involved, of lying in bed with him, late in the night, listening while he hatched yet another great idea that likely would never come to fruition, left me, frankly, exhausted.

"Colin seems to be pretty happy with Mark," I said, moving on to the other man Angie and Justin had invited to this little celebration. Colin, Angie's former co-host from her days when her acting career consisted of guiding a bunch of six-year-olds through an exercise program on *Rise and Shine,* was happily engaged in a conversation with his lover, Mark, at a nearby table. They looked adorable together—and happy. Colin, who once pined endlessly for a child to love, had gotten it all, I realized now, remembering that Mark was a single parent and that the two spent most of their weekends playing "My Two Dads" to Mark's son.

"Yeah," Angie said, her gaze softening as it fell on Colin. "Do you know, they're even talking about getting married?"

"Married?"

"Uh-huh. In Toronto." She smiled. "Now that it's legal in Canada. So all I have to do is find someone for you...." she said wistfully, her eyes cruising the room as if she were going to pluck my future husband out of the crowd.

"Marriage isn't for everyone," I said, suddenly defensive.

As if on cue, Angie's friend, Michelle Delgrosso popped out of the bathroom, her lips freshly glossed and her hair sprayed to new and frightening heights. Michelle was from the old neighborhood in Brooklyn. I had never cared for her myself, but somehow she had cleaved to Angie like an old piece of gum stuck to the bottom of Angie's scuffed yet fashionably urban shoes. I think Michelle, who subscribed to the theory that any man could be brought to the altar with a little arm twisting, even took credit for Angie's engagement to Justin.

I watched Michelle stalk past the couch where we lingered without sparing us a glance and head to the bar where Pete and Justin stood. Except for the official engagement toast we'd made once everyone had gathered together, Michelle had spent the evening hanging all over Justin's friend, which, I noticed, seemed to get Angie a bit miffed.

Not only was Michelle married—for over eight years now—she had, according to Angie, been to a marriage counselor and had even recently gone on a second honeymoon to Hawaii, all in the name of preserving whatever bond had driven her to marry Frankie Delgrosso at the ripe old age of twenty-four.

I studied her as she slinked by us—or should I say slithered, judging by how reptilian she managed to look in the black leather pants she'd donned for her big night out in Manhattan—heading straight for Pete once more, her monstrous wedding set winking at me even in the dim light of the bar.

Maybe that was why she stayed married to Frankie, I thought, noting the glitter that also twinkled from her wrists and ears. He was the heir apparent to Kings County Cadillac, his father's business, and was able to indulge Michelle's apparently insatiable passion for diamonds.

And speaking of glitter, I thought, my gaze falling once more upon the rock that now graced my best friend's hand…

Seeing where my attention had been drawn, Angie held her hand up, smiling somewhat dizzily at her rock for about the tenth time that evening.

I couldn't blame her. The ring was pretty magnificent. A one and a half carat Tiffany cut diamond set in platinum and flanked by baguettes.

Not that I was the type of woman to pine for jewelry. Angie hadn't been either, until she had gone engagement-ring shopping. No, not with Justin—with Kirk, her last boyfriend. The grand irony was that once she found the ring she wanted, she realized she didn't have the man she wanted. Now she had the ring, I thought, gazing over to where her gorgeous future husband stood by the bar, *and* the man.

But judging by the frown that I saw threatening her features, she still wasn't satisfied.

"What's wrong *now?*" I found myself asking.

"Nothing," Angie said, glancing over at Justin, who was now, along with Pete, leaning over Michelle as she demonstrated how to turn the new navel ring she had just gotten. This lurid little display was temporarily stalled when the bartender plunked down the freshly ordered drinks on the bar, which Justin proceeded to pass to Michelle and Pete.

I heard Angie sigh as Justin forked over the contents of

his wallet to the female bartender, who gazed up at him rapturously, either because Justin's golden-boy good looks inspired such worship or because he likely had included his usual fat tip. "Look at him—will we even have cab fare to get home tonight?" she said, incredulous.

Now I was frowning. "Angie, you live a few blocks away."

"That's not the point," she said, glancing down at the ring once more, then dropping her hand quickly, as if she was afraid to stare too long at that scintillating promise.

"So tell me what the point is, exactly?" I replied, starting to feel a bit exasperated with her. How had she managed to find a flaw in what appeared to be an utterly flawless man?

"He's too…generous," she said, with another quick glance down at her ring.

"You're kidding me, right?" I said. We should all have such problems.

She bit her lip, as if she were having trouble articulating what was clearly eating away at her, despite all the happiness that had recently been heaped on her plate. "Don't you think it's…it's *wrong* for a man who's about to take a chunk of his life savings and invest it in his next film project to be picking up the bar tab…or buying $9,000 engagement rings? At least we got a break there—the jeweler knocked a grand off the original price."

"Angie, as I recall, you were the one who wanted that ring."

"I know," she said, looking down at it once more as if the sight of it brought her pain. "It just doesn't seem…right."

"Right?" I asked, exasperated. *"Right?"* I shook my head. "Angie, the man just bought you a beautiful ring. Asked you to spend your life with him. And if that weren't good enough, he's even cast you as the star in his next movie!"

She frowned, and though she wasn't a nail biter, began to gnaw on the edge of that prettily clad finger.

I smacked her hand away. "Angie!"

"I know! I know I should be happy! And I *am* happy. It's just…" She blew out a sigh. "It's just that if they decide not to do a second season of *New York Beat,* I'm gonna be out of a job. And my health insurance is going to run out the minute I run out of money to pay for it. Justin is about to sink half his capital into this film… It's not that I don't believe in him, I do. But you can't trust that the industry is going to…to reward him for his talent. And if this movie fails, then where will we be? I'll be another out-of-work actor, and Justin—" She bit her lip. "This movie is everything to him. What if he doesn't recover from failure? What if—"

"Angie, need I remind you that no one has failed at anything here? Stop thinking about things that are out of your control. Life is going to happen no matter how much you angst over it. Just be glad you found someone you love to brave it with."

She looked at me then, and I saw that my lecture had caused her to transfer her worry to a new subject: me.

"What about you, Grace? Don't you want to find someone to brave it with?"

I shrugged noncommittally.

"Well, you're not going to if you never give a guy a chance," she said. "I mean, Pete's a nice guy," she continued, her gaze seeking him out in the crowd. Her eyes widened and my gaze followed hers, only to discover that Mr. Nice Guy was now doing a body shot of tequila, using Michelle's midriff as a salt lick.

Angie looked at me apologetically. "Well, he was. Until Michelle got her hands on him." She frowned. "What is *with* her?"

Or with him, I thought, but didn't say. I no longer felt a need to explain away the whimsies of men and women. It was clear to me that Pete and Michelle were just two more examples of the myriad commitment-phobic people I knew. Married or single, it seemed to me that, for some people at least, the longing for what you can't have never really goes away.

A warmth curled inside me at the memory of my own most recent longing for a child, but the feeling quickly died, leaving an emptiness as I also remembered that child was not to be. Not in the next nine months anyway.

Maybe not ever.

Somehow that thought made the longing come back.

And I wondered if I would ever be cured of this ache I felt inside.

What did I want? What would it take to make me truly happy?

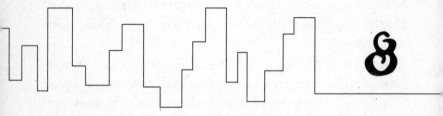

"A hard man is good to find."

—Mae West

What I wanted, I discovered when I came home later that night, my mind blurry with drink and my body thrumming with new anticipation, was a man. And fortunately, being a woman of means, I did still have a phone number at my disposal. After all, a woman didn't live in Manhattan for all these years without filling her arsenal with at least one good specimen of that breed of male who could be had as easily as she could access the address book on her cell phone.

Yes, I was no stranger to the booty call, though I hadn't had to resort to it in a while. Not since pre-Ethan days. To think I had given up Bad Billy Caldwell for Ethan Lederman the Third. Bad Billy was my prime booty call. Had been since we had hooked up for the first time in a bar on the Lower East Side six years ago, back in the days when I frequented places where the music was loud, the decor grungy and men even dirtier. Foolishly, I had tried to turn Billy into a boyfriend at first, and had nearly let my heart get into the mix before I discovered picking up women in bars on the Lower East Side was a habit Billy didn't want to break for anyone. But once I accepted the limitations of a relationship with Billy, I reveled in them. Because the cold, hard truth of it was that Billy was the best fuck I had ever had. It could have been his lean, well-muscled body, or that perfect, perfect penis of his—length, girth and a delightful little left hook designed, it seemed, to hit the G spot every time. Or it could have been that beautiful face—blue eyes, sooty lashes and a mouth so lush nothing short of nature could have created it.

It was the thought of that mouth that had me making the first move once I found myself alone in my apartment, which was dark save for the glitter of light pouring in through the windows.

Slipping my cell out of my purse, I quickly located his number and hit Talk.

And held my breath. Uncertain whether, after this time, Billy had moved on, as Ethan had likely done, or Michael clearly had....

"Ah, Gracie," that rich mellow voice purred into the phone and I felt relief, along with a rush of warmth a sudden memory of that hard body conjured up. "You're back, huh?"

"I'm back," I said, knowing that on some level, this was an admission of failure. Another relationship down the tubes. Not that Billy saw things that way.

"I've been thinking of you lately," he said.

"Yeah?" His words practically sounded like an admission of love, in my current state of longing.

"Thinking about those long, long legs. Those pretty eyes…"

I smiled. Love—what had I been thinking? This was better. Because if you couldn't count on love, you could certainly count on male libido.

"Come over," I said, and before I could even let out my breath, he had hung up and was, in all likelihood, already slipping on his boots, his leather jacket, and heading for the subway.

There is nothing like being with a man who worships women the way Billy does. From the moment he stepped through my door, his eyes raking over me as if he might devour me, I felt alive again. Powerful. Beautiful.

I *was* beautiful, I reminded myself, once he had tugged my dress down my shoulders and began kissing the tops of my breasts where they spilled from my lacy bra. He moved lower, pulling the dress down to reveal more flesh as he did, his hands and mouth moving over my rounded abdomen, over my buttocks, between my legs.

I cried out when his mouth made contact and he looked up at me from where he kneeled on the floor before me, still in his jacket, his face dusty with stubble and his eyes drunk, apparently with the sight of me.

"Ah, Gracie, you are so fucking gorgeous."

I let out a throaty chuckle. Billy always did have a way with words.

And with his hands and mouth, I remembered, once we were finally horizontal, his body naked and just as hard and lean as I remembered it to be. We fell into a rhythm the moment we hit the bed, as if we had been lovers uninterrupted these past six years, and not just strangers who liked to fuck when the mood, or desperation, drove us to it.

My hands roamed over his cock, grabbing hard, then tugging gently, the way I knew he liked.

His fingers massaged my breasts, trailed down my inner thighs, following old paths with the patience and the relish of a pioneer exploring them for the first time.

After he had secured himself in the latex he always seemed to have at the ready, he began that teasing dance of thrusts that would, within the space of a few hungry kisses, escalate to the kind of clawing, pounding heat a woman could only truly experience with a man as boundless, and as experienced, as Bad Billy was.

Afterward, as we lay breathing hard, side by side, I felt pure satisfaction, and it wasn't just the sex. It was the sight of this beautiful man in my bed, his eyes drifted shut. He and I were probably more alike than I had ever realized. Both of us fearless in the face of pleasure, yet running whenever the emotional heat got too high. I smiled then, at his gentle snoring, enjoying the comfortable companionship that had been between us since the day we'd met. And I wondered, if this could indeed be enough.

Claudia, on the hand, clearly needed a little more than what *she* was currently getting.

"Have we heard from the Sterling Agency today?" she asked, standing in my doorway, dressed in a deep fuchsia dress a tad on the sexy side for office wear. Come to think of it, I hadn't seen Claudia in anything other than her trademark black since the day she hired me.

I wondered at this now. "Were we supposed to hear from them this week?"

She frowned, running a hand over the front of the dress,

which was so bright my eyes were starting to ache from look-ing at her. "Larry did mention he would call me today…."

"Oh?"

Her dark eyes glittered, and I saw what might have been the shred of a smile touch her lips. "Yes, well, we did meet up for drinks last night."

"Oh, right," I said, remembering the drinks date she had set up with Larry in the hopes of securing her own booty, and with which Larry, I assumed, hoped to secure the Dubrow account. "So how'd that go?"

She stepped into my office, slamming the door shut behind her, and then, with what looked like a definite *glow* on her face, sidled into my guest chair, leaning forward confidingly.

"It was *fantastic,*" she said in the kind of hush that suggested she wasn't talking about the drinks.

"Claudia, you didn't *sleep* with him, did you?" I asked, sud-denly horrified that my boss was about to blow this campaign because she felt a desire to leave behind all battery-operated modes of pleasure.

"No, no," she said, shaking her head. "But I wanted to…"

That, in itself, was something. I had begun to think Clau-dia was asexual, judging by the number of dates she had ven-tured on in the few years I had known her. There had been precisely two. And one of them had been with her ex-hus-band to settle some lingering financial issues after their divorce.

I began to feel a flutter of hope for my termagant boss as she described the lovely lounge that Larry had taken her to down in SoHo, where he stared into her eyes and waxed po-etic about how he had always wanted to work for a com-pany like Roxanne Dubrow. And, he suggested, with a woman like Claudia. As I studied her new demeanor—a bit rosy but this may have had to do with the sudden injection of color into her wardrobe—I wondered if perhaps Claudia was going to get what she wanted from Laurence Bennett. Or at least, I thought, studying the tightly reined energy that radiated off her, what she clearly needed....

"I'm going to London," Lori said, stepping into my office after lunch.

"London?" I asked, looking up at her with alarm.

"With Dennis," she explained, placing a memo on the desk before me.

Relief sheeted through me as I saw the piece of paper before me was not a resignation, but a request for the two weeks surrounding Thanksgiving off. For a moment, I had thought Lori had resolved the Dennis dilemma by deciding to follow him across the pond.

And as she cheerfully explained how he had received an acceptance letter and an invitation to visit the campus, I wondered at how positive she suddenly seemed over the fact that her boyfriend might not be a boyfriend by next fall. "We're gonna check out the real estate situation, too," she continued. Then she blushed. "I mean, Dennis is..."

I realized then that maybe my first instinct *had* been right. Maybe she was going with him in the fall. But since I was her boss and not privy to the kind of details that might reveal whether she did have a resignation in her future, I simply signed off, listening while she babbled on about the sights she planned to see. I felt a burning need to offer her some sort of counsel, but what would I advise her? That she shouldn't follow the man she loved around the world? Maybe she was right to follow her heart, I reflected, thinking of how I was, at least, being led around by my libido these days. I'd even spent my session with Shelley the night before waxing

poetic about the therapeutic value of a good orgasm. But
whether I had shocked her with the subject matter, or with
the way I used it to avoid the topic of Kristina she tried to
prod me toward, I couldn't tell.

I handed back the memo, smiling a little sadly at the idea
that there would come a day when Lori wouldn't greet me
with her usual cheerful demeanor. But what had I expected?
That my assistant would stay forever my assistant? She was
young. She needed to explore. I just hoped her exploration
of what she wanted didn't stop with her boyfriend's dreams.

"Well, I suggest you put that vacation memo on Claudia's
desk ASAP. Claudia is floating on a cloud of something at
the moment," I said. "She'll sign off on anything."

"Good point," Lori said. "Thanks, Grace," she said merrily, bounding out of my office to do just that.

As it turned out, I was right about Claudia's mood. In fact,
she was so buoyed when Larry called to ask her out for dinner that very night, she might have signed off on a year-long
sabbatical, had Lori asked. And when she bounced in the next
day after her big date dressed in a winter-white frock (yes, I
would declare it a frock, complete with ruffles at the neck)
I began to wonder what exactly had transpired between her
and Larry. White was something for Claudia. But ruffles?

"Lori," I heard her say, "did you courier that contract to
the Sterling Agency like I asked?"

Contract to the Sterling Agency?

"Claudia," I called.

She turned to face me in my doorway, eyebrows raised
expectantly and what looked like a genuine smile on her
face. "Yes?"

"What's this about the contract?"

She looked at me. "I'm sending it over to the Sterling Agency."

Alarm shot through me. Was Claudia about to compromise this campaign because she'd finally found someone she was comfortable enough to drop her ice princess act—and likely those pretty little frocks she was now sporting—for? "But I thought we were going to review the Chase Agency's ideas, too. I think their proposal even came in with a lower bid."

"Cost isn't our only consideration, Grace. Besides, I really thought Larry's ideas were well put together."

Hmmph. Likely what she thought was well put together was Larry himself. "You slept with him, didn't you?"

"No," she protested immediately, and from the pensive look that came into her eyes, I believed her. "We just talked about the campaign...among other things." Then stepping further into my office and pushing the door half-closed, as if she were about to reveal a confidence, she continued, "But I did feel a...a *connection* with him, Grace. Working with Larry is going to be pure *pleasure*."

Dear God. What was wrong with her? She could at least get laid before *she* laid that contract on his desk. Because despite the flutter of hope I felt for her as she told me about her evening at La Caravelle, I had not put to rest my suspicions that Larry was motivated by something other than desire for the well-pampered but utterly charmless Claudia.

My eyes narrowed at her. "Is Dianne on board with this?"

I saw that familiar angry gleam return to her eyes. "Dianne trusts me to choose an advertising firm, Grace. I am, after all, the Vice President of Marketing."

My eyes dropped to the hint of cleavage pouring out of that frilly little dress of hers. "So are you like, gonna date this

guy?" *Date* was the polite term for what I sensed she hoped
to do with him.

As if my suspicions had suddenly cast doubt in her own
mind about what, exactly she was hoping to get out of Larry
Bennett, she dropped her eyes. "He did say something about
getting together next weekend." When she looked up again,
I saw that hopeful look had returned to her gaze, though this
time it was muted by a vulnerability I had never seen in Claudia before.

"Just be careful," I warned softly, suddenly realizing how
fragile she truly was.

"I'm a grown woman," she said angrily, standing up as if
to call this little female-bonding moment to a close. "I know
what I'm doing!"

I knew exactly what I was doing when I found myself
lying, breathless, beside Billy, later that night.

"That is some rib cage," he said, running his hands over
my frame after we lay back against the cool sheets, our bodies spent from yet another session of invigorating sex.

I glanced down at where his big hand roamed over my
ribs, then down over the smooth, pale skin of my stomach,
with a kind of reverence. "My rib cage?" I said, wondering,
as I had before with Billy, what new revelations he had had
about my body.

"That's right," he said, sliding his hand down my ribs,
across my hips. "You are a work of art, Grace."

I started to believe it. Believe that I was a woman so worthy of such worship from a man. After all, it appeared love—
or something like it anyway—was in the air. Claudia
practically bounced about the office every time the phone

rang and it was Larry on the other end, even though from what I could gather from my exuberant boss, it was usually to iron out the details of the contract. Even aspects Claudia normally left to our legal department were suddenly worthy of her attention. Lori was even more chipper than usual, probably because in between fielding calls, filing and doing the numerous tasks that came her way from Claudia, she was on the Internet, securing her flight, searching for bed and breakfasts and ordering up new clothes for her big trip overseas with Dennis. I was starting to believe that I had been too quick to judge the men in our lives. Maybe we could count on them to be there for us in some way. In fact, I was so caught up in this idea, that when my phone rang Friday afternoon and I discovered Ethan on the other end, I could not help the sharp intake of breath. Could not deny the sudden curl of satisfaction I felt at the sound of his deep, mellow and I have to say—concerned—voice.

I will admit, that over the course of that brief conversation, in which he inquired about my life, I fell victim to the belief that maybe he cared about me more than I had imagined. Perhaps I had misjudged him.

I couldn't have been more wrong.

"So, Grace, I was wondering," he said, once he had politely answered my inquiries into his own life. "Did you, uh, that is—did you ever get your period after that, uh, you know…incident?"

I felt the blood drain from my face, right along with any warm, fuzzy feelings about Ethan I might have conjured up during the cozy little conversation we'd just had. "Right on schedule," I lied, not wanting to share with him the mixture of fear and hope that had filled me in those two weeks when my cycle had gone awry.

Clearly, he was still the same self-absorbed jerk he always was.

And I was a damn fool for thinking otherwise.

Then, before I could give him the satisfaction of knowing he could still evoke boiling anger in me, I made some excuse about a meeting I had to prepare for, and hung up the phone.

Cursing the rush of emotion that clogged my throat, I swallowed it down and bent my head over the marketing plan I had been working on.

"Fuck them all," Claudia said as I shared the details of my latest Ethan fiasco with her over a cocktail later that evening. We had headed to Monkey Bar after work, a veritable haven for good-looking men, which was pretty ironic considering the reason we had found ourselves pouring down martinis like they were going out of style. Moments after I had hung up with Ethan, Claudia had appeared in my doorway, her face radiating the same fury I was feeling in that moment. Apparently, Larry Bennett of the Sterling Agency had canceled his dinner plans with Claudia for that evening and hadn't even bothered to reschedule, making some vague comment about being "busy" for the next few weeks. And why should he make room in his schedule for Claudia? He had just received the countersigned contract from Roxanne Dubrow, securing a big fat profit for his agency this year—and the contempt of at least one VP at Roxanne Dubrow.

"They're all bastards, every last one of them," Claudia continued, swallowing down the last of her martini and immediately signaling the bartender for another.

I had felt a certain camaraderie with her in light of my own recent man disaster, which was why I had agreed to her demand (she hadn't exactly asked) that I join her for drinks after work. Now, as I sat on the receiving end of all of Claudia's bitterness about the male species, I was starting to regret it.

"Did you know that Roger called me the other day to see if I was ready to sell him back the living room set his mother had given us when we got married? He claimed Heidi had admired it once before and wondered if I cared to part with it. Do you believe the fucking nerve of that idiot?"

Roger was Claudia's ex-husband. Heidi was half Claudia's age and had twice her bustline.

"I'll bet she admired it," Claudia muttered. "Do you know I found them fucking on that sofa?"

My eyes widened. "Maybe you don't want to keep it around then, Claudia."

She snorted with dissatisfaction, dismissing the subject as her hands reached for the sixth time in as many minutes, for the cigarettes she had tossed on the bar. Never mind that smoking was now banned from all bars and restaurants in New York City. "A woman can't have any vices in this city anymore."

Well, there was one vice she had left at her disposal, I thought after we had downed another cocktail and paid the tab. If she was smart enough to keep a man around who wasn't too egotistical, too self-absorbed, to make himself available for a woman's pleasure.

With my mind and body soft and achy with drink, it was the only vice I wanted to indulge in that evening.

I dialed Billy in the cab on the way back to my apartment. Delighted that he was not only available but eager to partake of whatever pleasures an evening together had to offer.

I had just enough time to slip out of my work clothes and

into a silky lavender negligee when my buzzer rang, and Malakai, with the resignation I always sensed in his voice whenever I resorted to what I was sure he recognized to be my booty call, announced Billy's arrival.

Once I threw the door open to Billy, I didn't give a damn what Malakai thought. Dressed in faded jeans, a baby blue T-shirt that outlined his v-shape and made his blue eyes sparkle, and a black leather jacket that looked just as sexy as his tousled dark hair, Billy was irresistible.

So I didn't resist when he pressed me up against the wall of my foyer and allowed me to feel the real reason he was the first number I called when the hour grew late and I found myself in need of a ready partner. His hands slid over my ass, dragging the negligee up. "So sweet," he said, grabbing hard and pressing his groin more firmly against me. His mouth hovered over mine, and I felt the scrape of stubble against my skin as our lips met.

We kissed like the old lovers we were, tongues tangling in a dance we'd been through over and over, teeth nipping playfully, teasingly, as if we still, despite the years, could not get enough of one another.

This probably was because we never did get too much of each other.

In fact, I might have taken him right there in the foyer and sent him on his merry way if it weren't for the draft that drifted over my bare feet, chilling them and distracting me from what was an otherwise drugging encounter.

"The bed," I whispered against his mouth, dragging him with me as I stumbled toward my bedroom.

Once I was on my back, gazing up at Billy as he stripped off his jacket, his jeans, his sweater and finally, his briefs, something changed for me. Suddenly I wanted to take everything slow and rather than allow him to do the honor of plunging that beautiful equipment of his inside, I coaxed him to kiss my breasts, watching lazily as he slid the straps of my negligee down and grazed each nipple with his lips and tongue. He caught on quickly to my new demand, moving his mouth slowly over my abdomen, then grabbing my hips as he placed his head between my thighs....

Really, what more did a woman need? I asked myself as I surrendered to his skilled tongue, crying out in warning as I neared climax.

Billy responded by lifting his head and, aware that I preferred him inside me for the climax, he slid up my body, a knowing look in those beautiful blue eyes as he gazed at me.

A smile graced his lips as he touched the tip of himself against me, teasing me. It wasn't like he had never done this before, but suddenly I found myself quivering with a need to have him inside immediately—and without barriers. In fact, the thought of having Billy that close, of his coming inside me, nearly caused me to come myself.

I shifted, bringing his shaft in alignment and maneuvering myself down on to him when his eyes widened, his smile broadened with surprise. "Whoa, gorgeous," he said, leaning away from me to grab his pants were they lay beside the bed. "Let me suit up first...."

"No," I said, surprising myself and pulling him back into position. "Let's do it in the raw, Billy."

"Grace—"

"Come on," I found myself pleading in earnest, driven hard by a desire I had yet to articulate to myself. "It would be amazing, Billy."

He smiled then, planted a soft kiss on my mouth. "I'm sure it would be, Gracie, but it would also be dangerous."

I looked at him then, really looked at him: his blue, blue eyes surrounded by sooty lashes, his fine nose and solid jaw. "We'd make a beautiful baby, don't you think?" I said, feeling a sense of déjà vu as I said the words.

He laughed. "And terrible parents."

I frowned at him. "I'm not so sure about that."

"Gracie, a baby? Come on. You're kidding me, right?"

Maybe it was the way he was staring at me in utter disbelief. Or maybe it was the sense I suddenly felt that I was fighting a losing battle—mostly with myself—but suddenly I found myself saying, "I had you going there for a minute, didn't I?"

"Shit, Grace," he said, shaking his head at me as he stood to retrieve his pants, pulling the ever-present packet of condoms out of one the pockets. "You sure did have me going." He laughed out loud. "A baby." He shook his head again. Then, once he had securely covered himself in latex, killing some little stab of hope that still gleamed inside me, his face turned mischievous. "Now you're gonna have to pay for that." And with one fast, hard thrust he was inside me.

But I was gone by then. So far gone I felt like my body was numb.

And I wondered if I'd ever experience the rush of pleasure the thought of that child—Billy's child, my child—had brought.

Wondered if I'd ever feel anything ever again.

I woke the next morning alone. Another side effect of my relationship with Billy, who never stayed the night.

Billy…

The memory of our little tussle the night before weighed me down and suddenly I felt very, very old.

I slid the sheet down, sat up in all my naked glory.

Well, my nakedness had felt glorious last night. While this morning…

This morning I felt an ache in my bones that I feared had little to do with the acrobatics of the night before.

Before I gave in to the urge to slide back under the covers for the day, I stood up, heading for the bathroom. On autopilot, I turned on the shower, adjusting it so that the spray was as hot as my body could bear, then stepped under the spray.

Only to discover nothing could wash away the sadness that had penetrated me.

Had it been there all along, waiting to swallow me up? My breakup with Ethan. The glow I had once seen in Michael's eyes…

Irritated, I shook my head and doused myself under the spray again as a memory filled me.

Of me and Michael making love on the beach. Well, not on the beach, but in the guest house at the Dubrow property in South Hampton. Not that we needed to stay in the guest house. It had been late September and the Dubrows had long since given up their weekly foray to the family vacation home. Yet Michael had opted for the little cottage closer to the shore, rather than staying in the main house. "We can hear the ocean better," he had said, though now I wondered if it was because he didn't want to muck up the pristine family home with our tawdry little affair. But that was just it. It wasn't tawdry. I had been in love and had thought he had been, too. So much so that we had taken other risks together, foregoing all methods of birth control aside from the pull-out method. Suddenly I remembered that feeling I had had—that same crazy wish that had washed over me last night. That Michael would let loose inside me, that we might possibly bring a child into this world together.

I realized that this longing that seemed to drive me now, with Billy, and yes, possibly even with Ethan, had originated then. In fact, I was so overcome by it that I had, while wrapped in Michael's arms in the cozy afterglow, admitted as much to him.

He had smiled softly, rubbed his nose into mine and run a hand possessively over my hips as he said, "You and I would make a beautiful baby."

Now I knew why I had felt that sense of déjà vu last night. Where I had heard those words I had uttered before. From Michael. I had taken it as a promise, I supposed. So much so, I realized now, that I had, on some level, been waiting for each man since to fulfill it.

I turned off the taps, stepped out of the shower and studied my reflection in the steamy mirror as realization dawned. Maybe that was what I had been doing wrong. Waiting. Waiting for some man to make me happy, I thought, my hand roaming to my gently rounded abs. Maybe I could have what I clearly wanted…on my terms.

9

"Carrying a baby is the most rewarding experience a woman can enjoy."
                              —Jayne Mansfield

"So you're going to have a child on your own then," Shelley said, when I informed her of my decision, which seemed to grow even firmer in my mind after a harrowing few days in the office. On Monday, Claudia received her assistant's resignation. Apparently Jeannie had decided life at home with her baby boy was more rewarding than being Claudia's personal slave. I couldn't blame her, especially after listening to Claudia rail against the injustice of her assistant leaving her in the middle of the biggest campaign this company had seen in a long time—you know, the campaign I was not even a real part of?

I decided to take it as a sign that perhaps my own happiness was to be found somewhere far from Claudia's clutching command. Somewhere free of the disappointments the men in my life had brought. Who needed a man nowadays, with all the new fertility technology? And with that thought I realized I had made another decision: I would not go the adoption route. Besides the hassles sure to be involved in single parent adoptions—my own happily married parents had had enough trouble securing me—I was certain that what I craved was the kind of motherhood bond that only could be made in blood.

And as I explained this part of my plan to Shelley, a stab of anxiety filled me—who even knew what really was involved in a donor search after all?—followed by a sense of anticipation. I could do this if I wanted to. The way I wanted to. That thought gave me pleasure.

Even Shelley was taking her own pleasure in my chattiness tonight. "Tell me, Grace, what having a child means to you."

For once, her question felt like an easy one. "It means having someone to love." I hesitated, searching for words to shape the longing—and the hope—that filled me. "It means always having someone there for you."

I saw Shelley's lips purse. "What?" I asked, suddenly fearful that she was about to burst this happy little bubble I had found myself living in.

"Think about what you just said."

"What did I say?" Now I felt defensive. And confused. What *had* I said? "That I want someone to love and be there for me?"

"Grace, you are talking about a child. Someone *you* must be there for. A child *you* must care for and love."

"I realize that." Did she think I was taking parenthood lightly? "I am perfectly capable of caring for a child." I certainly had enough experience mothering, I thought, remembering all the years I had helped Angie through the rough patches of her life, and even sometimes Lori. Hell, you might even call all that pandering Claudia required a kind of mothering. At least if I had a child on my own, I would get something in return. I'd even have someone to spend Saturday night with, I thought, realizing that despite all the mothering I had done in my life, I still was, essentially, alone, when it came right down to things. Angie was going to marry and live happily ever after. Lori would move on with Dennis, or move on, eventually. And Claudia…well I'd like to move her on…to the home for wayward adults.

"I think I would make a good parent," I said finally.

"I don't doubt that," Shelley said. "I'm just questioning what it is you want from parenthood."

Despite how embarrassingly needy it made me feel, I found myself blurting out. "I want someone to love me. Unconditionally. What the hell is wrong with that?"

I saw her shift in her chair, and I couldn't help but see this as impatience, as if I were some child who just didn't get it. I felt my old resentment toward Shelley rear its ugly head. "I deserve it, don't I?" I cried, surprised at the emotion behind my words.

Her face softened, and I nearly wept at the pure sympathy I saw there. Though I wanted to resent her for not giving me the guidance I sought, I realized that I needed something else from her now. And that something was the genuine caring I saw in her features just then. But it was only momentary. For Shelley folded that flickering emotion back behind her therapist facade just as easily as she smoothed the wrinkle that creased her pants as she crossed her legs once more, composing herself.

Ignoring my question, she said, "You can't hope to get from a child everything your mother didn't give you. And in this case I mean your biological mother," she said care-fully. "I think that's who we're talking about here, consider-ing the importance you seem to place on giving birth to this child you long for."

I felt the familiar resistance brewing in me. Now I knew why she had seemed so happy with my little sperm-donor plan. Probably because it validated that stupid psychological paradigm she had dreamed up ever since I had started com-ing to see her.

"Yes, the child will love you, but a child isn't a caregiver," she continued. "Your very language suggests that you are looking for a parent, Grace, not a child. You are trying to re-place your lost mother."

Whatever tears had threatened quickly died inside me, re-placed by mind-bending anger. I hated the idea that Kristina Morova—a woman who hadn't given me more than the nine months it had taken to form me—could have such power over my emotions. And I hated Shelley even more for sug-gesting it. "You know what, I'm tired of this," I said, folding my arms stiffly across my chest, whether to shield Shelley or myself from the wave of feeling shaking through me, I wasn't sure. "Why does everything I think, everything I feel, have to be about…about *her?*" I practically shouted. "Can't it just be that I want to have a fucking baby, for chrissakes? I'm al-most thirty-five years old!"

Shelley remained nonplussed, responding once more in that smooth, well-modulated voice. "Of course, a desire to have a child is common, especially among women your age," she said. "But you need to ask yourself why you are choos-ing to have a child alone, Grace."

Then, with a glance, I was sure, at the clock that ticked

ominously above my head, she said, "We're out of time for now. Let's pick up with this same topic next week, shall we?"

I decided to take up the topic the very next morning at work. And though I had made my decision to have a child out of the wisdom and, yes, the disappointments, only a thirty-four-year-old woman could have, I realized that when it came to modern-day babymaking, I would rely on the overused resource of the 18-to-24-year-old set, at least according to our recent focus group research.

The Internet.

It was amazing what a little search on "sperm donor" could yield.

Nearly 17,000 entries, the top results containing actual search engines where I could search for donors by race, education and most desirable physical attributes.

I was amazed at how easy it all seemed.

And how daunting.

Still, I downloaded some information from a few Web sites that seemed reputable—though that was quickly becoming a relative term—and tucked them into my bag to read at home, comforted by the idea that at least I had…options.

And I didn't need anyone else to pursue them.

The phone rang, startling me out my thoughts. "Grace Noonan," I said, picking up on the first ring.

"Gracie, it's Dad."

I froze, quickly shoving the last download into my bag, as if my father had just stepped into the room and caught me in the horizontal with a man. Ironic, yes, but the fact was, my father never called me at work. My father never called me period. It was my mother who did all the communicating for both of them. Which was why this little phone call coming in the midst of my little quest seemed stranger still.

"Is Mom okay?" I asked, grasping for the first reason I could come up with for why he was on the other end of the line and not her.

He chuckled. "What, a father can't call his daughter once in a while?" he replied.

I smiled, heartened by the idea that maybe my father did call just to say hi, though I was absolutely certain that wasn't the case. "What's up?"

"Well, now that you ask," he began, "as you know, your mother and I have a big wedding anniversary coming up."

Ah, it was all coming together now. The gift. He needed a little shopping inspiration for this momentous purchase he was about to make for my mom. My smile deepened. "Let me guess—you have no idea what to get her?"

"No, no, not at all. In fact, I have the perfect gift. And, as it turns out, it's just coming up for sale. Do you remember that painting your mother and I argued over when we met? *Mariella in the Afternoon* by Chevalier?"

I had never seen the painting, but the story had been told to me so often I could practically picture it. The painting featured a woman in the foreground, standing in her garden and gazing out, seemingly toward the road, where a figure approached in the distance. A figure so small it was difficult to know who the woman waited for. When my mother and father had found themselves standing before it at an art opening over forty years earlier, they had barely introduced themselves before their first argument began over whether it was a lover, a child or a friend the woman waited for, each basing their reasons on the enigmatic expression in the woman's eyes and a somewhat quixotic turn of her lips. My mother thought it was a child. My father, a lover. According to my father, the date on the painting was no help, as Chevalier often painted from a mixture of memory and photographs and didn't always adhere to historical veracity when it came to the subject matter. *Mariella in the Afternoon* was a modern-day Mona Lisa, though with a bit more scenery and narrative detail, painted by an up-and-coming French painter of the time, and now, according to my father, it was being shown at the Wingate Gallery down in SoHo.

"Wow," I said. "How did you manage to track it down?" I asked. I mean, it wasn't like we were talking about a Picasso here.

"I kept my eye on that painting," my father replied. "Knew that if I had the good fortune to make your mother my wife, I would one day buy it for her. That day has come. The painting came to New York through a private sale twenty years ago. To a collector—R.J. Sutherland, I think his name was. Anyway, Sutherland has passed on, and the painting was moved to the Wingate Gallery by his estate, to be sold on consignment. I had thought I might be able to fly in myself, make the arrangements, but with your mother and me preparing for our trip, I don't think I can get away. I wondered if perhaps you could go in my stead...."

"Dad, I don't know much about art..."

"Yes, you do, darling," he said, reminding me of the fact that I had studied fine arts before switching to business administration in my sophomore year of college. Not only had I discovered that I had more of an eye for art than a talent for it, I had decided I needed to get practical in my coursework if I hoped to get a job once I graduated.

"Besides," my father continued, "you don't need to know anything, as long as you have the asking price," he said, naming a figure that made my jaw drop.

"Dad, that's really generous of you, but can you and Mom afford that?"

"Of course we can. I've been keeping my own little nest egg for just this moment. I know your mother is going to throw a fit at first, but once she remembers that beautiful moment we stood before that painting, she'll understand why I did it."

I felt a fluttering in my stomach at the pure love I heard in his voice. "When is it, Dad?" I asked, feeling foolish for thinking, even momentarily, that I would not fulfill this romantic request for him. He gave me the date and time and the address for the opening of the show, and after I hung up, I felt a stab of longing so deep, I feared those downloads I planned to tote home could never satisfy.

"Have you set a date yet?" I said to Angie as we tried on clothes at Bloomingdale's that night. We were sharing a dressing room, partly because the early evening crowd prevented us from getting separate ones, but mostly because Angie was trying on bathing suits for the upcoming trip to L.A. she was taking Thanksgiving weekend with Justin and was anxious about it. And though angst was Angie's natural state, tonight she seemed even worse than usual.

"No, we *haven't,* okay?" she barked at me, stepping into the third pair of bikini bottoms she had brought in with her.

"Touchy, touchy," I said, holding a dress up against me to contemplate the color.

"I'm sorry." Angie stood up to look at me. "It's just that

my mother has been harping on that very same question ever since we told her about the engagement."

I looked at her. "Well, isn't that usually what happens? You get engaged, you plan a wedding."

"That's just it. Ever since Justin and I got engaged, this wedding has taken on a life of its own. My mother's got me schlepping out to Brooklyn every weekend, looking at halls. And you should see some of the places she's lined up—perfect settings for *Saturday Night Fever*. In fact, Justin should bring a film crew and we could do a remake."

"I didn't know you were getting married in Brooklyn."

She placed the bikini top against her chest. "*I* didn't know I was getting married in Brooklyn, until next thing you know, I'm packed in a car with my mother, Justin, Nonnie and Artie Matarrazzo—you know, my Nonnie's beau? He's become the family chauffeur ever since he started dating my grandmother, and now my mother's got him dragging us around from one horrifying wedding venue to another. Then my mother has the nerve—the nerve!—to yell at me for being too picky! Too picky! She's the one who insists I get married within a stone's throw of her house."

"What does Justin say?"

"You know Justin. He's happy with whatever makes me happy. I don't think he realizes that my mother is slowly driving me insane," she finished, her face flushed with frustration as she fastened the bikini top.

"Well, if you don't want to get married in Brooklyn, you need to tell your mother that."

Her face crumbled so much I feared for a moment that she would cry. "The truth is, I don't know what I want. I've been too worried about the show possibly ending and this film coming up." She sighed. "I suppose I could just let my mother run this whole wedding while I watch from the sidelines. I mean, she is paying for the damn thing."

"She is?"

Angie nodded. "Yeah, can you believe it? At first I felt kinda guilty. It's not like my mother's rich or anything. But I found out she's been saving for my wedding since I've been, like, *twelve.*"

I raised an eyebrow. "Wow."

"I know, right? I guess I *am* her only daughter. On the one hand, I'm relieved. But on the other…" She adjusted the bikini top. "I don't know. It's not like I've been dreaming all my life about my wedding, but I feel like I want the day I marry Justin to be about…*us.* And somehow doing the chicken dance under a disco ball at Lombardi's on the Bay isn't what I had in mind."

I stepped into the dress, pondering that for a moment. Like Angie, I hadn't given much thought to what my wedding day would be like. And, now, I realized, thinking of those downloads in my bag on the floor, I had mentally skipped right over the big day and gone straight to the…donor solution. I shivered, understanding why I had jumped all over this trip to Bloomie's when Angie had called me at work this afternoon to invite me along. I didn't want to go home and face the decision which had seemed so perfect…in theory. Somehow all those faceless possibilities I'd printed out from those Web sites depressed me.

"I'm almost relieved Justin and I are going to L.A. for Thanksgiving weekend just to have some time away from the whole scene. I told my mother we were going to visit with one of Justin's cousins who lives out there, and that's true, but mostly we're hoping to meet up with some potential investors for the film. And get in a little beach time," she said, turning to look at her reflection to contemplate her latest suit selection.

She sighed. "Well, this would be just lovely if I had some breasts." She looked at me. "You'd think there'd be some laws regarding fair distribution when it came to breasts."

I straightened, studying my own reflection in the dress, noting the way my breasts were practically bursting out of the top. "Trust me, I'd love to hand some over if I could." I supposed it didn't matter if the dress was no go. It wasn't like I needed any wardrobe additions. But then, that was the best time to shop, I rationalized, reaching for the black wool skirt I had dragged in, too. Besides, it would be nice to have something new for the holidays.

Then, remembering that I was going to be an orphan this Christmas, I said, "Do you think your mom would mind an extra person at Christmas dinner?"

Angie looked up as she untied the top. "Of course not." She frowned. "No New Mexico with Mom and Pop Noonan this year?"

"Nope, my mother and father will be spending the holidays in Paris this year. My father is giving a paper there, and since their fortieth anniversary is coming up, they've decided to stay on and celebrate it there," I explained, pulling the skirt up over my hips.

"That sounds amazing," Angie said, becoming dreamy-eyed. "God, maybe Justin and I should get married in Paris…." The dreamy expression dropped from her face. "But of course we can't do that. Do you know my mother refuses to get on an airplane? I mean, flying freaks me out, but at least it doesn't stop me from living." She tossed the top on the discard pile. "I have a feeling I wouldn't even be able to get my mother to cross the bridge to Manhattan to come to my wedding."

"Stop worrying," I insisted, turning sideways to study the way my abdomen protruded in the skirt. All that indulgent overeating had landed me with a little bit more of a bulge in my midsection. A swelling that I had grown to accept. Though I certainly wasn't the height of this season's stick-figure fashion, I had taken a comfort in my new shape.

"I'm thinking about having a baby," I found myself blurting out. After my disheartening session with Shelley, I hadn't planned on telling anyone else just yet. Least of all Angie, who I knew would stress over my decision more than I ever possibly could.

She didn't disappoint me. *"What?"*

"You heard me," I said, testing my decision once more now that I had dared to utter it aloud to my best friend.

Her eyes widened. "Don't tell me—Ethan. The condom—did you ever get your period?"

I shook my head. "I got my period, Ange. I'm not pregnant, if that's what you're asking."

"But how?" Angie asked, then blushed to the roots of her frizzy dark locks. "I mean, I know how. I guess the question I'm really asking is who?"

"You don't need a man in your life to have a baby nowadays, Angie," I said, slipping out of the skirt. "In fact, it's easier to have a baby on your own than you would think," I continued, my mouth pursing. This fact still…disturbed me somehow. Just as much as it bolstered me, I supposed. "I did a little Internet search. Just this afternoon. Do you realize how many clinics there are devoted to this kind of thing? I mean, you can even order up a 'dose'—that's what they call it—right on line. It's as easy as…ordering a bra from Victoria's Secret."

"Grace, do you realize what you're saying?"

I shrugged, hung up the skirt and reached for another. "A lot of women are doing it nowadays. Where do you think Melissa Etheridge got those cute kids of hers?"

Angie frowned. Apparently a celebrity endorsement was not enough for her. "Grace, Melissa Etheridge is a lesbian. She probably didn't have any other options, whereas you—"

"What options do I have, exactly?" I said, feeling fresh anger surging through me. "To wait around for some man who isn't a self-absorbed jerk? Justin notwithstanding, those are far and few between." I sighed. "Look, Ange, the truth is, when I thought I was pregnant with Ethan's baby, I felt like…like I was fulfilling some long-held dream I didn't even know I'd been dreaming. Then, suddenly I'm in bed with Billy and practically begging him to forego the condom—"

"Ohhhh, Grace!" Angie practically moaned. "Don't tell me you're tangled up with *that* guy again." Angie was not a fan of Bad Billy's. I think she saw my booty call as some kind of shallow replacement for what I really wanted. And she was right. Because ever since this baby lust had taken me over, I had lost all desire for Bad Billy. Even told him I'd started dating someone when he called me last week, which he accepted just as easily as he had in the past. Somehow even that made me sad. I mean, a girl does want a man to fight for her a little.

"So how long has that been going on?" Angie asked now.

"It's not going on," I replied. "Not anymore." Maybe not ever again, I thought, realizing bringing a baby into my life might require getting rid of a few…habits. "I have a new focus now."

"But a baby, Grace?" Angie said. "I mean, I love my god-child Carmella to pieces, but she scares the shit out of me. Do you know I was keeping an eye on her for my brother a few weeks back and I spent like the whole day trying to keep her from eating the potting soil in those stupid planters my sister-in-law keeps all over the place? By the time Sonny and Vanessa came home, I was exhausted."

"I'll have help—"

"Help?" Angie said. "Last I heard, those sperm donors don't change diapers or do midnight feedings. Have you heard about the midnight feedings, Grace?"

"I can hire help," I insisted, though I hadn't actually worked out all the details yet. My salary was pretty fat; still, if I was truly going to make this a reality, I was going to need to make a budget.

"All I'm saying, Grace, is that having a baby is a big deal. It requires sacrifice—"

"I'm willing to sacrifice," I said, realizing this was true. It seemed these past few years all I'd done was sacrifice. Sacrificed my time for men like Michael or Ethan or Drew, who gave me little or nothing in return. Sacrificed for my job, and it was clear now, as long as Claudia remained at the helm in Marketing, there would be no payoff for those sacrifices.

For once in my life, I wanted to work at something that might actually *get* me something. And I knew now, with a certainty I had not felt before, what that something was.

10

> "Life would be so wonderful if we only knew what to do with it."
>
> —Greta Garbo

I came home from Bloomingdale's laden with brown bags, from little to big, wondering what kind of madness had led to this sudden shopping frenzy when I had only gone to keep Angie company. But after she had finally found a bathing suit that didn't accentuate her butt, flatten her chest or wipe out her bank account, she went home, and I went...bananas. After finding a pair of trousers and two skirts on Level Two, I felt compelled to head to the shoe department, where I discovered a pair of stilettos that made me pine for a place to wear them, and a pair of knee-high boots that screamed chic go-go girl. Ironic, too, considering the new Saturday night I was envisioning would likely find me barefoot and breast-feeding.

Still, when I went home to my empty apartment, I took

satisfaction in putting away my purchases. Even contemplated doing an all-out closet weeding to make more room for my new wardrobe additions, until I realized I was just avoiding those downloads I'd dragged home.

As I closed the door on the overloaded closet in my bedroom and stepped into the living room, I realized there was another thing I was avoiding besides those downloads.

Like reality.

Had I really thought through all the changes a baby would require?

One glance around my stylish yet smallish living room and the first question bubbled up.

Where was I going to keep a baby?

I'd have to move, I decided, my eyes caressing the shiny hardwood floors, the way the city lights glittered through the wide window. I had always liked this apartment....

I shook off the thought. I had been living here six years. Maybe that's why my life had become so...stagnant. Maybe a change would do me good.

The phone rang then and I considered letting the machine pick up. It was my modus operandus these days. But something in me—probably some embarrassing loneliness I had felt lurking ever since I had come home—had me grabbing the receiver out of the cradle.

"Hello?"

"Is this Grace? Grace...Noonan?" came a familiar voice. The sound of it pierced me at first, as it always had every time I called that number in Brooklyn I had found under K. Morova in the phone book. The voice of someone I did not know, but recognized all the same. Well, thought I recognized. Because I had hung up on it often enough after sending my certified letter to Kristina Morova, believing it to be the voice of the woman who had given birth to me.

Now I knew otherwise. I steeled myself accordingly. "This is she."

She hesitated. "I'm sorry to bother you, Miss—Grace," she continued, as if testing the name. My own name sounded foreign to me coming from this stranger.

"My name is Katerina Morova. I sent you the letter back about…about my sister?"

I know who you are, I wanted to yell at her. But I kept my cool. What I really wanted to know was what she wanted. "Yes?"

"Well, I gave you my number and I know you are probably busy, but we so wanted to talk to you, Sasha and I…."

Is that right? I thought angrily. I sent my letter over seven months ago, only to hear back a few weeks ago. I guess some of us don't know what it is to wait, I thought, then began to feel like a sulky child. I mean, really, this woman had done nothing wrong to me. No one had. Not really. I would try to be civil. But brief. Mercifully brief. "What can I do for you?" I asked, cringing at the stiffness in my voice.

"We wondered—that is, I wondered—if maybe you wanted to come to our house in Brooklyn for…for dinner?"

A cold wave washed over me. Followed by heat. As the silence stretched over the line, I became achingly aware that I could not brush this woman off the phone the way I brushed off the men in my life.

Which was probably why I found myself reluctantly agreeing to go to Brooklyn on the following Sunday afternoon. Still, I felt the same relief I heard in Katerina Morova's voice when we finally said goodbye.

★ ★ ★

"Gracie, that's fantastic," Angie said, when I told her my plans. I had called her from the office the next day, probably in an effort to further procrastinate on starting any work. Besides, I did feel an obligation to tell someone about Katerina's call yesterday. And I wasn't sure I wanted it to be Shelley. In fact, I wasn't even sure I wanted to see my therapist anymore since our last conversation.

"I guess," I hedged, not sure how I felt about the whole thing. The truth was, I felt more like I was doing this for Katerina and Sasha, than I was for myself. For my part, I felt somewhat immune to the whole situation. A bystander unwittingly sucked in because I hadn't been able to devise a face-saving way out.

"WHERE IS THAT GIRL?" I heard Claudia bellow from the foyer.

"I have to go," I said. "Claud-zilla is on the loose."

"Okay," Angie replied. "Call me if you need me," she practically pleaded before I clicked off the line.

"What's up?" I said, once I reached the doorway and found Claudia, hovering over Lori's vacant desk as if to invoke her presence.

"Last time I checked, the work day began at 9:00 a.m. It's near eleven already and it seems our assistant is MIA."

Oops. I had forgotten to tell Claudia that Lori had mentioned yesterday that she'd be in late today. Late, as in ten o'clock, though. "Umm, she had to go to the passport office this morning."

Her eyes narrowed. "If that *girl* thinks she's running off on vacation in the middle of one of the biggest campaigns this company has ever seen—"

"She put in the request at least two weeks ago. You signed off on it, as I recall."

"I *what?*"

At just that moment, Lori popped into the foyer, carrying a shopping bag from Diesel and sporting a look of pure guilt on her face.

"Well, well, well," Claudia said, turning to glare at her. "Look who decided to drop by." I saw her gaze hone in on the Diesel bag. "I hope our little marketing plans aren't keeping you from your shopping?"

Though she should've known better by now, Lori started to babble. "I was on my way back from the passport office when I saw the cutest shirt in the window of Diesel and—"

"Enough!" Claudia demanded. "We have bigger things to worry about at the moment than you," she said contemptuously. "Irina is coming!"

"Yeah, so?" I said. Claudia had informed me a few days ago that the supermodel was planning a visit. She even had Lori working on a catered breakfast that might suit our little icon's dietary needs. "We've already set up the reception for next week."

Claudia shook her mane of black hair furiously—and somewhat unbecomingly. She was starting to look like some kind of crazed harpie. "No, no, no, NO!" she yelled. "Today! Irina Barbalovich is coming *today!*"

"Today?" Lori and I said in unison.

Claudia then explained, in a sort of strained calm, that Mimi had called that morning. It seemed there had been a change of plans. Irina had opted to go to Paris next week, and therefore, Mimi hoped we could "squeeze in our little reception" this afternoon. Right smack-dab in the middle of lunch.

"Get on the phone and order up something," Claudia barked at Lori. "Anything. Well, not anything," she said, probably remembering Irina's organic vegan lifestyle. "Something she'll eat, for chrissakes. And we need it by one o'clock!"

Lori's eyes widened and she nodded abruptly, darting behind her desk once Claudia had stalked to her office.

Though I was having a hard time working myself up into the same kind of lather, I followed Claudia, standing in her doorway and watching as she anxiously pawed through the small closet in her office, clearly looking for something to change into. Apparently an Armani power suit wasn't good enough for Irina.

"Does Dianne know?" I asked.

"Of course!" she said, fishing out another black suit, which looked similar to the one she was wearing, except that it had a skirt.

"Is she coming?" I asked, wondering really if the rest of the entourage was coming, too. Like Michael and his new bride-to-be...

"No, no," she said, shaking her head as she gave the suit a once-over. "She'll never make it in time. Besides, she's taking her mother to a specialist of some sort."

"Her mother?" I asked, wondering what the company's namesake needed a specialist for.

"Yes. Apparently the woman's losing her mind." She laughed bitterly. "That probably explains this whole stupid younger-is-better campaign. I wouldn't be surprised if Dianne were still taking advice from Mrs. Dubrow, despite the fact that the woman has Alzheimer's."

"Alzheimer's?" I said, shocked. I had no idea Roxanne Dubrow was ill. It explained a lot. Like why Dianne hadn't been spending much time in the New York office lately.

Claudia paused, hanging the suit on the back of her door as she turned to glare at me. "That's confidential, you know. Though in truth, I'm surprised the whole world hasn't figured it out yet, with the way this company is going to hell in a handbasket." She shrugged out of her jacket, reaching for a hanger.

I stood there for a moment, still dumbfounded at the idea. God, what Dianne must be going through. And Michael…

"Is Michael coming?" I asked.

"Please. He's off in Italy at the moment, visiting one of the plants there. Probably with Courtney. I swear, for the new VP of Product Development, she sure does get around. Especially in light of the fact that she should be working her ass off getting this new product ready for the spring launch."

This news didn't dismay me as it should have, probably because it only added to my assessment of Michael as careless and self-absorbed. Why should he bother about his ailing mother when there were other family members to do so?

"What are you going to stand there all day?" Claudia said, startling me out of my thoughts. "Get ready! We have—" she looked at her watch, her face paling "—less than two hours!"

Maybe because everyone else cared so much, I resolved to remain indifferent, shutting my office door against the flurry of activity in the halls as Claudia sent everyone in her path on some Irina-inspired task. If anyone asked I would say I was immersed in forecasting for the spring collection devoted to Roxanne Dubrow's older clients. After all, we couldn't forget about them. They were still, as Dianne Dubrow liked to say, our bread and butter—though in her case, it was more like caviar and crackers.

Dianne… Suddenly I thought of everything she was likely

dealing with, now that her mother was ill. I didn't know much about Alzheimer's, only that it tended to take a toll on the whole family. Fortunately, Dianne had a solid family to lean on. Her husband, Stuart. Her two daughters, Gabriella and Audrey, who must be in their early twenties right now. At least she had them to comfort her.

Before I knew what I was doing, I found myself dialing up my own mother.

"Hello, sweetheart. How's everything?" she said cheerfully.

"Good, good," I replied, suddenly remembering my impending visit to Brooklyn and wondering if I should tell her about it. Hell, there was a lot I should probably tell her, thinking of all those downloads from donor sites, which I had barely begun to peruse. Instead, I asked, "So how's your trip planning coming along?"

"Wonderful," she replied. "In fact, your father is in the attic right now, pulling down the luggage so we can start packing."

I smiled. My parents weren't leaving for a month, yet they were readying themselves for their big adventure as if they were boarding the plane in mere days. At least I might get to talk to my mother for a few minutes alone while my dad was occupied. But suddenly the weight of telling her all that was going on in my life seemed daunting.

"Listen, I'm glad you called," she said, saving me from spilling anything just yet. "Your father and I were wondering if you had made your plane reservations for Thanksgiving yet."

I had actually been avoiding making plans for the expected yearly trek. Now the thought of that rigorous day of travel seemed even more burdensome. "No, I haven't," I began.

"Good. Because we were hoping you might come in on

Wednesday so you could join us at the soup kitchen in the morning."

Oh, dear. I had forgotten about *that,* too. My parents, good liberal souls that they were, had volunteered to feed the vast, impoverished masses of New Mexico. When they first told me about their new cause, I had volunteered to pitch in when I came home for the holidays. But at the moment, I wasn't feeling all that charitable.

"And then the university where your father lectures is holding a potluck dinner. You'll get to meet all our new friends," she continued.

My stomach plummeted. Not that I had anything against the academic types my parents had always surrounded themselves with. But I had always felt like such an outsider, as a child growing up and rebelling against anything adult, and even more so after I became an adult myself and entered the corporate world, which was far, far removed from the lofty intellectual heights my parents and their ilk perpetually inhabited. Somehow, this year I didn't want to deal with it.

"You know, I was thinking," I began carefully. "Since you and Dad are leaving for Paris soon after Thanksgiving and I have so much to do at work with this new campaign, I thought maybe I should just stay in New York this year...." I hated to lie, but I needed to keep myself distant.

"Oh, Grace, what will you do? You can't be alone for both holidays."

"I won't be alone for both," I said quickly. "I'm going to Angie's for Christmas."

"But what will you do for Thanksgiving?"

What *would* I do? I wondered, remembering that Angie would be in L.A. Even so, solitude seemed better than being surrounded by strangers.

I saw Claudia stalk by my doorway. "Umm, actually Claudia and I were thinking of spending it together," I said, leaping on the first excuse I could come up with, though the thought of sharing anything with Claudia in light of the new level of malignant indifference she had shown to me was not appealing. Still, I persevered in what I saw as a little white lie. "I think she made us a reservation at the Four Seasons."

My mother paused. "Okay, if that's what you want to do…." She sounded a bit hurt, and I started to feel guilty.

"Come on, Mom, Thanksgiving's not such a big holiday anyway. They don't even celebrate it in Paris," I continued, hoping to bring the conversation back to her upcoming trip.

My mother leaped right on the happy wagon, though she tried to pull me on board, too, by turning my choice into some sort of triumph. "I guess it would be a good opportunity for you to…to bond a little more with your boss."

Though it was more likely that I would club Claudia if left alone in a room with her, I said, "That's right. And you know how important that is to a successful career."

And with that, I freed myself from all familial obligations, at least for the short term. Long enough to sort out all the decisions I needed to make regarding my life. Decisions I felt I needed to make alone if I hoped to see things clearly.

But after I hung up the phone the weight of everything that stood between me and any sort of future happiness made me feel very, very old.

11

> "Sex appeal is 50% what you've got and 50%
> what people think you've got."
> —Sophia Loren

If I thought Irina Barbalovich was beautiful in cover shots, photo spreads and billboards, I realized that was nothing compared to Irina Barbalovich in the flesh. Irina glowed. There was no other way to describe it.

Ever more so from where she stood center stage in the conference room as if she were wearing a ball gown rather than a trendy running suit and expensive-looking sneakers.

What was it about her? I wondered, as I stepped into what looked like the receiving line, awaiting an introduction once Claudia and everyone else within five feet of Irina got done with their groveling.

It was her skin, I realized once I got close. Soft, supple, with a subtle radiance. The kind of skin that all the moisturizing technology in the world couldn't bring back once a woman was past a certain age.

"This is Grace Noonan," Claudia was saying, as I stepped before Irina and experienced that glow full on.

Her eyes were a startling blue, as if Technicolor, and they stood out magnificently against her dewy skin. Her features were otherwise rather undistinctive, but in the best way. Straight nose, high, symmetrical cheekbones and a mouth that, though as pink as a baby's and nicely shaped, wasn't half as full and lush as it looked when fully lined and glossed and pouting at me from a magazine.

Still, there was no denying she was beautiful. But that was all I was willing to give her.

Well, not all. She was Roxanne Dubrow's next great hope, and since I still felt some need to be a dutiful employee, it was my job to kiss up to her.

"It's a pleasure to meet you, Irina. The spread you had in *Vogue* last month was magnificent."

No response. Unless you counted the gentle nod of that shiny head and the somewhat distracted look in her eyes. When she finally did open her pert little mouth to speak, it was to Mimi, who stood obediently behind her, smiling graciously and, at this point in the introductions, somewhat woodenly.

"See if they have Yum Yum Fruit Splash," Irina said over her shoulder, in a soft, accented voice. "Raspberry, please."

Mimi immediately dispatched someone to do Irina's bidding—in this case Lori, who stood nearby, probably at Claudia's insistence, waiting to meet Irina's every need.

Must be nice to be nineteen and have everyone at your beck and call, I thought, as I watched Lana, our VP of PR move in next, nodding and smiling at Irina, who stared back at her vacantly from her pretty blue eyes.

Those eyes weren't vacant for long. Because the minute Lori returned, a bottle of the flavored water in hand, I saw what looked like genuine *sorrow* seep into them the moment Irina spied the label. "No raspberry?" she said, turning to Mimi.

Mimi's mouth moved into that same patient smile. "Apparently they only have orange and lemon, Reny, darling," she said, just loud enough for Claudia to hear.

Claudia immediately stiffened, as if suddenly, horrifyingly aware of her inability to meet Irina's needs, and turned to glare at Lori, who darted out of the room, probably to hunt down the one gourmet grocery store that might have a Yum Yum selection wide enough to meet Irina's demand.

Not that this would likely satisfy Claudia, who had nearly gone ballistic on Lori just moments after Irina's arrival, when she learned from Mimi that Irina had just started a draconian new diet, though why this waif needed it was anyone's guess, and could hardly partake of the organic, vegetarian Asian Fusion feast Lori had ordered up from a nearby restaurant. Apparently, in addition to foregoing all meat, poultry and fish as part of her vegan promise, Irina was now giving up bread, sugar and any vegetable that broke down in the body like bread or sugar. In essence, all carbohydrates.

It was almost too much to bear. But as I studied Irina as she dazzled each employee, I wondered if there might not be something to it. Yes, she was young and beautiful, but that skin...

When Lori returned a short while later, several bottles of raspberry Yum Yum in hand, Irina was seated at the head of the table flanked by Claudia and Mimi, a plate in front of her filled with whatever food Mimi's own assistant, Bebe, had managed to scrounge up from the noodle laden feast, which amounted to a slice of tofu and two broccoli sprouts.

"Too squishy," Irina declared, after delicately spearing the tofu with a fork and pushing away the plate without even sparing the broccoli a glance. Then she actually smiled up at Lori, as Lori poured the Yum Yum into a glass. A veritable hush fell over the room as Irina picked up the drink and sipped gingerly, her nose wrinkling gently as if she were uncovering new tastebuds right before our eyes and in the process realized that, perhaps, raspberry wasn't her favorite flavored water.

The sight, frankly, exhausted me. For I suddenly remembered what it was to be young and restless and insatiable with ever-changing desires.

And felt glad that I no longer was.

By the time Saturday night rolled around, I was feeling even happier about the number of years I had walked the earth—or more specifically, the hallowed aisles of Bloomingdale's. Because the art opening was tonight and as I stood before a veritable history of wardrobe choices, I realized I was looking forward to what had started out as a daughterly duty. After all, an art opening wasn't a bad way to spend a Saturday night, and as far as my recent history of Saturday nights went, it was five-star. Besides, I needed something to take my mind off the promises and perils of the future I was hashing out as of late. I took great care with my hair and makeup. I even forewent the little black dress that was the uniform for such events, choosing a soft pink sweater dress, that rolled invitingly away from my shoulders and seemed to set a bit of a glow—albeit not of Irina proportions—to my skin. As if I were in love.

Well, I was on a mission of love, at least.

It was a beautiful evening; the sky clear and the air tinged with the scent of snow. I found myself getting out of the cab a few blocks early, to relish a brief walk down the streets of Soho. I almost felt a moment's disappointment when I realized I was, within moments, in front of the Wingate Gallery.

I stepped inside, reluctant to leave the crisp solitude of the street.

Even more so when I saw the black-clad shapes that had already filled that luminous space. Somehow the sight of the prototypical New York scene filled me with disappointment. What had I been expecting, a ball?

With a sigh, I relinquished my coat at the coat check, feeling glad that I had opted for the soft pink dress if only to set myself apart from the sleek ranks of Manhattanites clustered about, clasping long-stemmed glasses of wine while they chatted with the kind of merriment that could only come from the comforts of success, or at least the confident facade of style.

I bypassed the wine in favor of a flute of champagne, feeling as if I were celebrating something, though what I did not know.

I headed to the first painting on the right, pretending to immerse myself in the picture in order to avoid the eyes that strayed my way.

I did not have to fake it for very long. By the third oil, a portrait of a woman reclining before a mirror, I found myself truly drawn in by the lush colors and languorous shapes. I felt almost drugged by it, as I took in each painting, all featuring the same dark-haired woman in repose.

I recognized the now-legendary painting that began my parents' love affair the moment I stepped before it, though I had never actually seen it before. The woman's face, her lips pink as if she had just fed herself on the bright blooms that surrounded her, her eyes alight with some sort of recognition as she gazed into the distance beyond her overflowing garden at the tiny, tiny figure on the road. The silhouette was a mere brush stroke that suggested another human being, though whether male or female, child or adult, it was unclear. It was only the turn of her lips—almost sensual—that made me think it had to be a man she waited for.

As I studied her eyes for more clues, I became aware of a pair of eyes on me, the force of the gaze so palpable I felt compelled to turn and meet it.

The moment I did, those eyes moved on, but not before I caught a glimpse of them; a swirling sea of greens and browns, long-lashed, masculine.

Wow.

I tried not to stare, forcing my gaze away from the tall, lean form beside me; the dark haired dream who now carefully averted his eyes, focusing them so steadily on the picture before us that I thought he might burn a hole through it. And maybe it was because he was trying so hard not to acknowledge my presence that I felt forced to acknowledge his.

"Well, which is it?" I ventured. "Male, female?"

Startled, he looked at me, and I felt the force of those eyes once more. My God, this had to be the most beautiful man I had ever seen. Then I immediately amended that statement as I took in his somewhat crooked nose and jutting though delightfully cleft chin. No, not beautiful, I thought, my eyes meeting his again and feeling that ping inside once more. But there was something about him…something in his eyes…

"Excuse me?" he said, in a deep, disappointingly polite tone.

"The figure," I said, trying hard to keep my gaze from sliding down his broad chest, covered in a tweed sportscoat that clashed a bit with his sweater. "The figure in the painting," I continued. "I think it's a man she's waiting for. Probably her lover," I finished, meeting his gaze once more. Something about his shyness felt like a challenge, and suddenly all that was female in me was coming to life again.

He smiled, looking charmingly boyish. Then, in a tone that suggested I was a child in need of edifying, he replied, "Clearly it's a parent she's waiting for. Perhaps her father or her mother. She's too young to have a…a lover," he finished, as if the very word embarrassed him.

Cute, I thought, warming inside as I saw his eyes flit away from my breasts. He was obviously attracted to me. And clearly bothered by it. "Young? What makes you think she's young?" I asked. "You can always tell by the hands." I gestured to where her hand rested on the fence. "You see that?"

His brow furrowed, as if for the first time in his life, he had reason to doubt his assumptions. "Yes, well, that could simply be the rendering. She couldn't be more than a teenager."

"Have you seen a teenager lately?" I replied. I had. And though her skin had been just as flawless, Irina had lacked the sophistication of the woman pictured here. "Look at her eyes. There's no way a woman that young could have that kind of…knowing," I finished, satisfied that I had finally put a name to that quixotic gaze.

As if to verify my words, he looked into *my* eyes, and this time, at least, he seemed less shy about it. "Have we met before?" he asked.

I wasn't going to give him any points for originality, but at least he was finally making an effort. "I don't believe so. Grace Noonan," I said, holding out a hand, only to have him ignore it. I didn't take offense, considering the way he was now staring at me, as if he were scrambling to remember me, despite my words.

"Not Thomas Noonan's daughter?" he asked. "I believe he had a picture of you in his office. But you couldn't have been more than sixteen yourself in it," he said, his eyes narrowing on me as if it was clear to him that I was much more than sixteen, and the thought disturbed him somehow.

"The very one," I said, realizing this was probably one of my father's former student groupies. "And you are?"

"Jonathan Somerfield. Your father and I were colleagues at Columbia." He seemed to relax suddenly, as if now that my father stood between us as some mutual point of reference, he could do so. "Well, he was world history and I was art history, but we did an interdisciplinary symposium together once, and we've had lunch often enough ever since. That is, until he retired and headed west. We did catch up a bit last time he was in New York, but I haven't spoken to him in quite a few months. What's he up to nowadays?"

I filled him in on the upcoming trip to Paris, while he nodded, chin in hand, looking more and more irresistible by the minute. Which I found surprising. I didn't tend to go for those rumpled, academic types, but there was something about Jonathan Somerfield that drew me. And since I hadn't felt myself so taken with a man in a long time, I decided that I would, for a change, pour on the charm myself.

"So they've decided to celebrate their fortieth wedding anniversary while in Paris," I said. Then, gesturing to the painting before us and realizing, for the first time, the romantic happenstance of my meeting this compelling man in front of the very same painting my parents had met in front of more than forty years earlier, I continued, "In fact, I'm buying this painting for my father. He wants to give it as a gift to my mother when they return."

"This painting right here?" he said, his eyes going wide.

"My parents met in front of this painting. Forty years ago," I said, looking into those lush eyes and seeing a light glimmer in them—for the slightest moment—as if he might have, like me, perceived the fortuitous nature of our own meeting.

But if I saw something there, I clearly must have imagined it. For Jonathan Somerfield simply nodded again, murmuring something about forty years being a milestone worthy of such an acknowledgment. Then he held out his hand finally and, showing not the slightest flicker of emotion at the jolt I clearly perceived passing between our briefly joined fingers, made some declaration about it being a pleasure meeting me and asking if I could give his regards "to Dr. Noonan and his lovely wife." Then he disappeared into the crowd before I could even muster up more than a baffled "pleasure," and "will do."

I felt something start to sink inside of me, and realized it was that hope that had sprung to life the moment I found myself caught in Jonathan Somerfield's gaze.

I guess some things, like romantic dreams, a woman never really loses. Though I was starting to wish those dreams would just die. Maybe then I would be able to move on to the reality of my life.

I didn't see Jonathan Somerfield again that evening. It was as if he had disappeared completely, along with all those romantic notions I'd conjured up about him. I did, however, meet the artist, once I made my intention to purchase *Mariella in the Afternoon* known to the curator.

The curator, a reed-thin woman with short dark hair and a brittle smile, was naturally, delighted. "Well, it's fortunate you came tonight," she said, as if the coveted painting were in danger of being snatched up by a member of those black-clad ranks, who seemed more interested in their cocktail chat than the art that surrounded them. "The artist is here. You have the opportunity to meet him. Now where did he run off to?" she continued, gazing anxiously about the room.

That surprised me. I guess I had assumed Chevalier was dead, based on the tidy sum the painting was going for.

He might as well have been, I thought, once the curator, whose name, she told me, was Pamela Stone, led me through the crowd to the office at the back of the gallery, where we found a man stooped over a chair placed before a dark window, smoking.

"Oh!" Pamela said, as if startled herself to find him alive. Wrinkling her nose, she began to wave at the curl of smoke drifting from his cigarette; then, as if in fear of offending him, she clasped her hands before her. "Marcus," she called to him, as if he were a small child. "There's someone here I'd like you to meet."

The man, who looked ancient, glanced up at us, a weariness in his blue eyes. He was completely bald, and his flesh hung from his face, as if weighted down by the sadness that permeated his grayish features.

No, he wasn't dead. But there was an emptiness in his eyes that seemed to suggest he had already moved on from this life.

Pamela made the introductions, babbling on merrily about my interest in *Mariella in the Afternoon*. Chevalier didn't seem to move a facial muscle as she chattered on. In fact, the only reason I knew he was listening was the flicker of curiosity that passed through his eyes when the curator mentioned my intent to purchase his work.

"Come!" Pamela said now, holding out a hand to him. "Why don't we have a look together, shall we?"

He stood, looking much taller than his stooped frame had suggested and, somewhat mournfully, stubbed out his cigarette and this only after Pamela's suggestion.

We moved through the crowd, which seemed to part before Chevalier, though he kept his gaze high above it, until we reached the painting in question.

I watched the artist as his eyes came to rest on *Mariella in the Afternoon*. He looked almost startled to see it, as if its creation had little to do with him.

Pamela must have noticed, too, because suddenly she was going on and on about how *Mariella in the Afternoon* was representative of Chevalier's earlier career, with its use of color, its moodiness, as if the artist himself weren't standing right there to comment.

I, on the other hand, decided to take this opportunity to settle the dispute that raged, albeit tenderly, between my parents to this day. When Pamela came to a pause in her little discourse, I turned to Chevalier.

"The figure in the distance," I began, gesturing to that ambiguous form on the road that snaked away from the pretty little house, the even prettier woman. "Who is it?"

He glanced up to where I pointed, as if noticing the figure for the first time, a frown creasing his features.

"Who is she waiting for?" I asked, hoping to prod some sort of answer from him.

He turned to me, studying my face as if seeing it for the first time, then, finally, opened his mouth to speak.

"Who says she is waiting for anyone?"

★ ★ ★

I arrived at the house where Kristina Morova once lived a few minutes early the following Sunday afternoon. A sturdy brick structure attached seamlessly to its twin neighbor and set off only by the discoloration of the aluminum storm door that flanked its otherwise pristine entrance, it looked like any other house in this section of Brooklyn.

Though I had viewed that carefully edged lawn, that pretty little planter that now stood empty in the stone cold, at least twice before on my fruitless pilgrimages here, I had never, ever felt the shiver of pure anxiety that permeated my system the moment my taxi pulled up in front.

I was scared to death. And I didn't like the feeling one bit.

But I was going to have to deal with it, I thought, as I paid the driver and slid out of the car, almost wanting to throw him another fifty to wait outside for me. Just in case.

In case of what?

God only knew. But I knew that car service in Brooklyn was not as immediate as it was in Manhattan. If things went…awry, there was bound to be awkwardness. An awkwardness that would only escalate if I had to wait while a new car came to ferry me away.

I wished I could leave right now.

But I didn't leave. Instead, I summoned whatever courage I had left, pulling my cashmere coat more tightly around me against the wind. Underneath, I wore a wool pants suit more appropriate for the office than a Sunday afternoon dinner. Yet somehow a suit had felt right as I stood before my closet that morning. Like armor against whatever was to come.

Now it just made me feel foolish.

Even more so when the front door swung open to reveal a ruddy-faced woman who appeared to be as overdressed as

I was for a Sunday afternoon, in cranberry slacks and a ruffled, cream-colored blouse.

"Grace Noonan?" she said, as if still trying to get used to the name. "Katerina," she finished when I nodded. "Come in. Come in."

Once I had stepped into the tiny foyer, she leaned in to hug me and then thought better of it. Probably because I literally backed away from her gesture. I felt embarrassed, but only briefly. I was too busy studying her face for something familiar, but there was nothing in the slanted, mud-brown eyes and thick nose that said this woman was a relation of mine. She looked like someone I might have sat next to on the subway a thousand times before. Someone I would have never given a second thought to.

She smiled at me, made uncomfortable, I was sure, by the way I was staring at her. My gaze moved to her teeth, slightly askew and a tad yellow, before I remembered my manners. "You have a lovely, um, home," I said, then looked around to see if this statement was true.

We were only in the foyer, but it had a cozy feel, furnished with what looked like a small mahogany accent table and a pretty lamp.

"Thank you," she said, relief evident in her voice. Then, as if this was the invitation I had been waiting for, she said, "Come inside. Let me get you something to drink. Sasha should be home soon." Then she smiled again. "Your sister," she explained, her eyes gleaming with emotion and making me realize how very much I suddenly wanted to cry myself.

She left me in a comfortable living room, with overstuffed, fraying couches, a scuffed but shiny coffee table and a curio cabinet that held a myriad of trinkets. I barely looked at my surroundings until she was gone. Then I stood again, feeling antsy, and found myself face-to-face with a photo on the far wall that I might have said was myself, if not for the somewhat dated brown bouffant hairstyle.

I moved closer, my heart in my throat as I studied the laughing eyes, noting absently that they were more hazel than the blue gray of my own, but that pointed chin was mine, as was the slight tilt to the eyes....

"That is Kristina," came Katerina's voice, startling me.

I turned to acknowledge her return to the room, then watched as she placed two glasses of tea on the table before she turned to face the photo once more.

"She was just sixteen there," she said as I studied the eyes again. "That photo was taken by a professional photographer," she continued, her voice closer as she came to stand beside me. "He told Kristina she could be a model." I saw her shake her head out of the corner of my eye. "She spent all her savings on the pictures he took and then she never did anything with them!" She smiled, reaching one hand out reverently to touch the photo. "But she was so pretty. Too pretty," she said, almost wistfully.

Before I had time to wonder at this, I heard the rattle of locks, followed by the thud of heavy footfall. "Ah, this is Sasha," Katerina said, glancing at me in anticipation.

My sister, I thought, my mind mimicking Katerina's moniker for Sasha, though even calling her a half sister felt like a leap for me. But whatever label I gave this stranger, I could not have anticipated the fact of her, once she appeared in the oval entryway.

Standing at what looked like close to six feet tall in her thick-soled, metal-encrusted black knee-high boots, Sasha Morova was a giant. And not a very attractive one. Her unevenly chopped dark hair was dyed a bright red—at least patches of it were. Her skin was pale and her eyes shadowy above a nose that had been pierced twice—a hoop hung from the left nostril and a small pink gem graced the right. Her eyes might have been hazel like Kristina's, though it was hard to tell their color as they were thickly lined in black and practically covered by a hank of bright red hair. Her mouth might have been pretty—bow-shaped, full—if it wasn't for the hoop that popped out of it.

"Sasha, I told you to be home an hour ago," Katerina chastised her.

Sasha ignored the reprimand. "When are we eating? I'm *starved,*" she said, continuing though the archway to the next one, which would lead her out of the room and, I imagined, to the kitchen beyond.

"Sasha! Don't be rude, we have a…guest," Katerina said, the apologetic smile she turned on me a bit strained.

As if she had finally realized her aunt was not alone, Sasha paused, regarding me with what looked like suspicion.

Finally someone who feels just like I do, I thought, as I took my first good look at Sasha's face.

Because despite the piercings, the bad makeup and the somewhat sullen expression, it was my own, I realized. The eye color was different, as was the mouth. But the shape was there. The nose…

I felt a shiver move through me, followed by a wave of sorrow when I glimpsed something in her eyes that also mirrored my own. Something I could not fathom, yet understood on some level.

"Sasha, this is your sister," Katerina said with a finality that suggested simply by stating it she hoped to make it true. "Grace."

Sasha snorted at this, a smile—or a sneer, I couldn't tell

which—marring her features. I couldn't blame her. Sister? I would have snorted myself, if I weren't supposed to know better.

"Sasha," Katerina said again, the warning clear in her tone.

Sasha rolled her eyes, held out one hand, wreathed in leather-studded bracelets, and said, "Nice to meet you, *sis.*"

I took that hand in mine and almost smiled in recognition at the cold, leathery texture of it. Suddenly I knew what made her so familiar to me, besides the resemblance to Kristina that we shared. It was that at her age I had been very like Sasha. Wearing an air of rebellion and a lot of false bravado. The kind of confidence that had sent me out on the streets of Brooklyn clad much the way she was—though sans the piercings and the bad dye job—in a leather jacket that clearly couldn't hold out the cold, and no gloves. Even the fingernails I recognized, glancing at the bitten down nubs that hinted at her true confidence level—painted black of course—before Sasha quickly dropped her hand. I felt buoyed by this recognition, and saddened at the same time.

I remembered how hard it was to be sixteen. Almost as hard as it was to be thirty-four.

We sat down to dinner a short while later, and over tepid wine, dumplings and oddly spiced meats, I politely answered Katerina's questions about my life. She was amazed I had spent some growing-up time in Brooklyn, and impressed by my successful career at Roxanne Dubrow. It was a bit awkward, since Sasha seemed to preside in silent judgment over the whole thing, but once Katerina turned the subject to Kristina, I wouldn't have missed it for the world.

I learned how Kristina had come here when she was a young girl, with her mother and Katerina, hoping to set up a life with their father, who had emigrated ahead of them, only to discover he had set up a life already with someone else.

I learned of Kristina's desire to be an actress, thwarted, I suspected, by her pregnancy with me, though Katerina was polite enough not to say so.

I learned how she had loved Jean Harlow, Rita Hayworth, Jayne Mansfield. Had fashioned her hair after Marlene Dietrich once and kept her brows as finely shaped as well.

I learned she had a temper—surprise, surprise—and how, as a teen, she had left a boy standing on the stoop waiting for her for over an hour, because he hadn't thought to bring her flowers. I was starting to wonder if it was possible that I had inherited the title of Breakup Queen.

Finally, I asked about my father.

"He was killed in Vietnam," Katerina said with some hesitation. "While she was…while she was pregnant with you," she finished. "They had…had planned to marry."

Sasha, who had remained silent through most of the retelling of Kristina's history, shoveling in her food, snorted at this last statement. "She wasn't going to marry him and you know it," she said with a glare at her aunt. "She drove him away. Just like she drove my father away."

Katerina looked down at her hands, a sudden sorrow seeming to descend over her features. When she finally composed herself, she gave me a wan smile. "The Morova women—we've never had much luck with men. I told you about my mother, God rest her soul. Her life was never easy, raising two daughters alone. In fact, it was she who…well, my mother thought it was too much for Kristina to keep a baby when she was so young herself…."

She spoke so impersonally about the baby whose mother

was too young to raise her that it took me a moment to realize she was talking about me.

Katerina moved on quickly. "My own fiancé died just
weeks before our wedding. He was injured on the job." She
sighed. "It's hard after you lose your love to hope again."

"Yeah, sure," Sasha said. "My mother could have married
my father, but instead she acted like she was too good for
him. She wasn't too good to have sex with him."

"Sasha!"

Sasha ignored her, instead turning to me and addressing
me directly for the first time. "So what's your story?" she
asked. "You married?"

I started to shake my head.

"Got a boyfriend?"

The question seemed so ridiculously juvenile, yet I was
amazed at how annoyed I felt when Sasha snorted as I shook
my head once more.

"I do," she said. "Aunt Katerina doesn't like him because
he's black," she continued with a sneer.

"Sasha!" Katerina repeated, her expression horrified, as if
Sasha had cursed at the table.

"But I don't think Aunt Katerina likes men, do you,
Auntie?" Sasha continued. Then, looking at me once more,
a malicious gleam in her eye, she continued, "What about
you? You a dyke bitch, too?"

It seemed to me if anyone was a dyke at this table, it was
Sasha. She was about as butch as they came.

But it wasn't so much Sasha's question that concerned me
as the pure anger I felt coming off Sasha in waves. Anger at
me. I wondered, again, why I had subjected myself to the
scrutiny of these people. These strangers.

In truth, I was getting tired of Sasha's belligerent attitude.

As was Katerina. "That did it, young lady," she said. "You will go to your room."

Sasha shoved away from the table, laughing uproarishly as she slid her leather jacket off the back of the chair where she had hung it earlier, ever ready to make her escape. "Yeah, right. Where I'm going is none of your business," she practically spat at the older woman. Then, stalking from the room, she said, "Don't wait up for me. I might not be coming home tonight."

"You see how she is?" Katerina cried once Sasha was gone. "I can't handle her by myself," she said. "But Kristina made me promise. What can I do for my sister now? Nothing!" she said, looking at me with a kind of pleading expression.

I realized then that Katerina was looking for help in what appeared to be a hopeless situation. Sasha would do what she would do. Just as I had done when I was a teenager.

But then, I had always known I had parents waiting at home who could offer me a better alternative, a new vantage point, when I was ready to see it. As I studied Katerina's tired, bewildered face, I wondered what this woman could offer a girl like Sasha, who clearly longed for so much more than Katerina could ever possibly understand.

Then I realized that *I* might offer a vantage point Sasha could latch on to. I could help her....

I felt an immediate rebellion brewing in me. No way. I didn't even like the kid. Why would I subject myself to that? I didn't owe these people anything, I thought, looking away from Katerina's pleading eyes and trying not to feel a tug of sympathy for her.

No, I thought, gazing up at the photo of Kristina that

smiled blithely back at me through the arch that led to the living room.

I didn't owe anyone anything.

12

"It's better to be looked over…than overlooked."
—Mae West

"The deed is done," I said to my father when he called me at work first thing Monday morning. I had to admit, I was starting to enjoy this bit of subterfuge, if only because of the pleasure I felt picking up the phone to find my father on the other end. I realized now that the sometimes aloof man who had raised me may have been so simply because he didn't have anything specific to discuss with his daughter. I was glad to have a reason for us to speak now. Glad I could give something back….

"Good, good," my father replied, clearly pleased.

"There's just the matter of getting it shipped," I said. "The gallery offered to handle it, but they recommended insurance, of course. And we need a certificate of authenticity for that, according to the gallery manager."

"Right, right," my father said. "Did they have the paperwork?"

"Well, no. The gallery manager said it was just a matter of talking to the trustees of the estate that owns the painting. But they had better than the paperwork," I replied. "They had the artist himself."

"Chevalier? You met Chevalier?"

"Mm-hmm," I said, a smile in my voice. Then I told him about Chevalier's interpretation of the infamous painting that had waged war—and love—between my parents.

"He said that?" my father replied, his voice filled with disbelief.

"Yup. It appears you and Mom were both wrong. The woman in the painting—Mariella—she was simply…checking out the view." And what a view it was, I thought, remembering that lush landscape. It certainly could have put that smile on her face, that slumberous yet sensual look in her eyes.

"But the figure in the distance," my father said, clearly not ready to dismiss his interpretation. "Why paint him into the scene? Clearly a narrative was being set up."

"Maybe he was just a guy passing by," I said. "Or a woman."

"Nah," my father said. "Chevalier was obviously trying to put you off the track. He was always a tricky one. In fact, I would even wager that the figure in the distance is Chevalier himself!" he finished, clearly warming to his argument. "You do know that Mariella—the woman in the picture, hell, the woman in all his pictures during that period—was his lover? Though it's unclear when the relationship started. Probably because she was a tad young when they met. She started out as his muse. Or so the official record says, anyway."

"I didn't know that," I said, suddenly remembering the

sadness I had seen in Chevalier's gaze when he first approached the painting.

"Yes, yes. Why do you think I bother arguing with your mother over it?"

I almost laughed. It was clear why he argued with my mother over it. I think to this day my father takes pleasure in the battle that had begun their life together. Since my mother wasn't around to defend her point of view, I decided to take it up on her behalf. "So this Mariella, did she ever have children?"

"Three of them!" he announced, caught up in the game. Then he amended, "But her affair with Chevalier was well over and done by then."

"What are you saying?"

"What I'm saying is that Mariella married and had children. But with someone else. I think he was a Spanish noble. Anyway, Chevalier never recovered."

It all made sense now, I thought, remembering Chevalier's resignation as he stood before the painting. God, that painting was completed over forty years ago—could he still be mourning the loss of her? The idea was terribly romantic. And achingly sad.

So sad, I no longer wanted to dwell on it. "I ran into an old colleague of yours," I said, changing the subject. I wondered how old Jonathan actually was. He had to be around forty, though he wore forty very well.

"Is that right? Who was it?"

"Jonathan Somerfield?"

"Not Dr. Johnny?" my father said, pleasure filling his voice.

"Dr. Johnny?" I asked. Yeah, the rather aloof man whom I had met at the gallery was adorable, but he was no…Johnny.

"Oh, that's what I always used to call him. He'd just finished up his doctorate when he was invited to speak on an interdisciplinary panel I was working on about France after the Revolution. We got to be friends. But he was just a kid back then. Brilliant, but a bit wet behind the ears." He chuckled. "Hence the nickname. He hated when I called him that! But I felt a bit...fatherly toward him, you know? He was like the son I never had."

I ignored the stab of hurt my father's unthinking comment caused me. Long ago I had accepted that I was my mother's choice, and not necessarily my father's. Not that he hadn't wanted me, but I think he would have given my mother anything she asked for.

"So how is he doing?"

"He seemed...fine," I replied, remembering just how fine he was. And how unavailable. "He asked about you. And Mom."

"Is that right? He always was a fine young man," my father said. Then he sang the praises of paragon Dr. Jonathan Somerfield: smart, ambitious, well-published—which in academic circles, was better than being well-endowed, though I suspected he was that, too.

"You know," my father mused, "you might want to give him a call."

"Why?" I replied, fearful that he had somehow latched on to the attraction I felt for Jonathan but would never admit to, least of all to my father.

"Well, for one thing, with his background, he'd certainly be able to determine the validity of that certificate of authenticity we need for insurance purposes."

"I suppose..." I said, wondering if my father was only using this as an excuse for matchmaking.

"Besides," he continued, "Dr. Johnny was always a fan of

Chevalier, too. I'm sure he wouldn't mind having a look at the collection once more before it leaves town."

Clearly, if my father was matchmaking, he wasn't going to show his hand. I decided to play along. "Yes, the paintings were beautiful," I replied, remembering those sunset landscapes, the interiors bathed in light, with beloved Mariella at the center of them all. "I wouldn't mind seeing them again myself." Or Jonathan Somerfield, I thought but didn't say.

"Then it's settled," he said. Once he had located his address book, he rattled off a phone number. "That's his office at Columbia. I believe he's still there. He was up for tenure when I last saw him. Dr. Johnny," he said. "Imagine you running into him after all this time. And at a Chevalier show, no less!"

Apparently my father did have an interest here. I took comfort in the notion that, for a change, that interest was in my heart.

When I walked into Claudia's office that afternoon, I discovered *she* had developed a new interest, too.

I found her at her desk, leaning in close to the mirror she'd placed there, her fingers pressed to her tender skin beneath her eyes, and pulling gently...up.

"Don't hurt yourself," I mocked, startling her out of her strange pose.

"Don't you know how to knock?" she demanded, clearly discomfited.

"Door was open," I said, dropping some paperwork from the Sterling Agency on her desk. She hadn't had the heart to deal with it herself, especially since Laurence Bennett had now gotten his contract and Claudia hadn't even gotten a follow-up call. I was about to leave when I spotted the drawing on her desk.

Not exactly a drawing. More like a photocopied replica of a human face, which had been marked in dark pen around the eyes, the chin....

"What is *that?*" I demanded.

"Nothing!" Claudia insisted, sliding the paper beneath a magazine.

"Don't tell me you're considering plastic surgery?" I asked, realizing I had seen a similar drawing before in an article in a woman's magazine detailing the horrors—and the joys—of going under the knife.

"*Cosmetic* surgery," she said, as if it were as simple as choosing a new foundation.

"Claudia! Whatever happened to aging gracefully?" I asked, harking back to all those conversations we'd had over cocktails about how glorious our profession was for supplying us with the moisturizers, the color palettes, the illuminating creams, to do just that.

"Please," she said, "there is nothing graceful about growing old." Her eye fell on the blowup of Irina that now covered the back wall of her office. Claudia sniffed, returning her gaze to me. "Why do you think this company is banking all its *future profits* on that little chippy over there?" She gestured with her chin at the photo, as if she could no longer bear to look at it. "Beauty beyond thirty is a farce," she declared. Then she stood and walked up to the life-size Irina, her eyes scanning that insolent face as if to find some secret there. "Look at her!" she said. "That skin…"

"Claudia, that's been airbrushed."

She shook her head, a bit furiously. "Maybe. But you saw it. At the reception. She's practically flawless." Her voice lowered to a reverent whisper as she brushed a veiny, perfectly manicured hand over Irina's face, as if caressing a lover.

I stood behind her, also studying Irina's face. But all I saw was the blankness in her eyes, and a certain tilt to the chin that suggested Irina Barbalovich was selling the kind of confidence no girl of nineteen could have.

She's just a kid, I thought, suddenly seeing her cockiness, the kind of fearlessness that comes from not knowing what hurts, what disappointments, lie ahead. I recognized it as the same look I had seen on Sasha's face.

The phone rang then, though Claudia seemed not to notice, either because she was caught up in her adoration of Irina's virtual porelessness, or because she had forgotten Lori was now across the pond.

"Claudia? The phone? Do you want me to—"

She started then, picking up the phone and barking with her usual menace, "Claudia Stewart."

Her features slackened immediately, and her voice was positively ingratiating as she said, "Well, hello, Bebe."

Bebe was Irina's personal assistant. Though what a nineteen-year-old needed with a personal assistant was beyond me.

"Of course, I'm still coming," Claudia continued, in the same buttery tone. I saw her frown. "A car? I had thought we'd simply get a cab—" She paused, glanced at the window at the cloud-filled sky that brightened an otherwise cold and dreary evening. "Oh, right. No, of course. We wouldn't want Irina to catch a cold. Not with the shoot coming up. I'll order one right away. Shall we say, eight o'clock?" Her mouth moved into the smile that I suspected was more a cover for her gritted teeth. "Perfect. See you then." She hung up.

"What was that about?"

"Oh, some party down at Moomba I'm going to with Irina."

"You're actually hanging out with her?"

"Um-hmm," she said, digging through her Rolodex. "Her and that boy she hangs out with. The photographer? Phillip something or other. It seemed like a chance to meet new people—" She broke off, as if she realized that she had just revealed some new vulnerability—one I suspected had something to do with Larry Bennett's abrupt blow-off. "Though now that the party is here, I'm dreading it a bit. Can you believe that girl had the nerve to call us to order her a car?" Finding the number she sought, she pulled the card, then looked at the dial pad on her phone as if she'd never used it before. And maybe she hadn't. After all, she'd always had Jeannie—and now Lori—to complete such menial tasks as calling up cars or dialing up clients. She stabbed at the numbers, then stood, looking up at me, a kind of pleading look on her face I had never seen before.

"You want to come?" she asked, her tone implying she might get on her hands and knees and beg. In fact, the lost look on her face even lent her a kind of youthfulness. But maybe that was because I had never seen Claudia look so positively nervous.

"Um, no. Sorry. Can't unfortunately," I said, frowning as if dismayed by the idea of not joining Irina and her troop of followers as they traipsed all over town in search of whatever glories were to be had in NYC's bar scene. "I have plans," I lied.

I saw her visibly slump, resigned, before she focused her attention on her call. "Yes, I'd like a car," she began, then rattled off the address I knew to be Irina's brand-new loft in Soho, purchased before the ink was even dry on her million dollar contract with Roxanne Dubrow.

I turned to face my youthful counterpart, realizing suddenly where that bravado I saw cloaking her came from. Because I knew that whatever wisdom she couldn't possibly have didn't really matter in the face of what she did have. Like money. And most of all...

Power.

I felt a kind of power, too, when I dialed up Jonathan Somerfield the next afternoon. Maybe it was because my father had provided me with the opportunity to wield my charms on Jonathan Somerfield once more. The moment I announced myself to the assistant who answered the phone, I felt a kind of tingle of anticipation, as if I was certain the good doctor wouldn't outlast a second encounter.

"Hello, Dr. Somerfield," I practically purred into the phone when his deep, rich voice finally boomed a greeting over the line. "This is Grace Noonan."

I heard him hesitate and felt my heart begin to sink. Did he not remember me? Was it possible I had not made such a great impression on him as he had made on me? "Dr. Noonan's daughter?"

He cleared his throat. "Hello. What can I do for you?"

I bit back a disappointed sigh. Well, I could be all business, too, if that was how he wanted to play it. "Actually, my father recommended I contact you," I said, clearing up any misconceptions my somewhat breathy hello might have created. "He sends his regards and asks if you would do me—well, him, really," I added quickly, "a favor."

"Of course," he said, his tone clearly warming now that he recognized this to be a matter between him and his former colleague.

I explained that I had purchased the Chevalier, but that I needed an expert to review the certificate of authenticity before I could insure and ship the painting to my parents.

"We could meet at the gallery some night if you're free," I said.

I heard him suck in a breath and felt myself hold one of my own. What was with this guy? He was all raring to go until he realized this little favor for my father would bring him into contact with me again.

As if I could not bear what his pregnant pause might mean, I suddenly heard myself babbling into the phone. "It's open until six during the week. Or all day Saturday, if you're free. Just let me know what works for you, as I'd need to make an appointment with the gallery manager."

"Of course," he said, sounding somewhat reluctant. I heard him rifling through some papers on his desk, probably looking for a calendar. He blew out a breath, as if suddenly weighted down by a task that, up until five minutes ago, had been a joyous homage to Dr. Noonan. I felt a sudden burning need to make up some excuse to get off the phone, then realized what a child I was being. What the heck did I expect? The guy clearly wasn't interested. And while normally I took that as a challenge, this afternoon it made me…depressed.

"Well, I could do something on Thursday…around five?"

"Fine," I said, even knowing that meant I would have to leave work early. Now that this was feeling less and less like the romantic interlude I had imagined it might be, I just wanted to get it over with. Besides, it wasn't like anyone really needed me at the office these days. "I'll see you Thursday at five, then. Good night."

I hung up the phone, wondering when I was going to rid myself of this foolish desire for things—and men—I clearly had no business wanting.

I quickly dialed up the gallery to make an appointment with Pamela. When I was done, I looked up to find Claudia in my doorway. Or someone who resembled Claudia. She looked a bit…anxious. I had never before seen my boss in such a state.

Or such an outfit.

The pants were low slung, with a brightly colored embroidered design on the flare-cut legs and what looked like silver studs on the pockets. The shirt screamed hippie love child with a trust fund, with its wide sleeves and sleek cut high-tech fabric. I think I even saw Claudia's midriff peeking out at me, but I couldn't be sure from the way she kept smoothing her hands over the front of herself.

Wait—I had seen this look before. In the junior department at Bloomingdale's. It looked like a Mitzy Glam, a hot new designer catering to the fashion-forward teen.

Because I didn't know what else to say, I found myself asking, "Where've you been?"

"Bloomingdale's," she replied with a shrug, as if leaving midday for a shopping spree was ordinary behavior for her.

Uh-oh. It *was* a Mitzy Glam.

"I certainly couldn't meet up with Irina tonight in last year's Bob Mackie," she said.

Or this year's fashion for the fourteen-year-old set, I thought but didn't say. "You're going out with Irina again?" I asked, with no small amount of surprise.

She actually blushed, then said, "Well, I really had a nice time last night." She raised her chin, the gleam returning to her eyes. "In fact, Phillip seemed positively smitten with me."

Oh, dear. Clearly Claudia had lost it. Not only on a fashion level, but on a reality level. "Uh, Claudia, I hate to break it to you, but it's common knowledge that Phillip Landau is gay."

"I know *that*." She glared at me. Then, raising her chin once more, she declared, "He wants to take my picture.

In fact, we're thinking about approaching *W* with it," she said. Then, before I could accuse her of overreaching—after all, a supermodel Claudia was *not*—she added quickly, "For an article on Roxanne Dubrow's new face, of course." She smiled like a Cheshire cat. "With a feature on me, as the reigning queen of Roxanne Dubrow's beauty revolution."

I narrowed my eyes at her. "Does Dianne know about this?"

Claudia narrowed her eyes right back. "Of course!" Then she added, "I left a message with her assistant. I would have told her directly, if Dianne wasn't spending half her life at her mother's bedside." She rolled her eyes, as if tending to one's ailing mother was a nuisance better borne by others.

"How is Mrs. Dubrow?" I asked, thinking of the kindly elderly woman I had seen only at the yearly Christmas gatherings. She had been long retired by the time I had joined Roxanne Dubrow, but I knew of her legacy—and her radiant beauty as a younger woman, immortalized in the photos featured in numerous biographies written about her.

"The woman is *dying,* Grace. How should she be?" Claudia sniffed. "Anyway, I'm sure Dianne will get back to me if she sees a problem. Besides, it's good publicity for the company."

It wasn't the company I was thinking of when I rode home in a cab that night, but Dianne. Her mother was dying. Dying. How hard it must be to lose a parent....

My throat was clogged with tears, as if I were the one suffering this great loss. And even as my first tears fell, it occurred to me, with no small surprise, that I *had* suffered this loss. That I knew, at least on some level, how Dianne felt.

Oh, God, I thought, crumbling under the weight of the emotion that crashed over me like a wave.

Kristina Morova. She had never been my mother in any way that truly mattered, but I knew now that she had lived in my mind as some shadowy figure I could never quite grasp. Never would grasp now.

She was gone. Gone in a way that somehow seemed worse than I had ever imagined.

I had no plan anymore to make my way to see her. There were no more solitary cab rides to take me where I had believed her to be living all this time, hoping to confront her. Either to lash out in anger, or reach out to her in relief.

There was, I realized now, no more *hope* of her.

Nothing but a dream of her that up until this very moment, I had not allowed to die.

When I was a little girl, I used to run my finger over the arch in my grandmother's foot. "Your grandma's feet are shaped like stilettos!" she would say, chuckling over the arch that had deepened from the years she had spent in the high-heeled shoes she preferred.

I smiled at this memory now, running my finger over my own deep arch and realizing I had likely inherited my love of fancy footwear from my grandmother, judging by the way my feet were shaping up. I certainly hadn't gotten that taste from my adoptive mother, I thought, leaning into the phone as I listened to her inventory the comfortable flats and sneakers she was packing for her trip to Paris.

"You're going to be all right? Alone on Thanksgiving?" she said now, alerting me that beneath all her preparations, her excited chatter, lay the lingering fear that she was somehow causing emotional damage to her daughter by not sharing the holidays with me. It was my own fault really, for calling her midweek, compelled to by some lingering sense of malaise I had felt ever since leaving Shelley's that evening.

After hurriedly telling Shelley about my visit to Brooklyn and my decision never to return, I had tried to spend the rest of the session talking about real estate. Specifically, whether or not I should buy a new apartment to go along with my baby plans. Though the weight of everything involved in my single parent scheme had kept me from moving beyond the idea stage, I wasn't going to let Shelley know that. She went along with my chatter for a bit, even revealing that she had her own sweet deal in the West Village. But she still wanted to know why I felt a need to deal with everything alone. In particular, why I refused to discuss Kristina Morova's death with my parents.

"I'll be fine," I insisted to my mother for what felt like the umpteenth time. I realized once again that I had been right in not telling my parents about Kristina. Didn't Shelley understand that there were some things that you should just deal with alone, rather than drag the rest of the universe down with you? Needless to say, it was not a productive session. But I felt justified in holding fast to this point. I was certain if I told my mother about Kristina's death, she would cancel her trip out of some maternal desire to comfort me. It was enough for me to know that she would be there for me if I allowed her to. There was no way I would risk ruining this vacation for her.

I heard her sigh. "We should have flown you home for Thanksgiving."

"Mom, if I wanted to come home for Thanksgiving, I could have bought a ticket myself. It's not a big deal," I said, making light of it. "Besides, I could catch up on work, do a little winter cleaning."

"It's the perfect time of year to take advantage of the city," my father chimed in. "Black Friday is the best day of the year to do a little shopping. And I bet the museums and galleries are open."

I smiled, knowing he was likely wondering if I had succeeded in getting the certificate. "Dad's right," I said now. "In fact, I have plans to go down to SoHo to see a show tomorrow night."

"Good girl," my father said, as if my art education were at stake.

"Oh, that's lovely, Grace," my mother said. "A new artist?" she asked.

"Umm, no. Can't remember the name," I hedged. "I think it's French…. From the romantic period," I added at the last minute, as if to throw her off track.

"Oh, I love the romantics," my mother replied with a sigh. "Have a lovely time."

Lovely wasn't exactly how I felt when I stepped out of a cab in front of the Wingate Gallery the following night. Rather than the snow the recent cold bout had promised, a chilly rain had begun to fall, seemingly the moment I stepped out of my office, making it nearly impossible to find a cab. But find one I did when, after a full fifteen minutes of wielding my umbrella against the slanting rain, an off-duty cabbie took pity on my half-soaked self and pulled over.

After I had assessed the damage in my compact—rain-dampened hair and mascara shadows that I hastily rubbed away—I handed my knight-in-a-yellow-sedan a big, fat tip once we arrived in front of the gallery.

Pamela briskly unlocked the door and ushered me into the office, where Jonathan Somerfield already waited.

Liquid pooled inside of me at the sight of him, and even

tenderness at the sight of his brown loafers, the way the stripes on his oxford shirt clashed mercilessly with his tweed coat. Then he glanced at his watch impatiently, and I felt my armor go up, suspecting that my tardiness had not whetted his appetite, but only irritated him.

But it wasn't irritation in his eyes when he looked up, his gaze meeting mine and flickering with the kind of heat I had experienced myself moments earlier.

I almost smiled with pure feminine satisfaction. It seemed the good doctor was not immune to my charms after all.

"I have all the paperwork ready," Pamela said, clearly unaware of the temperature spike in the room. I might even have thought Jonathan Somerfield wasn't aware of it, by the way he dug right in, studying carefully the documents Pamela laid out before him, but for the way his gaze traveled over me once more when he was done, as if he would have loved to have taken me right there. Meanwhile Pamela was going on and on about how Chevalier's works would only become more valuable in years to come.

"Yes, he certainly is an interesting man," I said, my gaze still locked on Jonathan's.

"Oh, that's right. You met him the night of the opening, didn't you?" Pamela said, tucking all the necessary paperwork into a folder.

"Chevalier?" Jonathan said, frowning. "You met the artist?"

"Mm-hmm," I said, leaning over to sign the insurance forms. *You might have met him, too,* I thought, *if you hadn't run off like you did.*

I straightened, returning my gaze to Jonathan. "In fact, I asked him about the painting. You know, who the girl was waiting for." I felt a smile tugging at my lips. "Apparently she wasn't waiting at all," I continued, raking my eyes over him the way he had done moments earlier. "I guess she was merely…checking out the view." I smiled suggestively. "And why wouldn't she? It is, after all, a beautiful view."

I saw his pupils widen and I knew I had him now. Fresh heat curled through me. And I knew just what I wanted to do with him, too….

Even the weather seemed to comply with the fantasies now swirling through me when Jonathan and I stepped out of the gallery a half hour later. The rain had been transformed into fat, wet flakes, and the sight was so stirring I turned my face up to greet them as they fell, closing my eyes against the feel of the cool dampness cascading against my skin. I breathed deeply, savoring the feeling. There was nothing quite so beautiful as the first snowfall….

When I opened my eyes, I found Jonathan staring at me in a way that pierced me. His eyes held desire, yes, but also something else. Something I could not put a name to.

"Going uptown?" he queried, dropping his gaze and focusing his attention on the damp, empty street, which seemed oddly lit up by the whiteness whirling around us.

"Yes, Upper West Side," I replied, watching him carefully as he raised his hand to hail a cab.

He looked at me. "Me, too," he replied, but not joyfully— rather, as if disturbed by the synchronicity of our destinations. "Perhaps we should share a cab."

"Perhaps."

As it turned out, Dr. Jonathan Somerfield lived no less than six blocks below me, on W. 80th Street. And maybe it was the pull of what was starting to feel like fate, or a longing to dally in the delicious chemistry that only built between us once we were enclosed in the back of a cab together, that had me making a move on the somewhat elusive professor.

"You know there's a pretty little pub on W. 79th that makes a mean hot toddy," I ventured, entertaining visions of sharing this first snowfall in front of the crackling fireplace that was bound to be lit on a night like tonight.

He turned to me in the darkness, his face shadowed by the lights that whizzed by and I saw, clearly, that he wanted just as badly to check out the view. But then he looked down at his watch.

When his gaze returned to mine, the connection was gone, replaced by the same worry, the same *something,* I had witnessed earlier. "Well, that's tempting," he said carefully, "but I'm already running late for another engagement." He smiled, a bit patronizingly, I thought, and said, "Perhaps another time."

"Perhaps," I said, smiling back just as coolly and receding farther into the shadowy darkness, turning my gaze to the twinkling lights of the street and knowing, with the certainty that age and the kind of wisdom that only years of disappointment could bring, that there would be no next time.

At least he couldn't see the disappointment spiraling through me. Couldn't know how much I cared.

13

"It's not the having, it's the getting."
—*Elizabeth Taylor*

Though I was as loath to admit it now as I had been as a rebellious teen, I couldn't help but remember the old adage that said your mother was always right. Come Thanksgiving morning, when I awoke in bed alone, facing a day as empty and bleak as the cloud-filled sky that stared back at me from my window, I realized I was just as lonely as my mother had suspected I'd be. Even more so when I headed out to the street in search of sustenance and found the avenue beginning to flood with people, anticipating the festive parade that would start in a few hours.

Tourists, I thought with disdain. All the real New Yorkers had left town—except me. And Shelley, who I had avoided by canceling our appointment last night, figuring I had a handy enough excuse. It was a holiday, after all. I decided I was entitled to a holiday from her scrutiny.

I blustered through the crowds, hitting Zabar's and filling a basket with more food than a single woman with limited freezer space should ever purchase. Driven by a wave of pure nostalgia as I passed a display of fresh cranberries, I even went up to the deli counter and ordered a premade platter of sliced turkey, complete with a heap of stuffing, a woefully glazed-over bed of turnips, sliced mushrooms and cranberry sauce. I tried not to feel embarrassed as the cashier rang my sad, solitary little meal through the checkout, and felt something worse than shame as I headed back through the crowded streets to my too-quiet building.

Once I made my way through the empty lobby and took a mercifully brief elevator ride, I entered my apartment, my gaze flicking to the answering machine, which, of course, contained no messages.

Who would have called? Angie was in L.A. with Justin. "You could come with us, Grace!" she'd offered, not considering that I might feel superfluous when she and Justin sat down to the veritable family of friends they had in that city from their years in the entertainment industry. By the third phone call on this subject, during which she threatened to call her own mother to ask her to set a place for me, I found myself resorting to the same lie I had told my mother. "Claudia and I have decided to treat ourselves to dinner at the Four Seasons," I said, then crossed my fingers that Angie would just let the subject drop.

"You're going to spend Thanksgiving with Claud-zilla?" she said, incredulous.

"She's not so bad lately." That wasn't a lie, at least. In fact, in Claudia's own view she was doing fabulously. Indeed, my boss was spending her Thanksgiving in Milan, at the last-minute invitation of her new gal pal, Irina. I would have laughed, if the spectacle of Claudia running around trying to live like a teenager—a horrifically wealthy and up-to-the-moment fashionable teenager, but a teenager nonetheless—didn't depress me.

My mother had already called to wish me a good day, glee-fully reminding me that I would do well to share a little chardonnay and stuffing with my boss.

I did have some idea that I might use the day to further my career. I had dragged home a history of the marketing of Youth Elixir, planning to use all the free time I suddenly had to find a way—on a shoestring budget—to put this product in the public eye again.

So once I had packed away all my purchases—with the exception of the box of chocolate-covered cherries I had treated myself to—I sat down in the living room and began poring over every sales brochure, campaign strategy and print ad I had managed to dig up, from the day Youth Elixir first hit the market in the winter of 1982.

I smiled at the out-and-out glamour of the first campaign, which featured Daniella Swanson, a giant of a girl made even larger by the furs and jewels she was perpetually draped in for the print ads. "The time of your life" the ads proclaimed, positing Daniella, a buxom, aging film star, as the new model for beauty. Daniella *was* beautiful, but I was certain the sophisticated yet surprisingly fresh-faced glamour she was sporting had less to do with Youth Elixir than with the veritable spa she was reported to live in. I had been a teen at the time, but I remembered reading how Daniella had mineral water shipped into her secluded Santa Monica estate to bathe in and round-the-clock trainers, masseuses and nutritionists to keep her from looking even close to the late thirties she was reported to be. But whatever fantasy Roxanne Dubrow had been weaving at the time, it had worked. Because from the moment it hit the shelves, Youth Elixir shot to the top of the bestselling cosmetic products. Daniella was the new goddess of the over-thirty set, and Youth Elixir, the nectar of the new generation of thirtysomethings.

Of course, the spin was modified over the years. Daniella was replaced with the much-younger-and-much-more-all-American-looking Chloe Dawson, a blue-eyed blonde who might have been called bland in this day and age of multi-ethnic exotic looks, but who exuded a shining, wholesome appeal. No one seemed to care that she had barely hit the quarter-century mark yet was at the center of a campaign that attributed her youthfulness to the wondrous effects of Youth Elixir. "Beauty you can bank on" the ads read—it was, after all, the eighties. Skin care, like everything else, was a gamble on which the wisest might make their fortune. But it was Roxanne Dubrow laughing all the way to the bank, because although Chloe barely had a wrinkle to call her own, her sweet little countenance lured youth-obsessed clientele to Roxanne Dubrow counters.

There were other faces over the years, some prettier, some younger or older as the climate changed, but the Roxanne Dubrow message had always been the same: We have not forgotten you, oh neglected thirtysomething woman. We are here for you and we come bearing solutions. We are the fountain of youth.

Despite this soothing message—or maybe because of—sales went into decline around the mid-nineties. And it seemed no matter what new face was touting this miracle cream, or what fresh campaign was launched, Youth Elixir's sales remained stagnant.

No one had found a way to reverse the sales trend. In fact, after making my way through the history of the product, I couldn't even see what had precipitated the decline.

No wonder the company had decided to seek out a new savior in Roxy D.

I picked up the bottle of Youth Elixir I had placed on the coffee table, studying its clear, voluptuous design not unlike that of an hourglass-shaped female, the flowery font used for the name. I had always liked the way it looked on my bathroom shelf, had even taken a certain pride in it when I had first placed it there, just after I had begun working at Roxanne Dubrow. Now I noticed, for the first time, the thin layer of dust that had developed around the cap. It occurred to me that there was a reason this bottle had grown dusty on my toiletries tray. I couldn't remember the last time I had actually used Youth Elixir, even though I was a part of the post-thirty demographic it was intended for.

I opened it now, dabbing a little on the back of my hand and relishing its satiny texture. Raising my hand to my nose, I took a delicate sniff, and found myself flooded with memories of my grandmother.

My *grandmother?*

I sniffed again, taking stock of the floral notes that almost overwhelmed the hint of musk I knew was in there somewhere. No wonder I was reminded of my grandmother. This stuff smelled like old-lady perfume.

I studied the bottle again with new eyes, noting the overly ornate script, the fussy design, and realized the product itself looked dated.

As if to confirm my suspicions, I raided my medicine cab-

inet, marveling at the sharp fonts and sleek designs of the cosmetics that filled it. Yes, I was guilty of going to the competition. Roxanne Dubrow couldn't satisfy all my skin-care
needs. Or maybe that was just it, I thought, dabbing more of
the cream on my palm and noting how quickly it absorbed,
despite its richness. Maybe it *could*. Perhaps I just hadn't given
Youth Elixir a chance, because it didn't look like a product
someone like me—single, cosmopolitan and, yes, thirty-four,
but far from old-fashioned—would ever try.

I smiled at this revelation. Maybe the day had been well
spent after all.

My satisfaction was a bit short-lived when I realized what
my revelation would cost Roxanne Dubrow. A repackag-
ing—and a retempering of the fragrance—meant big bucks.
And in a year when Roxanne Dubrow was sinking a good
portion of profit back into the new Roxy D product line,
how the hell was I going to sell the corporate bigwigs on the
notion of giving Youth Elixir a face-lift? They'd all but given
up on it, from a financial point of view. Probably the only
reason they did keep it around nowadays was a PR maneuver. After all, they didn't want to alienate the customer who
had made Roxanne Dubrow the cosmetic giant it was today.
The problem was that customer was now likely edging toward fifty.

Still, I took a certain measure of satisfaction that even if I
hadn't solved Roxanne Dubrow's problems, I had potentially
discovered the root of them. Too, I had managed to spend
the day in a way that kept me from cringing every time I heard
the sounds of the Thanksgiving festivities of my neighbors.
Buoyed by my success, I decided to crack open a bottle of
red zinfandel, gratified that at least I knew how to conjure up
the proper wine for a turkey dinner, if not the company. As

I poured my first glass, I hoped it might conjure up my appetite, too, since I had downed no less than half a box of chocolate-covered cherries during my brainstorming session.

The wine made me hazy, but not any hungrier. So I gave in to my relaxed mood and drew a bath.

I wasn't much of a bath taker, but it seemed a lot of women were, judging by the number of bath salts and oils I had received as gifts over the years. Fishing through the selection, which I kept in a box in the back of my vanity, I chose a bottle that claimed to contain jasmine along with the healing aromas of chamomile. Though I wasn't entirely sure of what I needed to heal from, I dumped it into the steaming water, breathing deep as the vapors filled the room, then stepped to the bath.

Once I'd settled in, I picked up the glass from where I'd placed it on the floor and drank deeply, rolling the cool glass across my cheek against the sudden flush of heat I felt the moment I was submerged in the steaming water. Returning the glass to the floor, I sank lower, relishing the mix of scents and feeling the ease of some ache I had not even known my body held.

Old bones, I thought, smiling to myself. They weren't so bad. They helped me remember what it was to be alive. To feel…

Twenty minutes later, I was feeling a bit too much. I didn't know whether it was the wine I had consumed, or the now-suffocating heat, but my body was so relaxed, my mind so emptied, that something else had crept in when I wasn't looking. Something alarmingly close to melancholy….

Now I remembered why I didn't like baths. They made me feel depressed. Even more so today.

The sound of my phone ringing startled me out of my despondency, and also right out of the bath. Though I hated the thrill of anticipation that cheerful ring filled me with on this otherwise lonely day, I hurriedly wrapped myself in a thick terry robe, leaving a trail of water as I darted through the living room and practically dove for the receiver.

"Hello?" I said, a bit too eagerly, even to my own ears.

"Grace Noonan?" came a now-familiar voice.

"Katerina," I acknowledged, with a surge of—what? Surprise? Relief? Whatever it was, I felt my guard come up against it.

As if sensing my peculiar shift in mood, Katerina hesitated. "I just…called to…to wish you a…a happy holiday."

"Oh," I replied, then realizing some return greeting was required, I said, "Happy Thanksgiving to you, too."

She chuckled. "Thank you. We never celebrated this holiday when I was growing up. Kristina started the tradition after Sasha was born. My niece, after all, is American. My sister wanted her to live like an American."

I bit back a smile as an image of Sasha, the personification of punk American youth, rose before me. "So you and Sasha are sharing a turkey today?" I said, conjuring up a new image of that comfortable living room, laid with the traditional feast and surrounded with a family of people I could not really envision, except for Sasha and Katerina, of course. Still, I felt a twinge of something at the thought.

"Well, usually, yes." She sighed. "Sasha is spending the day…away. At her…her boyfriend's house."

The way Katerina bit out the word *boyfriend* clarified just what she thought of Sasha's plans. Then another thought occurred to me. "Are you…are you spending the day…alone then?" I asked. Somehow the thought of the seemingly vulnerable woman I had met spending the day alone bothered me.

"Oh, no, no," she said quickly. "My cousin Anna—well, she's not so much a cousin, more like a family friend—from the old country, too, she's making the dinner. I'm going there now. I just wanted...I just wanted to wish you a good holiday." She paused. "You are having dinner with your family?"

"Um, no. My family lives in New Mexico. It's too far a trip, really, for just a weekend."

An awkward silence followed, and I realized Katerina was now feeling sorry for me. "Um, I...I'll be joining some, some friends for dinner," I hedged, hoping to cut off the invitation I sensed would be forthcoming. Because I knew there was only one thing worse than spending a holiday alone—spending it with strangers. And Katerina and her family were strangers, no matter what bonds tied us.

"Oh, that's nice. Pretty girl like you. I bet you have lots of friends."

I smiled at that, a little sadly. "Yes, yes, I'm fortunate to have friends." *Just not strong enough to truly let them into my life,* another voice whispered.

"Well, I'll let you go then," Katerina said, as if she sensed I had already drifted off in my mind to that place where others waited with open arms.

I hung up a moment later, wishing, with a flood of pain, that someone was there to hold me.

And never let me go.

I left the house bright and early the next morning, knowing that another day alone in the apartment might do me in.

So I did the thing that never failed to bolster my spirits.

I went shopping.

No, I wasn't looking for a new pair of shoes to uplift my spirits or a flirty skirt that might soothe some momentary fashion whim. Christmas was coming, after all. Since this was the season of giving, I needed presents to give.

And as I sailed through Bloomingdale's, picking out a soft cashmere sweater my mother would adore once she chastised me over the cost and a navy turtleneck that would suit my dad's scholarly air, I started to look forward to the coming holiday. There was a certain joy in stumbling upon a gift I knew would be just perfect for someone on my list. Each find brought that deep satisfaction that came from knowing how to make another person happy.

I began to understand, in part, what might make me happy, too. Knew now it was something that a lifetime of solitude would never satisfy. I needed people.

Okay, Shelley? There, I said it.

By the time the afternoon rolled around, I had people—lots of them. Especially since, on a whim, I had headed down to Herald Square. I wondered what madness had driven me there, when after three hours of plowing through crowds, I stepped out onto an even more crowded and darkening sidewalk, only to realize it was close to five and conceivably the worst time of day to even attempt to hail a cab.

I would have to go underground, I realized with a sigh. It wasn't that I never took the subway. My commute to work just made a bus more convenient—or a cab, which I often indulged in.

The car was crowded, the ride longer than I remembered and I felt even more put upon when I got off at 86th and Broadway and discovered it had begun to snow. And not the harmless fluffy stuff I could simply have hurried home in. No, this stuff was wet. In fact, only an optimist would call it snow. It was more like rain than anything else.

When I saw the Cozy Café standing like a beacon on the

corner of 85th Street, I decided an impromptu meal was in order. Besides the fact that the Cozy Café made the best damn clam chowder, it was also a welcome respite from my lonely apartment. Funny how earlier I couldn't bear the crowds, and yet now the thought of being without them pained me even more.

I stepped inside, was just dusting off my collar with my one free hand, when I spotted him. Dr. Jonathan Somerfield, sitting all alone at a window table. I would have snubbed him if I could have, but he was looking up at me like a deer caught in the headlights.

"Well, hello," I said, deciding instead to confront the man head-on and stepping past the Please Wait To Be Seated sign to stand before him.

"Hello," he said, looking up at me as if I were…a sight for sore eyes. I wondered at that, just as I wondered how he could look so positively scrumptious, even on this somewhat soggy evening. He was dressed a bit better than previously, in a thick, braided Irish sweater and a pair of jeans that took away from his characteristic austerity. He surprised me further by saying, "Why don't you join me? I mean, if you aren't already meeting someone…" He glanced at the door as if someone might come in at any moment and swoop me away.

"No…no one," I said. Then, as if this admission embarrassed me, I explained how I had been Christmas shopping all day and was on my way home when I remembered how fantastic the clam chowder was here.

At the mention of food, he waxed poetic about the Reuben sandwich, noting however, that it was nothing compared to the one you could get at Delia's Bistro on 115th Street and Amsterdam.

"Oh, I've been there!" I said, realizing that we had been

frequenting the same haunts for quite some time. After all, Columbia was my alma mater, so I could lay claim to its nearby eateries, too. And just as I was about to launch into a review of Ziggy's Bistro—a little known find I had discovered during my freshman year—he, at least, remembered I was still standing there dripping and weighted down by one too many bags.

"Here, let me help you," he said, standing up to relieve me of some of those bags, carefully tucking them out of the way between the window and the table. Then he was helping me off with my coat, and I would have been suitably impressed by the chivalry of the gesture if I hadn't been completely blown away by the brush of his fingers on the nape of my neck.

My God, this man did something to me. And whatever it was, I wanted to bottle it.

But instead I hid my reaction, taking the seat he pulled out for me and watching as he walked to the rack by the front door and hung my coat.

When he sat down across from me once more, I was again in control. It was a good thing, too, because Dr. Jonathan Somerfield was looking at the way my sweater clung to my curves in a way that declared, yet again, that he was not as immune to me as he pretended to be, and he was clearly not happy about it.

Which only made me want to torture him further. So I slid my legs under the table until my knee came into contact with his.

I saw his eyes widen, felt him pull away before he began scrambling for conversation. "So, been Christmas shopping have you?" he said inanely. Then he picked up his coffee mug and practically gulped the still-steaming beverage.

"Mm-hmm," I replied, glancing up at the waiter who approached our table. "I'll have a bowl of the clam chowder."

When the waiter turned to Jonathan, he said, "I'll have the same," abandoning all memory of that Reuben sandwich he'd just gone on and on about.

"How about you?" I said now, my question startling him further. Clearly he had forgotten the thread of the conversation, probably because I had increased the pressure of my leg against his. I felt positively vampy, yet I couldn't seem to stop myself. "Christmas shopping? Have you started?"

He frowned, then glanced away at the falling snow outside, as if the thought of the coming holiday bothered him. "No, no. Not yet anyway," he said, meeting my gaze once more and allowing me a glimpse of that intangible emotion I had wondered at once before and now recognized because I had felt it myself so recently. Sadness. What did this man have to be sad about, exactly?

He looked away, as if he sensed he was showing his cards, then took another sip from his coffee mug before saying, "I'm not really one for the holidays."

"Why not?" I found myself asking.

He seemed even more disturbed by my question, and I felt a sudden urge to apologize for what now felt like an impropriety.

Fortunately, both of us were saved by the waiter, who placed two steaming bowls of clam chowder before us.

Jonathan seemed cheered by the sight of our meal. "Well, I see you were right about the clam chowder. It looks…delicious." He reached for his spoon, hesitated before digging in, as if the sight of that savory mixture were enough for him, then looked at me. "Aren't you—?"

I smiled. Wow, a gentleman, I thought, remembering the time I had returned from the rest room to find Ethan a third of the way through dinner. I picked up my spoon, as if to encourage Jonathan to eat, and watched as he ladled the soup into his mouth.

Do I know Manhattan clam chowder or what? I thought to myself as I watched him close his eyes to savor the taste.

When he opened his eyes, he nearly blushed, probably because *I* was devouring *him* with my eyes. "Kinda puts you in the mood," I said, causing his eyes to widen, much to my delight. "For Christmas," I finished, as if the answer had been obvious all along.

If my initial comment had shocked him, my explanation only confused him. "You know, Christmas Eve dinner." Then, realizing that seafood for Christmas Eve dinner was an Italian tradition I had shared in as an honorary Italian with the lovable DiFranco brood over the years, I explained the custom to Jonathan. "I think it might have some religious significance."

"Maybe," he replied, "but I believe it might have grown from economic factors as well." Then he went on to explain how in earlier times, the cost of meat was so much greater than that of fish. And as he outlined the historic and economic factors that had led up to the shrimp scampi I had enjoyed so often with the DiFranco family, I found myself biting back a smile. Jonathan Somerfield reminded me of my father, taking refuge in the certainty of academic facts and avoiding the more slippery terrain of emotion. I was certain now that this was his solution for avoiding the tension that buzzed between us every time we got within three feet of each other.

Now that I understood Jonathan better, I decided that if

I wasn't going to reach him on a sexual level, I'd take a back door. "So what is your area of specialization?" I asked.

"The French Romantics. Mostly Delacroix and Ingres. In fact, I did a little work with your father on post-Revolutionary art and culture. That's how we met. But I really got to know him at all those lunches we used to share. During his last semester at Columbia, we had the same four-hour gap between classes on Thursdays, and we sometimes headed over to the Met together to take in an exhibit. In fact, there's a great one going on right now that I'm sure he'd be interested in—'Foundations of the Modern.' It's too bad he's not around...."

"I'm around," I said, pouncing on my opportunity now that he'd opened the door. I don't know what came over me. I wasn't the type to run after a man. Had never really had to, since not many of the species could resist a big-chested blonde and alas, that was probably the problem with most. But something about this man—maybe his very aloofness— lured me. Challenged me.

He looked at me then, his brows furrowed. "Oh, I didn't know you had an interest in late-nineteenth-century art...."

Well, I was more of a twentieth-century art girl myself, but that was beside the point. "I dabbled a bit in school," I said, "but I always wanted to explore it further." Then, because my real motivation was to explore this man a little further, I prodded, "So how about it, Dr. Somerfield? You wanna give this interested bystander a personalized tour of the exhibit or what?"

14

"Being beautiful can never hurt, but you have to have more. You have to sparkle, you have to be fun, you have to make your brain work if you have one."
—Sophia Loren

It was curious that after protesting that he wasn't the best guide for this particular exhibit, since the paintings included were really outside of his area of expertise, Jonathan suddenly caved in. I mean, completely caved, suggesting we meet at the museum the very next evening. "Probably less of a crowd with everyone out of town for the holiday weekend," he added quickly, as if realizing he had gone from reluctant tour guide to eager companion in a heartbeat.

I began to wonder if he was as lonely as I was this holiday weekend. But rather than dwell on that thought, I accepted his invitation. I wasn't going to stand on some ridiculous rule of single life that said I shouldn't accept with so little advance notice. Besides, it wasn't really a date but more…an outing. A sharing of a common interest.

And perhaps it was this thought that had me dressing cautiously for my meeting with Jonathan, eschewing a skirt for a simple but flattering pair of slim-legged black pants and a sweater set in the softest shade of blue, which showed the color of my eyes without flaunting my other "assets." We were just going to a museum, after all. I didn't want to scare the man.

Being tall, I always chose my footwear for a date with great care, especially in a city where short men seemed to reign supreme. I couldn't seem to remember how tall Jonathan was, since we had been seated for most of our random encounter at the café, before he practically ran away once the bill was paid and we were left only to drink each other in.

I thought back to the night at the gallery when we first met, how I had looked into his eyes…. Warmth suffused me at the memory, but I pushed it away to consider more pragmatic issues. We had been eye-level. What shoes had I been wearing?

Clicking through my mental files, I remembered first that I had on the pink sweater dress, which I usually wore with my stilettos.

Which was followed by another realization: Jonathan Somerfield was a decent height, if I could look into his eyes in those shoes.

Mmm-hmm. I love a tall man.

Still, I opted for my ballet flats. They suited the Jackie O classic look I was going for anyway. It was just a trip to a museum, not a…ball.

But as I traveled uptown in a taxi I had been lucky enough to hail right outside my building, I felt as if I were going to a ball. My stomach was fluttering with butterflies. Butterflies!

I am not a butterflies kind of girl.

I was glad that I had volunteered to meet Jonathan at the museum, seeing as he was coming from an appointment he had at the university, which was all the way uptown. I clearly needed time to prepare myself for this event.

By the time I walked into the museum and found Jonathan waiting for me in front of the information desk, dressed in a pair of jeans and gray turtleneck, I was ready. And incredibly glad I had gone for a more casual look. At least my instincts when it came to men, and this man in particular, had been right.

So I followed instinct again and didn't launch myself at him the way I wanted to once I laid eyes on him. Not even a friendly kiss on the cheek. Probably because he seemed so reserved, even in blue jeans. Maybe it was the turtleneck.

"Well, here we are," he said, his eyes roaming over my face as if unable to believe I was there.

Cute, I thought, smiling up at him. He seemed so nervous.

"Yes, here we are," I confirmed, feeling a flutter of nervousness myself.

Then, as if he feared I *might* launch myself at him, he said, "Well, I've already purchased us some tickets. Shall we?"

So we did, heading for the second floor, where the "Foundations of the Modern" exhibit was located. And because we were following all the rules tonight, we started the exhibit from the beginning. As soon as we began to stroll through, I saw Jonathan gain his stride again, surrounded by a world he understood. Since I knew, like my father, he would be more at ease with intellectual subjects, I played the neophyte, asking questions about the paintings we stood before, which were arranged chronologically to show the beginnings of the modern period in artists as early as Velasquez, whose brush stroke technique, according to Jonathan, made him a very early precursor to the later Impressionist painters. The exhibit seemed to follow this line of thinking as well, since Monet and Sisley came next. And as we stood before each painting, I merely had to ask a few innocent questions and then stand back and listen as Jonathan gave a running discourse on historical factors contributing to late-nineteenth-century painting, some of which I already knew—not that he realized that. But I wasn't here to learn about art, though seeing these great works collected together was certainly stimulating. I was here, really, to learn about Jonathan. So I simply listened and watched and nodded my head in all the appropriate places.

And I did learn a few things. About art. And about the adorable Dr. Somerfield.

That he enjoyed the painterly style of some artists over the more restrained brush strokes of others. That historical subjects seemed to invigorate him somehow, while the landscapes made him ponderous.

That his eyes had gold flecks of color in them and his brows furrowed most becomingly whenever he stumbled upon a contentious subject.

By the time we were about to turn the corner on the twentieth century, *I* thought I might launch myself at him. The thing about Jonathan was that between his tall good looks and his keen intelligence, he was absolutely…irresistible.

And challenging. I had let him fly so long in those lofty intellectual heights I thought for a moment I might never bring him down. Maybe I should have worn a low-cut dress after all.

When we got to Cézanne's *Still Life with Fruit Basket,* I was bubbling over with something. And despite all those lush paintings Jonathan had just guided me through, I feared it had little do with art.

"Ah, here we are," he said, studying the painting, which featured exactly what its title implied. "The beginning of the end." His brows furrowed deliciously.

Whether it was the desire that shot through me at the sight of that now-irresistible expression, or the challenge of his somewhat blasphemous proclamation about the painting, I found myself ready to duel. After all, I was a modern girl myself, not only in my taste in art, but in my relationships with men.

"The end?" I said. "Maybe the end of this exhibit, but Cézanne laid the foundation for many of the abstract artists of the later period."

"I'll give you that, but just take a look here. See the way that table looks like it's tilted? He had no regard for reality. I mean, those fruits should be rolling off the table and on to the floor. The composition is…off."

I smiled, remembering how one of my favorite art history professors had argued that Cézanne had fashioned a whole new language for composition out of an inability to paint. It was the kind of argument that had given hope to a dreamy-eyed freshman with little artistic ability herself. After all, it had been hard to accept my lack of ability, especially in the face of all the accolades my mother had received for her talents as a musician. Or all the honors heaped on my father over the years for his academic writing. Of course, I was no Cézanne—in fact I had I finally given up and switched to business administration in my sophomore year. But the mythology of Cézanne's art had bolstered my spirits as a young woman still searching for her way in life.

The memory of that bolstered me now. Or maybe it was the way Jonathan was looking at me, with a kind of hungry anticipation of my next words.

"That may be true," I began, "but we couldn't have had a Picasso without a Cézanne. I think his disregard for the rules of composition is precisely what inspired later artists to explore a new language in their art making."

Those brows smoothed out once more. "Point taken," he said. Then, as if he wondered now at all the rather sophomoric questions I had lobbed at him through the rest of the exhibit, he said, "So I see someone isn't as unknowledgeable about her art history as she pretends to be."

I shrugged nonchalantly, then finally confessed. "Actually, I studied fine arts at Columbia before switching to business administration." Even as I said it, I felt that old insecurity rear its ugly head. Like I wasn't good enough to pursue those lofty dreams my own parents had pursued. "I loved the art history courses," I added, as if I were scrambling for common ground between us. "I guess I'm just more suited to analyzing budgets and monitoring trends than I am at…at painting landscapes."

A smile touched his features. And what a smile it was. "Clearly business was the best choice for you. I remember how proud your father was when you landed some big managerial position," he said. "A pharmaceutical firm, wasn't it?"

If I was surprised to have been a subject of conversation between Jonathan and my father, I was even more shocked that Jonathan remembered it. "That's right. Only I've moved on since then. Now I'm in cosmetics." Realizing I was in danger of sounding fluffy, I added, "More creative opportunities. And money, of course."

"Of course," he said, his smile deepening.

Then I discovered something else about Dr. Jonathan

Somerfield. That far from wanting to spend the evening es-
pousing his theories on art, he wanted to know about me.
In fact, I think he felt some sort of relief at giving up the
scholarly role I had maneuvered him into previously. Once
we made our way out of the gallery, he even suggested we
go to the balcony for a cocktail.

And as we sat overlooking the lovely lobby of the Met
from high above, he asked me all about myself. My job.
Growing up on Long Island. What it was like to have the illustrious Dr. Noonan for a dad.

I laughed at that. "According to my father, you're pretty
illustrious yourself. Imagine what your kids will feel like
someday…."

His expression became shuttered, and I wondered at that.
Wondered even more when he returned his gaze to mine
and I saw that same sadness I had seen there before. What
did this man have to be sad about? I found myself wondering once more.

As it turned out, I didn't find out that evening. Because I
also discovered that one of the reasons Jonathan wanted to
talk so much about me was so he could avoid talking about
himself.

It made him more of a mystery. And more of a challenge.
"So tell me your story," I said finally.

"Ah, it's the usual dull tale," he said with a smile. "Grew
up in Connecticut, went to Yale, then on to New York and
Columbia for grad school. I did some post-doc work at the
University of Chicago, even taught there for a while. But
when the Columbia position came up, I couldn't resist returning to New York." He looked around the beautiful
balcony we sat on. "I'm a slave to it really. All this…magnif-
icence." Then he met my gaze again, and I saw from the way

his eyes roamed over my face that he thought I was pretty magnificent, too.

Not that that got me anywhere. Because after we shared a cab back to the Upper West Side, with me plotting during the whole ride how to get him at least to my doorstep for that end-of-evening kiss I was anticipating in every part of my body, he simply smiled at me when we pulled up in front of my building and bid me a husky good-night.

It didn't worry me though. Because Jonathan clearly had been doing a little plotting of his own in the cab. Two blocks before my building, he had casually mentioned that he had tickets to a concert Tuesday night and just as casually asked me if I wanted to go.

It was enough to make a girl feel positively cheerful.

"'Allo, Grace!" Lori greeted me when I arrived back at work on Monday morning.

"Welcome back, Lori," I said, smiling at her. I hadn't realized how much I had missed her until I felt a wave of pure relief wash through me at the sight of her. "How was your trip?"

"It was fab!" she continued, her voice lilting oddly.

I raised an eyebrow at her, my smile still in place. "Really?"

"Oh, Grace, it was the best bloody vacation I've had in…in yonks!"

Yonks? Suddenly I understood that strange inflection in Lori's tone. It seemed our girl had taken on a bit of a British accent during her brief stay across the pond. She went on to explain how "brilliant" her trip was, describing the sights she and Dennis had taken in, the photos she had shot. The reminder of those photos caused her to pause in her discourse to dig into the knapsack beside her desk.

My smile grew wider as I remembered what it was to be young, to feel the freedom—or was it the naiveté—that allowed you to try on different hats and boldly wear them, no matter how silly they looked—or sounded.

"So how did Dennis's interview go at the school?" I asked.

Opening her packet of photos to show me, Lori rolled her eyes, looking like the all-American girl she clearly was. "The guy he met with was a bit of a wanker," she said, clearly pleased with her clever insertion of British slang, "but it went very well. Dennis liked the school, even met with one of the professors he hopes to study with. And the grounds were just…*fab.* Have a look for yourself," she continued, laying the photos out on the desk before her.

I leaned in to look, feeling keenly her anticipation of my opinion as I studied them. There were some shots of the campus, along with the typical tourist shots of Big Ben gleaming the sunlight, the Houses of Parliament. Dennis gazing out at the camera from beside the Thames and from within what looked like a castle turret. The photos were well executed, but they were nothing compared to the grouping she brought out next. A stormy sky sheltering a cobblestone path. A gray stone structure set off by a sweep of lush green landscape. A closeup of a child caught in a moment of surprise as she encountered a pigeon in Trafalgar Square.

"I especially like these," I said, pointing out the landscape she had captured and the photo of the cobblestone street.

"Yeah, I do, too. I was thinking of adding them to my portfolio," she said, gazing fondly on them.

"Portfolio?"

She looked up at me, her smile frozen on her face momentarily, before she finally relaxed. And confessed. "The truth is, I've always dreamed of being a photographer."

This was news to me. Probably because the only ambition Lori had revealed to me when I interviewed her almost two years ago was that she wanted to work in marketing in the fashion industry. But I suppose she had been in need of a job.

"Well, you are clearly talented," I said, looking her in the eye.

Perhaps it was my encouragement that made her come completely clean. "Thanks. Apparently the admissions committee at the School of Visual Arts agrees." She smiled shyly. "I've been accepted there for the fall…."

Now I understood the true source of her angst over Dennis's leaving. She had been deciding between Dennis and her dreams.

Clearly she was still angsting over it. "I did look at schools while I was in London, too. I mean, it can't hurt to apply other places," she added, her eyes a bit uncertain. "The London School of Photography has an excellent program, though it's very small. Which has its advantages…"

"Better than the School of Visual Arts?" I asked.

"Well, they are comparable," she said with a frown. Then, looking up at me, she continued, "But the London School is a short tube ride away from Dennis's campus. I mean we could get a flat together, somewhere in between…." Her voice trailed off and her eyes held a mixture of hopefulness and…sadness. I wondered at that.

"Of course, then I'd have to leave my job," she said, dropping her eyes as if this admission were a bit too premature to be making to her employer. "And my family…"

I smiled, realizing the true source of her sadness. Like your prototypical Long Islander, Lori was just as devoted to her family as I had always been. Because despite the rebellions of my youth, I had chosen a school a mere train ride away from my mother and father, as if the idea of being farther from them was somehow unthinkable. Of course, now that my own parents were off living their dream life in New Mexico, I knew that despite the lonely holiday I had suffered, no matter how far away your family was, they were still your family. This reminder comforted me. Buoyed me even. So much so, that I found myself taking Lori's hand in mine and giving it a quick squeeze.

"It's so difficult isn't it? When life is full of possibility?" I said.

She bit her lip, then sighed as she began gathering the photos up. "I guess I better put these away before that slag gets in…."

My eyes widened, and this time it wasn't at her Briticism. It seemed her trip to London had toughened Lori up a bit, at least where Claudia was concerned.

"That *slag,*" I said, mimicking her accent, "is in Milan. With none other than Irina and Phillip."

Now it was her turn to gawk. "Really?"

"Uh-huh. Until Wednesday at least. Apparently Phillip is going to take her portrait while he's there. For *W.*"

Her eyes widened even farther and I filled her in on Claudia's coup d'etat, at least from a publicity point of view.

"Wow," she said, suddenly losing her British accent. Then she shrugged. "Well, Phillip Landau is a genius with a camera," she continued. "I'm sure he could make even Claudia look human." Then, as she remembered that Claudia likely wasn't human enough to understand her future change in career plans, she added, "You won't tell her, will you? About my going to school? I haven't decided if it will be in London or New York. I mean, I have the whole winter really to make up my mind."

Hell, she had her whole life ahead of her.

Then, for the first time in a long time, I realized that I did, too.

It seemed Lori wasn't the only one with news.

"Okay, Grace, you ready for this?" Angie said sitting across from me on one of three couches that littered the apartment she shared with Justin. Justin sat beside her gazing dreamily at the soft red fabric that covered the couch they lovingly called "Sofa #3." I had given Angie little argument when she'd summoned me here after work, as I had missed her over the weekend. Besides, she mentioned she and Justin wanted to trim their Christmas tree, and I thought maybe a little holiday cheer after my less than cheerful holiday would be good for the soul.

Angie grabbed Justin's hand and he smiled at her, then she turned to face me once more.

"We're married," she said, her eyes barely containing the happiness those two words had brought to her.

"What?" I said, shell-shocked. "What happened to the…the swanky affair in Brooklyn? The disco ball and crystal chandeliers? Hell, the swan of ice?"

She laughed, as if the thought of doing the chicken dance with all her Brooklyn relatives no longer frightened her. "Oh, I'm sure we're not going to escape that circus in the making," she said, snuggling closer to Justin, who wrapped his arms around her as she spoke.

She turned to look at the man she had just tied her life to. "Justin and I decided we didn't want to wait. So we took a side trip to Vegas from L.A. And voilà!" She kissed Justin's cheek tenderly before turning back to me. "You should have seen it, Grace. We got married in a pink chapel. I think the altar was made of polyurethane! All we needed was an Elvis impersonator to complete the deal—but we settled for a pastor in a white Armani suit." She giggled. "Thinking about it now, it was probably gaudier than anything even my mother could dream up. But it was all ours. Every crazy, beautiful minute of it."

For a moment I got caught up in it—that look that passed between them, that silent communication that said what they shared was theirs alone and could not be spoiled by the madness of a DiFranco wedding.

But the thought of that family snapped me right out of it. "What did your mother say?" I said, imagining her disappointment—and downright outrage. Angie was her only daughter and her last unmarried child. I was certain Mrs. DiFranco saw planning Angie's wedding as her inalienable right.

"Umm, we didn't exactly tell her…" Angie said, biting her bottom lip.

"And the best part is," Justin said, standing up, "we don't even have to."

I looked at Angie the moment Justin disappeared into the bedroom. "You're not going to tell your mother you got married?"

She sighed happily, staring at the door Justin had just walked through, then popped up to join me on my sofa, sitting cross-legged in front of me. "I know it sounds crazy, but I feel calmer inside since we did the deed. It's the best of both worlds really. Now my mother can have her wedding, and I can have my peace of mind—"

"Wait a second, back up, I'm not getting this."

"Okay, let me start at the beginning. We're in L.A. We just had a meeting with some investors, and though everyone seemed interested, no one had jumped on board. But since we had gotten the business part of the trip out of the way, we spent the rest of the time puttering around, enjoying the city. We had just hit the beach to relax when my mother calls to tell me that the catering hall she wanted to book doesn't serve the Italian sausage she wanted for the cocktail hour—something about the place being kosher and the sausage non-kosher. I mean, she's hysterical over it, too! Yelling stuff like—"

"Whoever heard of a catering hall that won't serve Italian sausage!" Justin mimicked in his best Brooklyn accent, returning from the bedroom with a box labeled Ornaments.

Angie nodded frantically, glancing over at Justin as he laid the box on the floor and returned to the bedroom. "Then she's going on and on about how we needed to pick a date immediately because there was only one other hall she liked that wasn't kosher and that could hold the whole family. By the time I managed to calm her down and get off the phone, I was a mess. Suddenly I'm worrying—and not just about sausage. Like how Justin and I are going to manage together after the wedding. What's going to happen with the movie…with us. I mean, everything just felt so up in the air, and suddenly I was freaking out. So Justin and I got into a doozy of a fight, right there on the beach. Of course, we packed up our stuff and left—I think we were causing a scene. You know, Californians don't seem to get upset about *anything*. It's just not natural. I mean what kind of people are these?"

Justin popped into the room again with yet another box, this one bigger than the last. "There's nothing wrong with a little inner peace, Ange," he said, plopping the box on the floor next to the other one.

"I know, I know," she said, rolling her eyes at Justin's retreating back. "So anyway, we head back to the hotel, and there was tension between us—and not the good kind either. I never felt such a…a disconnect between Justin and me." Her eyes started to well up at the very memory. "He was mad at me for letting my mother's craziness come between us, and he was right—why *was* I letting her make me insane?" She sighed. "When we went to bed that night, everything felt wrong. Mostly because Justin and I never went to bed so…irritated with each other. But when we woke up in the morning, Justin looked over at me with those beautiful eyes—" she smiled, her eyes filling with fresh tears "—and I realized he was the man I would always love, no matter what happened. And he must have been feeling the same way about me, because suddenly he pulls me close and tells me he wants to get married—immediately. At first I thought he'd gone mad, but then there I was, throwing everything into a suitcase and hopping a plane with him to Vegas." She beamed, her gaze locking on mine. "As it turned out, he was right. I haven't had a care since we said 'I do.' It was like something…settled inside me. I wasn't even upset by the string of answering machine messages from my mother—apparently the Italian wedding band my brother Sonny had used for his wedding had disbanded and my mother didn't know if she could find anyone better. And how could we have a wedding without some short, bald Italian guy singing 'Amore'?"

Justin came back into the room again, this time with two boxes labeled Ornaments. Angie looked over at him and he smiled at her before returning to the bedroom, whistling "Amore" as he went.

When her gaze returned to mine, her face lit with a soft

smile, I saw, for the first time since I had known her, that the little hamster of anxiety that lurked behind her eyeballs was—miraculously—gone.

And I felt a certainty, too. That Angie had found with Justin a love that could weather whatever the future might bring.

A crash came from the bedroom.

Angie and I both looked at the door to see Justin, his face paralyzed with worry, as he lumbered in with a box big enough to hold a large screen TV. He put the box down quickly, opening a flap that was clearly labeled Ornaments. "God, I hope I didn't break any of these…."

"Justin!" Angie said, finally realizing that their living room now looked like Manhattan mini-storage, with all those boxes lying around. "What are you doing? We don't *need* this many ornaments—"

I glanced around, realizing that what they really needed, was a tree.

"Umm, where are you planning on hanging all these ornaments anyway?" I asked.

Justin looked up at me, a broad smile displacing the worry lines on his face. "On Bernadette, of course," he said, gesturing at the large plant that sat on the windowsill.

Bernadette was the azalea bush that had, inadvertently, brought Angie and Justin together. As part of a plot to win her last boyfriend's affections, Angie had ordered a dozen long-stemmed roses in a vain attempt to make Kirk jealous—and had wound up with an azalea that Justin had not only repotted and nurtured from day one, but had named and written a few songs for. Songs, I sensed now, that were really intended for Angie.

"Justin, Bernadette has gotten big, but not that big," Angie said, clearly exasperated. "What are we going to do with all these ornaments?"

Justin looked down at the boxes at his feet, as if never occurred to him that one little azalea couldn't possibly contain all that holiday adornment. "I dunno…I figured we could go through, pick out the best ones…." Then, as if he had just spied one of his favorites, he reached down and pulled out what looked like a stuffed Santa on a set of skis, his long fluffy beard yellow with age and one of his ski poles long gone. "Hey, my aunt Eleanor gave me this one when I was like, *five!*" he said joyfully, picking his way through the crowded room toward Bernadette and hanging the sadly worn Santa on a branch, front and center.

Angie looked at me then, and I knew from her expression that she was swallowing down the fact that her Christmas tree might not be the best one she'd ever had.

But her smile as she turned to her husband said that it just might be her best Christmas yet.

15

"It's time that the blonde glamour girl dropped her modern offhand manner and assumed the seductive ways of the traditional charmer. We should be dangerous characters."
—Kim Novak

Angie, of course, made a similar prediction for me, when I filled her in on my coup d'Jonathan, probably because I had embellished the tale of our would-be romance by beginning at our first chance meeting in front of the Chevalier painting my parents had met in front of forty years earlier. Which was probably a mistake, because Angie took it as an out-and-out sign of romantic happiness for me.

I got so caught up in that warm and fuzzy vision of the future Angie saw for me that I found myself taking measures to insure *something* happened between us, choosing a black wrap dress and a pair of knee-high stiletto boots for my date with Jonathan that evening. It was tasteful, but with just enough sex appeal to be…deadly.

Though the concert was somewhere up near Columbia—he hadn't said where exactly—he picked me up at my door, since he had no classes that day and he lived, I remembered with delightful anticipation, right in the neighborhood.

When he showed up, wearing dark trousers, a wool overcoat and a somewhat befuddled expression on his face, I knew I had hit my mark.

"Grace, you—that is, you look wonderful. Beautiful," he finished, though that last word sounded a bit…resigned. I didn't question it though, because his eyes told me everything else I needed to know.

He had it bad.

I smiled with pure female satisfaction. Even better, when we were seated in the back of the cab, the slit in front of my dress fell away to reveal a healthy length of leg. His eyes widened and I thought he might choke on his tongue as he sputtered, "112th and Amsterdam, please," to the driver.

When we pulled up in front of a church a short while later, I almost choked myself. "Oh, is this it?" I asked, realizing we were in front of the Cathedral of St. John the Divine.

Okay, so I was dressed a bit vampy for a church. But, at least, as far as churches went, St. John's was pretty sexy, with its Gothic spires and dimly lit, beautiful interior.

In fact, I had never felt so sexy in a church in all my life. We sat up in the balcony, and as the strains of Mozart's *Esultate Jubilate* wafted up to us from the orchestra and soloist at the front, I found myself overcome by a longing to press myself more firmly against the solid shape of Jonathan, who sat beside me looking handsome and subdued, except for the rapturous expression that came over his face as the music swelled.

Which only made me wonder what he would look like when he…

Uh-huh. I was going to hell.

And looking a little too forward to the burn.

"Are you enjoying the music?" Jonathan said during the brief break between pieces. I nodded, a bit too fervently. And whether because he shared my fervor, or was feeling some fervor of his own, he grabbed my hand and held it. And just in time.

For the music had begun again, and it was a piece I immediately recognized, having heard it enough times in my childhood during concerts my mother often took part in, when the demands of being a wife and mother didn't interfere. I remembered the first time I had gone to see her play, at a church that was not as grand as this one, though just as packed. I had been five at the time and sat in one of the front rows with my father, listening to the rise and fall of the melody and watching the dreamy expression come over my mother's face as she leaned into the cello to play.

I remembered thinking how different she looked. As if she were a stranger to me. And when the music reached a crescendo, as it did now, I remembered how my mother seemed to vibrate with it, her eyes closing, as if she were being transported to a place far, far away from where I sat beside my father in the crowd.

I had burst into tears at the time, bawling so loudly my father had to whisk me outside.

Of course, I could be forgiven. I was only a child at the time. Whereas now…

"You okay?" Jonathan whispered close to my ear.

I wondered at his question, until I realized tears—tears!—
were rolling down my face. Clearly, I had gone insane. Not
five minutes ago I had been aching with desire. And now…

Now, I was just…aching.

What the hell was wrong with me?

Since I didn't know—and probably wouldn't have shared
it if I did—I nodded briskly, accepting the fresh Kleenex
Jonathan procured from his coat pocket—so sweet!—and
wiped from my cheeks the remaining evidence of the emotion that swirled through me.

And when the piece came to an end I cleared away any misconceptions Jonathan might have harbored about my response
to the music, assuring him that it was simply nostalgia, even
though in my heart I sensed it was something more. "My
mother used to play that Elgar concerto when I was a child."

"It is a beautiful piece," he said, his eyes searching mine.

For what? I wondered, staring into those soft hazel-brown
depths. What did he want to know? Suddenly I was filled with
the feeling that I would tell him anything tonight. If he asked.

But he didn't. Which was okay, too. Instead, once the concert was over, we left the church and walked in companion-
able silence for a few blocks, as if savoring the evening.

At least *I* was savoring it. For the second Jonathan stopped,
I turned to him, hoping, perhaps, he might share my romantic
feelings as we stood in front of a tree that twinkled with white
Christmas lights, beneath a sky that glowed with the promise of snow.

But he only stepped to the curb and raised a hand to
hail a cab.

I shivered, feeling a bit bereft.

"You cold, Grace?" he asked.

I wasn't. Not exactly. Still, for a moment I considered parlaying his question into an opportunity to step beneath that black overcoat and gain a little body heat. But as luck would have it, a cab pulled up just then, and I yielded to Jonathan's gentlemanly attempt to usher me inside.

When the cab pulled up in front of my building, he gave me an all-too-brotherly hug. To hide the disappointment that washed through me, I ducked quickly out of the cab with a mumbled good-night.

"A hug is good! It's progress!" Angie said when I had lowered myself to that female vice of analyzing the male. In fact, I had called her bright and early the next morning to discuss this latest development. Or nondevelopment. I couldn't help myself. Because Dr. Jonathan Somerfield had me utterly perplexed.

"He probably thinks I'm a…a basketcase." Then I explained—worrying over the explanation as I did—the emotion that had come over me.

Angie was silent for a few moments, which scared me further. "Have you spoken to your parents lately?"

Now she was sounding like Shelley. "Not recently." I would have called, only the last time we spoke they had seemed so busy packing and making plans, I didn't want to destroy their merriment with my recent malaise. And now…now, I just wanted to protect whatever little happiness I had found by not placing too much on it. Because one mention of my recent outings with my father's former protégé, and I was certain my dreamy-eyed mother would turn it into the romance it was clearly not.

"I think I'm just…premenstrual," I said finally, rationalizing that perhaps it was the cyclical rhythms of my body that were making me feel so vulnerable.

Not that the feeling went away. It only seemed to multiply over the course of the day, so that as I sat listening patiently while Lori excitedly explained how she was readying her portfolio to send to the London School of Photography, all I could think about was whether Jonathan would be calling for another date.

I was positively wound up by the time I got to Shelley's that night.

Her attitude didn't help matters.

"I want to talk about last week," she began.

"Last week?" I said, blinking at her. It seemed like a million years ago. So much had happened. And not happened. "We didn't meet last week."

"That's right. That's what I want to talk about. Your reasons for canceling the session."

"It was a holiday—you know, Thanksgiving?" I said, latching on to the first excuse I could find for why I had blithely called her voice mail to cancel.

"Oh," she replied, studying me. "Did you go out of town? To see your parents?"

"No, no. It was too much of a bother, with them leaving for Paris so soon after. Besides, New Mexico isn't exactly a hop, skip and a jump. Do you know there's no direct flight from New York? It's a full day of travel, and it seemed like a bit much for just a long weekend...."

"So you stayed home then?"

"Yes, if you must know," I continued, frustrated with this line of questioning. "Had a little turkey." I didn't mention that the garbage disposal had had more. "Some wine. Got caught up on some work. You know, I think I may have figured out the key to the downturn in sales for Youth Elixir—the campaign I'm working on?" Then, eager to get on to the subject—i.e., the man—that was foremost on my mind, I continued, "Anyway, I was glad I did stay home. Because on Friday I—"

"So you could have come on Wednesday evening but decided…not to?" she asked, hanging on like a dog with a bone.

I blew out a breath. Clearly, this therapy business was for the birds. Wasn't I coming here so I could find a little peace of mind? And something about my last date with Jonathan had unsettled me. I felt a need to talk about it. And if I was paying for this session, I should at least have the benefit of angsting over a man when I chose to. "Look if it's the money you're worried about, I'll *pay* you for the missed session," I said finally.

"Is that what you think? That I'm upset about the money?"

"Well, you're acting pretty pissy about something. Look, I could pay you the fucking money—" I paused, and in a somewhat calmer tone, added, "I mean, if that's what you want."

"I want to understand why you're so angry."

"I'm not angry!" I yelled, then felt like a fool when she just stared at me. "Look, I'm sorry if you schlepped all the way out here from Brooklyn. You can charge me for car fare, too—"

"Brooklyn? Grace, I don't live in Brooklyn. I just told you a session or so ago that I live downtown."

"Brooklyn, downtown. What's the difference—"

"Well, there's a very big difference between Brooklyn and downtown Manhattan."

Didn't I know it. "Sorry if I…insulted you," I said sarcastically. "From a real estate point of view."

She stared at me.

"Not that there's anything wrong with Brooklyn," I babbled. "I mean, I lived there for a little while. Apparently, I was born there, too."

She raised her eyebrows. "So why do you think you said Brooklyn when you know I live in the Village?"

I had no idea where the hell she was going with this, but it was clear she saw some warped psychological motive here. So I stared back, trying to see into her head, to give her whatever stupidity she was looking for so we could just move on. I landed on it almost immediately.

"Oh, I get it. Kristina Morova." It always came back to her, didn't it? "So you think that Brooklyn slip was some kind of reference to her."

"I don't think anything. I'm asking you."

"Look, if it makes you feel better, I didn't go to Brooklyn either. I mean, Katerina called, but I told her I had plans." I blew out a breath. "I just didn't feel like seeing anyone last week, okay? And I didn't want to talk about it. Isn't that okay sometimes? If I don't come? Isn't this about making *me* happy, not you?"

"Were you trying to make me unhappy?"

"This is crazy. Okay, yes. I was trying to piss you off. Out of some warped need for revenge against Kristina. Okay? Can we move on now?"

"Interesting."

Interesting? Not very. "Look, can we change the subject?"

"I want to ask you something first."

I braced myself.

"If I *were* Kristina Morova, what would you want to say to me?"

I bit back the retort that had stood ready on the tip of my tongue, and suddenly found myself speechless. Because the truth was, I had no words for her, this woman who had given me life. She was just a shadow, a stranger….

"Look," I began, an ache rising up in my throat. "All I

wanted to tell you tonight was that I…that I met someone. Someone I really like…" I felt strangled suddenly and then very, very hot. Maybe I *was* premenstrual.

Then a sob shook through me, so uncontrollable I was powerless to stop it. And mortified. Even more mortified than I'd been last night, weeping over a goddamned piece of music.

The moment the tears broke free, I buried my face in my hands, as if I could hide my sudden weepfest from Shelley. But there was no hiding anything anymore. I was on a crying jag. And afraid. But of what?

Of wanting things, I realized. Things that seemed so impossible to have.

That thought sent another shudder of tears through me, and I let it flow. What else could I do? It was a fucking downpour.

And once it passed—because it did, *finally*, pass, I felt incredibly silly, crying like this in front of this woman, this stranger….

So I got a hold of myself, but then I saw a look of compassion on Shelley's face that made me want to cry even more.

As if she sensed it, she grabbed the box of tissues on her desk and held it out to me.

The gesture alone was enough to stop the tide, so ridiculously grateful was I for her acknowledgment that I was hurting. I just hoped I wasn't going to be asked to explain it, because I couldn't. Just as I couldn't have explained it to Jonathan last night.

"So tell me about this man you met," Shelley said.

Which surprised me even further. Finally we got to talk about something *I* wanted to talk about. So I told her about how we'd met, our day at the museum, the concert last night.

"I even cried in the middle of that, too," I said with wonder. "It's like I've become some kind of a…a head case." Of course, head cases were Shelley's specialty. She probably thought I was nearly certifiable.

"Now I'm sitting here like some…stupid love-sodden teenager," I continued, "wondering 'Is he gonna call, does he like me?' Isn't that *ridiculous?*"

"Yes, it is," she agreed.

I looked at her, and this time a laugh sputtered out of me. "Thanks a lot."

She smiled, too, and that was even more amazing. I'd never seen her smile before. It felt like some sort of…reward.

Then she gave me the first real piece of advice I had ever gotten at these crazy sessions. And it sounded an awful lot like the kind of solid, simple advice a friend might give. Or a mother.

"I think you should just call him yourself."

Yes, it was simple advice, yet so hard to follow for some reason. I usually had more balls than most men. Yet here I was acting like a scared little girl. The next morning at work I picked up the phone no less than half a dozen times, trying to think of some cool and casual way to wangle another date out of the elusive Dr. Somerfield—without it looking like I was trying too hard. During my last attempt I imagined pretending I had somehow dialed him by accident, and then chatting him up until I found an opening to ask him out.

Pathetic, right?

Even more pathetic, however, was the sight of Claudia, scurrying into the office a full two hours late and looking a bit jet-lagged from her trip from Milan. Or something. She positively slumped.

I might have said she was back to her old self again, if only because she seemed to have dropped her youthful garb for her former austere yet sophisticated wardrobe. But that was the only evidence we saw of the old Claudia. No shrill orders were barked from behind her desk, no impossible demands made at all hours. In fact, her door stood closed for most of the day, and when she did emerge, it was only to stalk silently to the ladies' room, or to drop some innocuous task into Lori's in-box, before she disappeared behind closed doors once more.

"Do you think she's ill?" Lori whispered to me.

I hoped it was something as temporary as illness. For as much as I despised Claudia's neo-Nazi management style, I couldn't bear this version of her. She seemed positively…meek. And somehow that was worse than her tyranny.

"Is everything all right?" I asked her when I managed to gain entrance to Claudia's office that afternoon to discuss a competitive report I had pulled together.

She looked up from the report, which she had already begun to page through diffidently. Her eyes were weary, and she sighed.

"I'm old, Grace."

I almost smiled. After all, admitting it was the first step. But knowing Claudia probably wouldn't find any humor in this response, I gave her the standard reply. "You're as old as you feel, Claudia."

She practically sneered at me. "Well, I feel about ninety today. My body is aching from riding coach from Milan to Newark—can you believe they only had two seats in first class on the return? And guess who got them. I was stuck in coach with Irina's assistant, Bebe, of all people. My head is aching, and I think I just had my first hot flash in the taxi coming here this morning. I nearly clubbed the cab driver for turning the heat up too high. Then he dumped me off in front of the building and I realized I was still sweating—and it's thirty degrees out there!"

I decided to hone in on what I suspected was the real source of Claudia's malaise. "What happened in Milan?"

She shuddered. "What didn't happen? The minute we stepped off the plane, Bebe came down with some crazy virus. So who do you think had to call all the restaurants in advance to see if Irina's dietary needs could be met? Then there were all the late-night parties Irina begged me to come to, though I have no idea why. She spent half the time voguing for Phillip on the dance floor and the rest of the time on her cell phone, telling whoever would listen what a fabulous time she was having. I was so relieved when she decided we should take a few days in the Lake Country. Then, when we arrived, I overheard the hostess asking Irina—" she squeezed her eyes shut, as if the memory still pained her "—if…if her *mother* would be joining her for dinner in the main dining room that evening." She scowled. "Do I look like anyone's *mother* to you?"

The menace on Claudia's face in that moment made her look far from maternal. But the truth was, Claudia *was* old enough to be Irina's mother. Not that I was dumb enough to point out that particular biological fact to her. I decided a change of topic was in order. "So how did the shoot go?"

Her features turned placid and her eyes lit up hopefully. "Oh, the shoot. Well, that was lovely. That Phillip…" She sighed. "He is a *genius*. He made me feel so comfortable, so feminine, the whole time the camera was on me. It's too bad he's gay. I bet he could make some woman very happy."

I smiled. "Well, apparently, he makes a lot of women happy, judging by the number of beautiful portraits he's done."

"It's true," she said dreamily, looking almost happy herself—and all the lovelier for it. She really was a stunning woman, but her strong nose, aristocratic features and exotic dark eyes often took on a hard edge from her shrewish temper. A temper that, I sensed, came from always having to fight to get what her money or her power couldn't get for her—and the cynicism that came from failing.

I saw that cynicism come back to her eyes as she regarded me now. "So what's going on with you?"

I shrugged nonchalantly, fearing she somehow saw evidence of all my recent emotional distress and would find a way to mock me for it. "Not much." Then I filled her in on what had happened in the office while she was gone, from a work point of view. I don't think she was even listening.

Or that she cared. "I would have gone right home to bed after lunch," she said when I was done, "except I have a conference call scheduled with Dianne, and you know we can't move that. It's the only hour today she won't be chained to her mother's bedside, feeding her pureed vegetables." She shuddered.

This image troubled me. "So I guess nothing has gotten any better with Mrs. Dubrow?"

Claudia shrugged. "I only know that she isn't coming to the Christmas party this year."

"Dianne?" I said, shocked that our CEO might not be able to preside over the annual bash the company threw at the Waldorf-Astoria during the week before Christmas.

"No, no. Of course, *she's* coming, and likely dressed in

something Escada designed with her in mind," Claudia said bitterly, as if she still held the wealth and relative ease of Dianne's life against her, no matter what trials the woman faced. "But her *mother* won't be coming, apparently."

That drove home to me how ill Roxanne Dubrow was. Despite her retirement over a decade ago, she had never missed the company Christmas party.

It seemed like the end of an era for Roxanne Dubrow now that its namesake was in deep decline.

It made me remember just how short life really was, and I could not escape the fact that I had waited too long for too many things. After all, it had taken me over thirty years to follow up on the questions that had haunted me about my biological mother for most of my life. Only to discover I was too late.

It was this thought, more than anything, that gave me the courage to call Jonathan. Even as I did, I formulated a plan. I knew the man desired me—I had seen it often enough in his eyes. Suddenly I wanted—no, *needed*—to confirm what I saw clearly in his gaze whenever he allowed himself to drink me in.

And as I waited for the young student who answered the phone to summon Jonathan, I began to plot. I would cook him dinner. At my place. Friday night.

He wouldn't have a prayer.

"Grace," he said, sounding surprised to hear from me.

"How are you?" I asked.

"Good, good," he replied. "Everything…okay with you?" he asked, as if searching for the reason behind my call.

Maybe he was clueless about how much I wanted him. I decided to give him a little hint. "Sure. I was just wondering if you'd like to join me for dinner Friday night." Okay, a big hint. "At my place."

Silence greeted my invitation, and suddenly I wanted to rescind it. Maybe I had gone too far. Or maybe I was too far gone, I thought, remembering how I had lain awake the night before, imagining just what Jonathan would look like once I got him out of those turtlenecks and trousers he favored.

"Actually, I have a previous engagement on Friday," he began.

I felt myself slump. *Here it comes. The blow-off.*

I listened as he explained that the university was throwing a reception for a benefactor of his department, and as one of their tenured professors, he was expected to go. "In truth, I'd sooner have dinner with you," he said. "This type of affair isn't really my cup of tea...."

He hesitated, giving me time to measure how much consolation I could actually take from this last statement, then completely astonished and delighted me when he added, "I suppose you could...you could come with me? That is, if you want to."

If I wanted to? *Heeellllllooo.* But because I didn't wish to seem too eager, especially after I had all but offered him my body, I said, in the coolest, most casual voice I could conjure up, "It might be nice to visit my alma mater again."

Angie, of course, was ecstatic, and seemed ready to print up invitations to my wedding, notwithstanding my explanation that Jonathan's invitation was really just a counterinvitation to my own. It wasn't like he had thought to invite me until I called.

"Who cares?" she practically shrieked at me. "You still get

to be with him. And think how romantic it will be! You and him, dancing together…"

I smiled. Yes, it could be romantic.

If I wanted it to be…

16

"Any woman can look her best if she feels good in her skin. It's not a question of clothes or makeup. It's how she sparkles."

—Sophia Loren

Believing in romance was one thing. Dressing for it, I discovered, was quite another.

Especially since the only information I had managed to eke out of Jonathan was that the affair was black tie. And that everyone from his department would be there.

Somehow that little bit of information unnerved me. And not just because I hadn't purchased any new formal wear this year. I could always go with last year's fashion for this crowd, who probably thought runway meant the tarmac at the airport. I knew these people, after all. Academics were the crowd my parents ran with all their lives.

All I needed was a little confidence.

And, of course, a great dress.

Fortunately, I had a closet full of them. Unfortunately, none of them seemed quite…right.

And trust me, I tried them all on. At least, all the ones appropriate for the season. There was the gold Cavalli wrap I had picked up at a sample sale, which hugged my curves and highlighted my hair color. But the hint of cleavage became a scandalous allegation the minute I leaned over. Next I pulled on my black Donna Karan sheath, which screamed sophistication—until I sat down to strap on my shoes and realized the slit up the front was a little too risqué. One good leg crossing and I would likely get a building named after my crotch.

When had my formal wardrobe gotten so positively vampy? I thought, standing before my mirror and eyeing the way my breasts were peeking out of the top of that sheath a bit more plumply than usual.

Suddenly I realized that my dresses hadn't gotten slinkier—it was that my curves had gotten a little…curvier since I last hit my closet. "Voluptuous" was the polite term. But when I turned and saw the way the dress was stretched against my somewhat fleshier rump, I was forced to admit I had gained a few pounds since my last formal event. More than a few, I realized, after I slipped into a soft silver halter dress and discovered my gently rounded abs weren't being so gentle on the seams.

While I had updated most of my everyday clothes to accommodate my extra curves, I hadn't had the time to do the same thing for my more sophisticated clothing. And I was certain sophistication was what I needed tonight.

An unease filled me at the thought of the distinguished men and women who would surely fill that party. I had seen them before, during the infrequent dinner parties my parents threw, or the events they had dragged me to before I was old enough to resist. Suddenly a memory filled me of one such event, a fund-raiser for the school of arts and science that I had been forced to endure at the age of fourteen. I remembered the staid faces of the women and the goggling eyes of the men when I had shown up in a seemingly innocent white frock, though nothing I had worn since I had sprouted to a C cup the year before looked truly innocent. "Where did she get *those?*" I had heard one usually reserved colleague of my father's whisper to his equally straitlaced associate. "Not from her mother," came the reply, causing me to seek out my mother in the crowd. She looked, as always, petite and lovely and positively perfect in a sedate cocktail dress.

Where did you come from? my mother had whispered time and time again, as she tucked me into bed or pulled me into a hug. I had sensed her question had been filled with the wonder of a woman who had gotten all she dreamed of when I had come into her life. She had told me so often enough.

Yet somehow the memory stabbed at me now as I prepared to step into my parents' world again. I realized that something in me—something about me—had never really truly felt a part of it.

The phone rang, startling me out of my thoughts. I grabbed for it, hoping for something—anything—to take me from this bad place I had gone.

"It's over, Grace," Angie said without preamble.

"Over?" I replied, confusion filling me. Followed by fear. It couldn't be. Justin and she were a unit. Soul mates—or as close to soul mates as I allowed myself to believe in these days. Had their hurried nuptials resulted in an even quicker demise?

"The show," she explained matter-of-factly. "My agent just called. The network decided not to go with a second season."

Relief sheeted through me, so much so that I was forced to admit to myself how important it was for me that Justin and Angie succeed where no one else I knew—outside of my parents—seemed to. I needed to believe that love happened, at least to some people. And I grew more and more sure of it as I listened to Angie give the details of the end of the show that had given such a boost to her career. She seemed so calm. So not in need of her usual dose of reassurance.

"So I guess this means you get to focus your energies on the film," I said, making an attempt at condolence any way, for old times' sake.

"Yeah," she said. Then, "Hey, I just called to tell you to have fun tonight."

"Fun?" I asked, looking at myself in the mirror once more and practically cringing at how obscenely that dress clung to me.

"Yeah," she replied, confused. "Isn't tonight your big date with Dr. Somerfield, I presume?"

"Yes, yes, it is," I said, dismay filling me as my gaze roamed over the myriad wardrobe choices I had strewn all about my bedroom. "But I have nothing to wear!"

Angie chuckled at me. "Gimme a break, Grace. You have more choices in your walk-in than the designer section in Bloomingdales'. In fact, that's your problem. You have too *many* things to wear."

"Not really," I said. "Nothing fits right. I gained a few pounds."

"Who cares?" Angie said. "You know it's not the dress, Grace. It's the girl inside the dress that counts."

I sighed. "In this case, there might be a little too *much* girl inside the dress."

"Well, in your case, that's probably a good thing. It's not like you ever let those men get enough of you anyway."

I knew what she meant. Also knew that was probably the source of my fear. I was allowing myself to step into Jonathan's world. Allowing myself to be vulnerable, when I swore never to open myself up to hurt again.

I hung up a few moments later and made a decision.

Chanel. Nothing less would do. Fortunately, I had one festive suit left over from my Drew days. As I fished through my closet, I remembered those days with horror. Sweater sets and pearls. Who had I been trying to be?

Drew's wife, I remembered with embarrassment. Or at least someone who didn't broadcast *sexpot* every time I stepped out on his pinstriped arm. Maybe that had been my mistake—trying to mold myself into something I could never be in order to please.

God, had I really done that? I thought, my eye flicking up to where my shoes were stacked neatly in boxes and spying a few from a designer known for her elegant yet sensible style.

I shook off the memory, reaching for the soft gray Chanel suit and yanking the skirt off the hanger with something bordering on anger. All those houses in Westport Drew dragged me to, painting some picture of our lives as the supremely successful couple, with a Mercedes in the driveway and 2.5 perfect little children....

I pulled on the skirt and felt a moment of horror when I realized I couldn't even get it past my hips. How long ago had it been? A year?

I couldn't wear this. And not just because it didn't fit. It

was a lovely suit yes, and would be perfect for me someday…when I was president of the PTA. But not for tonight.
Tonight, I needed to be Grace.

Grace with a few extra pounds.

Oh God, *what* was I going to wear?

Then I spotted it: a soft gold Ralph Lauren with a sweetheart neck and a somewhat full skirt that might turn my
newfound roundedness into tasteful voluptuousness.

Pulling it off the hanger, I slid the dress over my body. I
felt relief when the skirt came over my hips, let out a purr
of satisfaction when, after only a slight struggle, I got the zip-
per up, and gave a breathless sigh when I saw my reflection
in the mirror.

I looked very much like…a princess.

A princess with cleavage, I thought, adjusting the top of
the dress so it held me in a bit more.

Wow. Where had I been hiding this one? I thought, then
remembered I had bought it for a wedding Ethan had invited me to go to—a wedding that fell approximately four
weeks after our breakup.

Studying the soft elegance of the gown, I realized I was
going to make not a few heads turn tonight. Not in a bad
way—the dress was tasteful, elegant. But the color would
surely make me stand out, and I wasn't so sure I wanted
everyone to take notice. Just one man…

The thought of that man—the picture my brain conjured
up of his eyes as he took me in—confirmed my decision.

If I was going to catch a prince, then I needed to look like
a princess.

When the buzzer rang an hour later, I was just putting the
finishing touches on my lipstick—a kissable shade of red

with a little shimmer to keep it festive—and I felt a shiver of anxiety fill me.

Goddammit, what was wrong with me? You'd think I'd never been on a date before.

Then I remembered my last two dates with Jonathan, and that bit of hesitancy in his voice when it came to inviting me to this particular event.

That was just it. I knew he desired me, but it was unclear whether or not he really wanted me in his life.

I shook off the thought, taking another glance in the full length mirror in my dressing area and feeling emboldened by the woman I saw there.

She was beautiful.

And Jonathan was incredible, I realized, once I swung open the door and found him waiting there, wearing a black tux and a somewhat uncertain smile.

There was something to be said for formal wear. Because if I had thought this man was good-looking in his scholarly tweeds and turtlenecks, he was absolutely amazing in black and white.

And clearly amazed by me. I saw his eyes take me in appreciatively before coming to rest on my face with a look that seemed to be filled with…pain.

"Can I offer you a cocktail before we go?" I said, feeling a sudden need to soothe him with whatever means I had at my disposal. And I had a whole bar full of soothing means.

He cleared his throat, looking around my living room warily as if fearing that if he walked farther into that soft, romantic space, he might be swallowed up by it. "No, no. We'd better—that is, we should go."

I smiled to myself, nearly laughing in delight at the desire that clearly had him transfixed. "Let me just get my coat."

I pulled my most elegant coat from the closet and headed out the door behind a still somewhat befuddled Dr. Jonathan Somerfield.

He gained his footing once we reached the relative safety of the street, turning to me on the pavement, which sparkled with dampness under the streetlight. "You look beautiful, Grace."

There it was again—that tinge of regret in his tone. I shrugged it off. "You're not so bad yourself," I said, smiling at him as I took the arm he held out.

We headed to the corner to hail a cab, silence sealing in the intimacy that seemed to have sprung between us now that it was safe to bask in it, surrounded by the lights and murmuring traffic of a city street.

The silence continued even once we were enclosed inside a taxi and gliding up the avenue. I would have spoken, but I suddenly felt no need to. Instead, I felt a certain serenity sitting beside Jonathan. Maybe it was the sense that we were sealed off from that world that beckoned beyond, with all its demands and disappointments. Whatever it was, sitting here beside him, somehow, I felt…safe.

But it was only momentary, that feeling. Once we pulled into that stately and familiar campus all my fears rose up again. Crazy! This was my alma mater, I thought, remembering the first time I had come here as a student. I had been filled with all the hopefulness and, I realized, insecurities of a young woman who had enjoyed the privileges of an Ivy league education not only because of her good academic record, but also because of her father's great benefits package, which included full tuition for all immediate family members. Maybe that was it. Maybe it was because I believed I had gotten a leg up in this world due to my parents more than my own abilities. And suddenly I felt vastly out of my element, despite the fact that I had once called this campus home.

It wasn't looking very homey tonight, I thought, as we headed for the hall that housed tonight's event.

Fortunately, I had the benefit of Jonathan's good nature. I enjoyed the way he put his hand at my back as he guided me up the stairs and then took my coat to check before ushering me into the prettily appointed room where the event was being held. Still, I felt a bit wary as I stood beside him on the perimeter of that expansive, crowded space.

Jonathan must have sensed my unease, because suddenly I felt his reassuring hand at my back once more. "You okay?" he said, looking into my eyes. In his own, I saw the same sense of displacement. I didn't understand it, but I was oddly reassured. I wasn't alone in this, after all.

"Jon!" came a deep baritone from behind. A hand clapped Jonathan on the back, and within moments, a rather jowly albeit jolly-faced man who looked to be in his late sixties stood before us. "Glad you decided to finally join the living!" he said, bringing the hand up again momentarily to grip Jonathan's shoulder as his glance strayed speculatively to me.

"Professor Danforth, how are you?" Jonathan replied warmly.

This caused the older man to guffaw. "Jon, Jon—please!" Addressing me, Professor Danforth continued, "Do you know this young man and I have been colleagues for, what is it, now, Jon—nearly ten years?—and he *still* can't bring himself to call me Ignatius."

I smiled at this, wondering if anyone could wrap their tongue around a name like that.

"Dr. Danforth—" Jonathan began, turning to me. "That is, Ignatius—was on my dissertation committee."

"Jon was one of the brightest stars of our department," Ignatius declared. "Still is." He beamed at Jonathan. "The university was lucky they were able to snap you up after your post-doc." He turned to me again, the pride in his face quickly turning to chagrin. "So are you going to have me wonder all night about this lovely lady, Jon?" he chastised.

"Oh, sorry," Jonathan said, suddenly realizing his error. He hesitated a moment, then said simply, "This is Grace Noonan." As if still feeling a need to somehow explain my presence, he added, "Dr. Noonan's daughter. You know, Dr. Noonan from the history department?"

This information produced an effect I had seen probably one thousand times before. Ignatius Danforth's eyes widened, as if adjusting to the news that this amazon blonde was a product of a Black Irish father who probably reached my chin in height and an equally diminutive mother. But as usual, this double-take was quickly overridden by the genuine warmth the name of Dr. Thomas Noonan always inspired.

"Well, well, well! How is the old chap? My colleagues in the history department tell me it hasn't been the same without him."

I, of course, gave him the update—well, the only update a former colleague might be interested in. The panel in Paris. The paper my father was to give.

"Is that right?" Ignatius replied, his bushy eyebrows raising with approval. "That old rascal. Still landing the best lectures!" He chuckled good-naturedly, asking next after my mother and making me realize that he was likely one of those celebrated professors who had frequented my parents' dinner parties, though I didn't specifically remember him.

We chatted for a few minutes more before Ignatius released us from his amicable grip, imploring us "young people" to "have a good time." I smiled, thinking how much younger I might seem if I worked in academia, where the superstars were considerably older than Roxanne Dubrow's own nineteen-year-old superstar, usually by at least thirty years.

Except, that is, for Dr. Jonathan Somerfield, who, I was discovering as he ushered me through the crowd, was a bit of a superstar himself. Because a strange thing occurred as he introduced me to colleague after colleague, especially those who seemed to know him best. After eyeing us together—and assuming more intimacy between us than there actually was at this point—the esteemed colleague proceeded to wax poetic about the virtues of Dr. Jonathan Somerfield. "Did you know 'our boy' worked with the curator on the Ingres exhibit at the Met last year?" Or, "Did you know Jonathan won the Gunderman prize for his study of Delacroix?" It seemed *my* Dr. Somerfield—yes, some of them referred to him as "your young man"—was quite a respected man in his field.

Somehow that made him sexier in my eyes. I found myself stealing glances at his intelligent eyes—often muddled with embarrassment, for our boy was, if nothing else, modest—his broad shoulders and yes, those big hands, and believing him capable of just about anything.

Which was exactly what his colleagues intended, I think. It was as if they were trying to sell me on the idea of Dr. Jonathan Somerfield as a paragon of men. I was happy enough to stand on the sidelines and feel amused and even enchanted by the way everyone attempted to make the case for Dr. Jonathan Somerfield's perfection to me. I wondered at this, too. What made them think this guy had trouble landing women? I'd been wanting to crawl all over him from the moment I laid eyes on him.

I got my answer after dinner, when I escaped a conversation about transcendentalism and German romanticism that was way over my head by heading for the ladies' room. I was enclosed in a stall and was just smoothing down my dress when I caught the tail end of a conversation that stopped me in my tracks.

"Jonathan Somerfield? Why, yes, I was surprised to see him myself," came one female voice so near I figured she was standing at the sink before my stall. "And with a woman!"

My hand paused over the lock. What the hell did *that* mean?

"Well, it's about time he got back out there again," came a second voice. "It's been at least three years since—"

"I know, I know but it was such an absolute *tragedy.*"

"True. I can't imagine losing my husband—even at my age. He couldn't have been more than thirty-five when his wife died. And so suddenly!"

If curiosity held me hostage before, another emotion, far more overwhelming, paralyzed me now. My God, Jonathan had been married. Once.

Suddenly I understood, all too well, that intangible sadness I had glimpsed in his eyes so many times before. It was a sorrow I should I have recognized. The sorrow of loss.

"Well, I, for one, am glad to see him here tonight," the first voice said with finality. "He's still a young man. He has his whole life ahead of him. He couldn't stay in his self-imposed isolation forever…."

I felt an urge to isolate *myself* in that stall long after the two ladies of bad tidings had left. But although I felt my insides crumbling with a mixture of feelings I was powerless to analyze, I pulled myself together and headed out to find Jonathan again.

It cheered me to find him ensconced in conversation with a professor I had met earlier, and chuckling merrily over something his colleague said.

"Grace," Jonathan greeted me, one hand going to the small of my back in a gesture that now seemed alternatively tender and tentative. As if I were fragile—or he was.

But I held on, smiling at each new face until I thought my skin would crack with the effort. And just when I was wondering how long I could bear the facade of being his charming companion when questions about his past whirled through my mind, Jonathan turned to me and said, "What do you say we get out of here?"

I could have kissed him. And I would have, if I hadn't felt a new hesitancy in myself. As if I were treading on hallowed ground and suddenly didn't have the heart for it.

What was I so afraid of? I asked myself as I watched Jonathan walk to the front to retrieve our coats.

And had my answer once he returned, his gaze on mine brimming with the same mixture of sadness and light as before.

I was afraid that the gap that stretched between us every time he held back might swallow us both alive.

"Can we walk a bit?" I asked, once we stepped outside into the chilly night air. Somehow the thought of being in the cozy confines of a cab with him at this moment was daunting.

"Sure," he said, gazing at me curiously. I saw him glance back at the building we had left and felt fleetingly the sense that he wanted to return to the relative safety of that public space. But then he linked his arm in mine—so carefully, *too* carefully—and led me toward the exit to the street.

We walked in silence for a few moments and I relished it, breathing deep the cold air and praying I wouldn't start to shiver in the sub-degree temperatures, sending Jonathan chivalrously running across the campus to get us a cab.

Finally he spoke. I held my breath, as if I sensed he were about to share everything with me. I felt an odd sense of relief when instead he started to give me an architectural history of the buildings we passed. I saw again his propensity for escaping into the intellectual. It was easier to deal with matters of the mind, after all, than with those of the heart.

I was content to let him discourse, for the moment. Because as much as I needed him to tell me about his past, I feared it as well. I even started to believe, as I was lulled by his soothing baritone, that we could stay suspended forever in the heady present and never touch on all that sorrow that came before.

Moments after we had exited the campus, we passed a building site under construction and he stopped, studying the new foundation that had just been laid. "You know there used to be a beautiful little chapel right here," he said. "Do you remember it?"

I nodded. "Yes, yes, I do," I said, trying to pull myself from the pensive silence I had fallen into.

"It really was quite lovely, but I guess the developers think this might be more valuable if it had a new apartment building on it instead." He frowned, his brow furrowing. "That's the way this city has always been, I suppose. Tearing down the old in favor of the new." He sighed. "I guess not everything good can last...."

His words stung me, and I felt myself rebelling inside. "Why didn't you tell me about your...wife?"

He stopped, his arm dropping away from me as he faced me. His expression was a mixture of confusion and pain. "Grace, I'm sorry, I—"

"No, never mind," I said, no longer wanting to go there. "You don't have to tell me. I shouldn't have pried…"

"I wanted to tell you," he said, sincerity in his eyes. "I just thought…well, I feel so *good* when I'm with you. I guess I just didn't want to ruin it." He laughed, but without humor. "Maybe I was hoping that by not talking about it, it would just go away." He frowned. "I know—stupid, right?"

"No." I understood well that urge to stuff all the painful details of life into the recesses of the heart. Wasn't I guilty of the same?

Then, because I couldn't bear the thought of him suffering alone, I said, "Tell me about her."

He took my arm again, then started to walk down the avenue away from the campus. "Her name was Caroline," he began tentatively. "We met at Yale, and got to be good friends. By sophomore year we were dating, and I guess from the start it always seemed we'd be together. It made sense in light of our shared interests—she was in the art history program as well, except she stopped with her B.A. When I came to Columbia to study for my Ph.D., it seemed natural she would come, too. So she got a job at an art archive." He paused, and I glanced at his profile, saw the way his eyebrows drew together. "It wasn't her dream job or anything. I think Caroline mostly wanted to be a…a mother." He sighed. "Of course, I was in the middle of the graduate program, so we decided to wait. We married just after my coursework and planned to move back up to Connecticut at some point— Caroline was never as big a fan of the city as I was." He smiled sadly, as if that memory pained him.

I gave him a look that encouraged him to continue.

"Caroline wanted to start a family right away but I didn't… I didn't feel comfortable with it just yet. I wanted to finish my dissertation, secure a position. Caroline was okay with that. Then came my post-doc, and we were off to Chicago. When the position at Columbia came up, we moved back, agreeing we'd stay in the city for the first few years, save for a house. Caroline seemed satisfied to wait to start our family until we got our feet under us. Then, one morning, she woke up to go to work and could barely get out of bed. She said she was…nauseous, and I thought she had a migraine—she suffered from them a lot. So I got up to get her some water to take with her pills, and when I came back, she had collapsed."

He stared ahead of him now, as if the whole horrible scene were before him. "I called 9-1-1, but by the time we got to the hospital, she was in a coma. The doctors said she'd suffered a brain aneurism. Within four days, she was…gone." He paused, turning to me. "Apparently she'd been born with it. It was inside her that whole time, like a time bomb."

"Jonathan," I said, gazing into his face. His expression was bewildered, as if he still couldn't make sense of it. "I'm so sorry."

"I am, too," he said sadly, returning my gaze in a way that said it was more than just the past that pierced him now. As if that sorrow had marked him somehow for the future.

It was a sorrow I understood on some level, and before I could stop myself, I pulled him close, as if I could wipe it all away with some physical gesture. I felt his arms close around me and I breathed him in, relishing the feel of him, as if it might be my last. Because even as I leaned into his comforting strength, I could sense him drifting away. I felt myself loosen inside, as if I knew, that someday, inevitably, I would have to let go.

And so, as is my nature, I did let go, leaning back from the embrace to look again at his face, afraid of what I might find there.

I was startled by what I did find.

Desire, barely contained by his beautiful features. And hope shining in his eyes, which drew me in irresistibly.

I touched my mouth to his—or maybe he moved first, I wasn't sure—but suddenly we were joined, clutching at one another as if neither of us would ever let go.

But we did, of course, especially when the wind whipped up and reminded us that we were standing on Amsterdam Avenue in the freezing cold.

"Let's go home," he said, stepping away to the curb to hail a cab.

Home, I thought, imagining for a moment that there was such a place. For both of us.

Home turned out to be my apartment. Probably because Jonathan had every intention of remaining a gentleman and dropping me off, until the cab pulled up before my building and I stated rather than asked, "Come upstairs."

For the second time that night, I felt no resistance.

Even Malakai seemed happy with my selection; he was probably conjuring up a new name for my man friend. As I stood inches away from Jonathan in the elevator, gazing into those thickly lashed eyes as anticipation strummed between us, I decided Malakai's nickname for Jonathan should be "your Hazel-eyed Friend." He had such beautiful eyes…even as they shuttered closed when he leaned in to give me the softest, sweetest kiss.

A kiss so tender I ached for more. But I ordered myself to slow down, as I led him into my apartment and watched as his gaze roamed around my white living room, before coming to rest on me.

I saw his hesitation. "Grace, I—"

I stopped him with a kiss. Then, leaning away, I asked, "Cocktail?"

He smiled, his relief palpable. "That would be great."

I headed for the kitchen, dug through my makeshift bar for the scotch, glad that I had on hand the single malt he'd been drinking all night, and poured him two fingers and another one for myself. When I returned to the living room, his back was to me as he studied the glittering landscape outside my window. "Did you realize you can see the river from here, if you look just between those two buildings?" he said, turning to me.

"It's an amazing view," he added, his eyes roaming over my face.

I smiled and went to hand him his drink, only to have him take both glasses from me. Placing them on the small table beneath the window, he pulled me into his arms.

His kiss was even more tender than the earlier one and I felt tears collect in the corners of my eyes. I wondered at them, but only momentarily, before taking his hand and leading him to the bedroom.

I'd never thought of my bedroom as seductive until now, as I stood before the wrought-iron bed, noting how every available crevice that surrounded it was filled with candles. I worried that Jonathan might think of me as some kind of sex goddess from all the romantic apparatus everywhere, but it seemed he couldn't take his eyes—or his hands—off of me.

Nor I, him. Within moments, my princess dress was a

pool at my feet, and Jonathan was down to shirttails and un-buttoned trousers when he stepped back, taking me in.

"So beautiful," he said, and for a change, his words seemed tinged with anticipation.

We came together, falling onto the bed, hands roaming over each other, mouths seeking. It was as if we knew each other from long ago, the way we moved to each other's rhythm.

And when we had finally discarded all our clothes and I took in his firm, athletic build, I wanted to know him even better.

He kneeled at the bottom of the bed, pulling me down to meet his mouth, and began an act I might have called wor-ship, were I a believer in that sort of thing.

But I felt faith building in me, and something more—damn this man was talented—and I cried out with relief, reaching for him.

He was beside me again within moments, kissing my cheeks, my forehead, finally my mouth, before he poised himself over me, rock hard and more than ready to enter, ex-cept for one thing.

"I don't have anything," he said, "to…to protect you."

So sweet, I thought, gazing up at him. He would think of it that way—as him protecting me. I bit my lip, mentally going over the contents of my medicine cabinet and com-ing up empty. I had tossed Ethan's supply, along with every other personal item he had left in my apartment, within days of our breakup. And Billy had been on the Bring Your Own Condom policy.

I began to slide down Jonathan's body, kissing his chest, his stomach, moving lower, until he stopped me. "Let me—" he hesitated. "I just want to hold you," he said, pulling me up his body again until we were pressed together side by side, our faces inches apart.

I worried over that for a moment—I mean, a woman likes to please a man, especially a man this pleasing—but the way he was looking at me, as if I were gift enough— eased me inside. Eased him, I realized, feeling the tension flow out of his body when, a short while later, his eyes shuttered close.

We slept like that, twined together, for what seemed the full night, though it was dark when I awoke alone. Well, not exactly alone.

Jonathan was still there, a shadowy figure in the dim light, though it was clear what he was doing. Pulling on his tuxedo pants, his shirt and making preparations to leave.

"Hey," I called softly.

He turned, startled, then approached the bed, sitting where he had lain seemingly only moments before.

"Going somewhere?" I asked, trying to for a lightness I didn't feel. It meant something, this leaving. And it wasn't good. A man didn't walk away from the kind of intimacy we shared tonight unless he wasn't feeling as intimate.

"I've got a breakfast engagement at the university today."

I blinked, peering at the clock on the bedstand. "At 4:00 a.m.?"

"Well, I've got to stop at my apartment, change my clothes…"

Though it seemed to me that he couldn't possibly spend as much time on his wardrobe as he was allowing himself, I didn't argue. If he wanted to leave, there was nothing I could do to stop him.

"I'll call you," he said, leaning in to kiss my forehead.

Don't bother, my mind barked back, but I bit back the retort. He didn't deserve that, I knew. He had been a perfect gentleman in all ways.

Which was why I prayed he wasn't going to turn into a typical man.

17

"A gentleman is simply a patient wolf."
—Lana Turner

"It doesn't mean anything," Angie protested. I had wrestled with my doubts about Jonathan alone, wide-eyed and restless from the bed I had not been able to pull myself from since he'd left, despite the fact that I barely slept. I lost the battle just after eleven, when Angie called to find out how my big date went. I had filled her in from top to bottom—the dazzling dinner party, the startling bathroom stall discovery and Jonathan's sad rehash of the tale on a cold sidewalk just steps outside of the campus. Somehow Jonathan's widower status only made him more of a romantic figure in Angie's mind—she started rattling off myriad Mel Gibson roles in some strange attempt to explain away all Jonathan's hesitancy as the actions of man humbled by love—and the loss of it. Not that *that* made me feel any better about things. And though I was loath to conduct the kind of analysis Angie and I were already firmly in the midst of, I found myself suddenly, desperately, in need of answers.

"I don't know, Ange. Something seems wrong. I mean, the only men in my experience who didn't spend the night were the ones I threw out. And Bad Billy, of course."

"Jonathan Somerfield is not Bad Billy!"

At least I had always been able to rely on Billy to call, I thought, up until the moment I pulled the plug on our relationship. Whereas Jonathan...

"If he's such a great guy, then why hasn't he called me yet?"

"Didn't you just see him, like, hours ago?"

"Look, Ange, it's almost noon already, and in my book, when a man and a woman share the kind of intimacy Jonathan and I shared last night, I think a simple phone call is in order...."

"I thought you said you didn't have sex?"

Was my best friend really this thick when it came to men? Or was she already addicted to the idea that Dr. Jonathan Somerfield was Prince Fucking Charming? "Look, the act that he performed on me is, in my opinion, even more intimate on some levels." But with that comment came the memory that he hadn't allowed *me* to be so intimate with *him*. "The funny thing was," I said, "he didn't let me reciprocate."

"Wow, he *is* a dream," Angie said.

Angie, I knew, wasn't a fan of the blow job. She did it, of course, as an act of love. Which meant Justin was probably getting more than any man who came before him.

I, of course, found it odd that a man—especially a man as rock hard as Jonathan had been last night—turned down an offer like that. Prince Charming nothing. I think I might have been sleeping with a martyr.

My call waiting beeped, and a zing of anticipation zipped through me. "I got another call…."

"You better take that one!" Angie practically shouted, apparently certain who was on the other line. "Call me tonight!" she demanded before I clicked over.

"Hello," I said in the throatiest voice I could conjure up.

"Have you *seen* it yet?" came a strident and all-too-familiar voice.

Claudia. Disappointment pierced me. Followed by curiosity. The only time Claudia ever called me at home was during a crisis. Usually one of her own making.

"Seen what?" I asked.

"*W* magazine. The new issue is out. For some reason we didn't get our subscription copy in the office, so I picked it up on the stands this morning. I couldn't wait to see the article on Roxanne Dubrow, though I don't know why. It's a fucking disaster!"

Uh-oh. Apparently the media hadn't been kind to Roxanne Dubrow—or to Claudia herself. "I haven't seen it yet."

"You haven't?" she cried, as if the fact that I hadn't rushed out to pick up *W* was sacrilegious. She paused, then jumped on her next thought. "It's probably available online. Oh, *of course* it's available online. I'm sure it's everywhere by now, goddammit! For the whole fucking world to see! Oh, *God.*"

A moan came out of her, that was half-animal and all Claudia. It was probably the force of that unhappy sound that sent me scurrying over to the laptop I kept on the desk in one corner of my apartment. I quickly booted up and signed on to the Internet, listening all the while to Claudia's rant about the utter injustice of it all.

By the time I got to the site and located the article, I almost agreed with her.

Chasing Youth, the headline proclaimed. *Now that cosmetic giant Roxanne Dubrow is courting the younger market, is the party over for its older customer?*

The picture below, which featured Claudia, her head thrown back and her body angling awkwardly as she attempted to keep up with Irina on the dance floor, seemed to suggest the party was in full swing. Except that Claudia's expression was a bit…twisted, as if keeping up with Irina's beat pained her. And the way her head was thrown back made her neck look like a mass of veins.

"These were the photos Phillip shot of you?" I asked.

"Of course not!" Claudia said. "Do you think I'd let that boy go *near W* magazine with a picture like *this?*" She practically growled with anger. "No, we were at some fashion awards ceremony after party in Milan. Some paparazzo must have snapped this…this travesty!"

"It's not so bad," I hedged, though it was clear to both of us it *was* bad. "Your legs look good." Of course, the fact that a fortysomething woman was showing so much leg in the too youthful turquoise mini she was sporting was another issue entirely.

My eye roamed the page, falling on another photo, obviously taken years earlier, featuring a gracious, smiling Dianne shaking hands with Princess Diana. Dianne looked lovely, of course, and years younger than Claudia, though at the time the photo was taken she was probably not much older than Claudia was now.

"They didn't have a more recent photo of Dianne?" I asked.

"I'm sure they did. Just as I'm sure she took a moment from her bedside vigil to call in and make sure they didn't use it. She'd be sure not to showcase the fact that she's older than I am!"

That didn't sound like the Dianne I knew, but I wasn't about to reason with Claudia, who was positively inconsolable.

"I'm ruined!" she said. "I told everyone I know about the shoot. They probably all raced to the newsstands to get it, and now they're all laughing at me. Especially Roger and that little chippy of his."

"You told your ex-husband?"

"Well, not exactly," she said. "But I made sure Arianna Wainwright knew. You know, my old friend from Helena Rubenstein? And she's friends with Gloria Gibson, who works at Roger's firm…. Ohhh!" she said, the sound more a groan of pure pain than anything else. "Roger and Heidi will probably laugh at me all the way to the Puck building!"

"The Puck building?"

"Yes, yes," she said irritably. "Apparently that's where they're getting married."

"He's marrying her?"

"Yes," she said softly, followed by a noise that sounded suspiciously like a sob.

"Claudia, are you—"

"I'm fine!" she insisted. "It's just that I had always…" She sighed. "I guess I had always thought of Heidi as the other woman in Roger's life. And now—now she's going to be his wife. And I'm just going to be old."

"You're not old, Claudia."

"Well, forty-eight isn't exactly young!" she shrieked.

I heard her suck in a breath, just as I sucked in one of my own. Forty-eight? Claudia was forty-eight? That was impossible. She had only been thirty-nine when I first started at Roxanne Dubrow….

Well, well, well.

Realizing her slip, Claudia barked out, "That's confidential, you know," as if she had just revealed some corporate secret.

Now that I knew her true age, I was impressed. Claudia looked damn good for pushing fifty. Still, I felt a stab of sympathy for her. "Forty-eight is the new thirty-eight," I offered in consolation.

My words provided no comfort. "Old, young, what's the difference?" she cried, "I'm still going to be alone!"

I was beginning to think that being alone was to be my fate as well, especially after a day spent wondering if I was ever going to hear from Jonathan again. I hated that I needed so much affirmation. It really wasn't like me. So I went out to find myself again. In SoHo—specifically in Jimmy Choo, where I picked up a pair of shoes that were just sexy enough to remind me that I was a woman of means. I had nothing to worry about. But as I headed home again, anticipating a message—expecting it, really—I felt a frisson of fear. After all, we were way beyond the crucial morning after and into early evening already. There was no way in hell *I* could call *him* now and still maintain any self-respect, no matter how much I wanted to confirm that what had happened between us was more than just sex. It scared me how much more I wanted it to be.

My apartment, at least, stood witness to our romantic entanglement. Our drinks still sat abandoned on the table beneath the window. My shoes lay in a coupling of their own on the floor of my bedroom. And my dress remained in the same frothy heap it had fallen into when I stepped out of it the night before.

I shivered with the memory of the way Jonathan's eyes had drunk me in, a smile of pleasure touching my lips. Until

I remembered that I had seen that look in a man's eyes before. Desire, pure and simple. It didn't necessarily signify anything more.

I plucked up the dress, stuffing it unceremoniously in the dry cleaning bag I kept on the floor of my closet, then returned my shoes to the shelf above, placing my newly purchased pair right next to them, in the only vacant spot left. As I set about making up the bed, I wondered why I bothered—I would only be lying down in it again in a few hours.

I guess I had to maintain some sense of decorum for somebody. Why shouldn't it be me?

With that in mind, I slipped out of my clothes and into my silk lounge pants and a camisole, feeling the tension start to leave my body the moment I got out of that confining bra.

Yes, I decided, there was nothing like being home. No one to answer to. No one to cater to.

No one to have dinner with, I realized, as I headed to the kitchen.

See what happened when you invited a man into your world? The moment he was gone, you felt keenly that something was missing. Something you really hadn't needed so much before.

I decided a dinner of chocolate-covered cherries was in order, reaching for the remainder of the box I had broken out on Thanksgiving day. And a glass of red wine, I thought, feeling momentarily satisfied that I at least had a perfect companion on hand for my chocolates.

I had just settled on the sofa and was savoring my first bite of chocolate when the phone rang.

I popped the rest of the cherry into my mouth, sipped a bit of wine and contemplated letting the machine pick up, when some impulse I didn't want to examine had me reaching for the receiver. I assumed it was Angie, wanting the juicy details of the follow-up call she mistakenly thought I had received from Dr. Jonathan Somerfield....

Which was why I was utterly surprised to find the man himself on the other end of the line.

"Grace?" came his voice, seemingly at a distance.

"Well, hello," I replied, struggling to keep the surprise out of my voice.

"How are you?" he said. I heard the blare of horns in the background.

"Fine," I answered, "Where are you?"

He hesitated. "Downstairs."

The cherry felt like it had lodged in my throat. But that was nothing compared to the thrill that sang through my veins. "Well, what are you doing down there? Come up already."

I hung up the phone, leaping from the couch and rushing for the bathroom. One glance in the mirror was all I had time for before the buzzer rang. I rushed to the intercom and, pushing the talk button before my guest could be introduced, I said, "Send him up."

I licked my lips, hoping to wash away any trace of chocolate I had not detected in my fleeting inspection, gave my hair a quick tousle and flung open the door to find Jonathan ambling down the hall, somehow managing to look irresistible in a herringbone blazer that clashed alarmingly with the stripes on his sweater.

In one hand, he held a bouquet of soft pink roses.

He paused once he stood before me, his eyes roaming over me in that now-familiar mix of bewilderment and desire. "I was in the neighborhood, saw these and—"

I stopped him in the midst of his halting explanation, kissing him with all the confidence of a woman who knew exactly why he had come.

"Mmm," he said, pulling back momentarily from the kiss. "Is that…chocolate?"

"A poor substitute for what I really wanted," I said, looking into his eyes.

That finely held tension visibly left him, and I realized that he had likely worried over his decision to drop by uninvited. "I couldn't stop thinking of you," he admitted, pulling me close again.

Finally, I thought, leading him straight to the bedroom, *a man who's not afraid to say what he wants.*

Which made me feel free to show him exactly what *I* wanted.

Fortunately, roses weren't the only thing Jonathan brought over that night. Because that other bulge I felt when he first embraced me turned out to be a box of condoms. A big box of condoms.

And once we began working our way through them, I discovered Jonathan Somerfield was not only a thoughtful and giving man, but a tender and generous lover.

Very generous. In fact, it was nearing 2:00 a.m. when we finally gave in to exhaustion. Well, I did at least. For just moments before I relinquished myself completely to sleep, I felt his weight shift, heard his feet hit the floor.

Before I could stop myself, I found myself grasping his hand before he left the bed completely. He turned to look at me, startled.

"Please stay," I said, my embarrassment at uttering those two needy words clearly outweighed by my desire to have more of him. And I didn't just mean sex.

He hesitated, clearly wrestling with doubt.

"Tomorrow's Sunday," I said, hoping I had managed to steal away his one and only excuse for escape. He couldn't possible have class on Sunday.

Whether I had succeeded because I had managed to steal his only valid excuse for escape, or because he had decided to give in to my now-obvious need for some lingering intimacy, he relented, sliding back under the sheet and pulling me back against his chest as he curved his body around mine.

Despite the satisfaction I felt in his decision, I did not relax. Could not relax when I could tell by the way his fingers moved continually over my neck, my back, my thigh, that he couldn't sleep either. For what seemed like an impossibly long time.

At least as long as I could keep my own eyes open, which, I realized as I hazily watched the sun slant through the window at dawn, was a bit…too long.

I did sleep eventually. I must have. Because when I awoke to an empty bed, I felt a sense of shock. Followed by relief. I told myself I didn't want to face Jonathan if waking up to me was such a hardship for him. Being alone was a choice after all. The easier one, I was beginning to think.

I flopped onto my back, already organizing my day into useful parts, breathing deep to shake off the sadness fresh solitude always brought, and found myself wallowing in the miraculous scent of coffee and, oddly enough, bacon. Someone was starting off the day right, and I decided I would start my day off similarly, treating myself to a full breakfast. Maybe at the diner on Broadway. Or even the Cozy Café.

I heard a clatter come from my kitchen.

Or maybe at home, I thought, realizing joyfully that

Jonathan was not only here, but whipping up a breakfast that, judging from the scents wafting in, was fit for a king.

Or a princess.

I leaped out of bed, not even trying to curb the happiness that swirled through me. Pulling on a short baby blue silk robe and glancing quickly in the mirror to run my fingers through my bedhead and wipe the sleep from my eyes, I headed for the kitchen.

Then stopped in the entryway to drink in the sight.

Of Jonathan, clad in a pair of boxers and standing before my stove, whistling—yes, *whistling*—while he worked at a pan of sizzling bacon.

He glanced up at me, startled, then smiled sheepishly. "I hope you don't mind."

"Mind?" I said, my gaze roaming over his body and realizing, once again, how delicious he was.

"I kinda raided your fridge. You keep a pretty stocked freezer for a single woman."

He should only know.

"I found some bacon, eggs, a bit a cheese and even some salsa. Thought I'd make us some breakfast. It's been a long time since I…since I cooked anyone breakfast…."

I could have kissed him. So I stepped up to him and did just that.

He leaned away from me, his gaze on mine. "You're pretty nice to wake up to," he said with a smile.

And you're a dream, I thought. One I hoped I never had to wake up from.

We spent the rest of the day together, moving from the breakfast table to the bedroom where we wiled away the day making love and talking about everything from making art to making babies. No, not our own—that would've been premature. But I got the sense, as Jonathan spoke about the dreams he had once shared with his wife, of starting a family, of making a home, that he did so out of a desire to make those dreams seem tangible again. As if it all could still happen. And the way he looked at me as the afternoon faded into evening, I sensed he could see it happening with me.

So we fell under the spell of mutual possibility, shutting out the world, ordering in dinner. We even indulged in a video rental, which resulted in our first true argument right there in the video store, where he fixated on some old Civil War movie and I lobbied for *Casablanca*. We settled on *Braveheart* as a compromise. A little history. A lot of Mel. It seemed appropriate. Or at least Angie might have thought so, since she had Mel-Gibsonized Jonathan in her mind. I understood why, once Jonathan and I were snuggled in bed, watching Mel struggle with grief after the love of his life was brutally killed, before he moved on to conquer the world as he knew it, and even lay down with the queen.

I was feeling a bit like a queen myself when Jonathan treated me to a full-body massage before bedtime. I was about to maneuver the massage into a full-frontal attack, since those big hands were putting my body into a state of arousal, when the phone rang.

"You're a pretty popular lady," Jonathan commented. The phone *had* rung quite a few times over the course of the day, though I hadn't bothered to pick up. Once had been Claudia, trying to coax me off to a day at the spa, where she doubtless hoped to slough off her most recent rage. The second call had been my mother, and I might have picked up if I hadn't been in the midst of a most pleasant tangle with Jonathan. The sound of my mother's voice—followed by my father's, who chirped a cheery hello into my machine when my mother passed him the phone—seemed to send Jonathan into a strange spasm of momentary embarrassment. I guess it wasn't easy sharing a carnal moment with the daughter of the man he had exchanged some of his loftiest ideas with.

Then there was, of course, Angie, who gave me a momentary fright when I heard her voice on my machine. "I know you're there, Grace, pick up. Grace?" She hesitated, and for one paralyzing moment, I feared she might begin lecturing me on how I was avoiding talking about Jonathan. But something—perhaps some fluttering, romantic hope—stopped her. As if she sensed she might violate some Girlfriend pact of silence in the event that I wasn't alone. Thank God for that. The phone rang a few more times during the day, and the caller—likely Angie—wisely hung up. Now as it rang out, a bit late for a Sunday night, I grabbed the receiver, fearing Angie might go into a paroxysm of anxiety and be unable to hold her peace any longer.

"Hello?" I said somewhat throatily into the phone as Jonathan's hands moved down to the back of my thighs.

"Grace!" Angie shouted in my ear, clearly in a state of frenzy, just as I suspected. "Where have you *been?*"

"Right here," I said sleepily.

"Why haven't you been picking up the phone?" she demanded irritably. Then, as realization struck, "You're not alone, are you?"

"Uh-uh," I said, stifling a groan of pleasure as Jonathan massaged away a knot I had not even known I had in my calf. I heard him let out a little grunt of pleasure, himself, as if it satisfied him to find something on my body still in need of soothing.

"Grace, if that's Bad Billy I hear in the background, I'm going to kill you."

"What are you crazy?" I said, realizing suddenly how insane I had been to think a booty call, even one as bootylicious as Bad Billy, could keep me satisfied.

"Then it must be—oh, my God, Grace! Don't tell me—Jonathan is there?"

I smiled. "Okay, I won't tell you."

"Why didn't you *call* me? Oh never mind that, I want to hear everything!" she demanded. Then, before I could utter another word, she finished, "Tomorrow." And hung up.

Sending a bubble of laughter through me that shook my whole body.

Jonathan let go of my calf, flopping down on the pillow beside me and peering into my face.

"What's so funny?"

As I looked at him, that burst of laughter turned into an out-and-out belly laugh. I realized that I had not felt such an urge to laugh in a long, long time.

I gained control of myself and flipped over to face him. "Oh, nothing," I said, looking into Jonathan's beautiful eyes. "Well, everything."

He raised an eyebrow at me.

"I'm just happy, you know?"

His expression turned a bit puzzled, as if the idea of happiness were just as bewildering. Then he smiled, relenting. "Yes," he said, a bit shyly. "I know."

I suppose it was natural for a woman who had suffered as many heartaches as I had to worry that the bubble of happiness she found herself in would somehow burst. Because once Jonathan walked out the door on Monday morning,

leaving me at the corner with one tender, albeit brief kiss before we headed off to our different destinations, I found myself filled with the kind of icy fear that had done in lesser
relationships in my life. As I strolled across town, choosing
to face the bracing cold over the crowded bus when I
couldn't find a cab, I found myself mulling over the tenderness we had shared, the vulnerabilities we had revealed while
lying side by side. And felt a sense of déjà vu. I had been in
this happy little place before. With Michael, I realized, remembering well that feeling of possibility, of longing for all
that could be, that I had experienced with the Dubrow heir.
I might even have experienced this same floating feeling
with Drew and Ethan. At least in the beginning. Before reality had set in. And it always did.

Which was exactly why I had laid my emotional cards on
the table this weekend with Jonathan, telling him about
Kristina, how I had found her—and lost her. I worried he
might look at me differently once he discovered I didn't share
the same gene pool with his admirable former colleague Dr.
Thomas Noonan. I had learned the hard way that to some
men it mattered. Like Drew.

Whereas Jonathan…

Jonathan pulled me into his arms, holding me as if he could
wash away whatever sorrow I had suffered with the strength
of his touch. I very nearly cried.

But I didn't, of course. I didn't want the first man I felt I
could truly open up to thinking of me as some kind of emotional basketcase.

"Okay, give me all of it," Angie said as she sat across from
me at a sandwich shop near my office. She had cornered me
at high noon, calling from her cell phone to let me know she

was on her way uptown to have lunch and wouldn't take no for an answer. Apparently she believed whatever happened between me and Jonathan warranted a trip uptown, which only raised my romance-filled weekend to a level that positively frightened me.

So I did what I could to bring it down to earth. I shrugged, carefully pulling the wrap from my sandwich. "We spent the weekend together. It was nice."

Her eyebrows drew down. "Nice? C'mon, Grace, what happened? Start from the beginning! What happened when he called Saturday morning?"

"That was Claudia. Jonathan called around six. From the lobby of my building." I couldn't curtail the smile that tugged at the corner of my mouth.

"The lobby—holy cow! He obviously wasn't taking no for an answer." She sighed. "I bet he couldn't bear the thought of being without you!"

Or maybe he couldn't bear the thought of not finishing what he started the other night, I thought suddenly, remembering how quickly that box of condoms had come out.

"What was he wearing?"

I looked at her. "What does that matter?"

She rolled her eyes. "I'm trying to picture it!"

"A really bad sweater and a clashing wool blazer."

"So he's a fixer upper. Go on."

I sighed, realizing there was no way I could downplay these little interludes to Angie. So I gave in. Just a little. "He was carrying flowers. They were pink—pale pink...."

Angie clearly couldn't care if those roses were plaid. "Oh, my *God*, Grace! He's amazing! What did he say next? What did he *do?*"

I smiled, nearly blushing at the memory—and I'm not the type to blush. "Well, it was more like what *we* did."

Her eyes widened and her mouth opened on an "O" of understanding. Then she smiled, clearly pleased with herself. As if she had somehow orchestrated the whole thing. "So, uh, how was it?"

Then, as if I could no longer suppress the joy that had been simmering beneath the surface of my words, I said, somewhat breathily, "It was beautiful."

Angie sighed, her eyes going misty. It was almost more than I could bear. "Aren't you going to eat that?" I practically barked at her.

She looked down at her sandwich as if she'd forgotten about it, then picked it up and took a bite, chewing fiercely and swallowing quickly. "Then what?"

"Let's see," I said, remembering how we had lain back on the bed, just holding one another. Not that that had lasted very long. It seemed to me our breathing had barely returned to normal when his hand found my hip and he pulled me in for another round. "We, umm, we did it again," I said. Which had surprised me at the time. It was as if he'd just been released from prison. Then it occurred to me that maybe Jonathan had, in a sense, been released from a prison of his own making. Was it possible he hadn't had sex since his wife died? *No way,* my mind argued back, while another part of me wondered if that was what had driven him to my apartment, multipack of condoms in tow. Fear curled through me. Was that all I had been to him? A way to release all his pent-up sexual frustrations?

"Grace? *Heeellllo?*"

I came down to earth with a resounding thud. "What?" I asked, taking in her puzzled expression and realizing I'd never find the answers I needed there.

"I *asked* you a question."

"I'm sorry," I said, distractedly. I hadn't even heard her, my mind was so filled with the unbearable weight of other questions.

"What did you guys talk about? I mean you must have *talked* at some point."

"Right," I said, relief sheeting through me. We had talked. About our pasts. And more importantly, about our dreams for the future. But while I remembered the sadness and the hopefulness I had felt as Jonathan had told me how much he had wanted to start a family with his wife, I realized now that I might have read a little too much into his somewhat wistful tale. So much so, I realized, I had fallen asleep last night, filled with a vision of a hazel-eyed baby with thick, dark lashes.... My baby. And Jonathan's.

I know, crazy right? Even crazier when I remembered that I had heard a man pull out the baby banter in bed. Michael. And that had been merely...pillow talk.

"So when are you going to see him again?" Angie prodded.

I looked at her, feeling that arrow of fear hit its mark. "I don't know."

That was just it. It was too soon to know anything. Despite my realization that I was ready...for everything.

18

"All I wanted is just what everyone else wants, you know, to be loved."

—Rita Hayworth

Because I wasn't able to weave the kind of romantic fairy tale Angie tried to make out of my weekend with Jonathan without more to go on, I decided to take matters into my own hands and call him that afternoon. After all, the man had spent the weekend in my apartment—in my bed.

"Dr. Somerfield, please," I said into the phone once I was seated behind my desk and grounded firmly in reality once more.

"Uh, just a sec," came the youthful voice that answered.

"Dr. Somerfield speaking," he said a moment later.

Feeling suddenly like the naughty schoolgirl about to lure the innocent professor to a dirty deed, I said, "Well, hello, handsome."

"Grace," he replied, his voice a mixture of surprise and, I sensed, anticipation.

I warmed inside and decided to take the leap. "I need to see you. Soon."

He cleared his throat, becoming once again the befuddled professor I adored. "Well, let's see here," he began.

I heard the shuffle of papers and realized he was likely looking for his calendar. I had lived through this sort of thing with way too many New York men. You know, the ones who are so busy they need a Palm Pilot to keep track of everything from their next meeting to their next orgasm. It was clear to me, from all that paper rustling around, that Jonathan didn't own a Palm Pilot. I only hoped he had time for his next orgasm this week. Because I really didn't want to wait till the weekend for mine…

"I have class until six, then I'm meeting with a student right after…."

Oh my, the man wanted to see me all right. Tonight.

He did have it bad.

As I did. "Why don't I drop by your apartment? I could pick us up dinner at Zabar's. Some wine…"

He hesitated, but only for a moment. "Why don't I just come by your place? I'll get dinner. Besides, I'm not sure how long I'll be."

"That's fine," I said, though his sudden change of venue made me realize why I had suggested his apartment in the first place. He had already seen my world. I wanted to see his.

Still, I didn't push it. The point was to see *him,* wasn't it? To verify that all that had happened between us this weekend might have a follow-up act.

So I told him, in a low, husky voice designed to raise his temperature a few degrees, that I would be waiting for him.

And I *was* waiting for him that night…and the one after that, too. It was as if we couldn't get enough of one another. We made love and we talked and it was good. So good, I wanted more. Not too much more. Just an invitation, really. To his place, as I explained to Shelley during our session that week.

"Maybe he's a private person," Shelley said, once again becoming a fellow female with advice rather than the probing therapist she had been up until my little sob fest the week before. I think she saw the way I had opened up to her as progress. Because she seemed to be rewarding me with something that was starting to feel like friendship.

Of course, that didn't mean she stopped going where I didn't want to go.

"You're a pretty private person yourself from what I can see. The way you keep people at a distance," she said now.

I would have argued with her, but I could no longer hide from the truth. I hadn't let my own parents in on anything that was really going on with me as of late. Like Jonathan. Or Kristina…

I cringed. Yes, I was private. God, I was practically living in a…cell, I realized. I didn't want to let anyone in. The only one who *had* gotten in lately was Angie, probably because she was always pounding on the door. And Shelley, whom I was paying to pound on that door.

And Jonathan…

I sighed. "You know, I have opened up to *him*. I told him everything about me, I think."

"Yes, you probably did," she conceded. "Everything, of course, except how you feel."

I wasn't going to give Shelley that point. Because the truth was, I didn't know how I felt. Well, yes, I felt happy.

And positively lustful. But since I was overflowing with the possibility of more, especially given all the time Jonathan and I were spending together, I decided to pound on the door of *his* cell a bit.

"So what do you say we cook together on Saturday night?" I said, after we lay back on the sheets on Thursday, our bodies still buzzing from making love.

"Sounds good," he said, one hand going to caress my head as I laid it on his chest, probably to avoid his gaze, as I added, "at your place."

His hand paused and I held my breath, realizing that all my suspicions had been right. He was afraid. Afraid of letting me in. Literally.

I closed my eyes, bracing myself for rejection. Which probably accounted for the avalanche of relief that washed through me when he finally said, in the softest voice I had ever heard come out of him, "Sure."

I lifted my head, needing to see his eyes, to know whether or not his reply had come from politeness or some desire to take things a step further.

He gazed at me, and I saw sadness and worry and a bit of the usual bewilderment. But I also saw, shining beneath all that, hope.

"What's with *you?*" Claudia said as I sat across from her in the small conference room Friday morning, where we were finalizing our marketing plans for the consumer launch of Roxy D. We had been discussing the cost effectiveness of giving away a free sample of the Packs-a-Punch Pink lipstick with purchase and I had just turned away to start typing the financials into the Excel sheet on my laptop.

Lori paused in her note-taking and sat blinking at me, a smile tugging at her lips.

"What?" I replied, looking at them both.

Lori giggled. "Grace, you're *singing*."

The chorus of P.J. Harvey's "This Is Love" had been buzzing through my head—God, had I actually started singing out loud? I almost laughed myself.

Buoyed by the memory of the man who had inspired this happy little tune, I suddenly blurted out, "I have a date tonight."

The minute I confessed to my new relationship, I was sorry. Lori nearly bounded out of her seat with apparent joy. "Oh, Grace, what *fun!*"

Then, before she could leap into the next three questions that were clearly on the tip of her tongue—likely who, where and how—Claudia replied in a voice dripping with sarcasm, "Well, la-dee-da."

I should have expected that from Claudia. I knew well enough that no one was allowed to show even a glimmer of happiness in her presence, especially when *she* was miserable. And Claudia had hit an all time low since the publication of that harrowing photo of her in *W*. In fact, the only thing that seemed to keep her afloat was that she had used her considerable connections to get an appointment with the best plastic surgeon in New York City.

"Well, come on," she continued. "Out with it. Tell us all about this incredible new man you've managed to scrounge up from the muck."

Instinct told me to clam up lest Claudia's bitterness contaminate the well of hope I was feeling. But I was unable to resist when Lori leaned in, eyes sparkling and asked, "What's his name?"

"Jonathan," I said. "Dr. Jonathan Somerfield."

"Don't tell me you've managed to land a *doctor?*" Claudia's eyebrows flew upward. She had always been impressed with my resumé of men. Probably because she herself had spent a solid six years landing her investment banker husband, only to have him drop her for a younger model.

"He's a Ph.D. In art history."

"Oh, *that* kind of doctor," Claudia scoffed. I suppose she figured a man who spent his day atop the intellectual heights didn't have anything to offer financially.

It occurred to me then that maybe Jonathan *was* relatively poor. Maybe that was why he didn't want to show me his apartment. Could he be…ashamed of it?

That was ridiculous. Almost as ridiculous as the heady little refrain of "Love Will Keep Us Together" that wafted through my head.

I baked a cake that night. I'm actually quite a good little baker when I set my mind to it. Or, my heart, in this case. Because this wasn't just any dessert, but a rich chocolate layer cake I planned to drizzle with the freshly made strawberry sauce I also whipped up. At first, I told myself I was baking because I needed to do something to relax, and since Jonathan had insisted on doing all the shopping for the meal himself and I didn't want to show up empty-handed, I stopped at Zabar's for baking supplies on my way home. But as I whipped and stirred all those luscious ingredients together, I was forced to admit that my Betty Crocker act was more than the polite gesture of a prospective dinner guest. I liked caring for Jonathan—felt fulfilled by it in a way that I had never felt before.

Clearly I had sniffed a little too much cocoa, because

when the phone rang, I picked up the receiver and practically sang my hello into the receiver.

"Grace, sweetheart," my mother sang right back at me.

"Hello, darling," came my father's tenor to her soprano.

"Mom, Dad," I said, skittering back from my merriment
as guilt stabbed at me. I had never returned their call after
the message they had left on my machine last week. I guess
I had been a little…preoccupied.

Not that they noticed. Or if they had, they had forgotten
in light of what was currently preoccupying them.

"The Chevalier arrived," my father said happily. "Just this
afternoon."

"Oh, Grace," my mother said, practically on a sob. "I'm
positively overwhelmed by all you've done."

I smiled. "It was all Dad's doing, really."

"Please, I've already let him know just how insane it was
of him to spend all that money. And how romantic. I've never
been so—" She broke off, and I realized she was crying.

Which made me want to cry. With the same kind of happiness I sensed had caused her own tears.

When my mother finally recovered, I said, "I have to say,
it was really something for me to finally see that painting,"
realizing, even as I said the words, how much of a something.
If I hadn't gone to that opening, I wouldn't have met
Jonathan….

As if my father picked the thought of that man right out
of my head, he asked, "Have you spoken to Dr. Johnny? I
really must thank him for his hand in all this."

I bit back a smile, almost wanting to say that I had already
thanked him—over and over again. But, of course, I couldn't
share that with my parents.

I could, however, share something with them, I thought,

remembering my most recent session with Shelley. "Actually, I'm seeing him tonight."

"Jonathan Somerfield?" my mother asked, clearly delighted. "Oh, Grace, how did that come about?"

"We've been dating a bit," I said hesitantly, not sure how much I wanted to reveal.

"Is that right?" my father asked, a smile in his voice.

"Oh, Grace, that's *wonderful*," my mother breathed. "He was always such a nice young man."

Remembering that he had likely been a married man when my parents knew him, I asked, "Dad, why didn't you tell me he'd been married?"

My father paused. "I guess I didn't think of it."

I smiled, in spite of my chagrin. Of course he didn't think of it. He was a man. Did men ever think about these things? Especially men like my father, who spent most of his life studying world events, not personal ones.

"That was a few years ago, wasn't it, Tom?" my mother said now. "Such a tragedy…"

Her words brought all my fears to the surface once more. It *was* a tragedy. The kind of thing that might mark a man's heart forever.

As if my mother felt my anxiety over the phone line, she continued, "I think it's wonderful, Grace. He's wonderful. For you."

And as I lay in bed that night, bathed in the scent of chocolate that permeated my apartment, I thought he was, too.

This didn't stop me from feeling somehow less than wonderful myself as I readied myself to go to Jonathan's apartment the following evening. I changed my outfit no less than six times. It's tricky business, dinner at a man's house, especially when you know you'll be staying the night. I wanted to look casual yet sexy. Which would have been easy enough to do, if it weren't for the whole undergarment dilemma. And since the undergarments were likely going to have a starring role this evening, they needed to be good. But this is the problem when your bra size is a 38-C. No one seemed to cater to it except for those bra companies known more for sturdiness than sex appeal. If I wanted seamless support, I had to live with a bra that looked like it had been pulled from my grandmother's boudoir. Or was downright boring, which was what I usually had to resort to for everyday wear. Not that I didn't own better. I had a whole drawerful of the kind that generally were best worn when you were certain your man would be tearing it off you within minutes. A pretty little demi was out of the question, unless I wanted my breasts to enter the room before I did. And my lacy push-ups made the most unflattering lines under all my formfitting tops. And though I could have gone the bulky sweater route, I needed to have some sort of sex appeal *before* that sweater came off....

Finally I settled on stretch lace in black with a sexy French-cut brief, beneath a black sweater with a very deep v-neck that clung to me just enough to flatter my supremely female form while only hinting at what might be layered below. Of course, I paired this with an equally flattering pair of wool pants.

I topped it all off with my coziest cashmere coat. And, carefully fitting my cake into the baker's box I'd purchased, I tucked the cake, the strawberry sauce and a bottle of wine into a shopping bag and headed out the door.

I decided to walk, despite the cold. Or maybe because of it. I was starting to feel I'd lost it, considering all the angsting I'd done ever since I had proposed this tête-à-tête two days before. It wasn't like me to obsess over every detail as I was doing, and just as inexplicably I found myself letting the worry go. As I walked the short distance to Jonathan's apartment, I even began to relish the fact that he lived so nearby. If nothing else, he'd make a great booty call....

Stop that, I chided the demon voice that seemed to waft up from deep inside whenever I let down my guard. Or put it up, I thought, realizing it was probably a product of fear.

I saw the same fear in Jonathan's eyes when he greeted me at the outside door of the stately brownstone where he lived. It was as if he'd been waiting there for me, which seemed a bit odd. And the way he stood looking at me, I thought for a moment he might make up some excuse and quickly usher me out.

But he didn't. Instead, he took the shopping bag from my hand, then fumbled for his key when he realized he had let the inner door slam shut behind him.

"Jonathan," I said, grabbing his hand before he could reach for the lock. He looked up at me, a bit startled, as if seeing me for the first time.

"Hello," I said, leaning forward and brushing my mouth against his.

I felt some of the tension ease out of him, though it never left his eyes, I noticed when he finally pulled away to let us in.

It turned out, Jonathan's apartment was nothing to be embarrassed about. And it was located on the first floor, which at least somewhat explained why I had been greeted at the door rather than buzzed in. When we approached his apartment at the end of the hall, I noticed how small he looked against the tall wood door. Some ceiling, I thought, gazing up at the pretty woodwork at least twenty feet above me.

Some apartment, I thought, when he finally pushed the door open and stepped aside so I could enter. A large living room greeted me, which I might have called cozy due to the wood furnishings and Oriental rug, except for the sense of expansive space, created mostly by those amazingly high ceilings. And the fireplace. An image of Jonathan and me making love before it rose up in my mind, then quickly died away as I glanced about the room. No, not here, I thought. It almost didn't look lived in.

Then I saw a wall of books to one side, fronted by an armchair and a small table where a book lay open, as if he had just left it there, and an abandoned coffee mug. Apparently he was living in this room, yet somehow it felt lonely.

"So this is it," he said, startling me out of my thoughts. "See? You didn't miss much."

I turned to him. "Well, I haven't seen anything yet. Why don't you give me the tour?"

We started with the kitchen, where I noticed a couple of steaks, which lay on a plate on the counter looking like he had marinated them already. There was also something in a pot on the stove that Jonathan declared was a wild mushroom risotto.

"I see you have hidden talents," I said with a smile.

He blushed, then met my gaze. "I had to do something while I was waiting."

My smile widened. I guess I wasn't the only one who had been filled with nervous energy. I took comfort in that as he led me through the living room and down a hallway where we passed a bathroom and another door that was shut and that we would have passed by had I not paused before it.

"Closet?" I asked, curious as to whether he had been

blessed with what usually came at a premium in Manhattan: storage. I had already seen the generous front closet where he had deposited my coat and could only assume the bedroom held another closet.

"No, no. That's a second bedroom." And before the value of that real estate happenstance could sink in, he added, "A small one." As if the prosperity suggested by a two-bedroom brownstone apartment embarrassed him. "Caroline and I had hoped to use it as a…a nursery."

He looked away on that last word, and suddenly I understood what had hung so thickly between us since he had opened his home to me: the weight of his past and the pain of remembering what he had once hoped for his future. With someone else. Someone who I feared was still present, not only in these lovely rooms, but also in Jonathan's mind.

I struggled against the sorrow brought on by this realization, and got it under control by the time he looked at me again. "It's a study now," he said, frowning at the closed door as if, despite the rechristening, he hadn't completely come to terms with its new function.

I noted also that he didn't even touch the knob, as if he felt no need to show me that particular space.

Before I could wonder at that, he led me away toward the door at the end of the hall, which I saw, once we stepped through it, was the bedroom.

The bed was made up untidily in a plain blue spread, and one wall was lined with rows of books that were clearly constantly in use, judging by how they leaned haphazardly all over one another. A desk sat in one corner, which made me question how much of a study that other room really was, especially since this desk was clearly a working one, covered by a computer and piles of books and papers.

Still, I felt a momentary pleasure at the sight. This room, at least, was fully and completely inhabited by Jonathan, right down to the portable valet where some of those hopelessly outdated yet utterly Dr. Somerfield trousers were hung.

I smiled, finally feeling at home, and stepped into his arms. My hips came into contact with his and I felt his body come to life, which, of course, only boosted my spirits further. "Mmm-hmm," I murmured, placing my cheek against his delightfully rougher one, my lips against his ear, cradling his now-full erection in the apex of my thighs. "You sure do have a lovely…home."

Dinner got off to a late start, as Jonathan and I made a few more wrinkles in that bedspread before the call of hunger pulled us from post-lovemaking languor and we headed for the kitchen.

We cooked side by side, with me adding a marinade Mrs. DiFranco had taught me to the French string beans Jonathan had purchased, while he grilled on the kind of high-tech stovetop grill that could only have been a leftover from his married life. How else did a bachelor wind up with such so-phisticated cookware? But the reminder of his previous life was overridden by the new intimacy I felt as we stood in that small slice of a kitchen, cooking side by side, almost as if we were man and wife ourselves.

Our meal was even more intimate, with me draped in one of Jonathan's soft button-downs and my lacey briefs while seated across from him at a table awash in candlelight.

By the time we nestled together on the couch to eat dessert, my legs thrown over Jonathan's as he sat at one end and I reclined against the other, I was safely back in my comfort zone again, especially when I saw the way his eyes closed to savor his first bite of my cake from the plate we shared.

"Mmmm, Grace," he said opening his eyes and turning to look at me. "Is there nothing you can't do?"

I thought about this for a moment. "I'm not much of a chess player," I said, my gaze moving over to the pretty chess table set up in one corner of the room.

"We can remedy that." His eyes lit up as if the prospect of offering to teach me gave him joy. "Here, taste this," he said, holding out a forkful of the cake.

I leaned forward, holding his gaze as my mouth closed over the bite of chocolate. "Mmmm." I leaned back again to savor the rich taste. "I am good, aren't I?" I said with a wink.

"Where did you learn how to make this?" he asked, helping himself to another bite and then dishing up another for me.

"My mom," I replied, accepting the bite from his fork. "I used to make this cake with her when I was a little girl. Usually on Christmas Eve."

He frowned down at the cake as if the mention of the up-coming holiday disturbed him. I felt the temperature change—ever so slightly—in the room. Trying to purge the sudden awkwardness, I plunged forward, bringing up the subject that had lingered in the back of my mind since my lonely Thanksgiving.

"Of course, we won't be baking together this year, with her and my dad celebrating in Paris."

He glanced over at me. "Are you spending the holiday alone, then?"

"No, no," I answered quickly, not wanting him to think I was a friendless loner. "I'll be spending Christmas Day with the DiFrancos—you know, my friend Angie's family?"

"Ah, yes," he said, as if my having these plans filled him with some sort of relief. "So it will be a seafood dinner, then?"

"Well, that's on Christmas Eve." I was glad he was so focused on his cake that he couldn't see the question in my eyes. Because I hadn't made plans to go to the DiFrancos for that part of the holiday—Angie and Justin were celebrating a romantic Christmas Eve together at their apartment. I understood. Christmas Eve had always held a bit of romance for me, too, perhaps because it was so close to my parents' wedding anniversary. Yet somehow I never seemed to have a man in my life come Christmastimes. So after this brief but utterly romantic few weeks with Jonathan, I hoped that this year I would.

"You?" I said, venturing forth on that limb as carefully as possible. "Any plans for the holiday?"

I saw him chew thoughtfully, then offer the remainder of the cake to me before he answered. When I shook my head, he took the last bite himself, then placed the empty plate on the coffee table. "Well, my parents are in Connecticut, as you know, so I'll head up there for the day. My brother is usually there with his wife and their two little girls." His gaze turned pensive again.

"So no big Christmas Eve dinner for you either?" I said, feeling intensely the romantic wish that lay beneath my question.

He looked at me as if he sensed the direction my thoughts had taken. I saw his gaze darken with emotion and wondered at that, but the wondering got too much and before I knew what I was doing, I was putting my wish into words.

"Maybe we could spend it together…."

He reached for his coffee, only to stare down into the mug as if seeking an escape route in the bottom of that cup. My guard went up immediately, and just as I was about to rescind my proposal with some suddenly-remembered-invitation to help me save face, Jonathan looked up at me again, his gaze pensive as he said, "Maybe…" Then, as if he longed to shut the door on the subject altogether, he placed the mug back down on the table and stood. "So what do you say to a little Chess 101?"

It had been a mistake, I realized, to take that hopeful little step forward, for it had sent Jonathan retreating behind his wall of intellect. Gone was that searching intimacy I had earlier seen in his eyes. It was replaced by that scholarly-yet-once-removed air I had noted about him at our first few meetings, as he guided me through the steps of a game I no longer wanted to play.

"You sure you want to do that?" he said midgame, when I moved my knight over to the side of the board. "You left your pawn unprotected."

My pawn wasn't the only thing I had left unprotected.

"Why? Are you going to let me take it back?" I asked, thinking more of my little invitation that had apparently ruined everything.

Not that Jonathan noticed, looking at me as if I were a student in need of enlightenment, rather than a lover looking for more than her next maneuver. "Well, if you don't, I'll have your king in three moves. The game will be over."

More than the chess game was starting to feel over, that was for sure. The thought made me feel sad, and a bit angry. So I'd asked him out for Christmas Eve—why the hell had the thought of sharing that sacred romantic night with me scared him off?

"I'm sorry," I said finally, wearily moving my knight back into place. "I don't think I'm ever going to get this."

He looked at me. "Not everyone gets it at first. It takes some practice," he said.

Practice I had had enough of, at least in terms of relationships. I was so tired, suddenly, of having to learn how to be with another person.

As if he sensed my withdrawal, if not the source of it, Jonathan said, "Maybe we should wrap this up for the night. Get some sleep."

But sleep did not come for me after Jonathan had turned off the lights and kissed me—a bit too chastely—and rolled over to the other side of the bed. There was no spooning tonight, not even a late-night cuddle, and the gap that lay between us on the bed felt so wide I thought it might swallow me up. It seemed like hours before I heard Jonathan's breath move into the deep, even rhythm of sleep, and when it did, I felt that demon take me over again. Suddenly, before I even knew what I was doing, I was sliding quietly from the bed and creeping silently down the hall.

I knew it was wrong to pry, but a woman has to understand what she's up against if she hopes to gain an edge on the competition. And I sensed what stood between me and Jonathan somehow lay beyond that study door. I told myself I was only conducting a little market research. Because if I wanted this man—and I knew that I did—I needed to understand him, didn't I?

Pulling Jonathan's shirt around me against the shiver of cold I felt, I reached for the knob—and cringed at the loud click it made as I turned it to the right. When at first the door didn't budge, I feared it was locked, until finally it gave way and I stepped quickly into the gloomy interior before I could change my mind.

I could barely make out a thing, except that it did seem, as Jonathan had suggested, like a smallish space. And before I could stumble over what appeared to be boxes strewn on the floor, I slid my hand along the wall, made contact with the light switch, and flicked it on.

The room did appear to be some kind of a study, with a bit of storage thrown in. Beyond the few boxes at my feet stood a bookshelf holding yet more books and an antique desk strewn with papers, as if someone had only just been seated there, working. But when I stepped closer, I saw that everything was coated in a fine layer of dust, including the framed photos perched along the edge of the desk.

The first one I picked up was, of course, the wedding photo. Brushing away the film that coated it, I found myself staring into those eyes I had grown to know so well in so short a time. Except they seemed different. Younger, yes. And lighter. Happier, I supposed, finally moving my gaze to his bride.

Caroline Somerfield gazed radiantly out at me, and as I studied her straight nose and squarish face, I realized she looked a bit like a granola girl who'd gotten gussied up for her big day. But she was pretty, I had to admit, with straight brown hair that had been garlanded with a crown of flowers, and smiling brown eyes. She looked every inch the wife. The kind of woman you might see in a station wagon at a soccer game, ever ready to take home as many team members as would fit.

Someone you could rely on.

But she was gone, I remembered next, my heart filled with sudden sadness for Jonathan.

I put the picture down quickly, grabbing up the next, and this time the granola girl was in full earthy form, hair in two long braids as she laughed at whoever held the camera. Jonathan probably, I thought, this time feeling a stab of envy before I leaned down to peer at the final photo, which featured them both seated at a formal dinner, beaming at the camera like the loving couple they clearly were while a table of distinguished-looking people surrounded them.

I cringed when I found myself judging Caroline by her attire—as if I could reduce the impact she had had on Jonathan's life by reducing her to a fashion report card—when suddenly my eye caught sight of a scrawled note tucked into the corner of the blotter. And though the tattered page had gone a bit yellow with age, the words on it were from a woman who had seemingly been here moments before.

Off to Maggie's to see our new niece! See you at eight, darling.
Caroline

My throat thickened and my eyes blurred, and suddenly I felt like a voyeur, peering into Jonathan's cozy, intimate world of scrawled words of affection and family; a world he had lost forever. The kind of world I longed for; one I feared I would never be a true part of.

If the morning didn't bring me peace, it brought clarity. I knew what I had to do. I had to go home. To surround myself in the familiar if only to protect myself from the unknown.

So I dressed quickly, gathered up my things, and when I discovered Jonathan awake and regarding me warily from the bed, I quickly explained that I had to do some "catch-up" before work on Monday morning.

He made no argument, which only pierced me more. He only slid out of bed and probably out of that ingrained politeness I was beginning to abhor, he walked me to the door.

19

> "So long as a woman has twinkles in her eyes, no man notices whether she has wrinkles under them."
> —Dolores Del Rio

"So how was your big date with the big doc?" Lori asked when I walked into the office on Monday morning.

I paused before the coat closet. "It was...fine." As I turned away to hang my coat, I felt myself mustering up a dismissal of the most important relationship I had had in a long time. I knew it had been a mistake to allow my burst of romantic hope to infect Lori, who already suffered from a bit too much optimism. And since some part of me sensed there was little left to wish for when it came to Jonathan, I began the time-worn process of weaning myself—and Lori—from hope.

Closing the closet, I made my face a mask as I turned toward her. "I'm not so sure he's my type." Then, with a shrug designed to show my indifference, I headed for the safety of my office.

"Not your *type?*" Lori said, stopping me in my path. "Grace, you were practically *ga-ga* over him last week."

"Ga-ga?" I said with a frown. "I wouldn't say *ga-ga.*"

Claudia stormed in at that moment. "Who's ga-ga?" she demanded, shrugging out of her coat and regarding us both with interest.

"Grace," Lori said before I could stop her. "Over the professor."

Claudia paused, raised an eyebrow at me. "Ga-ga, are we?"

"Far from it," I replied, feeling myself go on the defensive. "Please," I continued, suddenly unable to control myself in the face of Claudia's questioning glance. "Do you really think I'd go ga-ga over a guy who doesn't know enough to separate his herringbones from his pinstripes?" Even as I said the words, I regretted them, especially since they conjured up an image of Jonathan looking adorably rumpled and irresistible in the hideous sweater he had donned on Saturday night.

Claudia sputtered out a laugh, meeting my gaze. "Well, that didn't take very long, now did it?" she said, referring to my seemingly quick reversal on Jonathan. Of course, she didn't know how far things had gone, didn't know that I had all but picked out his new wardrobe for the next forty or fifty years.

And wouldn't know, I decided. "Yes, well, you know me," I replied, with another shrug. "Easy come, easy go…"

The going was anything but easy. By two o'clock I had heard not so much as a peep out of Jonathan. No warm Monday morning hello. No tender words to tell me how much he enjoyed the evening we had spent. Nothing.

Of course, I could have called him. But by now I had turned this into some sort of test of his feelings for me. A test he had failed miserably when, come five o'clock, my only phone calls had been business-related and Angie, of course, barking out the inevitable "How's everything going with Jonathan?"

"I don't know, Ange, I don't see this one going anywhere," I said lightly, hoping to douse the excitement I had heard in her voice.

"Grace!" she said, clearly exasperated. "What happened *now?*"

I felt a pinch at her words, as if I had reinforced, once again, my image as the queen of the pre-emptive breakup. And maybe it was a desire to kill that image once and for all that had me confessing at least a few of my fears.

I told Angie about the shrine to Caroline I had found in the second bedroom, leaving out the note that had nearly brought me to tears.

"So what!" she said dismissively. "Guys are like that—they never throw away *anything.* Justin used to wear these bumble bee pattern boxers his last girlfriend bought him for, like, weeks after we got together. I didn't realize at first, until I discovered that the bumble bee over his crotch had a little 'mine' stitched beneath it."

"So what did you do?"

"I threw them out, of course. Not that *he* knew that," she added. "He still thinks the little Asian lady who did our laundry made off with them somehow. We had to change Laundromats after that. He instituted a boycott, all on account of those boxers. 'They were the softest pair I owned!' he whined. I nearly clubbed him."

I smiled, but my humor was short-lived. "It's not the same,

Ange. This isn't an ex-girlfriend we're talking about. She was his wife."

Angie blew out a sigh. "I don't mean to sound crass, Grace, but she is, uh, dead."

"Well, look at your mother," I argued. "She never remarried after your father passed away."

"My mother was in her fifties when my dad died, Grace. Not that that's so old, but in my mother's lunatic mind, her life ended with my father's. Her romantic life anyway. That's the way some people are, I guess. They just bury themselves with their dead."

Her words cut me to the quick, and a memory of that shadowed sadness I had seen in Jonathan's eyes in the early days of our relationship rose before me. Yes, that was what I'd seen: the resignation of a man who had let go of the living. I remembered seeing it in Chevalier's eyes as well.

And my own, I thought, suddenly realizing that a part of me had died the moment I had learned Kristina Morova was gone.

"So we're off," my mother said when I answered the phone that night, hoping for Jonathan. Hoping so much, apparently, that I had forgotten my parents were leaving for their two-week extravaganza in Paris.

"What time's your flight?"

"Ten o'clock," my father chimed in. "We'll be in Paris in the morning."

"How are you getting to the airport?" I asked, and followed up with a dozen other questions. Like, where were they staying? Had they packed enough warm clothes. Suddenly I felt a pressing need to know that they would be okay.

Which only made my mother start to wonder if *I* was okay.

"I'm fine," I insisted, feeling less so by the minute.

"How did your date with Jonathan go?" she asked next.

"Fine," I said again. "We had a nice time."

"I'm glad," my mother replied. "Makes me feel a bit better about leaving you alone on the holidays."

"I'm spending the holiday with the DiFrancos," I said, a bit defensively.

"I know, I know," my mother said hurriedly. "I just meant the season, you know. It's the perfect time for romance. Especially in New York City."

"Yes," I said, feeling depression threatening. "It is."

But I barely registered the lights that twinkled from the trees when I headed to Shelley's on Wednesday evening. Probably because I still hadn't heard from Jonathan. Or because I was practically running to her office to make it on time. I was positively anxious about getting my full forty-five minutes. Which was really weird for me.

Weirder still was the expression on Shelley's face when I handed her a jar of Youth Elixir, which I had grabbed on impulse on my way out the door from the supply of samples I kept in my office.

"What's this?" she asked, looking curiously at me.

And no wonder. I wasn't even sure why I had brought the gift now. As a thank-you for listening to me whine all these months? I was paying her so I could whine. Now I realized she might be taking my silly little gesture as an insult, judging by the way she was squinting at the label, which promised to dramatically take years away from the face.

"It's, uh, Youth Elixir. You know, that product I'm working on the campaign for? I thought…well, I thought you might like to try it. Not that I think you need it or anything…."

"Well, I appreciate this, Grace. It's very kind of you," she said in that same emotionless voice, "but not necessary."

I let out the breath I'd been holding. "I just thought…that is, I'm sorry. I guess I meant it as…as an apology for the way I treated you in the past." I realized it was true. I hadn't, after all, been very nice to her for all these months. And when I wasn't venting my anger, I was canceling appointments on the spur of the moment.

"Did you feel as if you'd hurt my feelings, Grace?"

I sighed, wishing I had not brought that stupid little jar with me. "Well, I did cancel a few appointments on short notice," I said by way of explanation. Then, hoping to move onto more even terrain, I joked, "Hell, the price of that stuff ought to cover at least half a session. Maybe I should have just brought you a case."

She looked at me. "As I said, this is a very nice gesture but not necessary. However, if you do plan to cancel in the future, I'd hope we could discuss it in advance if possible. I do keep a schedule, and I'm only in this office during my hours of appointment."

Suddenly the thought of her seated here alone, waiting fruitlessly for me to show up, filled me with unutterable guilt.

"I'm sorry," I said, feeling my throat thicken. Determined not to give into emotion again, I changed the subject, which was a mistake, too, because the next one was even more painful.

"Jonathan and I are over." I realized as I uttered the words that I had already made that decision when I didn't hear from him today. It was over. *Over.*

Now I really wanted to cry.

Shelley looked a bit down, too. Well, as much as she looked anything. "I don't understand."

So I explained how I had spent the night at Jonathan's place. How romantic it had been—up until the moment I realized that I had gotten behind the closed door of his life, only to discover there were no vacancies left at the inn.

"You're making an assumption, Grace, based on your own fears—"

"I'm not!" I practically yelled. Then, in a softer voice, I confessed to that room I had pried open, the photos I had found, the answers to all the questions I had had about why he held so much back….

"I know I'm right," I insisted. "He hasn't called yet—"

"Call him."

I shook my head. "No," I said firmly. "Not this time. You see, I can't change the past or how he feels about it. Just as I can't change my own past," I finished in a firmer voice, though I think this was the first time I truly understood that. "I can only change how I feel about it," I continued, my voice soft with wonder at this next realization.

Then I looked her in the eye. "You, of all people, should know that. Isn't that why I'm here? There's nothing I can do about my past—about Kristina, right? She's dead. The only thing to do is to accept that. And move on."

I could see Shelley was proud of me, since I had brought up Kristina without her usual prodding. I suddenly knew why I had come wielding that jar of Youth Elixir tonight. I had been scared of losing Shelley, too, now that we had formed a tentative bond. Maybe I had hoped to somehow secure her affections with that silly little gift.

I also understood now that I really hadn't needed to. Shelley *did* care about me. At least she cared what happened to me, I realized as she returned to the question of Jonathan as if he still could hold some key to my future happiness.

"How could you possibly know what he's feeling unless you ask, Grace?"

She had a very good point. "Because I know," I protested, somewhat weakly. "I saw…that study. I know what it's like to lose someone. Sometimes you never recover."

She stared at me. "Most of the time you do."

I felt a bit a relief at that, mostly because I knew now I *would* recover from whatever pain I was feeling about the woman I would never know. But I could not predict what Jonathan's future held. Or what place I had in it. And that was what scared me the most.

Because Shelley had managed to make me feel like a bit of a coward, I did call Jonathan the next day.

"Dr. Somerfield, please," I said coolly to the now-familiar assistant's voice, and once she put me on hold, I began to wonder if I was just as familiar to her. Did she see me as a regular part of Jonathan's life—or was I just another lady caller? Because now that I had come out of the paralysis of mind that accompanies the beginning of every new romance, it occurred to me that a man with such healthy desires like Jonathan's couldn't have lived like a monk during the years since his wife died.

"Hello?" came Jonathan's voice and the sound of it immediately unwound the coil of tension that had built in me as I had worked up my case against him.

"Hello," I began, surprised at how I practically whispered the word.

"Grace," he said. "How are you?"

"I'm good, good," I said. "How are *you?*"

"I'm fine. I…I'm sorry I haven't called," he said, making me aware that *he* was aware that he'd been remiss. "I've been so busy preparing for an upcoming lecture, and then the department had their annual Christmas party last night."

I felt my defenses rise, realizing that things *had* changed for him. During the last affair his department had held, I had been the woman on his arm. Now it seemed I was the woman he chose to leave home. I bit back on commenting as he went on to say it had been a smallish event. Maybe he hadn't been allowed to bring a date. It was this thought that gave me the strength to ask him what he was doing over the weekend. I knew now that what I needed most was to see Jonathan, to confirm that all the feelings that had sprung up so suddenly and so strongly between us were not imaginary.

"God, Grace, I would love to get together with you," he said. "But my brother and his wife are coming into the city this weekend with the kids." Then, as he went on to describe how they were going to see the tree in Rockefeller Center and do a little shopping in Herald Square, I felt once again like the girl pressed up against the glass of a world she would never truly be part of. And though I knew it was too soon to expect too much, I also felt like it was too late for me to accept so little. I cared about him too much. Too much to risk that hurt I felt sure would come. He wasn't ready to let me in. And I sensed he never would be.

"Hey, maybe we could have a little sleepover on Monday once they've gone," he offered.

It was that last statement that did me in, conjuring up for me as it did the history of my love life, which was strewn with men like Michael and Ethan. And though I knew Jonathan's reasons for not being able to open up might be a bit more sympathetic, I was tired of men who wanted me in their beds

but not in their lives. I knew what it would all add up to—
and I emphatically didn't want to do it again.

"You know," I found myself saying, "I'm going to be pretty
busy myself next week. I have my own office Christmas
party," I continued, hoping he might wonder—even for a
moment—if I would invite him. But since I was riding so
strongly on a tide of painful feeling, I didn't give him time
to wonder. Instead, I did the only thing I knew how to do
to protect myself.

"Maybe it's for the best," I said lightly. "The holidays are
coming, and I'm sure we're both going to be very busy."

"That's true," he agreed with a sigh. "I have finals to prepare for."

His easy agreement, the resignation in his tone, stabbed at
me. "And I have this campaign I'm working on, friends to
see. Parties to go to," I continued, making my life seem like
the big merry event it wasn't.

"I bet you do," he said softly. "A beautiful woman like you."
Then he chuckled, "God, I bet I'm putting a crimp in your
style. I'm not really one for the holidays…."

"Yeah, well, the holidays are rough," I replied philosoph-
ically, despite the tremor moving through me at my words.
"Maybe we should just take a little time," I said.

He was silent on the other end, and for one fleeting moment, I wished he would beg to see me. Which only made
tears flood to my eyes when he said finally, "If that's what you
want, Grace."

Swallowing hard against the thickness in my throat, I said
with as much firmness in my voice as I could muster, "Yes,
it's what I want."

And then, before I could cave to the crushing feeling of
loss, I quickly wished him all the best, and hung up.

The problem with learning the truth is that you have to live with it. I would have been fine, if not for the fact that everyone else was living in some other kind of reality.

Like Angie. "I sometimes think I get more attached to your boyfriends than you do," she said.

"I wouldn't exactly call Jonathan a boyfriend," I replied. "We didn't last very long."

"I know," she said, relenting. "But I guess I just thought he meant something to you."

He did, I thought, feeling the dart of pain that had lain beneath my rib cage ever since my conversation with Jonathan. He did….

I found myself resorting to my usual formula of all work and as little play as possible. Because idleness only brought on lonely thoughts. And social outings only brought out a longing that no one in my present company could possibly fulfill. So I worked and was more than glad to submerge myself. Claudia seemed in a better frame of mind now that she had met with the plastic surgeon, who called her the "perfect candidate." You'd think he'd just named her Miss America, the way she practically preened as she told me she was planning on going under the knife in the New Year. I think she felt like she had gained some control over her life, believing she could get one over on the aging process through the miracle of modern surgery. She even seemed cheerful. For Claudia, anyway. And though at first Lori and I questioned how long this chipper mood would last, eventually we started to count our blessings.

20

> *"A woman's dress should be like a barbed-wire fence: serving its purpose without obstructing the view."*
>
> —Sophia Loren

"**G**ood news, Gracie darling." Claudia dropped a copy of *Vogue* on my desk. "You're in."

I glanced down at the magazine cover, which featured Xander Oliva, a Brazilian beauty known as a model succeeding despite having a bit more in the hip area than a standard size 2 and verging just beyond a B cup. The Bombshell Is Back, the headline declared, and drawn in by this claim, notwithstanding it was for a model I probably could have shielded against a wind storm with my own body, I turned to the spread. It featured Xander posing in pencil skirts and tapered, feminine jackets as she pranced across a quasi-1940s setting. Yes, her lips were pouty and her eyes long-lashed and glamorous, but a bombshell she was not.

"So what do you think?" Claudia asked, heading for my file cabinet, which she proceeded to rifle through for something or other.

"I think I need to go on a diet," I said, my eye roaming over a new page, which featured Xander in a powder-blue Chanel suit, arm-in-arm with an equally waiflike counterpart in soft pink Chanel, as they pranced girlishly down a New York City street.

I looked up to find Claudia's speculative gaze move from my half-eaten muffin to my blouse, which, I noticed when I glanced down, appeared to be pulling. I sat up, giving my blouse a surreptitious yank, and said defensively, "What do these girls know about being a bombshell? They're barely out of their training bras."

Claudia raised an eyebrow, a smile curving the corners of her mouth, as if she found my sudden distaste for youth amusing. As if she were somehow above it all, now that she believed she had found a way to beat it.

Beat what, exactly? I wondered, looking at the blank gazes above the pouty lips and thinking of Sasha and Irina—how each of them, in her own way, wore her youth like some thorny crown. Then I thought of those bombshells of yesteryear—Jayne Mansfield, Rita Hayworth, Jean Harlow, Marlene Dietrich. Yes, they had been young, too, but somehow they seemed more like women. Maybe it was the wardrobe, but I sensed that it had more to do with their era. A time of sophistication. When men were men and women, were, well…women.

Whereas these two… "They look like they're playing dress-up. They're just…girls."

Claudia smiled even wider, resolve in her eyes. "These girls, Gracie, darling, are the future. Get used to it."

But I didn't want to get used to it. My eye skittered over the spread and landed on a movie still that had been juxtaposed against the laughing girls, featuring Rita Hayworth looking every inch the queen of an earlier era in a floor-length ball gown as she stood against an equally regal background. I was suddenly reminded of the picture of Roxanne Dubrow herself that I had seen in the family history album we kept at the office. She hadn't been quite as beautiful as Hayworth, but she had been dressed with the same sophistication, posing before the mantel of the Dubrow's Sutton Place home. I remembered that photo well; it had been captured for *Vogue* in 1942, when the Dubrow cosmetic empire had just exploded onto the fashion scene, and it had been featured prominently for years in the company sales catalogues.

That, to me, was a bombshell. And she had been there from the beginning, but buried away in the company's past.

An idea came to me then, so powerful that I nearly burst out with it on the spot. But I didn't, of course, knowing that this one was too good to share with Claudia, who would only claim it as her own.

If the bombshell was back, then why not bring back the bombshell who started it all?

I stayed late that night. In fact, I stayed late every night that week, watching my flash of inspiration grow into a bona fide brilliant idea for the new Youth Elixir campaign. Digging through a veritable library of Roxanne Dubrow sales catalogs, I pulled photos from the company's beginnings—including, of course, the famous fireplace shot of Madame

Dubrow—and juxtaposed them against the quasi-scientific
claims and smooth-skinned radiance of the models who had
launched Youth Elixir, crafting a proposal for a new campaign
that capitalized on the company's history as one of the first
major players in the cosmetics industry in the forties and the
leader in skin-care technology in the eighties. Yes, I thought,
at week's end, after enlisting Lori's help to design a polished
and dazzling proposal in full color, this proposal held all the
promise of my initial idea and more. I even included the front
cover of *Vogue,* since I had, after all, pilfered the headline as
the headpiece of the new campaign: The bombshell is back,
my positioning page declared. Only better. Smarter. She had
the Old World glamour and sophistication of the company's
early days—and Roxanne Dubrow herself—with the benefit of the new quasi-science that had taken the company to
further heights in the eighties: the formula that promised—
and in some ways even delivered—the skin that could carry
a woman through her best years. Youth Elixir.

For the bombshell who knew better than to rely on anything else, of course.

And because I knew better now, I waited until Claudia had
left on her annual pre-Christmas vacation—a long weekend
that she claimed she used to catch up on her Christmas
shopping but that the glow she always returned with suggested had more likely been spent in a spa—to send the proposal to Dianne myself. With a cc to Claudia, of course. It
wasn't that I meant to go over her head so much as fly under
her radar. By the time Claudia got her hands on my work
and either tore it down or claimed it as her own, Dianne
would already have judged for herself. And could give credit
where credit was due, for a change.

Besides, my deadline to propose a new budget was the end

of this year. And like the good employee I now aspired to be, I hoped the early bird would catch the campaign dollars.

With luck Dianne would read my proposal before the Christmas party. But then I remembered her ailing mother and wondered if she could do anything right now. How was she even going to handle the Christmas party, with the knowledge of her mother's illness weighing her down?

How was *I* going to handle the Christmas party? I asked myself two days before it. Especially when I realized that I would be facing Michael Dubrow again.

And single once more, to his nearly married.

As I passed the Armani store on my way home from work, I had my answer. I would handle my own personal crisis just as Dianne would surely handle hers.

With dignity. With style. And, of course, with a great dress.

Which was why I felt perfectly entitled to splurge on the positively devastating one I found the moment I walked into the store.

A stunning strapless floor-length sheath in a color the sales clerk dubbed "oxblood red." It fit me like a second skin, I discovered, after rushing into the dressing room with it. Even transformed those few extra pounds into a personal triumph, judging by how curvy I looked. I bought it without batting an eye. After all, I considered it an investment. In myself.

Yes, the bombshell was back.

And, I told myself confidently, when I donned the dress the following night, she was stunning.

The Waldorf, of course, was as lovely as ever. I took another measure of satisfaction in returning to this grand old dame for our holiday party. There had been talk of finding a newer, more trendy venue to go with the younger and ostensibly more chic vision for Roxanne Dubrow, but Dianne ultimately vetoed that. And I was glad, my eyes roaming around that elegant space once I'd checked my coat.

Everyone was here, from Marketing to Production to Research and Development. And our support staff, of course. I spotted Lori looking prettier than ever in a soft pink strapless gown and standing next to an adorable man. Ah, Dennis, I realized, watching as she leaned in close to him.

I didn't recognize him in a suit. He looked…like a man. No wonder Lori was angsting so much over losing him.

"It seems that girl isn't a complete idiot," came Claudia's voice in my ear as she suddenly appeared by my side. "That boy of hers is delish. I had hoped to take him home for dessert myself, until I realized it was none other than Dennis the Menace. All grown up, it seems."

"Hmm," I replied noncommittally, not wanting to encourage any sort of Lori-blasting on Claudia's part. I glanced at my boss, noting that she looked rather elegant herself in a slender column of black dress that fell to her ankles and which I suspected was Calvin due to its chic simplicity.

"Well, you look nice," I said, then realized how that might have sounded, especially considering that I had unintentionally injected a certain amount of surprise in my tone.

"So do you," she replied, her tone containing an equal dose of surprise.

I smiled. Yes, things were back to business as usual.

Almost, I thought, seeing Dianne across the room, presiding over the room as she usually did, with one exception. She was alone. Well, not alone. Her husband, Stuart, stood off to one side, greeting guests with his usual charm and grace. But her mother wasn't here this year, standing by Dianne's side and looking like the queen she once was although leaning heavily on a cane, or her daughter's arm.

I saw the crowd part temporarily, leaving a clear path to Dianne. Taking the opportunity, I excused myself from Claudia and stepped forward to say hello.

"Dianne, how good to see you," I said, and meant it. She hadn't been around the New York office much since her mother had taken ill. I realized now that I had missed her warmth, her elegance and, most of all, the inspiration her rallying spirit seemed to bring out in everyone she encountered.

"Grace," Dianne said, her eyes lighting up at the sight of me. "You look smashing, as always." Then she did something uncharacteristic, leaning forward to brush my cheek with a kiss and squeezing my hand in hers. When she drew back again, her corporate face was carefully back in place, but her eyes still glowed with what looked like need. I realized, in that moment, that despite all the devoted employees surrounding her and her husband lingering nearby, Dianne Dubrow was feeling very much alone tonight.

On some level, I recognized that loneliness. "I'm so sorry your mother couldn't attend."

Her eyes misted. "Thank you, Grace. She always loved coming to this party, and the fact that she—that she couldn't—was a...a real blow." She smiled wistfully. "I don't think I ever quite realized how much I counted on my mother to be there. Always."

I nodded, understanding what she meant. My mother and I didn't always have the closest of relationships, but I always knew that she was there, looking out for me. Suddenly that sole image I had of Kristina Morova, laughing glibly from a frame in her sister's dark and lonely living room, filled my mind. To my surprise, instead of the usual anger, I felt a well of sadness. If she had ever thought of me, I knew for sure she didn't now....

"Well," Dianne said, "at least the party is lovely."

"Yes, it is," I replied, "it always is."

She smiled. "Always let them see you sparkle," she said, taking my hand in hers and squeezing it again. "There's a strength in beauty. That bit of wisdom I learned from my mother." Her mouth moved into a wise smile. "And for that, I am very grateful."

She let go of my hand and seemed about to let go of me, but then she paused. "Oh, that reminds me, I read your proposal for the Youth Elixir campaign. I really like your ideas— harking back to the company's history to show what's possible for the future." Her eyes gleamed. "We'll need to put it in perspective in terms of our financial year, but I like it. I really do."

"Thank you, Dianne," I said, excitement thrumming through me.

"And I love how you included my mother. She was an icon back than. A real bombshell." Then she winked, her eyes roaming over my floor-length gown as she took me in once more. "A bit like you…"

It was just the boost I needed to get me through. Well, that and the second martini I helped myself to, the minute Michael Dubrow waltzed in with the ever-so-lovely Courtney Manchester on his arm for all the world to see.

I watched as Dianne greeted them both, feeling a shiver of need as they stood in a huddle, talking intimately. Well, at least Courtney and Dianne talked. Michael, on the other hand, was already scoping out the room.

Clearly, he hadn't changed. For a moment, I took a small satisfaction in that fact, even felt a sharp thrill of triumph when his eyes finally landed on me, moving slowing up my dress, pausing over my breasts, then widening with recognition when he saw my face.

Take that, you bastard.

Fortunately, I was saved from meeting his gaze when Lori popped up next to me. I turned to her, holding out my martini in a toast. "Here's to the happy couple," I said. Then, before she could even touch her glass to mine, I downed my drink in one fell swoop.

She looked at me in surprise. "The happy who?"

"Exactly," I said, feeling that martini move right through me. Strengthening me. Or shielding me.

"You having a good time?" I said to Lori.

She nodded, her gaze moving on to Dennis, who was chatting with one of the younger sales reps.

"And Dennis?"

She dropped her gaze. "Yes…"

"What's going on?"

She sighed, looking up at me again. "Well, I made my decision, Grace," she said. "I'm going to SVA in the fall. It's just a better program for me."

"Oh, Lori, that's wonderful!" I replied, and not just because it meant she'd probably stick around at Roxanne Dubrow a little longer. But I sensed she knew it was a good decision for her, despite the chagrin she clearly felt over leaving Dennis. Her gaze sought him out once more.

I turned to look at him, too. And for a moment, when I took in that handsome face, saw the way he looked up and smiled at Lori, I almost wanted to take back my warm affirmation of her choice. She was young, yes, but I had been just as young once. Who knew if she'd ever find a man she loved like that again?

After all, a man you could truly love wasn't so easy to find.

As if she read my mind, Lori looked at me again. "It's not like we'll never see each other again. In fact, we're planning on some time together next summer in London. And then there are school breaks…."

I smiled, somewhat ruefully, though I hoped she didn't notice.

Maybe it would work. Who really could tell about these things?

Since I certainly couldn't, I decided to give myself over to another power: Stolichnaya. And it seemed to work. Two martinis later, I was, conceivably, the belle of the ball. I spoke to everyone who was anyone—with the exception of Michael, of course. But I felt him watching me—and why shouldn't he? I was charming as hell, chatting up everyone from the pinch-faced research assistant from R & D to the Director of Northeast Sales. Which was probably why I felt so damn vulnerable the moment I found myself on the edge of the dance floor alone, after disentangling myself from Roland Barlow, an R&D researcher who'd had one too many himself.

Fortunately, when you wear a dress like the one I had on tonight, you didn't stay lonely for long.

"Grace Noonan, my God, you get more and more gorgeous every year."

"Ross, how are you?" I said, suddenly finding myself inexplicably delighted to be in the presence of Ross Davenport, aka Corporate Lech. Thrice-divorced and suspiciously tan in the dead of winter, Ross couldn't let a Christmas party go by without making his annual pass at me. He was the kind of guy who kept the party going long after they'd booted us out of the rented space, usually dragging his fellow rabble-rousers out for more drinks and mayhem. I wasn't normally among that group, though tonight I was feeling a bit like a good-time girl myself. And maybe it was all those martinis swimming in my system, but Ross, who was a handsome man despite his Long Island accent and lack of finesse, was looking quite delectable in his fresh-from-the-cleaners blue suit.

"I'm doing much better now, thank you very much," he said, meandering closer now that I hadn't given him my usual curt blow-off.

"You're looking well," I said, studying his tanned features and faded blue eyes. Could that tan be from time spent outdoors? I knew, from previous party chat, that he liked to fish. Men did that in winter, right? Maybe he wasn't a tanning-bed buffoon, but an outdoorsy sort.

That I could work with. "So how's life on Long Island?" I said, beginning the banter.

"Life is great, Grace," he replied, beaming a set of teeth at me that looked suspiciously white, considering that I knew him to be a chain smoker. "You ought to come out some time. I'll take you out on the boat," he said with touch of pride. There's nothing like having a good car, a good house and a good boat to make you the King of the Burbs. I'm sure Ross was a hot property out there, judging by the number of wives who had hooked themselves to his speedboat, hoping to zip off into the sunset with him.

Maybe I could be happy zipping off into the sunset with someone like Ross, I tried to persuade myself. Simple. Uncomplicated. And, I thought, remembering the three kids he had spawned with two of those wives, in…working order.

And just as I was envisioning a version of myself that was liposuctioned, lighter-haired and somewhat more fuzzy-headed from the drinking I imagined I'd have even more time and more reason to do, that prince of yesteryear stepped into my line of vision, which I was trying with difficulty to focus on Ross.

"Grace," Michael said, with a nod and a look into my eyes that said he was questioning my sanity at the moment. "Ross," he said, slapping his number-one plant manager on the back. He knew how to play with the little guys. And the somewhat bigger girls...

"Hey, Michael, my man," Ross replied, slurring his words in a way that said he would never make it as far as Michael, and not only because he wasn't a Dubrow.

Then, in a move that surprised me even more than the way Ross was visibly gawking at my breasts in his boss's presence, Michael reached for my hand, gently leading me out of the corner Ross had boxed me into. "Mind if I steal this pretty lady for a dance?"

Flabbergasted, Ross threw his hands up in the air, as if disavowing all claim to me. "Hey, no problem," he said, stepping back to make room as Michael led me to the dance floor.

"What the hell was that all about?" Michael said, once he'd pulled me into his arms.

"Hello to you, too," I replied, staring into those blue eyes and realizing how much I had missed them.

"Grace, you know what I mean," he said, smiling in spite of his admonishments. "Ross is a nice guy and all, but when it comes to women—" He grimaced. "You deserve better than that."

I do, I thought, warming, in spite of myself, to the feel of Michael's arms around me. Though I hated myself for it, I felt myself being drawn in all over again, this time by the wave of protectiveness he was showing me. I caught myself in time. "Yes, I do deserve better," I replied gamely, giving him a look that clearly questioned whether he was it. "How's Courtney?" I said, so tartly I was almost embarrassed.

"Grace, I wanted to call you so many times…."

"Call me? For what purpose?"

"Well, to talk to you about—"

I started to pull away, but his grip tightened. Not wanting to make a scene—not wanting anyone, least of all Michael, to get wind of the sudden emotion gaining ground within me—I swayed back into him again, feeling that same old electric zing when his groin made contact with my thigh.

God, this was madness. What a bastard he was. "Tell me what, exactly? That we weren't going to fuck anymore? I had already made that decision."

"Grace—"

"Oh wait, I know. You wanted to let me know that there had been a change in corporate policy. That you can't fuck employees anymore, but you can marry them…."

"Gracie—"

"Don't Gracie me," I said. "I'm not yours to play with anymore."

He sighed, letting his grip go loose on me. "You know you'll always have a place in my heart, Grace."

That little statement made me even more furious. "Which place, exactly?" I queried coolly. "Left ventricle or right? Or maybe you'll let me have the aortic valve, if I promise to stay real quiet and not clog the system—"

"Grace, you don't understand."

"No, Michael, that's where you're wrong," I replied, finally disentangling myself from his hold. "I understand you perfectly now."

★ ★ ★

I couldn't go home, I realized as the cab speeded uptown. Not alone anyway. Not when I was this drunk. The thought of sharing those walls with the weight of everything I was feeling was almost too much to bear. I felt desperate for human companionship—someone, anyone, to let me know that everything was okay. That I was okay.

I pulled out my cell, but the moment I had it in hand, I simply stared at it. Who would I call, exactly? Bad Billy? I supposed I could call Billy. He wasn't one to hold a grudge, especially if he stood to gain a little booty.

But the minute that thought arose came another: If I was looking for booty, why not go with the *best?*

"Make a right here," I found myself practically shouting to the cabbie when I looked up and realized we were at W. 80th Street. Jonathan's block.

The cabbie muttered something unintelligible. I was sure if I understood Arabic, it might have offended me. But I didn't care. I knew what I wanted now. Or more precisely, whom.

I glanced down at myself, noting the way my breasts rose most becomingly out of the red sheath, my skin looking positively shimmery in the dim light of the cab.

I smiled. And I was going to get him, too. Because if nothing else, I knew Jonathan desired me.

Once I stood outside of his building, feeling every inch a vamp in my red dress and stilettos and ready to make my mark, I suddenly wondered what the hell had hit *me.*

I couldn't just ring his doorbell for booty. Because I was sure there was something in the Booty Call Rulebook that said you couldn't turn a boyfriend into a…booty call.

He had been just as much a boyfriend as Billy had been

back in the day, the demon voice argued back, at least in terms of our length of tenure as an actual couple.

But as I gazed up at the single light that burned in the window, imagining Jonathan sitting quietly in his living room with a book, his solitude complete, the specter of all that had come between us rose up before me again. No, Jonathan was no Billy.

I had never been in love with Billy. And I was sure now, as I stared up at that window, longing for that man behind the glass, that love was what I had felt for Jonathan....

"Grace?"

I nearly jumped into the air at the sound of my name, then was pathetically glad I hadn't, seeing as I was teetering on four-inch stilettos and way too many martinis.

I turned, startled, to find Dr. Somerfield himself, strolling down the sidewalk toward me.

"Jonathan," I breathed, unbelievably glad to see him. God, he looked adorable, the thick collar of a deep brown turtleneck peeking out of his long dark overcoat and deepening the color of his eyes.

"What are you doing here?" he asked, stopping before me and gazing at me rather curiously.

And why wouldn't he be looking at me like that, standing in front of his apartment and gazing at his window like a bitch in heat? Suddenly I felt foolish, and desperate for a way to save face, I blurted out, "I, uh, I was just on my way to...to Zabar's," I said, latching onto the first excuse I could come up with. Yes, Zabar's. It was in between our apartments. Granted, it wasn't technically necessary for me to walk down W. 80th Street to get to it, but it was *conceivable*.

I saw that he was smiling at me now. "Do you always go grocery shopping in a ball gown?"

If I were the type of woman to blush, I would have gone red to the roots of my hair. Perhaps it was the alcohol in my system that kept me stabilized—or at least kept me in the kind of whirling state of mind that made anything possible.

"Well, you know—new dress, new shoes," I said, scrambling desperately to hang on to the ledge I had perched on. "I thought I'd break them in while I was at it. You know, it's not easy to spend a whole evening in a getup like this without a…a trial run," I finished, realizing I was now dangling off that ledge, and looking pretty ridiculous, too.

His smile faltered, and he looked at his watch. "It's ten o'clock, Grace. I hate to break it to you, but I think Zabar's is closed."

And with that one sentence, I was undone. "Right," I whispered, dropping my gaze to the sidewalk, as if I might find a crack in the pavement to slither into. Then, maybe because I saw no such escape, I finally came clean. Sort of. "The truth is, I just needed…to get out." Yes, that had been true, I thought, remembering how I had rushed out of the Waldorf as if it were on fire. Trying to escape the menacing loneliness I had felt in the midst of all those people after my showdown with Michael.

I looked up at Jonathan then, and saw something in his eyes that said he understood. It was almost too much to bear, that recognition. I felt suddenly, achingly vulnerable. "Well, I should go…." I began.

"Do you want to come inside?" he asked, studying my eyes again.

If only you knew, I thought, embarrassed about everything that had brought me to his doorstep tonight. "No, I…I should go," I repeated, backing away.

"Let me walk you," he said.

"Oh, no, that's fine." I backed away even farther, feeling more shaky with every step I took. Then, like a savior in the night, a cab came rolling down the street. "It's too cold to…to walk," I explained, and with a hurried good-night, I flagged down the taxi and nearly leaped inside.

And just in time, too. Because, much to my surprise—and my horror—I realized I was crying.

My phone was ringing when I walked into my apartment, and the sound sobered me. Who could be calling me? I wondered. Jonathan? It had to be Jonathan. He must have sensed my state of distress, and now—noble soul that he was—he was calling to offer me comfort. He was so good. Too good, I thought, my hand closing over the receiver before I could even collect myself.

"Grace!" came my mother's voice, sounding surprisingly strong considering how far away she was. "We're just heading out to Versailles for the day and thought we'd check in. How are you, darling?"

It was the simplest of questions, and usually I was fully prepared to give the simplest of answers, but suddenly I found myself choking out around the sob in my throat, "I'm not so great…."

"Gracie, sweetheart, what's wrong? What's *happened?*"

"Nothing really," I said, struggling to get a hold of myself. It was true, nothing had happened. Not between me and Jonathan. Or me and Michael, for that matter. In truth, nothing *ever* really happened, I realized, suddenly seeing the fruits of every effort I had made over the past few years as just that: a whole heap of nothing. Not even the glimmer of hope about my campaign idea that Dianne had given me last night could save me now.

A tidal wave of feeling crashed over me, and suddenly I was crying in a way I could not control. Or hide.

"Oh, God, Grace, are you hurt? Please. Oh, Tom, something has happened to Grace."

Then, before I could stop myself—or before they hung up and called the nearest New York hospital to send an ambulance to carry me away—I told her everything. And not the everything I thought I was going to tell her.

No, what I told my mother about was Kristina. How I had finally learned the startling truth behind all those months of silence. How she was gone…

"Oh, Grace," my mother replied, her own voice filled with tears now. "Why didn't you tell us sooner? My God, what you've been handling. And all alone!"

"I'm sorry I didn't tell you…." I began.

"*You're* sorry," my mother said, her voice breaking. "I feel terrible that you felt…you felt you couldn't talk to us. Oh, Grace, we always raised you to be so independent. Maybe that was a mistake."

Now I felt guilty. "No, no. It wasn't that," I said. "You've always been the best, Mom. I just…I just thought I was okay."

I heard her muffle the phone as she asked my father a question. "Grace, we're going to call the airline right now and book the next flight to New York."

"No!" I said, realizing I had done exactly what I hadn't wanted to do. Ruined their first real vacation in years. "I want you to stay. Celebrate your anniversary, like you planned."

"Please! Grace, we want to be there for you."

I felt myself soften inside at her words, and fearing I would burst into tears again, I said, "No, please. I would feel really bad if you did that. And I feel better now. Much better." I realized that I did. I hadn't even understood what a burden

I had been carrying until I unloaded it. Until my mother showed she was more than capable of bearing the weight. I wondered now why I hadn't trusted that.

"Well, we're flying through New York on our way back. And we're coming to see you!"

"You are?" I asked. "Didn't you fly through Houston on your way to Paris?"

"We'll just change the ticket!" she said.

I frowned. "Mom, that could cost you a small fortune...."

"What do I care?" she cried. "You're my daughter! I'd do anything for you!"

I felt myself smile, now that she had confirmed what I had always known deep down inside but had been so unwilling to test. That she really loved me. And would be there for me. No matter what.

21

"You can't bottle happiness, but with the right attitude, you sure can bring it on."

—Grace Noonan

There is nothing like the sight of my apartment awash in candlelight. Which is exactly why, on Christmas Eve, I pulled out every single candle I owned—a considerable collection. Candles littered my dining table and lined every windowsill, sending soothing light all around the room and creating an atmosphere that was, in a word, romantic.

Or would have been, had I not been all alone.

But I was used to being alone on Christmas Eve. And nevertheless, I had always considered it the most romantic holiday of all. Maybe because my parents had been married so soon afterward, I thought, imagining them in Paris, about to share their long-awaited celebration of their life together and feeling inexplicably glad that they were.

Because it made everything seem possible again. That you could love like that, could share a life with someone worth celebrating, even after so many years.

I guess that's what had always made Christmas Eve so romantic for me anyway. The sense of anticipation. The hope…

And, of course, the food. Yes, I had foregone the annual Christmas Eve dinner at the DiFranco house, knowing I would spend the day with them tomorrow along with Angie and Justin. But that didn't mean I had to give up the Italian tradition I had grown up with, as the adopted member of their family.

I was making a seafood marinara, taught to me by Nonnie herself, when I was sixteen. It had been a while since I tested the recipe, but judging by the amount of calamari, shrimp and mussels I'd tossed in, I couldn't really go wrong.

So I gave the sauce a final stir, turning down the heat to let it simmer. Then, taking the glass of wine I had poured myself, I headed into the kitchen to wrap my gifts.

Another indulgence, I thought, kneeling next to the pile of presents on my living room floor and pulling out the boxes of paper and ribbon I had picked up at Kate's Paperie. I had spent almost as much on the gift wrap as I had on my mother's cashmere sweater, I realized, as I pulled out a pretty gold and purple sheet.

But it was worth it, I thought, feeling satisfaction as I laid paper out and cut it down to size to fit the first box, which was baby Carmella's tea set. Besides, I was a hell of a gift-wrapper, I thought, imagining Carmella's delight when she saw the whirls of ribbon I used to secure the top once I had covered the box in paper. And according to Angie, who always sweated over gift selection herself when it came to her little niece, I was a hell of an aunt.

I would likely make a good mother, I thought, smiling at the idea that someday I might just be that. All I needed was a little courage....

The phone rang, startling me out of my reverie. I almost let the machine pick up, I was enjoying my solitude so much, but then I realized that it was probably my mother, calling to wish me a happy holiday. And to remind me that their plane was landing in New York on the 28th and that they would be at my apartment no later than 4:00 p.m., as she had already reminded me no less than six times since she had changed the reservation.

"Hello," I said, waiting for the static that usually prefaced one of my mother's international calls.

"You're home," came a startled male voice over the line.

Jonathan. Calling me. On Christmas Eve, of all times.

As if he were equally aware of the significance, he started to backpedal. "I had thought for sure you'd be out celebrating."

I frowned. The coward. He knew I was going to be home. 'Fess up! I wanted to scream.

"Is that Mozart's *Esultate Jubilate* I hear?"

"Yes," I said, heading to the stereo to turn down the volume.

"Oh, I'm sorry if I'm interrupting something...."

I smiled, realizing I had caught Jonathan in the same kind of stupor I had found myself in when I was standing out front of his apartment in the freezing cold in a flaming red dress. Expectant, yet not wanting to expect too much.

I decided to help him out a little. "No, no. I'm alone." Then, not wanting him to think I was in the same pathetically lonely state I had been in when standing out in front of his apartment in a ball gown, I added, "I mean, I'm still going to celebrate tomorrow with my friend Angie's fam-

ily, but I thought I'd take tonight to myself. You know, wrap
a few gifts..."

"Of course," he said, as if this made perfect sense to him.

"You?" I asked.

"Me?"

"Yes, any plans?"

He cleared his throat. "Why, yes, of course. That is, tomorrow I'm going to my parents' home. They wanted me
to come tonight, but since my brother and his family are already there, I thought I might just add to the confusion. You
know, with the sleeping arrangements. My brother and his
wife have two kids and, well, anyway, I'll see them all tomorrow. Like you, I thought I'd take the evening for myself."
He paused again. "I guess I always found Christmas Eve to
be..." He struggled for words.

I decided to help him out. "Romantic?"

He hesitated. "Well, now that you mention it..."

I smiled. It was all the confirmation I needed. He did
want to be with me. Just as much as I wanted to be with him.
"You know, I've got a pot of sauce on the stove...."

"Seafood?" he asked.

He remembered, I thought, hoping that perhaps he had
been savoring our every conversation just as much as I had.

"Why, yes, it is," I replied. Then, taking the opening he
had finally—finally!—given me, I asked, "Care to join me?"

I'll admit that despite my coolly proffered invitation, I went
into a bit of a tizzy after he accepted. Hanging up the phone
and spying the pile of gifts on the floor, I realized I had nothing to give Jonathan. Not that I hadn't seen a half a zillion
things I wanted to give him....

This thought was quickly obliterated by a quick glance
down at the comfy—read: worn-out—sweater and faded

jeans I wore. Forget the gift. What really needed wrapping was…me.

I rushed to my bedroom, only to discover I hadn't even made the bed that day, so caught up had I been in last-minute shopping. I quickly grabbed up the clothes that littered the bed, tossing them into the hamper in the closet, then smoothed out the sheets and threw the comforter over them.

But not fast enough. I barely had a chance to rake my fingers through my more-tousled-than-usual hair, never mind slip into something more alluring, when the buzzer rang.

Damn, what did he do, run here? I gave myself one last glance in the full-length mirror, realizing I would have to do, just the way I was….

I opened the door and found Jonathan standing there, a bottle of wine in one hand and the largest bouquet of red roses I had ever seen in the other. His eyes roamed over me as I stood in all that candlelight as if I were the most beautiful woman on earth.

Just the way I was.

The roses, he told me, after we had dined on a pasta made only headier by the magnificent wine he had brought over, reminded him of me. "I couldn't resist them," he confessed, then became shy after the admission. We were seated on the living room floor, our plates on the coffee table before us, since neither one of us had had the heart to clear the dining table of all those candles.

Maybe it was the wine, but he seemed to have dropped his usual reserve. He looked up at me, catching my gaze once more. "That is, they reminded me of you in that dress. You know, that night in front of my apartment?"

Now it was my turn to be embarrassed. Picking up my

wineglass, I took a healthy sip before I met his gaze again, feeling even more shy, despite the soothing warmth that flowed through my veins. I opened my mouth to answer for myself, and discovered I didn't have to.

"It was strange that night," he continued, staring into one of the candles. "I was just coming home from an event at the university. It had run a little late, and I was hurrying across campus to grab a cab when I came to the college walk. Did you ever see it lit up for Christmas?"

I nodded, recalling the awesome sight.

"It made me think of you. How beautiful you are. Almost too beautiful…" He picked up his glass, wrapping his hand around it as if to brace himself. "I felt like you were a gift. A gift almost too precious to take…" He looked at me then, and I saw all the sorrow, all the loneliness, I had seen in his eyes since the beginning. "Which was why when you called to say you wanted to take a break, I had to let you go. I felt like I had nothing to offer you. You have so much—"

"But you do, too," I argued.

He shook his head. "I guess I didn't feel that way. I felt like it was best to let you go on your way. Have the wonderful, happy life I was sure you were destined for. But I missed you. Hell, I missed you so much, it was almost as if I was trying to conjure you up." He smiled, reaching out to touch my cheek. "And suddenly there you were. Standing in front of my apartment. Like a dream come true," he finished, his eyes widening as he remembered. "And you seemed to be wait-ing…for something." He smiled even wider. "Despite all that stuff about new shoes and Zabar's, I knew, Grace. Knew that you were waiting for me. That you needed me. It surprised me at first," he continued, "until I realized how much I un-derstood it. How much I needed you, too." He took my hands in his. "And when I saw that you were there, I wanted to be there for you, too."

My friend Angie will tell you that everything happens for a reason. Which was why, on Christmas Day, when we sat down to a sumptuous feast at the DiFranco home in Brooklyn, and Angie discovered her mother had replaced the traditional Italian sausage with a turkey-sausage substitute, she took it as a very bad sign, especially considering her mother's fanaticism about Italian sausage.

Of course, Angie couldn't let it slide, seeing it as her mother's attempt to push her to set a date for the big day she didn't know had already happened by showing her daughter the importance of a homage to the proper meat products when it came to special occasions. Like weddings, for example.

So Angie decided to get to the bottom of it, once the rest of the family was in the living room recovering from the huge meal, and Angie, her mother and I were cleaning up in the kitchen.

"What was with the sausage, Ma?" Angie asked, practically yanking the plate out of Mrs. DiFranco's hands to dry it. I looked up from where I was wiping down the table, biting back a smile.

"What?" Mrs. DiFranco said, her eyes going wide with innocence. "You didn't like it?"

"I don't like you trying to get at me using…meat products."

"Angie, I have no idea—"

"Look, Ma, I know you only put that turkey sausage in the sauce to get at me because I won't set a date for the wedding at Lombardi's. But I told you already that with production beginning in the spring—"

Her mother stopped her washing, turning off the tap and

wiping her hands off on the towel with a barely harnessed fury. "You think I would ruin a perfectly good meal to get at you?" she said.

"It wasn't ruined, exactly," I offered. In truth, Mrs. DiFranco made such a killer sauce, it really was hard to ruin it.

They both ignored me. "Yes, I do," Angie declared. "Ever since Justin and I got engaged, you've been harping at me over this…this wedding, and I can't take it anymore!"

Mrs. DiFranco's expression hardened. "You listen to me, young lady, that turkey sausage had nothing to do with you. That sausage was for your grandmother's benefit."

I saw Angie's face flush red before she paled. Even I held my breath.

"Oh, my God, Ma, is Nonnie okay? I mean, is she not taking care of herself?"

"Of course she is. I make sure she is," Mrs. DiFranco said. "You think I don't take care of my mother?" She sniffed. "But she's not getting any younger, Angie. She's not gonna be here forever. And at the rate you're going, who knows if she'll even make it to your wedding!"

Angie's eyes narrowed, and I nearly laughed at Mrs. D's slyness. Then, before she could stop herself, Angie burst out with, "Well, I'll have you know, Ma, that Justin and I are already married!" Then, as if to prove her words, she pulled out the necklace where she had kept her wedding band hanging from around her neck, and all but waved that pretty piece of platinum in her mother's face.

Which, of course, was the wrong thing to do. Because within moments, the whole house was in an uproar, especially since Mrs. DiFranco rushed into the living room to declare her daughter's treason to the entire family.

Nonnie was tickled pink and, with Artie's help, heaved

herself off the couch immediately to hug her new grandson, Justin.

Sonny thought it was hilarious.

His wife, Vanessa, jokingly asked if she could keep the espresso maker she had purchased for them.

Angie's brother Joey and his wife, Miranda, struggled to contain their kids, who were jumping up and down, clearly thrilled they wouldn't have to wear the starchy, itchy and utterly uncomfortable wedding clothes their grandmother had not only bought for them, but had forced them to parade around the living room in one Sunday after dinner.

Baby Carmella started to cry in the confusion, until Sonny scooped her off the carpet to soothe her, all the while struggling to contain his mirth.

Mrs. DiFranco turned to me, as if hoping I might be the sole person to take her side, considering that I, at least, had allowed her to show me all the wedding gown photos she had clipped from various magazines.

"Grace! Did you know about this?"

"I did," I admitted guiltily.

"And what do you make of it?"

I smiled, looking at Angie and Justin, who stood arm and arm, as if bracing themselves against the onslaught that was sure to come from Mrs. D.

"I think…I think they are going to be very happy together. For a very long time."

Just as I trusted that I was going to be happy for a very long time, judging from the romantic Christmas Eve I had spent with Jonathan.

Not that I knew what would happen with Jonathan. But we *had* shared Christmas Eve. And Christmas Eve was all about anticipation, right?

★ ★ ★

"It's a charm bracelet," my mother said once I had un-wrapped the exquisite package she had pulled out of her suit-case. My apartment floor was positively overflowing with the gifts she and my father had hauled back from Paris, which was surprising for my usually frugal mother.

We were sitting in my living room, and after sharing a meal I had ordered in for us, we had talked for hours. About Kristina. Her family in Brooklyn, whom I had opted to visit on my way home from the DiFrancos. Just for dessert. It was a quiet evening—just me, Katerina and Sasha, but I could tell they were glad I had decided to come. I think Katerina saw it as some holiday homage to her sister, and Sasha, once she got past her usual anger, even took some comfort, too. I re-alized then how keenly my half-sister was suffering, and un-derstood that I had been just as unable to acknowledge her pain as I had been unable to acknowledge my own. I didn't know what it was to lose a mother in the way Sasha had, but I understood loss in a way I never really did before. Real-ized, too, that not only did I have something to offer Sasha, but she had a wisdom she might offer me. A faith that de-spite all the pain life could bring, it also brought hope. A hope I saw shining in her eyes when she opened up just enough to show me that far from merely being a surly teen, she was a talented artist who made jewelry for all her friends—and aspired to one day make it for the marketplace. She even shyly offered me a bracelet in return for the Roxy D samples I had brought her. But her reaction to my gift was nothing com-pared to the thrill in her eyes when I disclosed that I had not only had some part in the campaign Irina was fronting this spring, but that I had met the supermodel. Of course, Sasha was a fan. Wasn't every woman under a certain age? And I think I might have even made Sasha *my* fan when I promised to introduce her to her idol. After all, Irina was turning twenty this January, and according to the invitation I had received, was having a hell of a celebration at one of the hottest new clubs in New York City. I guess every woman deserves a ball as she moves on to the next phase of her life. And since it was reportedly going to be a big bash, I was sure Irina wouldn't mind…or wouldn't notice…if I brought along an extra guest or, two….

"Do you like it?" my mother said now as I fingered the pretty little charms strung together on a thick gold chain. "The lady at the jewelry store told me charm bracelets were all the rage in Paris right now!"

I looked up at her, saw the mixture of hopefulness and worry in my mother's eyes, and realized, for the first time, that she was anxious over the gift. As if I wouldn't accept it. Or her…

"It's beautiful," I said, reaching over to her to hug her tightly.

"See, I told you she would like it, Serena. All that worrying over nothing!" My father smiled at us from where he sat in a wingback chair across from us. Of course, whatever worries my father had about me were put to rest when I told him and my mother about my Christmas Eve with Jonathan. I got the feeling, from my father's hopeful expression, that he had been matchmaking all along.

My mother ignored his comment, touching the little charms one by one as if she still felt a need to explain her gift to me.

"This one here is a little artist's palette. Remember how you used to love to paint as a girl?"

I smiled, studying the pretty gold charm. "I remember."

"And this is a little calendar. You see the date marked there?"

I looked more closely, expecting to see my birth date marked, as was typical of this type of charm. But the little gold tablet was a calendar for May. And the date marked with a little heart was the fifth. "I don't understand...."

"That's the day you came to us, sweetheart," she said, beaming at me. Then she frowned at my father. "I guess that day has more meaning for us than it would for Grace. Maybe we should have gotten the birthday charm, like you suggested...." She looked at me again and sighed. "I guess it's just that that day in May—well, it was one of the happiest days of our lives...."

My eyes misted at her words, because even though she had told me the story of my homecoming at least a hundred times, it seemed like the first time I was hearing it.

"And this here is a 'G' charm, of course, for Grace," she continued. "You do know why we called you Grace, don't you?"

"After Grace Kelly," I said, looking at my father for confirmation. It was he, after all, who had always called me Princess Grace when I was a child.

My mother waved her hand. "How could we know you would grow up to look like her? Only prettier," she said with a wink. "No, no. We named you Grace because it means 'gift from God.' And you were, after all, our miracle. You still are," she continued, reaching out and hugging me again like she'd never let me go. "You know that, don't you,

Grace?" she whispered fiercely in my ear. "Please tell me you know that."

"I do," I said, relishing her embrace. "I really do."

I knew for certain in that moment that my life was a gift.

And a perfectly beautiful one.

If I did say so myself.

More great reads by Lynda Curnyn:

Engaging Men

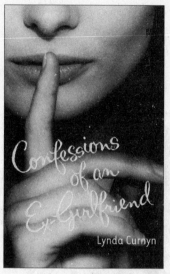

Confessions of an Ex-Girlfriend

"Sex and the City with more heart...a winner."
—*Publishers Weekly* on *Confessions of an Ex-Girlfriend*

"Readers will eagerly turn the pages..."
—*Booklist* on *Confessions of an Ex-Girlfriend*